I0685266

Fire In The Knight

Louise Dawn

Let curiosity burn like a flame.
Always keep dancing,
and learning new steps.
Find your song.

To my guardian angel, my grandmother.
Your inquiring mind and passion for knowledge
rubbed off on your stubborn granddaughter.
Love you granny. Miss you always.

Prologue

Saint Julian's, Republic of Malta.

With no sign of potential witnesses in the hall, the man pulled the apartment door shut with a soft click. He adjusted his hoodie and ran down the steps before stepping onto the damp pavement. The sun had set and on a wet November night in Malta, the streets surrounding Spinola Bay were deserted.

It was time to settle in and wait. The mark—Joseph Da Silva— had only just sat down for dinner at one of the nearby restaurants. It would be at least an hour before he returned to his rental villa facing the water.

With quick and efficient movements, the assassin made his way to the docked speedboat. Villas and hotels pressed together around the inlet, stacked like Legos in the small cove. He ignored the colorful skiffs floating alongside his craft. Traditional Maltese Luzzu fishing boats painted a patchwork of color both on and off the water. Clambering onto a small speedboat, he adjusted the tarp that added concealment before settling in his seat. He glanced at his watch. Nineteen minutes and 28 seconds. The efficient time it took to gain access to the apartment—and to set the pressure switch—pleased him.

1

Setting up the Semtex charge inside the water tank took skill, but connecting the explosives to a double pressure switch between the toilet bowl and the seat had made him sweat. It was foolproof. Mr. Da Silva would return from his dinner. If he needed to piss, he'd raise the toilet seat which would trigger the switch and blow him to pieces. However, if Da Silva decided to sit on the crapper, the second pressure switch would also activate the water charge.

He reached into a packed cooler and pulled out a Tupperware filled with Bigilla, carrots and crackers. He loved the Maltese version of Hummus. No one made better Bigilla than his mama and he was grateful for the packed dinner.

Toilets were foolproof when it came to eliminating a mark. People may not use a fridge or an oven—mainly if they eat out or don't know how to cook—but at some point, everybody responded to the call of nature.

He thought about the mark. This would be his fifth kill, not bad considering he'd only been in the killing game for ten months. He did the work that others were afraid to do, and his work was meticulous. Joseph Da Silva shouldn't have asked questions. The private detective should've stayed in Italy. Instead, he began investigating links between the Sicilian Mafia and wealthy Maltese families. Over the past decade, the police had made arrests, linking Maltese individuals to Libyan fuel smuggling and illegal gaming activities. But now that the dust had settled, new investigations would open a can of laundering worms.

The detective was bad for business. He had to die.

As the killer waited, he slipped a hand in his jacket pocket and pulled out his talisman, rolling it between his thumb and fingers. He took great care. One wrong move would mean death.

He looked down at the small green object. The smallest grenade in the world. A replica of the V40 Fragmentation Grenade initially manufactured in the Netherlands. He carried the shell on every mission. It kept him alert and careful in the field.

The contained explosive energy lying in the palm of his hand made his heart pump a little faster. Explosive devices fascinated him. That and the fires they caused, after ripping through space with shredded mayhem. He placed the fragmentation device carefully back in his pocket, opened a soda and returned to watching the apartment entrance.

Two hours later, the detective walked up the chilly street and then up the stairs. Rain pattered on the tarp, sounding peaceful as the sea gently rocked the boat. Ten minutes later, an explosion shattered the silence. Fiery missiles blew outwards, then showered onto the harbor below. The killer could feel the concussive blast from across the water and the sight energized him. Although he wanted to hang back and watch the flames flicker in the night's sky, it was time for him to leave. He turned on the motor and made his way towards the open water, blocking out the screams and never once looking back.

Wyoming.
Six months later.

Dave "Donnie" Wilson grabbed another beer from Johnny's fridge. When back home in the States, Donnie liked the road trips on his Harley. It sure beat staring at the four walls of his apartment every day. Even though he'd moved to Utah to be closer to his team, he still felt the isolation. Their team leader—Erik "Max" Andersen—spent much of his time with his new family. His wife had just given birth to a baby girl. Between that and their three-year-old, Max barely had time to sleep, never mind hang with Donnie and the rest of the team.

So, Donnie had decided to stop over at James "Johnny" Cane's cabin on the way to Montana for a fishing trip. Johnny—the medic on their black ops team—was a former Ranger and a bear of a man who loved having friends over whenever they were in town.

Donnie worked for the Mobile Intelligence Team Taskforce, known as MIT for short. His team—MIT2—were based in the East African region and were responsible for shutting down newly formed extremist groups who threatened not only local governments and their people, but American facilities and interests. MIT2 went after the leaders of these violent groups—protected men that were normally inaccessible by local military.

Donnie loved his job as the Information Specialist—or Analyst—on MIT2 and felt like he made a difference in the fight against terror. His family and friends had no idea what he did for a living. As far as they knew, Donnie was a tactical salesman who sold military clothing and equipment for global companies. They knew he'd served as a Green Beret, but when he was offered his current position with the covert taskforce, his work life became a government secret. Only present and future wives were allowed to know what the teams did for a living. The MIT men were as mysterious as Delta Force Operators—Ghosts who worked in high-risk areas and never left an identifying mark.

This time, they'd been Stateside for longer than Donnie would've liked. MIT2 were training their new team member—Dylan "Atlas" Jenkins—as the new Force Protection Specialist and Sniper.

Donnie shouldn't have stopped over at the farm. He was the

awkward third wheel as Johnny and his girlfriend, Lizzy, canoodled every chance they got. This was a natural response to their harrowing brush with death just weeks earlier. They hadn't come through the brutal nightmare unscathed. Aside from PTSD issues, Lizzy lost half a finger in her fight to survive. Relieved to be re-united and safe, they clung to each other like monkeys, even when eating their meals.

When Donnie wasn't avoiding the love fest, he was thinking about Charlotte Quinn. Her father owned the land that Johnny's cabin sat on, and although Donnie and Charlie didn't get along, he couldn't stop thinking about the pretty redhead.

Donnie walked out and admired the setting sun. He glanced to the left and winced at the couple on the porch. "Jeez, will you two get a room? If you're not squabbling, you're sticking your tongues down each other's throats."

Johnny growled. "Be a good houseguest. Hassle someone else—like Charlie. You're good at getting her all riled up."

Donnie had time; he had a whole week at the farmhouse. Johnny and Lizzy were moving to Salt Lake City, and Donnie would help them pack before he drove to Montana. Then after a short fishing trip, the team would be flying back out to Kenya. Maybe if he spent time getting to know Charlie, she wouldn't look as if she wanted to poke his eyes out with a sharpened stick.

"How is she? How's her father?"

"Not doing so well. Charlie is going through a tough time. She's in the barn if you want to see her."

"Shit," Donnie said and headed for the steps. He knew what it was like to lose someone. Those last precious weeks of clinging on to their final haunting moments. Waiting, watching and praying for hope.

"Take a cold shower, brother, while I'm gone. Your tented

sword is scaring off the wildlife."

"Screw off, tech boy," Johnny said as he picked up their service dog, Ray, and carried her inside.

Donnie headed down the grassy path that cut across to the gate linking the properties. He slipped through then ducked under a fence, heading to the barn. The doors were locked for the night and the stables next door were quiet. Donnie turned, ready to head back when he heard raised voices.

The commotion came from Jack Quinn's farmhouse. Donnie loped up the hill, following the sound of Charlie yelling.

"I've called the police. Get off the property now."

"I'll sue you and your old man. You owe me a week's worth of pay; I'm not leaving without it."

Donnie came around the corner and stopped short, then took off running. He recognized Peter Billings. They'd had issues with the large ass-wipe for months, and Charlie had fired him last week. When he'd refused to leave, Johnny had kicked him off the property. Apparently, Peter hadn't gotten the message. Donnie never liked the man. The few times Donnie had seen him, the massive asshole had skulked around with an even bigger chip on his shoulder. And Donnie didn't like the way he looked at Charlie. The only reason she'd kept him around for so long was that his wealthy father was a friend of her dad's. They'd thought some hard-manual labor would fix the boy. Instead, he'd stolen tools from the storage shed and beaten one of her horses—resulting in his instant dismissal.

Her father, Jack Quinn, stood at the bottom of the stairs as Peter bellowed. The older man swayed. He'd lost even more weight over the past few weeks and looked like he could barely stand. Peter lunged, Charlie stepped between and shoved him back. Donnie got there a second too late. Lightning quick, Peter swung and caught Charlie on the chin. Before Peter could swing again, Donnie grabbed his arm from behind and circled, while twisting the wrist. Peter screamed and fell to his knees. Donnie kept twisting until he heard the shoulder pop. Then he used a front kick to knock Peter to the ground.

The man wasn't going anywhere anytime soon. Peter groaned, flopping in the dirt. Bending over, Donnie twisted Peter's useless arm behind his back and called back to Charlie.

"Are you okay? Is the jaw okay?"

"I think so. Did you dislocate Pete's shoulder?" she asked as she lowered her father to the stairs.

"Yup. I need something to secure his hands with until the police get here. Do you have duct tape?"

She nodded and ran inside.

"You're going to pay, bitch!" Peter screamed through the muddy spittle covering his lips. Donnie didn't want the nut job focusing on Charlie. The guy was a tank with hands that could crush steel.

Donnie pulled hard on his wrist. "Shut up, asshole, or I'll pop the other shoulder."

Peter's lizard eyes didn't even glance Donnie's way, and when Charlie emerged from the house, he spat out more threats. "Your daddy ain't gonna be around for long. I'll come by and take my time hurting you. You got me arrested and now I have a record. You fucking ruined my life, bitch! Do you know who I am, who my daddy is?"

Donnie reached his limit. Grabbing hair, he pulled Peter's head back. "If you come near her or this property ever again, I will end you. You will be slaughtered. Do you understand?"

"Fuck you, asshole. I have friends in high places that will finish you both."

"Here's the tape." Charlie placed it on the ground. She now held a shotgun loosely in her right hand. "Pete, you won't get one up on me again. If you come back, I'll shoot you in the dick, and then I'll let my friends beat your sorry ass and bury you beneath that apple tree."

"Is that a threat?"

"No, honey, that's a promise, and this is for trying to hurt my daddy." She kicked him in the ribs, then kicked again. "And that was for hurting my horse." Peter groaned as she sauntered away. Donnie couldn't help grinning as he watched her sexy ass sway in the moonlight. Charlie Quinn and her fiery temper were quite a combination.

Once he'd secured Peter, he sat down on the steps next to the Quinns. "Are you sure you're both all right?" Donnie placed two fingers under Charlie's chin and turned her head to the light. Her jaw looked red and swollen.

Jack's hands shook, and Charlie had her arms wrapped around the fragile man.

"I want my father to rest, but he refuses to move his stubborn ass until the police get here."

Jack shot her a look. "You're the one that got punched in the face. Aside from that, I haven't had this much fun in months. All I do is lie in that damn bed and stare at the ceiling."

"Bullshit. I'm always entertaining you. If I have to play one more game of Monopoly."

Jack's brown eye's twinkled. "You're just a sore loser. I beat you at everything, including Rummy."

"That's 'cause you're a darn cheater." Charlie grinned and kissed Jack on the cheek. Donnie smiled at the bittersweet interaction. Jack grew weaker each day and the next few months would be hard on Charlie. She already looked exhausted—

judging from the dark shadows beneath her eyes.

"Tell you what," Donnie said. "I'll take you inside to rest and at the same time, pick up a bag of peas from the freezer for Charlie's poor face."

Jack's eyes narrowed. "I know your angle, you want my daughter all to yourself."

Charlie snorted. "Hardly. I'm not his type."

Donnie frowned but didn't argue. Instead, he lifted Jack in his arms and with direction, carried him to the back bedroom. It looked inviting. Drawn back covers and an old Elvis tune crooned in the background. Donnie removed Jack's shoes and tucked the quilt around his delicate bones.

"Do you need anything?"

"I'm all good, boy, just taking my truckload of meds." He reached for his pill box, and Donnie handed him the full glass of water from the bedside table. A framed photograph caught Donnie's eye. He barely recognized Jack who looked like a brawnier version of Robert Redford. A little girl clung to his waist—Charlie—she was around ten years old. Even back then, her hair glowed with that unusual fire. A much older teenage boy stood in the back with his arms looped around a distinguished lady.

"My little family." Jack pointed a shaking finger at the framed picture. "Not so much a family anymore, but I still have my Charlie." His eyes filled. "I worry for her. She has such a big heart and an even bigger mouth." Donnie chuckled and Jack smiled. "She'll make something of herself. My hardworking girl puts most men to shame." His hand flopped to the bed and Donnie eased the frail man's head back against the pillow. Just like that, Jack was snoring and out like a light. Wondering about her sibling and mother, Donnie picked up the frame and traced a finger over Charlie's cute grin. She wore breeches and riding boots with a riding helmet tucked under her arm. Blazing tendrils fell around her mischievous face and Donnie couldn't help but smile at her eyes twinkling with joy.

He stopped by the freezer then sat back on the steps, close enough that his leg rubbed up against hers. Donnie grabbed her hand, ignoring the zing of electricity that shot between them. "Put this on your jaw. Don't take it off for at least an hour."

He handed her the towel-wrapped bag of frozen sliced carrots. Charlie placed it on her chin. Her hair fell haphazardly around her face from a high ponytail. Charlie had the sweetest profile—a slightly upturned nose sat above generous lips. And those wide eyes had the longest lashes that brushed her cheeks every time she looked down.

"Well, aren't you a bossy pants," she said.

"You know it."

"Thanks for stepping in, but I would've come back fighting. I should've had my rifle with me, but I'd just returned from the stables when I saw him hassling my father."

"Where are your farmhands? Where is your foreman?" Donnie asked.

"I gave them the night off; it's karaoke night in town. A couple of the guys are good crooners."

Donnie felt his jaw tick as he stared at her profile.

"Say it, Donnie. What's itching your butt?"

"Nothing."

"What a pile of crap." She glared his way. "Your bottom lip twitches when you're pissed about something."

"I worry. What's going to happen when you're running this farm on your own."

"Don't you dare go there. I know what you're saying, you

mean when my daddy eventually dies." She stood and dropped the bag from her face.

"Safety is an issue."

"Why, because I'm a girl—because a woman will be running such a large operation all by her lonesome? Well, I got news for you, I've been taking care of this farm for years now and I can run it in my sleep. I might not seem capable—"

"I never said that and put the frozen pack back on your face."

"You don't say a lot of things—at least none of the nice things. You always have to criticize."

"Shit, okay. So, we're going there." Donnie got to his feet.

"We're going nowhere. When we're done, you're heading back to Jamie's place and I'm heading to bed."

Charlie referred to Johnny as Jamie. She had no clue what Johnny did for a living, and since they'd grown up together, she only knew him by his birth name.

"Sharls, I didn't mean to say that about your dad. I'm sorry, and I hope he pulls through." He reached out to touch her arm and she shook him off.

"Don't call me that—acting all sweet—and don't think that you know me, or what's best for my daddy and me. He's all that I have, and you have no right to talk about his future or mine. You should know better."

"I know, I'm sorry." He'd pissed her off again—for the hundredth time.

Headlights hit the path as a truck pulled into the drive. A door slammed.

"Charlie?" A familiar looking man ran around the corner. Donnie had seen him around the farm. Judging by his graying temples, the well-built and capable man looked to be in his mid to late forties.

"Earl."

"What the hell happened? A cruiser is barreling in behind me."

Sure enough, flashing lights hit the side of the house as the officer parked behind Earl's truck.

"Pete decided to pay us another visit."

"That shithole." Earl looked like he wanted to crush skulls. Instead he eyed Donnie. "You're a friend of James, I've seen you around."

"Donnie Wilson."

"Earl Taylor."

"He's my foreman," Charlie supplied.

Donnie exchanged small talk with Earl, then withdrew. It's best he forgot about Charlie and got on with his life. An officer rounded the building, and with one last glare his way, Charlie turned her back to give her statement.

Chapter One

Valletta, Republic of Malta.
Four months later.

Ruzar Comino watched the woman take a sip of her red wine as she leaned over the wooden railing—gazing down at the streets below. He started down the steps, slowly winding his way through seated tourists and standing partygoers. On a Friday night, the *Bridge Bar* offered a casual experience for travelers on the wide candlelit steps just above the *Victoria Gate.* Jazz musicians played live music on the terrace, and the audience lounged on red pillows dotting the steps or they sat at one of the small tables decorating the streets.

Tourists loved Malta—the island country that sat just fifty miles below Italy in the Mediterranean. Overcrowded streets and heavy traffic defined the Summer months. Mid-October meant that Malta's cobbled avenues had calmed after the recent populous season.

There was still enough of a crowd to cloak his interest in the fiery redhead. Her hair fell in silky, thick tresses down her back. That glowing red color couldn't be natural, yet he had a burning need to know. Compared to the rowdy revelers, she seemed sad—pensive. It was their destiny to meet. Her tall, blonde, female sidekick walked inside the pub with one of the bartenders, and within half a minute, a man sidled up to the lonely scarlet beauty. In contrast, his hair shone unnaturally under the street light. Oil-slicked hair weighed down enough to sink an island of penguins.

With barely a glance, she turned her back on the drunk stranger. His greasy friend approached, and they both stepped closer, insisting on buying her a drink. She refused. They asked again. She stepped sideways. The slick bastard reached out for her arm and Ruzar stepped in.

He spoke rapidly in Maltese with the two locals. Two well-placed sentences later, and they apologized to her in English before retreating.

Ruzar turned, addressing her in English. "I'm sorry you had to deal with that. Not all Maltese men behave like imbeciles around beautiful tourists."

She gave him a considering look. "How do you know I'm a tourist?"

"Honey, with hair like that, you wouldn't have been hidden for long. Malta is a small republic, and you would have been famous in a heartbeat."

She smiled.

"Plus, the American accent gives you away."

Sighing dramatically, she swayed against the railing. "I concede defeat. My damn hair and mid-western accent paint a giant target on my jet-setting ass."

Ruzar raised his brows. "Jet-setting ass?"

"Maybe jet-setting is the wrong word. After all, this is my first trip out of the States. It's a big deal." She took a sip of her wine and gave him a wink.

Her warm brown eyes sparkled, and he couldn't help grinning at the sweet picture she made. The wine had stained her full lips, the color matching her maroon dress. A scattering of freckles traced her pert nose. He felt himself relaxing around her, and he leaned against the railing mirroring her open stance. Her eyes ran over him, and Ruzar couldn't help but inwardly preen. Thanks to a strict diet and fitness regimen, he was all wide shoulders and roped muscle. His hair—worn longer than most—was pulled back into a low pony. The trim goatee and beard gave him a dangerous edge, one that worked against him as he registered a flicker of uncertainty in her honest eyes. Before she could retreat, he stepped closer and presented his hand.

"Ruzar Comino, at your service. Use me however you need, as a friend, or a tour guide or a bodyguard for the occasional drunk ass that dares to step in your sweet shadow."

"Wow. Ruzar Comino, you know how to chat up the ladies."

He kept his hand extended and waited.

She bit her top lip as she considered her next move, then took his hand in hers.

"Charlotte Quinn. Only ever a friend. Might enjoy having a local tour guide. Can take care of drunk asses on my own, but thanks for the offer."

Laughing, Ruzar gestured her towards the pub. "In that case, let's go and find your blonde friend you were with earlier. I'll buy you both a drink. No strings, you know."

Turning, she said, "My blonde friend, huh? Sorry to break it to you, but we're not into threesomes. And we're not looking to hook up. We're here to work."

"I can accept that," he said as he opened the door for her. "What kind of work?"

"Fire dancing, baby…. we play with fire and get paid to do it."

◊ ◊ ◊

Her words stopped Ruzar in his tracks and Charlie wanted to laugh at his flummoxed expression. She slipped past, ignoring his expensive cologne or the way the jeans molded to his muscled legs. His shirt whispered against her skin as he escorted her inside the quiet bar. All the patrons sat outdoors. A hand stroked her back; her stomach did a small flip. Not because of an attraction to a rough-looking stranger, but because it reminded her of another capable man. One that occupied too much space in her head. Considering that she consumed hardly any space in his, now wasn't the time to moon over Donnie Wilson. A man that despised her and a man who'd seen her at her most vulnerable. His hawkish face kept intruding on her thoughts. The way those green eyes rimmed with dark lashes would watch her from the shadows. Squinting and sizing her up under slashing brows as he threw quiet jabs her way. He was a handsome man if you were into the mysterious, arrogant vibe. All she knew was that he worked with her friend Jamie, loved to ride motorbikes and embraced the loner vibe. Pity that they had nothing in common. Charlie had no space in her world for high maintenance men.

The last four weeks meant significant changes in her life. She'd lost her dad, and although she'd known that day would come, it hurt so damn much. Charlie had lost a father, a best friend, her mentor and her confidant, all in one devastating moment. A week before he'd died, her father had told her to live out her dream. To dance, and see the world, to get lost and to forget. Then, when she'd healed, and the time was right, to return and re-shoulder her responsibilities.

After the funeral, she'd chosen to run from the black dresses, the familiar faces, and sweet memories. Along with her dancing colleagues, leaping into the wide world, spelled fresh anonymity for a small-town farm girl. Her invisibility now held peace, and it could also mean fun, she thought while admiring Ruzar's muscular physique.

His natural confidence drew her in, and she smiled at him over her shoulder as she made her way to her friend's side. Elana, however, did not smile his way, as he extended a hand in greeting. Instead, she frowned at Charlie.

"I leave you for five minutes, and you get picked up by a smooth-talking local?"

"He rescued me from a pair of drunk idiots."

"Oh, I'm sure he did."

Charlie loved Elana like a sister. They'd grown up together in Wyoming. Elana's first day of middle school was also her first day of school in America. Elana spent her younger years in Turkey. At eleven years of age, her parents decided to move to her mother's hometown of Jackson Hole. It took time for her Turkish Muslim father to acclimate to small-town life. He threw himself into the real estate industry and at the same time spent years decking out their farm property—which he transformed into a modern stone and glass mansion with a massive infinity pool, overlooking the Tetons.

Unlike Charlie, Elana spent a great deal of her life traveling. She spoke four languages and thanks to her over-protective parents, Elana was an all-around self-defense expert who held wary regard for strangers.

Charlie could see why they'd be overprotective. Their daughter was stunning. Tall with long, honey-blonde hair and light green, slanted eyes. Her super model looks were a honey trap for slathering men. Except she always kept the boys at arm's length.

Elana was the woman that Charlie wished she could be. Sophisticated and worldly.

Confidence came easily to Charlie when it concerned the farm or her studies. She knew what she was capable of and was damn proud of who'd she become, but she was a small-town girl of average height. The girl next door who smelled like fresh farm and horse. The girl who had no clue how to apply eyeshadow or how to even ride the subway. Hell, Lizzy, had only just taught Charlie to flat iron her hair—she could now contain the frizzy mess. This trip was about challenging herself to learn new things, experiencing new cultures and meeting new people.

"Elana, don't be rude. Say hello to Ruzar. He's been nothing but a gentleman."

Elana leaned against the bar while staring at the Maltese man. She then chatted with the bartender in Arabic—obviously asking his opinion. Ruzar chose a barstool and folded his arms.

Once they were done, Ruzar addressed them both in what Charlie assumed was also Arabic. Elana's surprise registered. Charlie wasn't sure what the conversation entailed but she tired of being the outsider.

"English, please? Someone?" Charlie grumbled while taking a seat.

"I just ordered you a drink. A local beer called a Cisk in Malta," Ruzar said.

"Impressive—that you speak Arabic, although it's the origin of Maltese. You look Maltese—from the Italian side?" Elana asked.

"I am. My family has Sicilian roots. But I also have some Arabic friends on the island."

Elana raised her brows. "So, you speak…"

"Maltese, Italian, and a little Arabic—"

"And English," Charlie supplied.

He laughed. "That too."

"To seduce naive travelers?" Elana said.

"To meet wonderful new friends. Besides, most locals speak English. It is an official language—we were under British protection until 1964."

"Fair enough. What do you want with my friend?" Elana asked as she took a sip of her beer.

"Friendship, ma'am. And to show you some of the local sights. How long are you girls here for?"

"Three days," Charlie said. She saw Elana scowling from the corner of her eye.

"And how did the fire dancing thing come about?" Ruzar seemed fascinated.

Charlie answered, "Elana learned to belly dance through her relatives in Turkey. I wanted to learn, and she taught me. A good friend of ours—Zach—taught himself to juggle fire from online videos. We all joined forces and the rest is history."

"That's damn cool, but why Malta?"

"I've always dreamt of visiting Malta. We've already visited the Three Cities and Fort St. Angelo and St. John's Co-Cathedral."

Ruzar ran a finger along the rim of his beer mug. "Excellent, since you've already hit some of the typical tourist hotspots, I'll rent a couple of mopeds in the morning and take you to Marsaxlokk. It's a small fishing village to the south. They sell the best seafood on the island."

Elana scowled. "I don't know about—"

Charlie scowled back. "Don't be a shitty stick in the mud.

I'm going with or without you."

Ruzar and Charlie exchanged numbers. Elana relented like Charlie knew she would. Elana protected her friend like a lion would her cub. Charlie couldn't wait to start new adventures. She adored the main island. Malta was everything she'd dreamt it would be—magical, mysterious and breathtaking.

◊ ◊ ◊

Marsaxlokk, Malta.

He wanted to be that peach, so fucking badly. Ruzar watched Charlotte take another bite of the juicy fruit. Her full lips caressed the fuzzy skin as her straight, white teeth sank into its flesh. Unaware of the riot she'd caused in his pants, Charlotte leaned over to examine a silver bracelet—one of many on display. She licked her lower lip before chewing and Ruzar almost groaned. She traced a finger over the Maltese cross dangling off the delicate silver chain.

"You want it?"

Charlotte looked at him with wide eyes. "You're not buying that for me. I can pay for it myself." She turned to wander off.

"Come here, you." He grabbed her hand. "It's nothing, and it will look pretty on your wrist."

Wandering through the market, they'd bought freshly cooked fish. After moans of delight from the ladies, they'd bought peaches at a fruit stand before strolling past the silverware on display. It wasn't an expensive or well-made bracelet by any means, but Charlotte liked it, so he'd buy it. The more time Ruzar spent with her, the more he wanted her. Her direct humor and refreshing honesty were like nothing he'd experienced. She looked at everything with open wonder. Before the market, they'd stopped at St. Peter's Pool—a natural pool located near the village.

The still chilly morning air meant that they had the clear azure pool to themselves. Elana sunbathed on the rocks as Ruzar splashed in the cool water. With his encouragement, he got Charlotte to slip in while holding onto the edge. He was surprised to learn she couldn't swim. Ruzar held her tight as he paddled in the cove. Once they'd dried off, her hair dried into a thick curly mass. Each ringlet shimmered like fire as she moved and Ruzar had no problem trailing behind her as he gazed at the glowing tresses.

After spending most of the day exploring the area and surrounding cafes, he drove them to Pretty Bay, a sandy cove decorated with palm trees and surrounded by holiday apartments. The sun was beginning to set, casting a golden glow over the bay. Elana walked off to call her parents and Charlotte sat beside him, staring at the horizon.

"I wish my father was here. He loved this time of the day."

She'd told him that morning about her father's recent passing.

"I'm sorry for your loss."

Charlotte continued as if she hadn't heard him. "He'd pour a whiskey and sit on the porch, not moving 'til night had fallen. He said it was a magical time when day creatures went to sleep and night creatures woke."

"It does sound magical." Ruzar rubbed sand through his fingers.

"He'd tell me stories as we watched the sun fall from the sky. Every evening. Stories of his youth, of growing up in the mid-west. Of buying the farm and starting with nothing. Now we have over five thousand head of sheep."

"It sounds like hard work."

"It is. I'm considering..." Charlotte paused, then sighed.

"Considering what?"

"Selling. While I'm away, I have a foreman running things, but I want a life outside of sheep and cattle and endless chores."

Ruzar reached up and tried to tuck her hair behind her ear. The tresses caught on his hand and he studied the fiery strands falling through his fingers. His hand wrapped around the back of her neck and he pulled her towards him.

"My Firefly," he said before crushing her mouth to his.

She smelled like flowers and salt water. Ruzar ravaged, moaning as he melded his tongue with hers, angling her head and licking deeper.

◊ ◊ ◊

This had to be the most romantic setting on earth. Charlie sat on a Mediterranean beach, being thoroughly kissed by a man who looked like a swarthy pirate. This was what she'd hoped for—adventure and romance in a foreign land—except all she could think of was Donnie. His stubbled, sarcastic mouth haunted her dreams. Sitting on a beach next to a strange man suddenly felt all wrong and Charlie placed a hand on Ruzar's chest.

"I can't do this."

"I know... you'll be leaving soon. I don't expect anything, one night together. Let me spoil you and give you everything you deserve. Let me touch you, baby."

His hand ran down her side and Charlie leaned away. She opened her mouth to say something as his phone rang.

"One second..."

He answered in another language. Maltese, she presumed.

The conversation started casually, then he turned angry—words rapid-firing from his lips. He stood and paced before hanging up and staring out at sea.

"Everything okay?"

He offered her a forced smile. "Fine."

"Do you want to talk about it?"

"My father can be challenging. I wish I had the same relationship you've had with yours, but he pushes all my buttons."

"What does he want you to do?"

"Play a larger role in the family business. He wants me to mentor my cousin, who's an idiot—to work on a contract with him. I told them all to fuck off. I'm taking a break. I'm always fucking working to line his pockets. I don't like where the business is going."

"In what way?"

"My family is wealthy, and they used to care about the Maltese people. They'd invest in the economy. It's a great place to stay. You could easily come and live here. Low taxes, free healthcare, good job opportunities, genuine and hardworking people. Malta deserves loyalty but my father only cares about extending his business empire. He'll work his staff, including me, to the bone. I deserve happiness."

"Looks like we're in the same boat. Happiness isn't that lofty a goal." She winked as he pulled her up, then spoke again. "Ruzar. I like you, but I'm not ready for more than friendship."

He considered her words. "Okay, little Firefly, how about we take it slow. I will be your friend for the moment. Tomorrow we can drive to Golden Bay; I'll show you the north part of the island."

"That sounds wonderful, but the following morning, we're

heading out to the cliffs of Gozo for a video shoot. Then we'll be heading to Morocco to meet up with the rest of our dance group."

"I have one day left to win you over?"

Charlie picked up her sandals as Elana moved towards them. "No, you have one day left to have fun with your new friends."

"Party pooper." He winked.

Charlie laughed and shoved him sideways before running for the bikes.

◊ ◊ ◊

Fort Bragg, North Carolina.

Donnie sidestepped, narrowly avoiding his opponent's jab. He followed through by pushing the man's elbow across his body and punching the target in the ribs. At the last second, he softened the blow before twisting back around to face the enemy.

The target's face reddened, and Donnie braced himself for retribution. Instead of taking the standard Krav Maga stance that most covert operatives used, he switched over into a Kung-Fu tiger stance. Unlike most special ops soldiers on base, Donnie had grown up on martial arts and defense techniques. He'd studied Shaolin Kung Fu from a young age and he was now a Sifu. The second highest tier in the Chinese martial art. Donnie was introduced to Pekita-Tirsia Kali as a teenager when he'd traveled to the Philippines with his mother. He'd mastered the art that had an emphasis on tactical application. In short, if an opponent carried a weapon, Donnie could easily disarm and kill them in a matter of seconds.

Unofficially, Donnie's hands were known as the deadliest in the covert community. He'd like to think it was because of his work as an analyst, but he knew better. He knew hundreds of ways to kill someone, and he didn't even need a weapon.

He didn't look like a killer, and that's the way he liked it. Donnie wasn't tall or built like a truck like Johnny. Or a lanky, pretty boy like his ex-teammate, Derek "Slater" Banez. Donnie was the shortest man on the team—give or take an inch—slightly shorter than Max.

He liked to blend into the background. He wanted to be underestimated and lived the saying *still waters run deep*. Donnie was the mother-fucking Mariana Trench at the bottom of the deepest ocean.

The enemy charged, and Donnie kicked out low, sweeping him off his feet. The man stumbled for balance as Donnie caught him around the waist and slammed him to the floor. Donnie locked the target's hand behind his back and straddled him.

"Jesus. Enough," the man said before moaning and tapping out.

"How long?" Donnie asked.

Another soldier stepped up to the ring. "One minute, fifty seconds."

Donnie smiled, getting up. "That's a new Delta takedown record."

"Screw you, Wilson!" The large Delta Force soldier rolled into a seated position, rubbing his wrist and Donnie extended a hand to help him up.

"Train harder, Mike. Maybe next time you'll make it past the two-minute mark."

"One of these days, I'm going to own your tech-ass in that ring," Mike said, as he shook out his wrist.

"Yeah, yeah. Heard it all before." Donnie ducked under the ropes as he unraveled his wrapped hands. "Are you going to sulk or come and hug your friend?" Donnie said, walking over to the dark corner near the back.

The chair scraped, and Derek "Slater" Banez stepped out of the shadows, pointing at Donnie's chin. "You're slipping, old man, that Delta fucker hit you on the button."

"I was feeling generous." Donnie grinned. "Shit, I've missed you. What are you doing at Fort Bragg?"

"I could ask you the same thing?"

"Some new fancy drone I'm training on. The thing is the size of a damn bee."

"Nice. I'm swinging by HQ to sign the last of the paperwork."

After being injured in the field in an explosion, Slater had decided to retire from their unit. Donnie felt the loss. Not only had they lost an experienced teammate, but a good friend in the field.

Donnie examined Slater's arm—still trussed up in a sling. Slater Banez fought through four months of healing and therapy. Sadly, the sniper's right arm may never fully recover after being shattered in numerous places.

"How's life been with your sister?"

"We're about to kill each other. After Fort Bragg, I may be heading to Salt Lake City. I've decided to take a job with the FBI."

"Holy crap, buddy!" Donnie slapped Slater on the back. "Well, in that case, give me fifteen to take a shower, and then lunch is on you."

They chose a Mexican place off base, chatting easily about past assignments and plans to hook up. Donnie finished the last of his burrito when Slater mentioned her name.

"How's Charlie doing? I believe her father passed away—like a month ago."

The spicy mouthful of chicken suddenly tasted dry, and Donnie twisted off the cap, taking a large gulp of water. "She's... um... fine."

"Did you go to the funeral?"

Donnie shook his head. "We were called away—on deployment. Since getting back, I've been at Fort Bragg."

"Is she doing okay?" Slater asked as he grabbed a tortilla. "Her father was her everything."

"I don't know. I heard she's in Turkey or Cyprus... or maybe Malta." Donnie pushed his plate away.

"I know you guys don't like each other much—"

"Jesus, Slater. It's not that I don't like her..."

"Chill, bro. Wait. I'm confused. You do like her?"

Donnie felt his ears flame, ignoring his friend's grin.

Slater leaned back and stretched out his legs. "Holy crap, buddy, you really like her!"

"No. I really don't. Charlotte Quinn is the opposite of what I want in a woman. She's loud and annoying and ignorant of those around her."

"Are we talking about the same Charlie?"

"She's loud!" The death glare he sent Slater's way had little effect.

"All right, calm down. Is this because of your disastrous date. That high-strung chick you brought to Johnny's party?"

Jesus. The famous Wyoming get-together from three months ago. Slater must've heard about that disastrous evening from one of the boys. Donnie would never live that down. He gathered their leftovers to toss in the garbage, ignoring the smirk on his best friend's handsome face.

Chapter Two

Somewhere near Gozo, Malta.

The speedboat bounced, skimming over small waves and Charlie clutched the side. Although the morning air felt like biting needles piercing through layers, the trip was exhilarating.

Dim light to the east indicated the sun would soon begin to rise, and they'd need to hurry to get set up in time. Thankfully, Ruzar knew of a shortcut to the top of the cliffs. He'd also arranged transport on the other side, paying a taxi driver to meet them at the dock. They'd make their way to an isolated area of the cliffs—a location without paved roads, hotels or buildings nearby—essential for the right backdrop. Elana would be the one filming, and Charlie would be the dancer—executing a fire dancing routine on the edge of the Ta'Cenc Cliffs as the sun rose.

Charlie scratched her nose and winced at the sunburn. The previous day was worth the burn. They'd gone horseback riding on the Golden Bay beach. All three of them were competent riders and loved exploring the coastline via horse.

Now it would soon be time to say goodbye to Ruzar. Once they'd wrapped up filming, they'd head to the hotel to pick up their bags. Charlie breathed in the salty air and freedom while riding through the dawn on a speedboat around the 120-meter-high cliffs. Her stomach tingled with butterflies as Ruzar maneuvered the boat towards the small jetty. Within the hour, she'd be dancing precariously on what might feel like the edge of the world.

An old silver Mercedes waited for them. The driver stayed at the wheel as another man stepped out the passenger side. Ruzar paused before walking ahead to greet the man. Charlie stepped forward to introduce herself and Ruzar pushed her hand away. "Leave it."

"What's wrong?" she whispered.

"Nothing. I don't like the way he's looking at you."

"Should we tell them to leave?" Charlie asked.

"They're harmless. Probably just out to make an extra buck." Ruzar smiled easily.

His explanation didn't make sense, but Ruzar was the local and Charlie trusted his judgment. They all helped Elana to load the equipment in the trunk, then Ruzar climbed in the back with the ladies. He spoke with the driver in Maltese. Charlie couldn't help noticing Ruzar's sudden stiffness or his glances at the driver and the passenger—he didn't like the men.

Elana noticed it too and turned to study the other occupants and Charlie did the same. Nothing seemed out of place. Both looked to be in their mid to late twenties, about the same age as Charlie and Elana.

The driver wore a flat tweed cap, pulled low over his eyes. His jacket looked like a common everyday item. Aside from his thumb tapping against the wheel, Charlie didn't notice anything unusual about the man. They drove at a safe speed, winding up towards the top of the cliffs.

Once on the plateau, the tar road fell away, and the sandy

path narrowed. The old car bumped and groaned over rough tracks, rolling to a stop as the sky began to turn pink.

The three men exchanged words, and Charlie wished she could understand Maltese. Ruzar opened his door and told the women to get out as this was the best view they'd get.

The lightening sky galvanized Elana into action and she raced ahead, carrying as many bags as she could manage. Charlie ran behind, skidding to a stop a few yards away from the most spectacular sight she'd ever seen. The land fell away in an almost vertical drop. Although it wasn't quite light enough to see the sea near the bottom, the view was enough to make her feel like an insignificant speck on the edge of an infinite abyss.

"Stop gawking and strip, woman!" Elana yelled. "We have five minutes to set up before we lose the sunrise."

Ruzar walked up beside Charlie as she sprang into action.

Ignoring the chilly breeze, Charlie shed layers, until she stood in lycra yoga pants and a bejeweled halter top. She ripped the wraparound skirt from her bag and tied it around her waist. Then she grabbed the fire staff with a double-sided wick. Next came the flower steel-kevlar fans for spinning. She unzipped the safety kit, pulled out the fuel bottle and readied the emergency equipment they always kept on hand, in case of emergencies— fire blankets, burn gel and an extinguisher. Ruzar stood too close, getting in Charlie's way. She ignored his bulk as she prepped the rest of the equipment, which took another couple of minutes.

Elana cursed beside her. "I can't find a stable base for the camera stand. Hold this for a second."

She passed the tripod to Charlie, who stood and shivered as Elana scurried around in the dirt a few yards away. Charlie scanned the rugged landscape, Elana was correct in cursing. The irregular rocky surface provided a viable challenge.

Charlie would need to be cautious when dancing near the edge. She glanced back, looking at the misty sea. Thudding footsteps over the rocky shelf gave little warning, and a flash of movement had Charlie turning. The driver ran towards her like a battering ram. Charlie didn't think—just reacted. She swung the heavy tripod in an arc. It connected with the attacker's nose before continuing its trajectory, slamming into Ruzar's temple. Both men fell, but the driver staggered back to his feet, veering sideways as he zoned back in on Charlie.

The passenger joined in on the attack, rushing towards Elana who scrambled behind a boulder.

"Run, Charlie!" her friend screamed as she grabbed a large rock.

It was too late to run. Charlie slammed the legs of the tripod into his shoulder. He grabbed the weapon and pulled, then shoved, swinging her towards the edge of the cliff. Scrambling for purchase on the graveled surface, she pushed back. He twisted the tripod, and she fell. Something sharp sliced her forearm. She had little time to react before he kicked her in the side.

"Fuck you, asshole!" Charlie screamed.

He tried to slam the tripod into her chest. Refusing to let go, her elbows banged painfully into the ground. Charlie glanced past him and saw Elana slam a rock into the side of the second attacker's head. He screamed and grabbed Elana's hair. She swung again, this time with a direct hit to his balls.

Charlie kicked out, hitting the driver's knee. He shouted and tried to move out of range, but a now furious Charlie kicked at his thigh then pulled the tripod towards her with all her might. He stumbled over her body and with one last shove, she let go. Both man and tripod disappeared off the edge.

The momentum rolled her over onto her stomach and

Charlie scrambled to stop herself from sliding over the cliff. The dizzying drop made her want to vomit as she glanced down at her foot dangling over the side.

"Please, God, no," she sobbed. Visions of the second assailant tipping her over, had her frozen on the brink of oblivion. Nails tore as she dug fingers into rock. Blood coating her left hand made it slip. The rising sun lit the sky with shimmering golds, water expanded in all directions, and a sea breeze cooled her sweat-covered forehead. Not a bad last view of planet Earth before one died.

"Charlie!" Elana called. "Don't move, honey. I'm coming to get you."

"The other man?" Charlie asked.

"I de-brained the dickhead."

Charlie sobbed out a laugh, then froze as gravel shifted beneath her.

A minute later, Elana called out. Her voice sounding loud through Charlie's buzzing shock. "Easy, don't move; I've got you. I'm going to grab your arm and scoot back."

"If you slip, we might both go over." Charlie re-adjusted her grip.

"It's not as bad as it seems. I'm holding onto an outcropping of rock."

Elana grabbed Charlie's arm. Painfully—inch by inch—they shifted back. When the girls were a safe distance away, they fell into each other's arms, hugging out their relief.

Elana pulled a thin satin scarf from a backpack and wrapped Charlie's arm. "Keep pressure on it."

"How's Ruzar?"

"Still out cold. You really hammered him upside the head— not sure if he's even alive. There's a gaping cut across his temple."

"It was a mistake. We need to call the paramedics."

"I know. I'll drive that evil-ass taxi to the nearest hotel. Stay here with Ruzar, see to his head."

"Are... are you sure the other guy is dead?"

Elana nodded, looking like she wanted to hurl, as she began to tremble.

"What if the driver's keys went over the edge... with him?"

"There's only one way to find out. If so, then I'll walk for help." Elana took off back to the car, and Charlie curled her knees to her chest as she shook violently. She had a nasty feeling that the evil from this day would follow her off the cliffs like a poisonous fog, curling down past the dock and across the sea.

Chapter Three

Clicking his pen, Donnie looked at his watch. The instructor took way too long to wrap up the day's training. He prattled on about new advances in propulsion which could reduce a drone's engine heat signature, thus reducing detection via vibration and heat. Donnie closely followed advancements in the unmanned aerial vehicle—drone—arena. Thanks to independent research, he'd already covered much of the day's curriculum. His heart pumped a little faster, though, at getting his hands on the newly released insect-sized drones. The rumors were true. Drones were now that tiny, and just that morning, he'd held the prototype in his hands. The valuable bastard looked like a yellow hornet, capable of flying a distance of three kilometers, at more than 18 kilometers per hour, equipped with a thermal micro-camera.

Chasing high-value targets for a living meant that the small drone was a distinctly desirable tool for the MIT teams. And the rumors were—MIT2 would test that prototype in the field. Every analyst's wet dream.

As soon as the instructor excused them for the day, Donnie pulled out his phone. The conversation he'd had with Slater bothered him, and he couldn't stop thinking of how he'd left things off with Charlie.

The phone rang, and Dylan "Atlas" Jenkins picked up. The Utahan sniper—originally from the 19th Special Forces Group—was a great asset to the team. Both he and Donnie were stationed Stateside, temporarily forced to be away from MIT2. Donnie hated that replacements had been rotated in for them in the field.

Two weeks ago, just days before MIT2's deployment, a drunk driver t-boned Atlas's Dodge Challenger. The accident strained ligaments in the operator's back. After a week of bed rest, Atlas still felt tender, and like Donnie, he was eager to get back to MIT2.

"How's the back feeling?"

"I may have overworked it at the gym. I saw the doc this morning, I'll be returning to duty in two weeks."

"Two weeks, huh? You still in the Fort Bragg area?"

"Yup. Scratching my balls in the locker room as we speak."

"Meet me at the Cross Creek Mall. I have a proposal."

Thirty minutes later, Donnie sat opposite the laid-back operator at a well-known coffee spot. Atlas was the opposite of Donnie in many ways. He looked like a hippie surfer, and not one of the deadliest snipers in Special Operations. Atlas ran a hand through sun-bleached, wavy hair, as he gingerly stretched out his back.

Donnie leaned on the table. "I have one day left of training."

"Bully for you. You still can't join the team. MIT2 has just gone radio silent. Last time I spoke to Max, he mentioned a new target embedded in South Sudan. We'll have to wait until they've returned to Nairobi before we swap out, and that could take weeks."

"I know. I spoke with Johnny yesterday before they left. I still want to fly out."

"To Kenya?"

"To Italy or possibly Malta."

"What the fuck is in Malta?"

Atlas hadn't yet been to Johnny's farm or met Charlie. That made things easier for Donnie. He wouldn't get ragged for showing an interest in a girl he'd kept at arm's length for way too long.

"Not what—who. A friend from Wyoming is visiting and I thought we could all hook up; it beats sitting in North Carolina."

"A lady-friend? Mate, I'm not gonna be your third wheel."

"You won't have to, Charlie has a friend with her. A single friend—as far as I can tell."

"Screw that. You ain't setting me up with some random chick!"

Donnie pulled out his phone and tapped away, pulling up Elana's Facebook profile and handing it over. He'd met Charlie's friend at Johnny's notorious party a few months before. "You're welcome to stay behind. This way, we're only twelve hours away from the team, as opposed to twenty hours."

"Holy shit, she's not a human, she's a Victoria Secret model."

"In the flesh. Are you coming?"

"Hell, yes. I'm coming."

"I'll call Charlie and determine where we can meet. Stop ogling." Donnie had to wrench the phone from his mate's hand. He walked out the door, bracing himself for a potentially awkward conversation.

Johnny had shared Charlie's number with the team when she'd told him that she'd be country hopping for the next three months. Johnny watched over her like a big brother, except he wasn't the one lying awake and thinking of her in the early hours—wondering who Charlie was with and if she was safe.

Taking a deep breath, Donnie dialed the number. It rang and

rang. Just as he was about to hang up, she answered.

"Um. Hello?"

"Charlie?"

"Who is this?"

"It's Donnie."

She didn't say anything.

"You know. James's friend…"

"Donnie, of course, I know who you are. What do you want?"

This might be a harder sell than he'd first thought. He contemplated backing out of the call but chose honesty instead.

"I can't stop thinking about you. After your dad died, we didn't get to talk, and I need to know if you're okay."

Silence. For a second, he thought she'd hung up. A hitched breath came through the line. *Shit.* He'd upset her.

"I'm sorry. I didn't mean to bring up your father—"

"It's not that. I didn't expect a call from you or from anyone back home. It's nice, especially after the week I've had."

"Wait. What do you mean? Where are you?"

More silence.

"Charlie, talk to me."

"I'm still in Malta. Something happened… it's not a big deal. I'm fine now."

"As opposed to what? What happened?"

"Two men attacked us. Three days ago, in Gozo."

"Define attacked. Attacked as in 'mugged' or attacked as in—"

"They tried to kill us."

"How badly are you hurt?"

"Both of us are okay. Bruises and stitches. A friend of ours is in the hospital; he's just woken from an induced coma and I'm on my way to see him."

She relayed the chilling story. Of how she'd fought for her

life, how she'd almost fallen to her death and Donnie wanted to put a fist through the wall.

"We've spent the last few days with the police and at the hospital. The authorities have been after a serial killer. Seven women have fallen to their deaths on the cliffs over the last two years. They think it was the men that attacked us, and the locals are hailing us as heroes."

Donnie's gut felt like ice. He needed to be by her side, to watch over the woman who was like a baby sister to Johnny. At least that's what Donnie told himself.

"Stay where you are, I'll be there as soon as possible."

"I don't want you flying over. I told you, we're fine. Besides, we had to reschedule our flights around the attack, but thankfully, we're heading out tomorrow for Morocco."

"Do you think that's wise?"

"We're meeting up with the rest of our dance group and a film crew. We have three photo shoots planned and two performances scheduled in Marrakesh. Plus, we'll be training with some of the local belly dancers."

"I don't like this. Come home."

"Morocco is a whole other country. We can escape the ugliness and the violence…"

She couldn't carry on, and he heard the tears in her voice. Donnie rubbed a hand over his eyes. Charlie didn't deserve any of this. Her father had just died. She'd run to find peace and instead run into violence. The two women, traveling alone after such an ordeal—their vulnerable situation bothered him. Arguing with Charlie would make her dig in her heels.

"I'll check in with you tomorrow. Keep your phone nearby."

"Thanks, Donnie, I appreciate the concern. I have to go."

"Charlie," he called out, reluctant to end the call.

"Yes?"

"If you feel afraid in any way, call me. No matter what time of the day or night, I'm here. Even if it's just to talk."

After Donnie hung up, he relayed the information to Atlas. Next, he stopped by the boxing gym, releasing his frustration on a bag. Later that night—as he lay in bed—he couldn't shake the worry that phone call invoked. The Intelligence Specialist in him prodded Donnie to rise and pull out his military grade laptop. After establishing a secure line, he researched the recent attacks in Gozo. Seven women had died—beaten and tossed onto the rocks below. The eighth victim had survived. The murders were significant as the Republic of Malta had low crime rates.

It was one of the safer tourist destinations in the EU. Donnie used his cyber hacking abilities to gain access to the survivor's file. Martina Denaro. Attacked a year ago while walking her dog along the cliffs. According to her statement, a masked man had assaulted her. She described her attacker as a large man—over six feet tall and close to two hundred pounds. He wore brass knuckles, punched her in the face and cracked her cheekbone. Luckily, she wore a fanny pack that contained her police grade mace. She'd managed to spray him repeatedly before screaming at the top of her lungs. By the time help arrived, the man was gone.

Donnie rubbed his neck, knowing what came next. Re-focusing, he tapped away furiously, hacking into the Imgar Police station in Gozo and locating the online file. He opened the report and froze. Charlie's image sat front and center—a photograph—taken just days before. One of many that cataloged her injuries. Fine, my ass, he thought. The son of a bitch had torn her up, both mentally and physically. He sifted through her nasty scrapes and cuts, including her sliced up forearm. The dazed look in her eyes—reflecting shock—had his gut clenching.

Donnie zoned in on their statements. According to Charlie and Elana, the perps were of average height. Unmasked. No mention of knuckle dusters. Hacking into more files, Donnie sifted through autopsic reports from the last twenty-four months. Two of the female Gozo bodies were too battered from the fall and the eroding sea, to recover much evidence. But the other five victims showed bruising, indicative of being punched in the face with a metal object. Best guess from the pulverized patterns? Brass knuckles. Different assailants had attacked Elana and Charlie. The men were dead—the threat permanently removed. Then why did the back of Donnie's neck prickle?

He never ignored his gut instincts in the field. As an analyst, facts and hard evidence led every mission, but that didn't mean that intuition never played a role. As an intelligence professional, collecting data and developing knowledge of the enemy's intent, was a critical objective of any mission. Did these assailants even connect to the Gozo serial killer? If so, then what was their plan? Patterns and links were always present, and the analyst in Donnie needed answers.

Donnie considered the long list of items he'd need to prep. Decision made, he called Atlas as he pulled up connecting flights. "Wake up, asshole. We're heading to Marrakesh."

Gozo, Malta.

An elderly couple hobbled out the door and Charlie took one of their now open seats in the busy waiting room. Visiting hours started in ten minutes. Thankfully, after three long days, Ruzar was now awake. She hadn't yet seen him, electing to keep her distance while his family kept vigilance. Charlie had checked in with the ward on a daily basis, relieved to hear that he was awake and talking.

She'd come alone to Gozo, leaving Elana at the house in Valletta to finalize the details of the next leg of their trip.

They were still staying with friends in Malta. Well, technically they were Charlie's brother's friends. After her father passed, her sibling decided to step back into her life. It wasn't like they never spoke, but the relationship between her brother—Nathan—and their father was a strained affair. They were always at loggerheads. Nate was much older than Charlie—eight years older. And although they battled to connect, she still relied on his substantial presence. He'd always hated the farm, electing to move to California when Charlie was just a kid. Apart from rare visits, he lived a life entirely separate to hers. He ran a string of successful Michelin Star restaurants. When Nate heard she'd be traveling for the next few months, he'd offered to help with her overseas accommodation, and volunteered to look after the books on the farm. Without his generosity, she'd never have been able to take a break from the grinding work in running such a large farming operation. She'd left a capable team in place, thus retaining her sanity.

Charlie looked up at the clock, wanting to delay the inevitable—an awkward visit. *'Hi, Ruzar... I didn't mean to hit you over the head with a tripod... just wanted to say hello before I disappear off into the sunset. Hope we can still be friends.'*

God forbid she ran into one of his family members. *'Sorry for de-braining Ruzar. My name is Charlie—by the way.'*

Her hands still trembled. Even after three days of rest. Every time she closed her eyes, she saw the stomach-turning view of rocks below dizzying cliffs, as she'd clawed and scrambled her way back to safety. Swallowing back nausea, Charlie fingered her mobile phone, thinking about the call from Donnie earlier in the day. He'd actually called her.

The whole conversation felt confusing. Why was Jamie's brooding friend suddenly so interested in her welfare? Brooding was a good word to describe Donnie. Whenever she was around, he'd step back in the shadows, and squint at her with those narrow eyes that spoke of heated, wicked things. He rarely smiled or showed emotion. The brutal look that settled most of the time on his hawkish face, motivated her to "poke the bear." Unfortunately, he poked back, and his verbal jabs sometimes drew blood.

A woman's pitiful cries had Charlie glancing up. An older lady dressed in a black, tailored suit stepped from Ruzar's room, her eyes wet with tears. Charlies stomach flipped. Had he taken a turn? The elegant woman turned back and spoke in another language before switching to English. "Rest up, my son. I'll bring you some treats. Your father will come by later, don't make him angry. Be a good boy."

Ruzar's mother? She sounded like she had a Russian accent, but Charlie was no expert. Two burly men flanked her, as they made their way to the elevator. His mother never looked Charlie's way, and Charlie felt grateful for the crowded room.

She stood, groaning at her still bruised limbs, and limped up the passage to Ruzar's private room. Second to the left. Nudging the door open, she stepped in.

Ruzar stared out the window, still hooked up to beeping machines and an IV line. Taking a breath, she called his name. He stiffened before slowly turning.

Charlie smiled nervously. "Hey slugger, how are you feeling?"

"Shit. Charlotte." His already pale face turned gray.

"That bad huh?"

"No. What are you doing here?" He looked over her intently, his eyes pausing at her bandaged arm.

"I came to see you." She walked up to the bed and placed a hand on his broad shoulder.

"Honey, you need to go. Now." His gaze was like a soft caress as he traced a finger along her jaw.

"I know you probably don't want to see me. I socked you across the head and I'm so, so sorry. I was aiming for the driver. I didn't—"

"No! Firefly. Stop. Jesus, listen to me. You have to go." Grasping her hand, he tried to sit up and the movement had him groaning.

"Don't move. Oh, my God, I'm upsetting you."

His eyes shot to hers, and he pulled her close. The grip on her wrist felt like a manacle. "Go back to America," he said between gritted teeth. "The men that you killed, their families want vengeance."

"How would you know that? You've just woken—"

"When it's safe, I'll come and find you. We can be together, fuck them all."

She stood there, stunned while frowning at his words. His babbling made no sense and the vengeance part caused a roaring din. Her ears buzzed as her skin grew clammy. Charlie's pause had him pulling her onto his chest. He grasped a hand to the back of her head and mashed her lips to his.

Charlie wrenched herself out of his hold and stumbled back. "What are you doing? Are you crazy?"

"I can protect you. You and me against the world. When I've healed, we'll meet up. I don't care where you are, I'll—"

"Ruzar, stop. I told you on the beach that I wasn't ready for anything but friendship."

"Screw friendship, I've risked everything for you! My relationship with my family and my career."

"What are you talking about?"

He erupted. "You want to leave me? Then go, see how far you get!"

His expression—darkening with dangerous emotion—had her stepping back. She hardly knew this man. She'd stupidly trusted him, and his obsessive words made her ill.

"I know these men—the ones that will hunt you—they're notoriously good at what they do. Killing stupid, naive Americans like you. Start running now, Firefly."

"Why are you saying this? You're trying to scare me into staying with you. Is this all a game? Seduce the silly tourist. Well, screw you. The men that attacked us also killed other women on those cliffs. They were a serial killing duo, and now they are dead. The police sergeant says we have nothing to worry about."

His eyes turned cold. "You're right. I did try to seduce you. I wanted a quick fuck with a pretty redhead. Except you can't shut that twangy mouth, and thanks to you, I'm lying in this bed instead of sitting behind my desk. You've cost me a big contract."

His vile words broke the last of the threads that linked her to his Maltese world. She gave him a hostile glare. "I wish you luck. Get well and have a nice life."

Charlie walked to the door on shaky legs. It had been a mistake coming here.

"Charlotte, I'm sorry."

"So am I."

"Firefly, please stay."

She walked out, not looking back. Charlie stopped by the pharmacy before using the bathroom. She washed her hands robotically in the sink. When a wave of nausea hit, she ran for the toilet. Sinking onto her butt in the quiet cubicle, she cursed the direction her trip had taken. This vacation was supposed to be a fun getaway, and a time for healing. Instead, she felt like broken shards, all exposed and bruised as constant explosions rocked her sanity. She rubbed a temple, and her wrist twitched in pain. Something buzzed against her ass, Charlie reached for the phone. *Donnie.* Fantastic, another complication to add to her mixed-up world. She rubbed her stomach and answered.

"How are you feeling?" he asked. That deep voice sounding like a growl.

"Don't ask."

"Are you at the hospital—visiting your friend?"

He said the word 'friend' with disdain. Charlie hadn't told him much about Ruzar—fudging over the details of her failed holiday romance—but Donnie naturally fitted the pieces together.

"I am. Ruzar is no longer my friend. I barely recognize him, not that I knew him before."

"What happened?" Concern colored his words.

"He's not making any sense. Told me that there are men out there that will be hunting me. That he seduced... never mind."

"Wait. Go back. He said that men are hunting you?"

"He's delirious from the head wound and being dramatic. I spoke to the sergeant again this morning. They've wrapped up the case in a neat little bow and we're perfectly safe. Elana and I were just in the wrong place, at the wrong time."

"I need his full name."

"The sergeant's name?"

"Both. Your friend—in the hospital—and the sergeant's."

"Okay. What will you do with it, give it to an Army buddy?"

She knew Donnie was a veteran—like Jamie—and now they sold military clothing.

He didn't answer her question. Instead, he asked, "Where are you?"

"In the hospital bathroom."

"Tell me you're leaving soon for Morocco. Even better, tell me you've changed your mind and you're heading back to the States."

"We fly out in two hours for Casablanca, then we're heading to Marrakesh."

"I'll meet you there."

"Wait. What?"

"We'll be arriving a day behind you. I'll call when I land in Morocco."

"I don't understand. You're flying over because of me?"

"I need a vacation and thought I might annoy you with my presence at the same time. I'm bringing along a friend, a work colleague."

Donnie went over the details as Charlie sat in stunned silence. Once they'd hung up, she placed the phone to her chest. Charlie could've fought him on his decision and told him to stay away. Except she wanted Donnie there. He was the very last man she needed and the very first man she craved.

Chapter Four

Gozo, Republic of Malta.

"Harra." Ruzar swore in Maltese.

His head pounded, grounding him into the mattress, as he seethed with mounting rage. She'd turned her back and walked out the door—like he'd meant nothing. Like the last week was a waste of her time. Charlotte was his Firefly, a light dancing in his dark world, with dazzling energy and blazing hair. She'd made him smile and laugh, and he hadn't done that in a long while. The door swung open, and Ruzar turned his aching head, praying she'd come back.

His father stood on the threshold, flanked by three bodyguards and his second in command.

Ruzar knew this moment would come, and he clenched the white sheets as his father looked him over. Luca Comino was a good-looking bastard who'd produced handsome sons. Ruzar felt grateful for at least that. If daddy dearest disowned him, Ruzar still had his looks. He waited patiently as the alpha fucker walked to the window. Two men remained outside as the third scanned the room for bugs. His father then turned, looking down at his prone son.

"I give you one job—one small fucking job—and you screw the family over."

"Papa—"

"Don't talk when I'm speaking." Luca Comino's profile spoke of ageless power as he stared out the window. "Your mother is a wreck. Thanks to you, her third cousin is dead."

"Andrej was an idiot. I told him to hold off. Told—"

"You told him shit. Literal shit is all that comes out of your mouth. Like manure from a cow's ass. Andrej called me, the day before and told me you had second thoughts about killing the American women. Said you'd acted like a pussy."

"The location was all wrong. You shouldn't have dragged the family into it! I work alone. You forced me to depart from what I do by bringing my imbecile cousin and his sidekick into my business."

"Your business? Your shit-hole business? Do you think I don't know what your plans are? You work for the family, and any killing gets done through the family. Except you don't see it that way. You want to go off—half-cocked—and become an infamous assassin asshole. Why can't you be like your brother?"

The prodigal son. Ruzar had tried for many years to be like his perfect sibling, but no-one could be that much of a brown noser.

"I killed for you—last year—blew up that detective, and I eliminated those two Russians last month. Investigations have never traced any of our kills back to the family. I'm precise and never leave a trail. Now, you want to lick Serbian ass, merge the two families, and bring in their idiot son?"

His father spoke carefully. "That was your cousin. The body, now lying in the morgue is family. You chose some red-haired bitch over blood—over Andrej who's not even left in one piece?

They couldn't recover all his smashed-up body parts at the bottom of the damn cliff. And look at your face. The bitch marked you."

Ruzar restrained himself from running a hand over the bandaged scar at his temple.

His father's prime henchman—Eddie Zarafa—spoke up. "You're not thinking clearly, son." Ruzar hated when Eddie called him "son," because Eddie had been more a father to Ruzar than Luca Comino had. Even in his fifties, Eddie still wore his hair in a short military cut. His proud stature and built physique spoke of the hours he spent at the gym. Ruzar and Eddie worked out regularly together and had a connection that transcended friendship. Ruzar truly cared for Eddie Zarafa. The fact that Eddie sided with his father hurt.

"Andrej should never have gone ahead with it—out in the open like that. His impatience got him tossed over that bloody cliff." Ruzar couldn't stop the defensive tone.

His father responded. "Bull. It was the perfect alibi—kill the women and blame it on the serial killer. Now, I have to cover up this bungling mess. Do you know how many officials I've paid off? How much I must do to protect your mother's family? Or how I've paced in this fucking room as you've lain in a coma. I almost lost you over that Yankee whore."

Ruzar didn't say anything. He couldn't. His father was right, he'd screwed over family. The Comino family and his mother's Borjan clan. The Cominos might be Maltese mafia—confined to a small island—but his father's operation rivaled those across the water. Ruzar's family knew the benefits of working with their extended family in Serbia. Not only had both families grown their gambling syndicates together, but they now dipped their toes into cocaine smuggling and arms trafficking operations across North Africa. And Ruzar risked it all by falling for an American firefly. Charlotte wouldn't be his downfall.

Ruzar turned to his father as his stomach rebelled against the promise he was about to make. "Fine, I'll fix this. I know where Charlotte Quinn is heading. I've planted a tracking device in her phone."

"You'll stay in Malta and heal. I have it under control. The *Crimson Quarter* will find the two women."

Ruzar's stomach burned. The *Crimson Quarter*—run by his mother's extended family—were not just Serbian assassins; they were one of the cruelest gangs in Europe. If they had a chance, they raped and tortured their victims for hours. Ruzar might be a killer, but he cleanly disposed of his targets. Aside from the fact that he didn't have the stomach for gore, he had a professional reputation to uphold.

A hand grasped his wrist, making him jump. He looked up into his father's impassive face. Cold, dead eyes stared back. Even as a child, he'd never seen warmth in that face, only judgment and scorn. Now his father shot him a shark-like smile. "Easy, my boy. Tell me her location, then lie back and let Papa take care of the rest."

◊ ◊ ◊

Atlas dozed in the seat next to Donnie. Sleep would be a welcome friend, except Donnie needed to finalize mission details. Technically this wasn't a mission, just two friendly parties meeting up in colorful Morocco. Except Donnie had the same jittery feeling he'd felt before every mission, and he itched to land on Moroccan soil.

Blocking out the hum of the aircraft engines, Donnie cataloged the tools and weapons he had at his disposal as he ran through a timeline. The two men had seven days before MIT2 possibly returned to Nairobi. If the Sudan mission delayed the team in the field, then Donnie may have extra time. They'd packed as much as they could get away with… under a plane… on a domestic flight. Tactical pens, two small drones, survival gear and knives.

MIT3 had contacts in Morocco and Tunisia. One of their assets in Marrakesh—a former British SAS lad—would provide weaponry, MRE's, burner phones and radios. Donnie knew he might be swimming up a Rambo stream, but his gut told him it was the right move. Things were likely to be fine. They'd protect the dance group while enjoying the sunny country and its happy people, aside from the occasional scammers and con artists that cluttered the main tourist jaunts. Donnie was keen to taste the Moroccan cuisine. If he was honest, he was equally as eager to taste someone else, a girl who smelled of roses and bad ideas.

First, Donnie needed to make sure Charlie was safe, and under his protection. His mind wandered back to the night of Johnny's party in Wyoming. Donnie shut down the memories and got back to work.

Chapter Five

Marrakesh, Morocco.

Noise and a kaleidoscope of chaos assaulted Charlie the second she stepped out of the Riad. The traditional Moroccan townhouse surrounded by a tiled courtyard embodied tranquility, that was until the rest of the dance group and film crew arrived. Charlie barely had time for a morning walk to Marrakesh's main square, before the group adjusted their plans. All she wanted to do was explore the vibrant narrow streets and curl up for a nap. Charlie settled for a refreshing shower, before readying herself for the next leg of the journey. Instead of remaining in Marrakesh, the group decided to travel to Merzouga—a small town in the Sahara Desert near the Algerian border. Zach thought the endless expanses of fiery dunes would make an incredible backdrop for their photographic shoots and YouTube videos. He was particularly excited to capture Charlie's deep crimson locks, blowing in the breeze—her hair was the exact color of the sand. Zach's energy was contagious, and Charlie couldn't wait to see the group's fire dancing skills set against such exotic backdrops. Wyoming fields and mountains were incredible, but this was where their art was meant to be performed.

They'd travel the nine hours, then would spend the night before heading back to Marrakesh. Later in the week, the dancers planned to take belly dancing lessons with a local group. Charlie couldn't wait. Over the years, she'd devoured every belly dancing technique and craved tips from the Moroccan women. It would be a truly magical experience.

Charlie looked around the narrow streets and ached to walk the labyrinth. Instead, she pulled out her phone, and called Donnie. The smell of fresh spices and bread baking drifted down the lane and made her mouth water. The call went straight to voicemail. Her dance group would probably make it back to Marrakesh—from the Saharan trip—half a day after he'd arrive from the States. As she waited for the beep, she noticed a man lingering at the mouth of the alley wearing black jeans and a navy shirt. His large belt buckle glinted in the sun. Their eyes collided, his cold glance turned away.

The touristy vibe seemed absent, yet the unnerving man wasn't a local. Charlie slipped back into the Riad, and when she glanced back, the man was gone. Dead air drifted through the line, and she realized she hadn't left a message.

"Uh... Donnie. It's me. Plans have changed. We're heading up to Merzouga for the night. I'm not sure if we'll have cell coverage. I'll call you when we're heading back... travel safe... anyway... thanks. I'll call you. Shit, I already said that. Uh, anyway, bye."

That went well. Wrinkling her nose, Charlie sunk against the wall. Her rowdy friends spilled into the courtyard, scuttling around the fountain. Grabbing her backpack and trolley bag, Charlie ran to catch up. The bus left at eight-thirty. They had half an hour to get to the station.

As they hurried through the narrow streets dodging loaded

carts and random piles of manure, Charlie glanced back catching a glimpse of the same man she'd seen earlier. Was she being paranoid? Being victimized in a violent assault had her seeing boogeymen lurking in every corner. She wouldn't allow her neurotic state to run the show. Catching up, she grabbed Elana's hand. "Hooah. Time for some dune dancing, baby."

Her friend grinned. "Girlfriend, we're going to the Sahara freaking Desert."

◊ ◊ ◊

An hour before dawn, Donnie walked onto the narrow street and quickly opened the trunk. The lane was empty of curious eyes. Their asset lived in Gueliz, the European quarter of Marrakesh, a mile from the old city and just over half a mile from the train station. Those were details that Donnie took note of, in case things went FUBAR.

They weren't exactly there for morning tea. Atlas slipped out of the small home facing the street with two heavy bags, depositing them in the trunk. Looking both ways, Donnie nodded once to their British contact standing in the shadow of the entryway, before climbing in behind the wheel. Atlas slipped in beside him. The tension rolling off the usually sedate warrior was warranted. They'd picked up enough firepower to flatten a souk. Not only were they locked and loaded for action, but their arsenal contained MRE's, survival gear, GPS trackers, night vision goggles, a new laptop, burner phones, and medical supplies. For the first time in twenty-four hours, Donnie felt like he could breathe—aside from the fact that Charlie wasn't even in the same town. Her vexing voicemail had him cursing and wanting to punch the dash. As far as he was aware, they should shortly be heading back after a sunrise video shoot on the dunes.

He needed Charlie to check in. Her phone went straight to voicemail—probably out of range.

He navigated carefully to their rental apartment, keeping an eye out for police. The last thing they needed was to be pulled over.

"You don't think you're overreacting, dude?" Atlas asked as he shifted to stretch in the small sedan.

"I'm following instinct combined with what I've researched online. Buddy, nothing adds up. After barely three days, Gozo police closed the case. The women were allowed and even encouraged to leave Malta by the local authorities, and there has been no coverage of the attacks by the Maltese media."

The constabulary swept the whole incident under an ornate Maltese carpet, one that made Donnie's skin itch.

"And because the tangos were illegal Serbians?" Atlas asked.

"Serbians who supposedly lived off the radar for three years in Gozo. Do you know how small that island is? Yet none of the townsfolk had ever seen the attackers before, so they'd just emerged from where, the sea caves below the cliffs? Marked as serial killers who'd killed seven women over the last couple of years, and yet I can't access any of their records. The two bastards have fucking aliases." Flexing his fingers against the steering wheel, he glanced over at Atlas. "What?"

"Nothing. Don't shoot my nuts off."

"Atlas, what's that look for?"

Atlas cracked his fingers as he yawned. "Why are we messing around Morocco instead of heading to Malta to investigate?"

"Because I need to ensure that the girls are safe. Hopefully, we'll coast under the radar and won't even need the shit in the trunk."

"For sure. You care about her?"

"She's a friend," Donnie said carefully.

"I see how it is. Like, possibly a friend with benefits?"

Donnie elected not to answer as they approached the rental accommodation. They'd pack gear while waiting for the call that would have them back on the move.

Charlie felt like she could conquer the world and that truly alive feeling had her grinning from ear to ear. The sand in her teeth and grainy residue coating her skin did nothing to dampen her mood. Nor did the chill in the air. Surrounded by a red sea, she never wanted to board the bus and drive away from the wind-swept dunes. Reluctantly, she wrapped her Pashmina close and stepped up into the large bus before swinging herself into the window seat.

The engine sputtered to life and Charlie blocked out the voices of her teammates as she gazed at the passing scenery. For the first time in months, she felt at peace. It seemed ridiculous, but she'd felt her father's spirit, out there in the desert—on the undulating sand. As they'd climbed to the top of a dune, she'd dropped back from the rest of her group, and taken her time to absorb the energy of the land. The wind sifted the sand in endless waves, the movement reminding her of windy Wyoming grasslands back home. Her feet had sunk into the still chilled sand, pulling her downwards as she'd struggled to balance. The air smelled different to home, just as dry, but she'd tasted exotic freedom on the breeze. One moment of suspended bliss was all it took for the tears to burn beneath her eyelids. The sacred breeze wrapped her in its silence, telling her it would be all right.

Now bumping over sanded potholes, Charlie smothered her mourning heartache and tuned back into the conversation dominating the vehicle space.

Zach leaned towards her. "We'll still be in time to practice. Marrakesh isn't going anywhere. How often do we get to film with such an impressive backdrop? It's a five-hour drive away."

"Wait, what's a five-hour drive away?" Charlie asked.

"Ait Benhaddou," Elana said before chatting to the driver in Arabic. They negotiated the new destination stopover, and he nodded.

Back in Wyoming, Charlie remembered researching Ait Benhaddou as a potential location for a photo shoot, but due to time constraints, the group had nixed the idea. Now, they were caught up in the romance of the trip and the old village was foolishly back on the map. A cluster of earthen buildings layered in steppes and surrounded by high walls made up the ancient town. It lay in the foothills of the High Atlas Mountains. The dramatic pre-Saharan architecture and defensive walls reinforced with corner towers, made such an astounding backdrop, that many filmmakers used the location.

"We don't have time—"

"C'mon, Charlie, it's on the way. We'll schedule a sunset photo shoot, then stay the night. We'll drive the four-hour drive to Marrakesh in the morning. We're only meeting the belly dancing biddies in two days' time."

Elana confirmed their altered plans with the film crew at the back of the bus, then yelled, "I'll book a hotel as soon as we get signal."

Crap. That meant Charlie would have to call Donnie. She felt like she was giving him the runaround and she hoped he'd give up and enjoy Marrakesh without her. Besides, they were perfectly fine. Three hours later—as they stopped for gas in a small town—Elana booked accommodation. Charlie powered up her phone and it beeped with incoming messages. Two texts and three voicemails from the man. All said the same thing. "Charlie. Call me."

Taking a breath, she pressed redial.

"Are you okay?" Donnie asked.

"Fine," Charlie said. "Are you in Marrakesh?"

"Yes. How far out are you?"

"We've been traveling for a few hours, but Donnie, we're staying in Ait Benhaddou for the night."

Silence greeted her statement. She paced dusty circles behind the bus, twirling a lock of windswept red hair as she spoke. Charlie continued, "Look, why don't we call it a day. We keep missing each other, and I'm sure you want to relax and do some sightseeing. Maybe go to Casablanca or Rabat…"

Still nothing. "Are you there?"

"Yes, I am. Where are you staying in Ait Benhaddou?"

"What?"

"Where are you staying? Hotel-wise?" Donnie asked.

"Umm. Some new fancy place. As it's offseason, we got a group discount."

"I need a name," Donnie said.

"Ahmar Hulm Hotel and Spa."

"We'll be there in just under four hours. Keep in touch."

"Wait—"

Donnie hung up. Hell and shit, her life was getting mighty complicated. The bus groaned as the dance group climbed back on. Turning, Charlie froze. A man stood across the street. He wore local clothes, but his eyes drew her attention. That same hardened look as the man in Marrakesh and he watched her with the same predatory gaze. He was all hard muscle with a vicious look around his mouth. A scooter drove past. Kids chased a ball, yelling as they ran. Charlie smiled at the stranger. His expression didn't alter and he didn't look away or even blink. Instead, the now corrupted air made it hard for her to breathe. Palms damp, she wrapped the lavender scarf around herself and hurried around the bus to the stairs. Her heart pumped in a primitive rhythm as she stumbled to her seat. *Close the door. Close the door.* Her silent chanting fell on deaf ears as the driver chatted with a British tourist through the open entryway.

Her eyes darted back across the street. Her onlooker was gone. She checked the perimeter but couldn't see the creepster amongst the scattering of tourists.

"Charlie, what's wrong?"

Elana's question had her jumping.

"Why do you look like you're expecting a sandstorm to rain down upon us?"

"Don't be crazy. I just thought I saw someone I know."

"Yeah right," Elana said as the bus pulled away.

Charlie barely noticed, her entire focus was on any vehicles following their group. Sitting back in her seat, she pulled out her phone. Then she slipped it back in her sling bag. What good would a text to Donnie do? *A scary looking man looked at me funny... I have a foolish imagination.* Besides, Donnie was just a salesman... on vacation... with a buddy... at least four hours away. What could he do? With one last glance out the back window, she settled back, mentally going over her newest dance routine.

Chapter Six

Ait Benhaddou, Morocco.

"I cannot believe I'm standing in a place where they filmed *Game of Thrones*. Holy shit!" Zach squealed like a kid.

Charlie glanced around for the hundredth time. It was an impressive sight and she felt like she'd stepped back—to the time of the gladiators. She balanced on the edge of the crumbling rampart in the walled ksar—the ancient fortified village. The red clay buildings below provided a burning backdrop to the setting sun. A small crowd had gathered to watch their video shoot. Tourists snapped away and local merchants watched from shadowed doorways. The sequence that Charlie was about to perform was the last reel to be captured before they wrapped for the evening. It had taken all afternoon to get set up and to film three of the routines. Elana and Zach had danced their hearts out, and now it was Charlie's turn.

Standing in a tribal tiered ruched skirt, with a cinched and corseted half blouse covered in gold coins, Charlie felt powerful and female. The layered skirt shone with golds, turquoise, and olive greens. A coined belt tinkled at her waist as she situated herself for the final act.

Thanks to the make-up artist and small professional film crew, Charlie felt feminine and beautiful. She'd never worn this much make-up in her life. The false eyelashes felt heavy, adding emphasis to her darkly rimmed kohl eyes. They'd even plucked, groomed and colored her eyebrows into manicured slashes that set off her overly styled hair. With so much damn hairspray, Charlie would be cautious in brushing the candled flames near the proximity of her head.

The music began, and as the cameras rolled, Charlie let the seductive rhythm take over. Her skirts danced as a cold breeze swept around her. The coming winter season made itself known, and Charlie welcomed the brisk wind as she worked up a sweat. They stopped a few times to re-position her and to shoot from various angles. After the impromptu show, the courtyard quickly emptied as dusk fell.

With the help of Zach, Charlie handed off the candles and stepped down off the wide ledge. Eager to get out of the elaborate costume, she slipped into an empty chamber they'd used as a dressing room. Elana, who'd already changed out of her dance getup, stood guard as Charlie slipped on her jeans and sneakers in the dusty space. After pulling on a pale blue, pin-striped, fitted T-shirt, she slid on a white button-up shirt. Finally, she pulled on a denim jacket. Loosening some of the hairpins, Charlie shook out the stiff hairdo, happy when her mane fell softly down her back.

Elana slipped into the room. "Hurry up, slow coach. We want to walk the village before dinner."

"But all the storefronts are closing for the night." Many of the local merchants lived in a modernized town on the other side of the river. The ancient village of Ait Benhaddou, without basic resources, wasn't set up for comfortable living. By nightfall, aside from five Berber homes, there would be no-one left.

"Fifteen minutes. We'll run the streets to the top ramparts, snap a couple of photos, and then we're done. We'll meet the rest of the group back at the hotel. One of the camera guys will take our kit to the bus."

Charlie hesitated, pulling out a scarf and Zach poked his head in the doorway. "We're leaving too early in the morning for sightseeing. We've been stuck in a bus for most of the day. Get those dancing legs moving. C'mon. I'll beat you to the top."

Charlie hurried to keep up with them in the maze of narrow alleys. Every turn looked the same.

"Do any of you have a map?" she called.

"Nope," Elana yelled back. "Don't need one. Winding uphill will eventually get us to the top. There's a loft at the top of the village."

They stopped to glance inside a few of the crumbling dwellings. Some looked like small urban castles. Others were rebuilt with authentic tools and furniture, making the merchant houses look like something from *The Mummy*.

While her friends poked around, Charlie stepped out to look at the view. Lights from the hotels began to twinkle as dusk fell. She glanced down and froze. A man stood below. The same man who'd watched her at the bus stop that morning. The same man who now glanced up. Their eyes met, and Charlie held in panic. Her phone vibrated in her pocket, and she casually pulled it out, ignoring the man's friend who'd now joined him—a companion with a silver belt buckle and icy eyes.

Donnie didn't bother with a greeting. "The rest of your crew are in the parking area. Where the fuck are you?"

"You're here?" She breathed out her relief.

"Yes. Where are you?"

"Still in the village. I'm with Elana and Zach." She stepped out of view of the voyeurs below and plastered herself against the wall. "I think we're being followed. I've spotted the men before, in Marrakesh and at a bus stop—"

"Get out now. How far up are you?"

"Two-thirds of the way, I guess. Oh shit, I think they have buddies." Two more males stepped from the shadows of a dwelling down the path and Charlie snaked along the wall, slipping back into the room where she'd left her friends. Empty.

"Shit. I'm coming to you. I need you to descend—find a way. Make your way westwards, and veer to the left."

Stepping out of a back exit, she spotted Elana's blonde hair up ahead. "Why left?"

"That side of the village is in disrepair. There may be an exit point along the outer ramparts. Trust me on this and keep your phone on."

"Elana!" Charlie ran and grabbed her arm. "There's no time to explain. I think there are men after us. They have the same look as the two thugs on Gozo. We need to move."

Charlie thanked the stars for her pragmatic friend. With only a moment's hesitation, she nodded then called to Zach.

"Donnie is coming. He has a buddy with him," Charlie said as they caught up to their male friend.

"What? You mean he's in Morocco? In Ait Benhaddou."

"Yeah—"

"The sulky dude from the barbecue. The one who gaped at you dancing yet sneered at you like you were mud on his shoe? I'm only finding out about this now?"

"We'll talk about it later." Charlie yelled Zach's name in a low shout.

Just as he turned back, a goon stepped out a doorway and

grabbed Charlie's arm. She let out a scream and kicked him in the knee. Someone grabbed her jacket from behind and Zach launched himself at the second assailant. Charlie used her clutched phone to punch at the thug twisting her arm. The blow broke his nose on impact and with a howl, he let go.

Although Donnie had never visited Ait Benhaddou—or Morocco—he still had a good idea of the town's design. When he'd discovered that the dance group detoured to the tiny village on the way back to Marrakesh, he'd taken a moment to study the layout and exit points. Luckily after checking into the hotel, Donnie's instincts had pushed them to travel the short distance to the crumbling village, making their way over the low river where they'd run into the film crew and dancers emerging from the Ait Benhaddou Ksar.

Now both operators took off through the labyrinth of dark passages, intent on locating the three remaining dancers in the earthen maze. The men wore Mystery Ranch backpacks built for high-speed tier one operators. They also wore concealable holsters but preferred not to use their weapons to contain a situation. Drawing attention would be the last thing they needed. Besides, Donnie was comfortable using his hands. Unless he was shot at, pulling his newly acquired Glock was the last resort. Now, as they moved higher into the maze, leaping over low walls and racing through narrow passages, Donnie heard the sound he'd been dreading. The muffled thwap of a suppressed weapon. He swore and pushed himself harder than he'd ever done before.

Zach landed a lucky punch about the same time as Charlie's assailant fell against the wall. All three dancers took off, running and stumbling over rough ground.

"Stick to the left!" Charlie said as they approached a split in the path ahead. It was getting harder to see. During the day, these passages held little light. Now, as night fell, Charlie felt almost blind as she barreled her way through twists and turns. She sensed, rather than saw the hulking mass rocketing towards her. The muscled attacker ambushed her from a side lane, slamming her into the wall. The impact knocked the wind from her, and she collapsed, gasping. The man with the silver buckle. His reptilian eyes glinted as he raised a gun. Before he could aim, Zach barreled into him.

"Run, Charlie!"

The men struggled for the weapon as Charlie used the wall to drag herself to her feet.

"Elana, take Charlie, go," Zach yelled.

"No!" Charlie gasped as she stumbled towards the fighting men. More mercenaries spilled around the corner. Doing as Zach asked, Elana dragged Charlie away and down a passage.

The buckled thug threw Zach to the ground and pointed his gun. Time slowed as Charlie heard the discharge and saw her friend jerk. The gun fired again, and again.

"Zach!" she screamed.

"Move!" Elana pulled her around the corner and they took off running. Zach was dead, they'd just seen their kind and loyal friend die. If they slowed, they'd be next. And Donnie? He'd walk into an ambush. She'd invited him into a maze of vipers. Charlie tried not to hyperventilate as she stumbled over a doorway. Footsteps echoed, and Elana pulled them into the shadows. Three men ran past. The women paused before moving down a new passage. They rounded a corner, and shapes came at them from all sides. The girls kicked and screamed as men dragged them into a darkened room. Remembering a self-defense move that Jamie had taught her, Charlie reared back, headbutting the bastard holding her from behind. He dropped her, and she immediately kicked out, while fighting the rough hands grabbing for her hair.

Elana fought just as hard. Charlie heard something crash. One of the men yelled. A shot rang out in the enclosed space and Elana yelped. Panic had Charlie kicking hard, her foot slammed into her attacker's thigh and he stumbled back before falling into a crumbling wall. Mud bricks gave way and he tumbled from the towering structure to his death below.

Before Charlie could register what she'd done, an arm wrapped around her throat in a wrestler's grip and threw her onto her stomach. Her basic self-defense skills were no match for the trained killer ramming a knee in her back. She choked on dust as a hand wrapped around her hair, bending her head back at an impossible angle. Charlie gasped, trying to breathe against the brutal pressure. A second later, something sharp pricked her throat.

"Twitch, and not only will I slice your pretty throat, but I'll hack your head off."

Charlie listened to the gravelly voice, not moving against the blade pressed to her neck. He sounded Eastern European. Muscles screamed as he released his knee, and re-settled himself. She felt his crotch ride up against her ass. "Do you have the blonde bitch under control?" he asked, addressing the other shit-head in the room. Charlie couldn't see Elana, but she heard her friend moan.

"Hell yeah. Feisty fucking hell-cat. She has some moves,"

another man answered with the same accent. "Do we off them now or take them somewhere else?"

"Here." The word uttered by her brutal captor sealed her fate. A dark, musty village under the High Atlas Mountains would be where Charlie drew her last breath.

"No-one else is around. Why don't we play? How often do we get two American girls alone?"

"We don't have time."

"C'mon. I saw your hard-on when you watched her dance. You want the bitch—ride the mare."

The knife bit down and Charlie felt blood trickle down her neck. Her assailant rolled his hips as he wrenched her head further back. Charlie gasped against the pain. "Like that?"

Both men sniggered and the man above her stilled. "Tempting, but I have a job to do. Say goodbye, sweetheart."

◊ ◊ ◊

It took Donnie longer than he'd liked to locate the women. They'd slowed to eliminate two tangos along the way. Coming across Zach's bullet-ridden body had Donnie's chest tightening with worry. This shit had gotten real.

"You know him?" Atlas asked.

"I met him a few months ago at a party. He's Charlie's friend."

Atlas raised his weapon in unison with Donnie as they saw a shadowed body fall from the structure on the edge of overhanging quarters. They clambered over the next level. A target stood guard with his back to them. Donnie stepped in behind, suffocating then lowering the man to the ground. Both operators ran the passage to the dark entrance. Donnie adjusted his NVG's hooked to a thin headband and took in the disturbing scene.

Two men. Two women. One asshole held a gun to Elana's head as she lay unconscious in the corner. Another savage fucker straddled a facedown Charlie and he held a knife to her neck. From the guy's readying stance, he was about to eliminate her. Like Atlas, Donnie was already positioning himself, weighing up what action to take. Charlie could be wiped from existence if Donnie made a wrong move.

Charlie couldn't twitch in the brutal hold, helpless as she waited for the brute to draw the knife across her throat. She thought of her dad and of Donnie. Saddened that she'd let Elana down. A sharp thunk of a discharged weapon and the hand that held her hair with such savagery clutched even harder, yet the knife hand slipped from her throat—more like it jerked, then fell away. The heavy body above her felt awkward and slid to the side.

"Easy, honey." The deep American voice in her ear had her jerking. "I'm now holding you by the hair, not him. I'm lowering you back down while re-situating his knife hand. I don't want it to cut you. Just relax. I've got you."

Charlie groaned in relief. Donnie lowered her head, then let go of her hair. Too drained to move, she felt him drag the dead man's legs off her back.

Another American voice spoke softly. "Here I am—using restraint by snapping the guy's neck—and you decide to shoot your tango? I thought you said no guns."

"Shut up, Atlas," Donnie said.

Charlie didn't recognize the other man. She didn't recognize a lot of things. The shock pounded her into the ground, holding her prisoner as the world swayed around her.

"I had no choice. I couldn't risk the target's hand jerking. It had to be a shot to the brain stem."

Turning her head, Charlie regretted the small move. Sightless eyes stared back at her from a mangled face. Donnie had blown half of her attacker's head away—the bottom half. The head lay barely attached to a body. All that was left intact were the pale eyes, but she still recognized the Marrakesh Man with the silver belt buckle lying beside her. She groaned against nausea as Donnie turned her over. He immediately clamped a hand on her neck injury as he spoke to the man called Atlas.

"Is Elana conscious?" Donnie asked.

"Barely."

"We need to move them to a new location to assess and possibly treat injuries before attempting an exfil out of this damned village."

"Agree," Atlas answered. "Let's move."

Donnie turned back to her, his voice gentled. "Sharls, put your arm around my shoulder. Let me help you up."

She could hardly stand. She knew it had a lot to do with shock, at least she hoped that was the cause and she wasn't leaking from a severe neck injury. Charlie also knew that Donnie needed both hands free for protection purposes. Having to carry her along might put him at a disadvantage. Once upright, she let go of the substantial man and placed her hand over his fingers at her throat. "I've got this," she whispered. "Get us out of here."

She'd long suspected that her friend Jamie and his band of merry men were not regular salesmen like they claimed to be. The way they moved. That watchful look in their hardened faces, not only spoke of a past in specialized military units but a possible current and active contract with the US government. She wasn't ready to analyze the ease of which Donnie dispatched her assailants; she needed help. She craved safety, and he was her lifeline.

He slowly released her, expecting her to collapse in a shocked heap. Instead, Charlie placed one shaky foot in front of another and slipped past him. "Donnie, move that cocky ass. We don't have all day."

And he took the lead. Grasping Charlie by the arm and pulling her behind him as they eased out of the dwelling. Elana seemed to be coming around. Donnie's tall, well-built friend easily carried her in his muscled arms as they eased into the dark shadows. Charlie hooked a finger into Donnie's belt, walking then pausing as he led the group deeper into the maze. She had no idea how much time passed, every narrowed lane seemed the same as the last, and she knew this otherworldly web of corridors would haunt her nightmares for years to come.

A light flickered up in a doorway ahead. Donnie asked them to hold as he ducked through. He spoke another language to someone on the other side. A woman's voice answered him. Charlie stood shivering, not taking much notice as she waited in the chilly air. Her friend lay too still in the blond combatant's arms. Atlas lowered his head and spoke softly in Elana's ear. Charlie absently took note of their similarities. Both tall and blond. They looked like a fierce Celtic couple and reminded her of the Elfin warriors in *Lord of the Rings*.

Donnie stepped out then led them into the room. His hand on the curve of her back felt reassuring and warm. The dwelling felt just as toasty and smelled like slow-cooked tagine. An old Berber woman stood up from beside a fireplace. She pointed to a back room, and the four Americans made their way back where a senior man gestured to a bed. Atlas lowered Elana to the mattress and Charlie gasped as she saw the blood soaking the right side of her friend's body.

"Sit," Donnie ordered, and Charlie didn't protest. She lowered herself beside Elana.

"I've got this." Donnie said to Atlas, "Fly the drone. If we're about to have a neighborhood block party, I need to know about it." Atlas paused then nodded. He looked reluctant to leave Elana's side. The men tore open their backpacks and pulled out their respective equipment.

Atlas stepped back outside, concern evident before disappearing.

"He'll stand guard," Donnie said to Charlie by way of explanation. "We'll remain here long enough to patch up the both of you. I have a feeling more men are lurking below."

Charlie agreed. "They'll find us." Her voice sounded raspy. Probably from sucking in dust through a bruised throat.

"How's the neck?" he asked as he pulled a gadgety-looking strap off his head.

Her fingers felt sticky, but the bleeding had slowed. "Good. I think."

"I'll take care of it. Elana first."

Charlie agreed as he passed her a flashlight. The light jiggled in her trembling hands, and she gritted her teeth, trying to hold it steady. Digging in his bag, Donnie produced a strap with a flashlight attached, which he slipped onto his head and switched on.

"You can turn the flashlight off. Too much light will draw attention. Looks like he hit Elana on the back of the head. I feel a bump." Donnie pressed around the injury, and Elana groaned. He then ripped open Elana's shirt sleeve before examining her upper arm.

"She's lucky. The bullet sliced through muscle and exited without causing major damage." He swabbed the site with antiseptic wipes and wrapped her arm in gauze. "This is QuikClot Combat Gauze. It contains kaolin and will slow the bleed."

Once he'd bandaged up the arm, he turned his attention to Charlie. He tilted her head away as he studied her neck. She couldn't stop herself from rubbing her bloodstained hand on her jeans.

"Shit, Sharls. This was too close," he said, as a thumb rubbed along her collarbone below the injury site. The gentle stroke eased her racing heartbeat.

"Is... is it bad?"

"I can glue it. You may have a scar."

"I have my life. He wanted... he said he wanted to hack my head off. If you hadn't found us..."

Donnie's thumb stilled. She couldn't see him behind the light shining in her face, but she sensed his coiled tension. Being the quietest man she'd ever met didn't mean that Donnie wasn't the deadliest. On this night, he'd unleashed all that lethal energy she'd sensed from their first meeting. Charlie had a feeling that the biggest predator in this terracotta labyrinth hovered an inch away from her.

"Who are you?" she asked as he cleaned her neck.

Silence was the answer Donnie gave.

"What are you? A mercenary?"

"I sell military clothing. You know what I—"

"I know nothing. I don't know why those men tried to kill me. Why they shot Zach." Her voice shook. "Or why you turned up in Morocco with guns and fancy goggles and headlamp shit. I know fuck all."

Wrapping her arms around her waist, she wanted to turn away, to hide from him and the violence that had waltzed into her life. Why did she come here? If they'd stayed in Wyoming, Zach would still be alive.

"Hold still. I need to apply the glue."

"That's all you have to say? If you want to act like a cold bastard, then—"

"Jesus, woman. I'm trying to help. I'm trying to save your ass. Would you rather I leave you here?"

The thought of him walking away, into the night had her grabbing his wrist. "I'm sorry. Please don't leave us. I know you hate me, but Elana needs you."

She heard him take in a measured breath as he lowered his arm. The flashlight clicked off, and she blinked as her eyes adjusted to the sudden dark. A hand snaked around the back of her head, pulling her to his chest. "Honey, you're in shock and you might not know me all that well, but you know James. He's like my brother and best friend all rolled into one. We're alike in many ways. He would rather die than abandon his friends and I would do the same. I won't leave you here. I swear, I'm not going anywhere."

His fingers massaged her scalp, and for a moment, she relaxed into the reassuring hold. His warm breath whispered near her ear. "And I don't hate you. 'Hate' is a word that holds a lot of weight. Just because I might occasionally want to strangle you, and you might wanna kick me in the balls doesn't mean we hate each other."

"I don't want to kick you in the balls."

"Don't deny it, I've seen that bloodthirsty look in your eyes."

She giggled against his chest then sucked in a breath.

"Now can I glue your neck while you get your shit together?"

Pulling back, she nodded then winced against the sting. Donnie worked quickly and the ease at which he worked told Charlie that he'd done this many times before.

"You look different," Donnie said. Her eyes darted his way and he elaborated. "I barely recognized you with all that make-up."

"It was for the video shoot."

"I know. You're pretty without all the face paint, but I like what they've done with your eyes."

"You think I'm pretty?" she teased.

"I… You need to let this dry. Hold still."

Did Mr. Articulate- Donnie-Wilson just stumble over his words?

The bed creaked as Elana shifted and clutched her head. Reaching out, without moving her neck, Charlie grabbed her friend's hand and offered reassurance. "You're okay, sweetie. Shallow breaths."

"Welcome back, Elana," Donnie said, supporting her as she sat up. He began to assess her dazed condition as Atlas stepped back in.

"Stoked to see you awake, sweetheart." Atlas crouched next to Donnie. "Five men—to the east. We need to move."

◊ ◊ ◊

Odds were improving in the biggest goat fuck operation in North Africa. Both women were now ambulatory. Well almost both, Atlas held Elana around the waist as they ran down yet another narrow lane. Donnie paused and held up a fist as he scoped the small tunnel ahead. This village was an ambush haven. He felt Charlie brush up behind him, and her perfume wrapped around him. Oranges and Rose. The most delicious scent he'd ever smelled. He always equated rose perfume with old ladies' scented drawers, powdered and ancient English Rose. Charlie smelled like a rose creamsicle, all velvety with a juicy and carnal accent. It reminded him of authentic Turkish Delight—the traditional sweets found in the Middle East—flavored with rosewater. Sweet, rich and sitting beside a glass of cold orange juice.

He glanced back at her quiet profile, barely making it out in the dark. He'd bet she still carried that glazed look in those big brown eyes. Her friend was just shot to death in a remote village somewhere in Morocco and seeing that knife pressed to her neck by that asshole highlighted the gravity of the situation. Both women were in the center of a shit storm. Donnie wasn't going anywhere until they were safe. From the determined stance of his teammate, he knew Atlas felt the same. They headed west, emerging from the sprawling village into an open and craggy area. The men helped their charges over a low wall, and they edged along a rock face towards another higher boundary wall.

Sure enough, thanks to flying a mini UAV over the area, they found a weak spot—a crumbling gap in the clay barrier. Donnie clambered up and lifted the girls. Once Atlas scaled the wall, Donnie lowered them back over on the other side. Instead of crossing the river near the main entrance, they circled—taking cover behind boulders, palm trees, and scrubby bush. By the time they crept into the hotel parking lot, the women were breathing heavily.

As the foursome crouched behind a wall, Donnie tapped Charlie on the shoulder and whispered, "That silver Dacia Duster. That's our vehicle. Keep low and move fast. Here are the keys, don't press the unlock button as it'll beep. Use the key to open the door. I'll cover you."

"Wait. What about our bags at the hotel?"

"It's too dangerous. I guarantee that there will be men waiting for you to return to your rooms."

Atlas clicked his tongue at that exact moment and pointed his head in the direction of two suspected mercenaries emerging from the entrance.

"Move. Now, Charlie."

Instead of arguing, she did as he asked. Crouching low, she crab-walked between vehicles to their silver sedan. Thankfully, Elana seemed more alert and managed to hunch over beside Atlas. Once they were all in, Donnie made his way to the driver's side. Taking care not to draw attention, he slowly pulled out onto the gravel road. After five minutes of negotiating the dark side roads, Donnie glanced over at Charlie in the passenger seat.

"How are you holding up?

"Are we going to the police?" she asked.

"We can't."

"Why not?" Her voice rose. "Zach is lying dead in some dirty alley. They killed him! He's dead and—"

"Sharls, breathe. I know. I also know that those men are well trained. Too well trained to be opportunists singling out tourists. They were targeting you specifically."

"How does that stop us from going to the police?"

"Because it's linked to the Maltese attack. These super custom dicks have you on their radar." This time Atlas spoke and Charlie whipped her head around to stare at him.

"Are you saying that those dick-weeds followed us here?"

"You said it yourself. You told me on the phone that you'd spotted the tangos before tonight."

Charlie grabbed the dashboard and turned to face Donnie and Atlas. "Then let's get their thug buddies arrested."

"We can't. The sergeant in Gozo, the Maltese official who dealt with your case, is dirty."

Charlie gaped at Donnie. "He was the nicest man. Compassionate and—"

"He's on a payroll and already closed the case; they sent you on your way for a reason."

In the rearview mirror, Donnie saw Elana shift painfully in

the backseat. "You're saying that these bastards have connections and that they may be operating with local support in Morocco?"

Elana's quick deduction had Donnie raising a brow. She'd read the situation accurately and immediately. Charlie persisted, and the hitch in her voice had Donnie's hands fisting around the wheel.

"We can't leave Zach there, lying in the dark. His mom needs to know what happened. He's all by himself." Charlie huffed out a shaky breath.

"We don't have a choice," Elana said tiredly. "Once we're safe, we'll tell his story and how he saved us."

Donnie turned onto the main road as silence descended.

"Where are we going?" Elana's question cut through the silence.

"The fastest route to American soil," Atlas answered.

"The US Embassy in Rabat is our first choice. I have a contact there," Donnie said as he stretched out his hand. "Give me your phones."

"Excuse me?"

"Phones. Now. The easiest way to track a target is to use their fancy smartphones."

Charlie groaned as she whipped out her iPhone. "You're going to destroy them, aren't you?"

"Not him, me." Atlas leaned forward and grabbed the mobile device. He turned it off, then removed her black phone cover. "Dude, you were right." Atlas flashed the back of the phone at Donnie who swore.

Charlie grabbed his wrist. "Right about what?" When she spotted the small, flat, circular object stuck to the back of the phone, she sucked in a breath.

"That's a tracker, honey. And now the whole shitting device

is going out the window." Donnie grabbed the phone and tossed it. He did the same with Elana's phone.

"What does that mean?" Charlie asked as she stared back at the open road.

"It means we're about to have company." Donnie had barely said the words when a truck pulled onto the road from ahead, trying to veer into them as Donnie swerved.

◊ ◊ ◊

A hard hand shoved Charlie to the floor.

"Stay down!" Donnie said as he straightened and accelerated. A yelp from Elana meant that Atlas had done the same.

"Get the AR-15," Donnie ordered as he braked then sped up.

"Copy." Atlas shoved down the back seat and pulled a black bag from the trunk. From between the seats, Charlie watched him ready the assault rifle. The passenger window exploded. Glass rained down on Charlie as the car lurched sideways and bullets punched through metal.

"Tires, now! Atlas!" Donnie pulled a handgun.

"I know how to do my fucking job. Keep us steady."

Two deafening cracks filled the air, followed by a third. Tires screeched, and something slammed into the tarmac next to Charlie's side. A vehicle rolled away into the night. The force of it had her flinching as she covered her face against the seat.

"Got the Mercedes," Atlas said as he switched sides. "Second vehicle coming from the rear."

He fired his weapon at the same time as someone shot back. Donnie stepped on the brakes, and the car slammed forward when the vehicles made impact. Crying out, Charlie tried to wedge herself into the tight space. Her body tingled with adrenaline as she squeezed her eyes shut. She felt the vehicle accelerate as Atlas shouted, "No luck, they're still behind us."

She heard the rifle fire twice before a returning shot had their car skidding.

"Brace!" Splintering metal drowned out Donnie's shout as they slithered then flipped sideways. The impact flung Charlie into the air, in a concussive blur of carnage.

Chapter Seven

With every blast, her ears rung. Charlie tried to cover them, but someone pulled her hands away.

"Charlie! Wake up."

"Just a little longer," she said drifting away from the chaos. Her leg scraped over something sharp and another burst of noise slammed through her aching head. Someone groaned as they dragged her through a narrow space. Charlie's hair caught, she opened her eyes and tried to free it. Expansive black sky… and stars filled her vision. Strong arms lowered her and her head flopped to the side. Her jeans were hooked on a piece of metal. Charlie glanced down just as the large body holding her yanked her back. Her legs came loose from a gaping back window of a car and she fell against a slab of granite—a hard body that held her tight. Panic broke as a voice whispered in her ear.

"Sharls, don't fight. It's Donnie. You're okay. I'm going to prop you up behind the engine." He dragged her over to where Elana lay.

Their car now lay on its side and they hunkered down behind its underbelly. Shots cracked the air and echoed through the hills, some pinging against their fragile metal shelter. In one smooth move, Donnie stood and stepped to the side, firing his handgun.

He crouched back down to reload.

"Where... where is Atlas?" Charlie asked through gritted teeth. Her body ached, and she shifted to get comfortable.

"He's circling around to ambush the bastards."

"How many... many are there?"

"Three men." Donnie stood, aimed and fired. "More like two—I just shot the third."

Charlie grasped Elana's arm. "Are you okay?"

"Just dandy. Squatting on a remote desert road in the middle of a gunfight—like I'm in a damn Bond movie."

Aside from a graze on her cheek, Elana looked alert as she rolled to her knees.

"What are you doing?" Charlie asked.

Elana ignored her as Donnie ducked back down. "Hey, Schwarzenegger, do you have a gun I can borrow?"

He gave her a disbelieving look.

"Charlie and I can both shoot. Let us help."

Charlie nudged her. "I can use a shotgun or a rifle. I've never shot a handgun before."

"You wanna get picky or help out Mr. GI Joe here?"

Another louder volley of shots echoed through the hills.

"Thank fuck," Donnie said and bowed his head for a moment.

"I take it that's the blond cavalry sweeping in from the left?" Elana asked.

Donnie nodded, confirming that Atlas had indeed taken out the two shooters. He swiped his forehead on his sleeve; blood covered the right side of his face. Charlie visually checked him for more injuries, but aside from the leaking head wound, he seemed just as virile and stable as he ever was.

"Stay put until we confirm it's clear." He slid out of sight and

Charlie leaned her head back as she surveyed the rocky terrain rolling into the darkness. It looked and felt like they were on Mars. The only lights that flickered in the endless expanse before her were the stars.

The road sat quiet. The silence was suddenly strange after the explosions and gunfire, like the land collectively held its breath. Her ears rang as she cautiously moved her limbs. Nothing seemed broken. Her ribs felt bruised and her head throbbed. Charlie explored the egg-shaped swelling at the back of her head while lying in numb stupefaction.

Elana's words echoed her own surreal thoughts. "How the living hell, did we end up with busted up asses on the side of a deserted road in the middle of Africa? With two scary Robocops mowing down the bad guys as they clear a path for our sorry butts?"

Charlie tried not to laugh as pain lanced through her side. Tears pricked the back of her eyes as the chuckle turned into a sob. "Poor Zach."

"I know," Elana soothed. "We couldn't save him."

They held each other's hands as they stared at the thousands of stars speckling the black canvas before them.

The earthy smells in the vast space grounded Charlie, and she rubbed a palm in the cool sand and sighed. "To get out of this alive, I'm guessing we'll need to transform into Amazonian warrior women."

Squeezing her hand, Elana smiled. "We've always been Amazonians. We kick butt on a slow day, but you're right. It's time to step up our game. Besides, I'm not sure how safe it is lying up against a battered-up gas tank."

Charlie loved her childhood friend. They'd met on the playground on the first day of middle school and had taken an instant dislike to each other. Elana pulled Charlie's braid and Charlie then shoved the skinny firecracker down a hill. It took three teachers wading into the melee to separate the angry eleven-year-olds who held onto each other's hair like limpets. Both sets of parents were pulled into the office and the pre-teen monsters were forced to hug out their apologies. They'd been best friends ever since.

With one last squeeze, Charlie let go of her friend's hand and rolled to her side, and then her knees. "Shit, that hurts. Shitty shit, shit, shit... and stop laughing."

"I can't help it!" Elana giggled. "You look like you're eighty years old."

Charlie tried to give her the middle finger as she staggered to her feet. "Let me help you up—slowpoke."

"I've got this."

When both women were standing, they held onto each other for support as they chuckled.

Elana grew serious and grasped Charlie's shoulder. "Don't you dare die on me. You're the only sister I've ever had."

Both women were upright and Donnie huffed out his relief. The last ten minutes had shaved years off his life. After the car flipped, he'd blacked out for a second and then woken to Atlas kicking out the back window as he'd called Donnie's name. The sniper had slipped out and moved around quickly enough to stave off an attack. He'd drilled five assailants down to three, while covering Donnie's scramble to pull the women to safety. Seeing Charlie lying so still over the dash, had done funny things to Donnie and he'd taken a second in the mangled cab to clutch her to his chest, chanting her name as he'd checked her pulse.

Now all five tangos lay in bloody heaps next to their still running BMW. After checking the bodies for both identification and signs of life, Donnie went back to retrieve the girls. They needed to find a secure hidey hole. Night traveling through Morocco during the offseason would draw too much attention. Their best hope was to blend in as tourists during the day, when foot and road traffic was at its busiest.

"There may be more assailants on the way. We need to disappear and fast. We'll take the beamer."

He led them to the tangos' vehicle and couldn't resist rubbing a hand down Charlie's back. Instead of stepping away, she moved closer and seemed comfortable with his touch. As they emerged into the open, Donnie switched back into operator mode while they swapped vehicles. Atlas had already loaded the go-bags and weapons into the new trunk.

"Donnie, wipe the evidence."

"Already on it." Donnie grabbed a bag and loped back to the up-sided vehicle. Atlas pulled the BMW further down the road, and waited with the engine running.

Once Donnie returned and climbed into the passenger seat, they pulled away in a dusty cloud. The old vehicle exploded from behind, and Charlie squeaked with fright.

She looked back at the fiery ball lighting up the night's sky. "Why did you do that? And you have explosives?"

"Our DNA and fingerprints are all over that sucker," Donnie replied.

As Atlas drove, Donnie's entire focus was on finding a safe location until contingency plans could be hashed out. He pulled out his laptop and examined a satellite map of the area.

Charlie's husky voice broke in from the back seat. "All this equipment, and your weapons. The way you fight and how easily you kill. You're trained mercenaries."

No-one answered as Donnie tapped away.

Bitterness bled. "Ordinarily, I wouldn't give a damn, but a few months ago, one of my farmhands died. A good man. I know you were all involved. I didn't buy that bullshit story that some vagrant wandered onto our land."

Donnie swallowed and re-focused on the map on the screen. That was classified and Johnny's story to tell.

She took Elana's hand. "A good, kind man was murdered on my farm. Like Zach, he had a family. Elana and I deserve to know what we're up against and who's in our corner. What kind of men do we have fighting by our sides?"

Atlas shot him a glance. Donnie barely blinked as he zoomed in on coordinates and addressed Atlas.

"According to satellite imagery, there's a village five clicks out. It doesn't appear on the traditional tourist maps. We'll have to go off-road but due to its location, we can't get boxed in. There are smaller farm roads nearby that lead to the N9 and N10 freeways."

"You know what, Donnie? Screw you. Ignore me then," Charlie said.

He gritted his teeth and turned to the vexing redhead. "I'm trying to get us to safety. When I have us all situated, we'll talk. Let me first help you, and then you're welcome to chew up my ass."

Atlas leaned over to glance at the new coordinates. "This is some bad juju. If these mercs are as powerful as we think they are, then they'll have the N9 closely monitored. Any attempt to get to Marrakesh or Casablanca might go sideways."

"Roger that. I'm working around it."

"We'll need supplies," Atlas said as they turned onto a smaller sand road.

"Hopefully a four-hour hunkering down session would give us time to gather resources."

"Give who time?" Elana asked Donnie. Her voice sounded thready and Atlas glanced in the rearview mirror.

"Are you holding up okay?"

She raised a thumb in a half-hearted gesture. "Enjoying my off-road safari."

Donnie closed his laptop as he eyed the occupants in the back. He needed to give them a heads-up of what lay ahead.

"To get you out of country, you'll need new identities. I gather you have your passports on you?"

Both girls nodded.

"We'll need to destroy them."

"You're kidding—"

"You'll also go through purses, pockets and your satchels and remove anything that could be linked to your old identity. We'll get dye for your hair." Donnie also had sets of colored contacts. The team kept those on them. A covert team like MIT2 changed up their appearance regularly in the field. Especially Max. His ghostly gray eyes drew too much attention.

"You want me to dye my hair?" Charlie touched her thick red waves and Donnie felt a twinge of regret. Her natural hair color rippled with burning intensity that always fascinated him. Unfortunately, it made her stand out like a red cherry in a bowl of bland grapes.

"It's your most recognizable feature. We'll try to arrange for a temporary hair dye."

"Arrange with who?"

"Leave that up to me. Stick to an identity which is close to who you are in real life. You're not going to say you're a neurosurgeon if you're a plumber. If we're stopped by law enforcement, your story will need to hold up."

Shifting to get comfortable, Elana said, "I think we're making this way more complicated than it needs to be."

Donnie passed a document over to them. "That's one of the dead men's passports. I found it on him. Like all five of his colleagues, he's Serbian."

Charlie frowned. "And that's bad because?"

"It looks like he's part of a criminal organization, one that equips their men with top of the line weaponry. Three of the men carried the latest CZ 75 pistol. The favorite handgun for Police and Military across Europe, except theirs were fitted with custom, permanent extensions—suppressors. Two wore ballistic vests and all were well trained. All that takes resources. Once I have a secure connection, I'll run their names." He leaned over and grasped her hand. "Sharls, they're paid goons, and I think they're not the only ones on a powerful payroll. To attack so brazenly in a tourist hotspot, they'd have to have Moroccan connections."

Blinking rapidly, Charlie turned away to look out the window. Her fear punched him like a fist, but he wouldn't gloss over the reality of their situation. Now she knew. Donnie needed to crush her optimism bias—an affliction that affected many tourists. The misperception that because you're in an exotic location, surrounded by palm trees and other foreign visitors, that bad things could never happen.

Many petty criminals capitalize on the naivety. Scammers and pickpockets littered cities like Paris and London. Tourists in all the major Moroccan cities were equally targeted. Overcharged in taxis, taken to select hotels by hired men who jumped on travelers like vultures at the ports or railway stations. And occasionally in places like Karachi or Acapulco, travelers disappeared. The fact was that bad things happened to foreign travelers all over the globe, and Charlie was in a desperate situation. Donnie wouldn't let her disappear or get hurt, not while she was under his protection and while he was still breathing.

Chapter Eight

They parked in the shadows near the enclosed village. In a predominantly Berber area, Donnie expected humble and generally hospitable inhabitants. They'd be used to visitors, not the typical snap happy tourist—more along the lines of backpackers who passed through. Still, Donnie didn't climb out. Instead, he pulled a pack of antiseptic wipes from his backpack and began wiping the blood and dust from his face.

"Aren't we going in?" Charlie asked, her arms folded tightly over her chest.

Atlas shook his head. "We're chilling until we find a target."

"Like a... a target for us to kill?"

"No," Donnie answered. "Like a target that we can convert into an asset."

The entrance sat quiet, and Charlie shifted. "We could wait all night. This isn't exactly a teeming city like Casablanca."

"Patience," Donnie said as he pulled off his soiled tee. Working an asset with a blood-spattered shirt didn't exactly inspire trust. He dug in the pack for the replacement and glanced sideways at Charlie. Her eyes glittered in the dark cab, tracing the contours of his chest. Donnie ignored the warm flush spreading over his neck as he pulled the black t-shirt over his head.

He fished out a small box from a side pocket and handed it back to Charlie. "I did a rush job on those, but they should work." She flipped open the lid. Two sets of small silver earrings lay in the box.

"Uh. You shouldn't have?"

"They're trackers with hidden GPS chips. I made them as small as possible not to draw attention. I need you to put them on. I'll activate them if we get separated."

"You made them?" Charlie said as she handed Elana a pair, and then slipped one through her left ear.

"Heads-up," Atlas said softly.

Four pairs of eyes watched the elderly man herding three goats towards the village. Donnie shook his head; the old man seemed too observant, and wasn't the right fit. Ten minutes later, two young men wandered out and leaned against the wall. The taller one lit up a cigarette. Donnie studied them carefully, estimating them to be in their early twenties. A couple of children ran by and the smoker lunged for one kid and grabbed him by the arm. They argued, then the little boy produced a pack of gum and handed it over. The tall man grinned and shoved the child away. Donnie saw enough. He needed to buy an ally and the ciggy smoking bully fit the profile. He clipped on a geeky fanny pack before opening the door and stepping out into the chilly night.

Both men straightened as he walked over. His cheesy smile had them narrowing their eyes. Once he was close enough to engage, he played up the American accent.

"Howdy guys. Thank God we found this place. I've been trying to find the N9 like forever."

Both men sized him up as he extended his hand. "Jim Colby." He whistled. "This is an authentic looking village. Don't get shit like this in Colorado."

"You're a tourist?"

"I am indeed. A lost tourist, and a stupid one. Decided to convince my friends to go hiking." He pointed at the BMW. "My wife and her friend took a nasty tumble, and we didn't bring any water."

"You want water?" The tall kid glanced at Donnie's bulging fanny pack, probably guessing how much he could charge for a handful of waters.

"We'd appreciate a place to stay. I don't trust my sense of direction, and it's getting late."

The shorter man stepped closer. "My name is Safrian and this is Brahim. There's a hotel just inside. We can arrange accommodation."

Donnie ran an assessing eye over the pair noting how Safrian looked to Brahim for confirmation.

Donnie focused all his attention on Brahim. "That's mighty generous, but if possible, we'd like to stay with a Berber family— you know—get the authentic experience and all. But I don't want any young men staying in the home. I get a little jealous. My wife has a wandering eye."

Before Brahim could consider the odd request, Donnie unzipped the fanny pack and produced a wad of cash. "We can pay. How does a thousand dollars sound? Five hundred now, and five hundred when we leave in the morning?"

Both men's expressions slackened, as they stared at the thick stack of fifty-dollar bills.

"You want to pay a thousand dollars for one night? Why?"

"The exotic setting gets my wife all hot." Donnie added a sleazy wink.

Brahim smiled. "I can appreciate that."

Donnie guessed right. These men may have grown up in the

village, but they'd traveled enough and interacted with enough travelers that they knew how to play the game.

"I want a quiet spot, away from the noise of the town square. We need our rest."

"Sure you do." Safrian grinned. Brahim pulled him aside, and they whispered between themselves. Donnie knew the men weren't used to this much money. He counted on their greed to secure a safe spot tucked away from prying eyes.

Brahim turned back. "For an extra five hundred dollars, we give you a rooftop apartment with a prime view of the stars."

Donnie smiled. "For an extra five hundred dollars, I'll take my chances of finding my way to the next village." He turned, and the men shouted.

"Okay, okay. Come, come. We take you around the side. Give us five minutes to speak to the family."

"I'll follow in my car."

He walked quickly back to the BMW and they trailed the men down a side lane. After a few twists and turns, they were directed to pull the car under a small makeshift garage. A tin roof covered in a rotting tarp now hid the vehicle comfortably from view.

Phase two of the evening was about to begin and Charlie would like him even less by the end of it. Not that Donnie cared, he thought as he watched Atlas assist her from the vehicle.

Charlie wore a scarf, covering up the neck injury, and Donnie slipped a jacket over Elana's shoulders to hide the bullet wound. He supported Elana's weight as he pulled her from the backseat. The blonde beauty looked fatigued as he guided her inside.

An elderly man stood to the side and spoke with Brahim in hushed tones. Brahim handed him a hundred dollars. The elderly man led them through a door to an open area that held an old sofa set, a fridge, and a stove. Two bedrooms led off the main suite. They'd westernized the home enough that Donnie suspected it accommodated regular foreign tourists. Hikers or climbers. Charlie collapsed on the sofa as Donnie walked Elana to a bedroom to lay her on the bed. Once he'd assessed their surroundings and was comfortable with the positioning of the women, he made his move.

Charlie felt like she'd run a hundred miles. Everything ached, including her head, neck, and back. Her throat felt bruised around the neck injury. Swallowing hurt—hell—breathing hurt. They may not be safe for long, but Charlie felt grateful for the soft sofa. The worn velvety set had lost most of its springs, but she didn't care. This might be her bed for the night—her sore ass had made the silent announcement.

Charlie leaned her head back as Donnie emerged from the bedroom. Atlas stepped just inside the entrance. The three local men spoke in another language as Donnie casually stepped around them. In one fluid motion, he grabbed the taller teenager in a choke hold. The sudden violence had Charlie launching up.

She stared at tendons rippling in Donnie's arm as he held the groaning man still. A wicked looking drop point knife sat against the man's carotid artery. The way Donnie held it, spoke of a practiced comfort with the weapon. It didn't face forward. Instead, it rested backward along Donnie's wrist—he kept it pointing down. The sharp edge sat snug against the young man's neck. Charlie knew a little about weapons. She'd studied and even collected ancient knives and swords and Donnie held a knife ideal for slicing. The cold warrior watched the room. Atlas blocked the other men as they turned to run.

"What are you doing?" Charlie breathed the words in a whisper.

Donnie didn't look her way, instead he focused on the other two local men.

"Safrian, does he speak English—the old man?" Donnie asked.

The smaller man—plastered to the wall—nodded with wide eyes.

"Good, because I don't speak Amazigh."

Charlie guessed that referred to the local Berber language.

"I do speak Arabic, so I'll repeat what I'm about to say in Arabic. Do you understand?" Donnie asked.

Both men nodded. The third man in Donnie's grip barely breathed.

"I've killed many men. More than I'd like to count. Killing comes easily to a man like me. I protect things of value and I won't stop until I've destroyed all those involved in threatening those close to me. Nod if you understand."

The locals looked confused but nodded. Donnie repeated his words in Arabic.

"There are bad soldiers after us. Foreign mercenaries. If they find us tonight, it will be on your heads, and I'll conclude that you sold us out."

Atlas stepped forward, raised a phone and snapped pictures of the men.

"My friend is sending your photos and our location to the rest of my colleagues—killers just like me, who protect their own. If you betray us or if we die, you will be hunted down like dogs. Next, they'll find your families."

Charlie sucked in a breath as they paled.

Again, Donnie spoke in Arabic, then switched back to

English. "If the mercenaries hurt these women under your watch, I will find you and kill you. Now, if you cooperate, you'll get paid handsomely. I'll give you that additional five hundred dollars in the morning. I'll also ensure that in the future, your village gets sent regular food packages."

Donnie's hostage whimpered in the uncomfortable hold, and his friends agreed wildly that they would never betray them.

"There are conditions attached. Safrian and Brahim here," Donnie squeezed, "will keep watch throughout the night. If mercenaries come to the village, you will deflect them and warn me. My big buddy and I will also take turns watching. I also need you to fill a shopping list, and I'll need every item by daybreak. Can you do that?"

"Yes, sir." Safrian held out his hands in complacency. "We are friends, and we help, okay? We help."

Loosening his hold, Donnie looked down at Brahim. "Will you betray me?"

"N… no. No, sir."

"Good." Donnie released the skinny man with a quick shove before calmly re-sheathing his knife. "Safrian, wait here for the list." Turning his back, Donnie walked to the car. Realizing her mouth hung open, Charlie snapped it shut. Donnie wrote out a list and placed it in Safrian's shaking hands.

Charlie frowned at the men's expressions. Still terrified but they looked at Donnie with a trace of awe. Even Brahim seemed to idol worship his recent assailant. The older man fussed and offered her a blanket before placing pots on the stove and chopping up vegetables. Atlas and Donnie discussed shifts, conversing like they hadn't just held the room hostage.

Atlas must've taken first shift, as he grabbed the rifle and left. Donnie walked into the kitchen area and offered to help the old man. They chatted easily, switching between Arabic and English. All went about their business as if Donnie had never held a knife to an innocent man's throat. Charlie stared, she was in the twilight zone.

When Donnie knelt before her, she tried to meld the man she knew with the scary attacker in the room from five minutes before. The thing was, she barely knew him. She knew nothing about this green-eyed, dark-haired wolf.

"Don't look at me like that."

"Like what?"

"Like I would ever hurt you."

She swallowed and looked away.

"What about those men? Would you hurt their families like you said you would?"

Leaning close, Donnie whispered, "Do you think I'm capable of hurting innocents?"

Charlie considered the question and shook her head.

He visibly relaxed. "We need their cooperation and they need to know who's in charge."

After facing the brutal American, Charlie was sure that the villagers would cooperate. Hell, she was ready to simultaneously pee her pants… and stand and salute.

"We need to talk." Donnie rose. "First, I need to look in on Elana and check her arm."

"I'll help." Charlie rose stiffly. When Donnie placed a hand at her back, she pulled away.

"What supplies did you ask for—on that list?" she asked.

"Mainly things for you and Elana. Hair dye, scissors, fresh clothes, burner phones, and some additional first aid items. At this time of night, I don't expect them to find everything— especially here—but the Berber community is close-knit. They help each other out. I'm sure some of the shop owners will make a plan."

The QuikClot did its job, Elana's arm had stopped bleeding. Donnie cleaned out and examined the bullet wound. Elana woke briefly, then fell back to sleep.

"Providing she doesn't get an infection—with rest—she should be ambulatory tomorrow."

"I'm sleeping with her tonight," Charlie stated as she walked over to the bench in the corner and toed off her sneakers. "In case she has bad dreams. Plus, I'll monitor her."

Donnie followed her to the bench and sat beside her. She ignored his stare.

"What about your bad dreams? You're hurting too."

"Of course, I'm damn hurting. What do you think? My father just died. My friend just got shot to death. I killed two men. Two human beings who... who—"

"Who tried to kill you."

"Oh, God." She couldn't stop the shaking and couldn't prevent her brawny companion from pulling her into his arms.

"My world... has gone mad. It's all gone mad."

Donnie whispered soft nothings as she rocked in his arms. She didn't cry. Charlotte Quinn would fight this and walk away. Deliberately slowing her breaths, Charlie reined in terror and pulled back. Donnie tucked a curl behind her ear before resting his hand on her shoulder.

"Your hair is so shiny and straight and there's so much of it. I'm used to your curls."

"It's a red jungle. Try going to school with a mop of corkscrew curls as a kid. It's been yanked more times than I can remember."

"Kids yanked your hair?" Donnie frowned.

"Sometimes pulled out whole chunks. I was the ginger pariah on the playground."

"Little bastards." His hand tightened on her arm.

"Daddy taught me to kick butt at a young age, and I was a strong little girl. When the school bully—nasty Tom Lemkus—pulled me down the stairs by my hair, I punched him in the nose."

"Good for you, Sharls."

She smiled at the memory and rubbed a thumb. Then she gnawed her bottom lip before looking up. "I want to fight alongside you."

His dark brows furrowed. "What do you mean?"

"I can shoot and fight dirty. I need to know what weapons you have and what I can do to help."

"Honey, you're untrained."

"And you're trained." She waited, watching as he dropped his arm. "Don't let me fight in the dark on my own. I've got you, and you've got me... dawg."

He shook his head then rubbed a hand over his goatee. "Shit. Shit. Shit."

He must've decided because he grasped her hand. The shock of his touch had them both looking up, but he didn't let go. Charlie tightened her hold around his broad palm.

"I work for the US government."

"Not as a clothing salesman," she said wryly.

"Not selling military clothing. Have you heard of Delta Force?"

"Kind of. They're like the SEALS."

"Not the same, none of their missions are public knowledge. They operate under the black ops umbrella. My team does something similar. We're ghosts, like the Delta boys and that's all I can tell you."

"Is Jamie on your team?"

"Johnny—James—serves on the same team."

"So… this is a mission?"

"No. This was me, coming to find you—on my days off."

"Why?"

"Because I care and because of the party—the barbeque. Because of Wyoming."

She stood.

"Sharls…" He reached out as Atlas walked in.

"Brahim has some borrowed clothing for the girls in the sitting room. He says there's a shower next door if they want to freshen up in the morning. He's paying the neighbor for the use of their modern facilities."

"Is there a toilet nearby?" Charlie needed a moment alone with her churning stomach.

"Yes," Atlas said as he stole a glance Elana's way. "There's an outhouse with a squatter, but I think the neighbor has a western toilet. I'll show you on my way out."

Grabbing her satchel bag, Charlie followed Atlas, refusing to look at the grim soldier still seated in the quiet room.

◊ ◊ ◊

At three in the morning, Donnie stood by the bed. Two bodies lay entwined, clutching each other for comfort—both small-town girls from Wyoming looking so fragile as they slept. But looks could be deceiving. Elana had traveled extensively with her family, and her worldly savviness would work in her favor. Charlie might be a little more sheltered, but she was capable, a fast learner and physically strong. Charlie's red hair spread out across the pillows. She lay on her back, her dark make-up now slightly smudged beneath her eyes. Her knuckles lay against her cheek as her other hand held onto Elana's uninjured arm. Elana rested on her good side, wrapped around a pillow and her bandaged arm rested on top. Tiny snores escaped her slightly open lips, shifting blonde tendrils lying across her face.

What had they gotten themselves into? Donnie had sent out feelers into his intelligence community and photos of the dead men along with their fake passports. He'd know who the Serbians worked for within the next twelve hours. It was time to wake the women. He'd just woken Atlas. Both men rotated shifts and caught a couple of hours of sleep; they'd exfil before dawn. He sat the paper packet on the edge of the bed and fingered a lock of Charlie's fine red hair. It glistened like liquid fire, reminding him of her temperament. Flashy, impulsive and quick-tempered. Now he would ask her to paint over the glowing embers with brown sludge.

Donnie looked up as Atlas walked in.

"She's cranking out those snores in the cutest way." Atlas used one finger to drag the loose strands of hair from Elana's face. He then felt her forehead. "No fever."

Donnie shook them awake.

"Holy crap, I feel shitty." Curling to her side, Charlie tried to snuggle into the scratchy covers.

"Get up. We need to dye your hair. Then we need to leave." Donnie stroked her shivering arm.

It was cold—fucking freezing. An indication of the coming winter and he could understand her reluctance to leave the bed. "We need to go over the game plan."

"We now have a game plan? Does it involve us rolling our car and getting shot at?" Elana asked as she gingerly rolled onto her back.

"Hopefully not."

Charlie stood as Donnie laid out supplies. She looked washed-out with arms wrapped around her waist. The cut on her neck stood out against her smooth skin. "I need to use the bathroom first."

Atlas unwrapped Elana's bandage and checked the site for infection, before cleaning the bullet wound. Donnie briefed Elana while Atlas worked. "We found temporary dyes. You can choose a traditional henna red or go for pink or a lilac spray-on color. You'd need to embrace a hippy hitch-hiking type vibe. With Atlas's laid-back surfer personality and his long blond hair, you could both pull it off." Donnie added a tie-dyed scarf, brown contacts and garish looped earrings to the mix.

"Atlas and I are a couple?" Elana asked.

"Correct. We'll split and go our separate ways. You'll go with Atlas to the US Consulate in Casablanca. Charlie and I will head to the US Embassy in Rabat. Once there, we'll inform them of the mess, and secure flights to the States."

"I'm not leaving my friend. Elana and I stick together," Charlie said from the door.

"They're looking for two women that match your description. Staying together will get you killed."

"We're changing our appearance," Charlie persisted as she stalked into the bedroom.

Donnie rubbed his eyes. "That won't be enough. Are you willing to bet your lives on lack of observances of the enemy?"

"This is our best chance," Elana said as she moved to the edge of the bed, careful not to jar her arm. "We can move faster and adapt quicker, and I trust Atlas to get me to safety." Elana looked up at the tall man assisting her.

Charlie raised her brows at their sudden familiarity. Trust wasn't something Elana gave easily. Called an ice queen

---

throughout high school, she never dated, preferring to keep an arm's length from the opposite sex. Elana's next statement had Charlie's eyes widening in surprise.

"And Donnie will look after you. He has your back," Elana added.

"You don't know that, you barely know him."

"I don't need to know or even like Donnie to know that he'll protect you. He's done a good job so far." Elana turned to Donnie. "I'll shoot off your nuts if she gets hurt. I don't care if you're bigger and badder, I'll fucking kill you."

"Message received, ma'am."

Picking up the packet of dark brown dye, Charlie groaned. "This goes on my hair?"

"You're like a fire engine out there, you betcha."

"Screw you, Donnie," she said halfheartedly. "But I do like the blue contacts."

"You have an hour. Get cracking."

◊ ◊ ◊

The walk over to the neighbor's shower and toilet extension was a chilly one. Cold rose from the bare and trampled ground. Rustic smells filled the fresh air—manure and goats and the coming frost. The basic design of the small, white-washed room held a shower in one corner and a toilet and a rickety stool in the other. The pink and purple streaks were easy to apply in Elana's hair. Only taking twenty minutes to set before Charlie helped her to shower and re-bandage her injured arm. A soft pink djellaba fell over Elana's jeans—covering the bloodstains near the pocket. The traditional Moroccan hooded long-sleeved dress would help her to blend in with the eclectic tourists. Charlie braided Elana's hair into two long braids, giving her a playful and artsy vibe.

Elana looked worn out after her shower. Encouraging her to rest, Charlie gritted her teeth and asked Donnie to help her dye the forest that was her hair. She didn't want him near, never mind touching her, but with Atlas patrolling the village she had little choice.

Donnie hovered at the edge of the tiny bathroom before entering. Emerald flashed as his eyes ran over her hair then over her chest. His eyes narrowed before traveling down and lingering on her belly. Charlie wore a black tank top and had wrapped a towel around her waist, but still felt naked under his assessing gaze. The stark space made her feel vulnerable as she waited for him to step in.

"There's a stool. I can sit while you apply that gunk," she said by way of explanation.

He didn't say anything—didn't move. Charlie sat, and the rusty, three-legged chair protested, squeaking beneath her weight. Heat shot down her back, but she tried not to fiddle under his scrutiny.

"Are you going to stand there all day?" she asked.

He cleared his throat, then moved into the small space before closing the flimsy door. "You're all tanned. Your arms and even your legs."

"Thanks to the Maltese beaches."

She felt a warm hand brush her back and she jumped. Donnie moved like a phantom knight.

"Easy. How do I do this?" he asked.

"I have no clue. I just slapped that shit in Elana's hair and hoped for the best. I've never had to color my hair. There's a hair clip and a hair tie. I'm guessing you section it off and paint on the stuff. I've already mixed it—we'll need both boxes."

She heard him slipping on the gloves. A hand traced her neck before running through her hair. Goosebumps broke out and Charlie bit back a moan of pleasure. His fingers drew her hair to one side exposing her neck and then he stilled. Frowning, she stared ahead and waited, not sure what he was planning.

A finger ran over a bruise on the back of her shoulder. It traced a path down to the center of her back, where her tank top began. He traced her spine.

"Is this where he knelt on you. Where he shoved a knee in your back?"

Did he mean the bastard who held a knife to her throat?

"Yes…. Uh, yeah."

"Does it hurt?"

"About as much as all my other bruises."

She felt him shift. His hand ran back up to her shoulder and then his breath whispered along her spine, a second before his lips touched the bruise.

Charlie froze. "Donnie, what are you doing?"

His mouth worked up to her neck as strong hands gripped her shoulders. "What I've wanted to do since the last time I saw you in Wyoming." Teeth nipped at her earlobe as a hand wrapped around her hair, pulling her head sideways and exposing her to a neck nibbling experience. "You smell good and taste so damn good. Like oranges and flowers. Shit."

Aside from a dripping tap, the only sounds that filled the intimate space were her harsh breaths. Her pulse pounded as a hot ache grew between her legs. He sucked the hollow between her shoulder and neck before working back beneath her ear.

The white walls and harsh lighting made her feel like his captive in an interrogation room. There was no doubt that Donnie controlled the invasion. Pulling shivers of delight from her moaning lips as he bit and sucked. When she groaned, he swung in front and straddled her, cupping her jaw. Bending, Donnie traced his lips over hers once. He drew back and stared down with laser intensity before covering her mouth hungrily with his. She met his urgent kiss in a wild swirl as he grabbed the back of her neck, angling them for better access. Blood pounded as he deepened the kiss. Her thoughts spun as she clutched him close.

His hand pulled down the strap of her top, and the move jarred her away from raw need.

"Stop. Donnie. Stop."

He immediately pulled back and raised his hands. Both of them panted as they stared at each other in disbelief.

"I'm sorry. I lost my mind." He licked his lips.

"We both did. Holy shit."

Standing, he ran fingers through his cropped hair. "We're not the best fit... for each other."

"So, you keep saying."

"Sharls—"

"You've made it clear that I'm not your type. Then what was that, Donnie? Wanted to squeeze in a quick fuck before we set out? Is that what you want? Casual screwing until we go back to our designated lives?"

"I didn't mean for that to happen. I shouldn't have touched you."

"Yeah, wouldn't want to touch the horsey girl next door. Charlotte, the chump..." She stood and placed her hands on her hips.

His lips thinned. "Jesus. That's why we don't get along because you always have to have the last harpy word."

"Are you going to whine for the next hour or color my hair?"

"Sit back down."

She stuck out her tongue and did as he asked. He began to work with brisk efficiency. Despite his evident frustration, he tried not to tug or rip her hair as he worked through the thick tangle. When he'd covered the last strands, he dropped the application brush and left the room. Charlie slumped and folded her arms before tracing a finger over her swollen lips.

Donnie Wilson could kiss. He seduced her mouth with dominant expertise, sweeping away all her defenses. When it came to him, her position was a weak one. She'd always had the biggest crush on the reserved man from the first time she'd seen him—three years ago—when he'd ambled down Jamie's front steps, trailing behind his friends. She'd ached to embrace the stranger with the burning eyes. Jamie had told her about Donnie's dying wife. After his wife's passing, Charlie had stayed away, only seeing him from a distance over the years. Then one night, she'd met up with Jamie and his friends at a local music festival.

She'd got all gussied up that day, feeling pretty in a white sundress and cowboy boots. It was the only dress she'd owned. Waiting until the time felt right and walking up to ask Donnie to dance had taken courage. And she'd never forgotten his rejection.

"No, thanks. I don't do country dancing, and I don't do country bumpkins."

Her cheeks had flamed as she'd clutched at her stupid dress. He'd tried taking back the words the second after they'd spilled.

"Shit. I didn't mean, I'm sorry—" He'd reached out.

"It's all good. I don't do uncoordinated dickheads who obviously don't know how to dance or how to speak to a lady." She'd turned and raced through the crowd.

Donnie had chased her, eager to apologize, but she'd never

forgiven him for embarrassing her in front of Jamie or the townsfolk. Logically she'd known that was the grief talking. The man wasn't ready to date and even if he were, why would he choose her? Still, those bitter words had her running back to the farm. Abandoning the festivities meant dragging on a pair of jeans and settling for an evening in the stables.

Now, they were alone together in a foreign country while Charlie's world blew apart. Looking for scraps of kindness from Donnie should be the last thing on her mind. As she sat waiting for the color to set, she rested her head on her knees, never feeling more alone than in that moment.

Chapter Nine

Charlie's now curly dark hair and her blue eyes changed her appearance. She still wore her jeans paired with a newly gifted, pale blue, embroidered tunic, which she wore under her denim jacket. She stood to the side as the men split their supplies. Donnie couldn't stop thinking about sinking into that delectable mouth.

And why did she look so breakable? The look in her eyes undid him. Charlie was one of the strongest women that Donnie knew. Hell, if she'd joined the military, she would've kicked some serious ass. Everything about her spoke of strength. She had a well-proportioned and firm body that wasn't just for show. Years of hard grafting on a farm developed working muscle. She could give most men a run for their money. Her confidence never wavered. She executed everything with smooth—and sometimes loud—aplomb.

Thrown out of her comfort zone on the other side of the globe—straight after her father's passing—might have something to do with her uncertainty. Donnie wanted to kill the sons of bitches that had attacked her all over again. Donnie zoned back on the weaponry before him.

"Atlas, you're taking the assault rifle."

"Hell, no. All you'll have is the Glock and your back-up weapon."

"You'll need the rifle more than I will. Elana is injured and that puts you at a disadvantage. Besides, I have my hands."

Reluctantly, Atlas placed the AR-15 next to his supplies. And Donnie pulled the group in for a huddle for the final run-through. He laid out a map of Morocco on Elana's bed and outlined the plan and the latest developments.

"I've received Intel on the identities of the team that attacked us. It's not good news." His eyes locked with Charlie's. "They're part of the Serbian mob. A sect that calls themselves the *Crimson Quarter*. Based in Sicily, they're involved in everything from cigarette smuggling, arms trafficking and dappling in the heroin trade."

"But why would they target us? Because we killed their mob brothers in Gozo?"

"I'm not sure yet. All I know is that they'll keep coming. The *Crimson Quarter* have endless resources and connections across Europe and Africa."

"This is bigger than we thought," Atlas said. "We're gonna have to contact Max."

Donnie didn't want to contact his team leader to tell him that they were balls deep in mob malarkey in Morocco. Or that they were leaving a trail of bodies. First, before the bastards boxed them in, they needed to get moving, and Donnie went over the plan.

Atlas and Elana would avoid the obvious route—through Marrakesh. Instead, they'd work their way through the smaller towns like Demnat and El Borouj while taking the R305. The last sector of their trip to the Consulate may be the most stressful—going through Berrechid into Casablanca. An ambush could occur on that route.

Donnie and Charlie would head to Rabat via Khenifra, then to Meknes. They'd then circle to Rabat. The men hunting them wouldn't expect them to take the winding route. It added a few hours onto travel time, but they had little choice.

Once they'd loaded up on rations, Donnie gifted their local hosts with the almost new BMW and the money promised to them. Safrian and Brahim turned out to be reliable allies. The bleary-eyed men had kept watch all night. In exchange for their generosity, Brahim provided both couples with new transport. A rusty-looking truck for Donnie and Charlie, and an ancient Peugeot for Atlas and Elana. It was the best they'd find. The Serbian syndicate would know by now that the women stole the BMW and that they had professional help. Now it was time to play hide and seek. If they ever found Charlie, they'd need to get through him first.

Her foot tapped away as she stared out the window at the arid terrain. Charlie didn't know much about automotive shit, but she guessed that either the suspension or the axle was shot because it was one bouncy ride. A slit in the vinyl seat meant that every time her ass shifted, something pinched against her back or snagged her hair. She didn't care about that or the black exhaust smoke drifting from behind. At least they had gas and the engine ran. Plus, she loved watching the stark terrain passing by. Every now and then, she'd point out a valley, a village or even a bird to Donnie. The joyous blue color of the sky contrasted with her divided heart. With each mile, Elana drifted in the opposite direction. Had Charlie made the right decision? Letting her best friend drive away? Did she have a choice, and what if they were caught? Charlie sensed Donnie's growing tension as the miles passed; the N10 highway was still a main thoroughfare that drew traffic. The Serbian's could easily monitor the main stretch.

"Tap any harder, and you'll drill a hole through the floorboard," Donnie said with a smile. The first words he'd spoken in over an hour.

"Oh, I'm sorry, am I dampening your mojo? I just had to say goodbye to my injured and shot-up best friend."

She expected him to retaliate. Instead, he shot her a compassionate glance that only served to piss her off.

He glanced in the rearview mirror for the hundredth time before asking, "Have you and Elana been friends for long?"

Suddenly the man found his tongue. She wasn't sure if she wanted "Yapper Wilson" as her new travel mate. He'd kept quiet despite her running commentary on the passing countryside. She answered the question anyway.

"Since we were eleven. She's like the sister I never had. I do have a brother, but that's not the same."

"Wait, you have a brother? I've never seen him at the farm."

"Daddy and Nate had a falling out and didn't speak for fifteen years. He lives in California and is much older than I am. We're not all that close. Although he is helping out at the farm while I'm traveling. Both him and Earl."

"Earl Tanner... or Earl Taylor? He is your foreman, right?"

"Earl Taylor. Yeah. He's great. We've worked alongside each other for years. Mostly since daddy got sick. Without him, I wouldn't have been able to plan this trip with Elana."

Donnie shot her a look. "I think Atlas has the hots for Elana. Be honest, will she chew him up and spit him out?"

Grinning, Charlie agreed. "Oh. Hell, yeah. He's toast..."

"I get the vibe that she's a man hater," said Donnie.

"No. At least I don't think she is. Elana has a unique

perspective. She's never had much time for boys and says that a guy must be really special before she'd even consider him as a fit for her life."

Donnie nodded. "I get that. I'm the same way."

They fell into a comfortable silence and stopped for gas before pulling back on the N10. When Donnie dialed his hyper vigilance back a notch, Charlie asked the question that had been eating away at her for far too long.

"Why did you say no?"

He frowned. "No to what?"

"To me. To that dance. Like a year and a half ago."

"Oh, hell, Sharls. Don't go there."

"I wanna know why you acted like a turd biscuit. I felt mortified."

His knuckles turned white as he stared ahead, and it seemed as if he might not answer. Miles passed, and she gave up and scratched for her lip balm in her bag.

"I'd lost Sophie the year before, and I was still in a dark place. That's no excuse for the way I spoke to you, but it was a definite asshole period in my life."

"It's fine—"

"It's not fine. Let me explain. I wasn't ready to date or look at other women. I loved my wife. She was everything—she was my life."

"I'm sorry."

"Watching her die, it broke me and every day I lived to survive to the next. Time passed, and that night at the dance—when I saw you walk across the room—for the first time in a long time, I wanted to drag a woman home and fuck her blind."

He met her gaze head-on—the mix of desire and anger keeping her glued to his next words.

"That reaction angered me. I wasn't supposed to feel anything, not yet. I only welcomed the numb grief, and suddenly I felt something more. Something fuckable and savage and raw. It scared me... I acted like a dick."

"I thought you didn't like me... physically."

"Oh, I liked you, Sharls. But aside from our obvious chemistry, we have nothing in common. We're oil and water."

"Bullshit."

"We're the opposite in every way. You're loud. I'm quiet. You're a country girl, and I'm a city boy. You're—"

"Double bullshit. We're exactly alike." She ignored his look of disbelief and continued, "We both value physical activity and like to keep fit. We're both direct and honest, but we express it differently. I think we're both comfortable with who we are. We're hardworking human beings. Like me, you're a realist. You have a quick temper, and hell, I have a huge one—we'll blame that on my red hair—and you and I value loyalty above all else."

He didn't say anything. His slight frown meant he was considering her words. Good. He tried to fit her into a neat little box where he could justify his attraction to her, explain it away as just a chemical nuisance. He could lie to himself all he wanted, but she wouldn't allow him to do the same to her. If they were going to bonk like rabbits in the coming future, they'd do it with their eyes wide open. Was that what Charlie wanted, Donnie Wilson in her bed? He complicated the hell out of her life, adding to her existential crisis in an uncontrollable environment. He didn't want her—not all of her. Attempting a relationship— even a casual one—would break her heart.

Maybe they'd get lucky and get to the Embassy without incident, thus spending a minimal amount of time together. She prayed that would be the case because if Donnie kissed her again, like he did in that bathroom, she'd go up in flames and her heart be damned.

◊ ◊ ◊

She'd drifted off to sleep after they'd fallen into silence—curled up into the door frame. He recognized the exhaustion that came with surfing on a drawn-out adrenaline rush. Donnie trained to deal with stresses that came with being shot at. He forgot what it was like for a civilian and as she dozed, he missed her constant commentary from the passenger seat. Drowning in danger and yet she gazed at the passing scenery with admiration.

He didn't want to like her. Charlie wasn't what he needed, but the more time he spent with her, the more he wanted to get to know her. While being attacked, she'd kept her shit together. Her common sense and fighting spirit garnered his respect. Grateful for having a non-hysterical target as a partner, Donnie checked his mirrors and changed lanes. The truck stuttered, and white smoke poured from the hood.

Swearing a blue streak, Donnie steered the vehicle to the curb as it cruised to a stop. He climbed out as Charlie sat up.

"What is it? The radiator?"

"No shitting idea. Pop the hood; it should be near your feet."

Charlie did as he asked and then opened her door.

"No! Stay inside and duck down. The last thing we need is a nosy driver getting a glimpse of your face."

"But it's quiet. There isn't a car for miles."

"Sharls, do it and don't argue."

After rooting around, he climbed back in. He felt the need to break something and took a couple of calming breaths.

"I gather it's not good news."

"Probably a coolant leak. The engine is fucked."

"Well, I guess we're thumbing a lift."

"I'm flagging someone down. You're staying in the truck until it's safe." He checked his weapon and slipped a second smaller pistol in his ankle holster.

"If you look like Rambo, no-one will stop," Charlie called as he slammed the door. He ignored her and waited in the warm sunshine. It was a mild day and he assessed the horizon. The road curved around a shale hill. A sparse valley spread out below with a splash of greenery in the far distance. The arid section reminded him of Southern Utah—rock climbing in the state was one of his favorite past times.

The fifth car stopped. Keeping his hand at a close distance to his weapon, Donnie watched the middle-aged lady climb from her Ford Truck. Roughly clipped gray hair, a loose blouse, men's trousers and sensible looking sneakers. Nothing she wore matched and seemed to fall in line with her bustling gait as she hurried over.

"Tourists?" she asked. She had a cultured British accent that spoke of years of private education. She smelled of incense and patchouli and he'd bet that she'd spent many years in Morocco.

"Yes, ma'am."

"Where are you heading?"

"Fes." He lied as he met the older woman's shrewd eyes.

"Well, you're not getting there with that bloody wreck of a car."

"No, ma'am."

"Are you on your own?" Her keen eyes surveyed his battered truck.

"My wife is in the truck. This is our honeymoon."

"Well, why in the blazes would you drag her around the countryside in that wreck?"

"We paid a bus driver to take us to Ait Benhaddou, but he conned us out of a hundred dollars and left us at a fuel stop. I rented this truck from a local villager."

She considered his story. Jesus, CIA spooks had nothing on this old coot. Donnie heard Charlie close the truck door and walk over.

"Hello, I'm Sharla Walcott and this is my husband, Donnie." Charlie leaned over to shake hands. She'd remembered their cover story and embraced her new identity with ease. He knew she'd be a natural and slipped an arm around her waist as they secured potential transport.

"Barbara Pritchard. You can call me Barb."

"Hi, Barb. I'm sorry, this is turning out to be a doozy of a trip. My darn husband decided that camping in North Africa would be a great honeymoon. Hot water and a soft bed are all I ask for."

"Sharls—"

Charlie gave him the cold shoulder. "Don't you dare. Sitting on the side of a freeway for hours is not my idea of romance. You're so far up poop creek, mister, stay in that canoe and keep rowing."

He tried not to smile. Charlie played up her country twang. That combined with her now big baby blues and her sweet snub nose and she looked like Bambi.

She raised her chin as Barb harrumphed. "These men are frightful buggers. Luv, I can take you as far as Tinghir. You should be able to arrange transport from there, but I wouldn't advise continuing this afternoon. There's an awful accident just before Agoudal—up one of the passes—the authorities will close it for most of the day."

That was the last thing they needed. More delays, but Donnie wouldn't chance getting stuck on a narrow pass that could expose them to an attack. Plus, the local police would be handling the accident and may stop them with his stockpile in the trunk.

"Hope no-one was hurt. What happened?" he asked casually.

"A friend called me. He's stuck in the chaos. A bus overturned. They overload them to capacity. Unscrupulous bus companies don't give a flying fig about their passengers. Third bus accident this year. Unfortunately, there are fatalities. I run a hotel in Tinghir, more like a large Riad. You're welcome to stay; I'll charge my honeymoon rate."

"Well, then it's fortuitous that we've run into you. What do you say, sweetheart?" Donnie asked Charlie.

Charlie stood on her toes and kissed his cheek. "I say, it's a good start in making it up to me."

Itching to get moving, he threw his kit bags in the trunk as Charlie settled in the front seat. With one last glance down the dusty road, he climbed in the back. His skin crawled, and Donnie knew without a doubt that if they'd stayed any longer, they'd have had unwelcome visitors. They were being hunted, and Donnie didn't like the feeling one bit.

Chapter Ten

The warm water washed the last of the shampoo down the drain and Donnie didn't want to step out. He turned in the walk-in shower, admiring the intricate green tile work and gold finishing in the luxury bathroom. As Charlie had already taken her shower and he'd hopped in straight after, the mirrors were now completely misted over. As heavenly as the spray felt, he'd stayed away from her for too long.

Thanks to the unscheduled stopover and the choice to travel a less popular route, they should be safe. At least for the moment. Tinghir was a fairly large oasis town with a population numbering around forty thousand. Unless the Serbian's had direct Intel—for now—they were out of danger. Donnie may not be operating under condition red, but he'd still take precautions. Aside from a security check, he needed to contact Atlas and then Max. He dreaded that call to his team leader. Max Andersen wouldn't be happy knowing that bogies in North Africa were chasing two members of his elite team.

Donnie dried off and pulled a fresh change of clothes from his backpack. He'd packed three sets of trousers, three shirts and six t-shirts for the trip. Hopefully, they could utilize the laundry facilities before they left in the morning. Opening the door had him freezing. Expecting to see Charlie on the bed, he clenched the door handle, scanning the space. Their empty lunch tray sat in the corner.

Quietly calling her name provided little help. Donnie holstered his Glock 19 under his shirt, clipped his Kukri knife into the waistband of his pants and left the room. The hotel was set out like a typical Riad. Rooms faced a large central courtyard which contained a tiled aquamarine pool and palm trees. Lanterns and luxury sofas filled the exotic area. The hotel played up the lush feel of Tinghir—a town based on the foothills of the Atlas Mountains—at the center of one of the most attractive oases in Southern Morocco. Thirty miles of lush palm trees grew along the Wadi Todgha—a seasonal ravine. Thanks to irrigation channels, the green gorge was a beautiful tourist spot that still retained many of its Arabic traditions.

With no sign of Barb at the check-in desk, Donnie walked the lobby looking for signs of his pretend wife, his pulse thrumming in his temple. He was about to reach for the entrance door when it swung open.

"Hey, sweetheart," Charlie chirped as she held the door open for their new British acquaintance. "I told Barb that I under packed on this trip and she took me to the best boutique, just a block away." Charlie held up a shopping bag, ignoring his gritted teeth as she slipped by. "I used some of my cash. It didn't take long."

At least she didn't use a trackable credit card. Thank God for small miracles. But parading around town on a busy afternoon was a foolish move. Not telling him made him even angrier. Donnie tried to smile as he slipped an arm around Charlie's waist and steered her towards the stairs.

"Great, honey. But I thought we were having an afternoon nap."

"Is that what you young Americans call it these days?" Barb chuckled. "Dinner's at six, but I can send the plates up to your room. Get on with your honeymoon snogging, and I'll see you in the morning."

Once they were back in the safety of the room, Donnie rounded on his so-called wife. "I thought you had better sense than to wander around in public, exposing yourself to an attack."

"I needed western clothes or at least acceptable looking Moroccan clothes. I stand out like a sore thumb. A newly wedded American woman wearing the same worn Berber shirt day after day attracts scrutiny."

She had a point but Donnie still felt the need to shake sense into her.

"Relax, Chuck Norris, I bought a couple of shirts, a pair of sneakers and a new pair of jeans."

"We need to go over some ground rules."

Charlie rolled her eyes and Donnie caught her arm. "If we're attacked or separated, we'll both need to be on the same page."

"And that would be?"

"First rule. Movement saves lives. It's called getting off the X."

"Getting off the what?"

"The X. If someone tries to stab you, how would you save yourself? You'd jump out of the way. If you're in a plane crash, escaping the wreckage immediately quadruples your chances of survival. Those that could move but stay frozen in their seats will either die from toxic smoke or fire. It's about finding that small window of escape and taking it."

"How does a plane crash relate to our situation?"

"If someone is shooting at you, it's harder to hit a moving target. It's not foolproof but your chances of survival increase with movement. If I ever tell you to get off the X, you'll do it. I don't need a debate or hesitation. If I tell you to move, you'll move."

Charlie sat on the bed and crossed her legs as she listened, now looking interested. Donnie continued as he dug for his burner phones in his go-bag. "Also, you have strong legs and arms. Put those defined muscles to good use."

"If you mean apply self-defense, I have minimal training. Jamie showed me a couple of moves. I could shoot if need be."

"You're a natural. You've killed two men using your bare hands."

"And legs," she added.

"Exactly. I don't have the time to teach you, that would take weeks. However, if you use your feet, legs, knees, head, and elbows, you can do some lasting damage. Elbows are particularly effective. Jab and strike out as much as you can. Go for bellies, noses, and throats. Years of manual work on the farm gives you an advantage, throw yourself behind every punch and kick."

Charlie nodded and licked her lips. Fingers fiddled nervously with the hem of her shirt.

Donnie knelt before her. "I'm hoping it never gets to that. To hurt you, they'd need to get through me first."

"It doesn't feel right—hurting another human being even if they've hurt me. I keep having nightmares about that cliff, about watching that man fall to his death. I know he was trying to kill me but..."

"That could've been you."

She nodded and looked away. Donnie climbed on the bed, wrapped his arms around her and shifted them onto the pillows. "I can't promise anything, but as long as I'm around, I'll do my best to make sure you're safe and that you'll never have to kill anyone else again. Leave that to me. It's what I'm good at."

She didn't say anything, just tightened her arms around his waist. A breeze whispered, and Donnie stared out the grated window. Wispy white curtains that matched the bedcovers drifted as the light fell across the bottom of the wide bed. Aside from the occasional yell from down below, the streets were quiet, and the peace made him almost forget the danger.

Charlie felt good in his arms. Too good. She was the perfect height—only a few inches shorter than his nearly six feet, and her head rested comfortably on his shoulder. Her fingers played with the neck of his shirt as he took in a mix of the hotel shampoo and a warm spicy smell that was hers alone. When she eventually fell asleep, Donnie resisted listening to her raspy breaths and instead rolled her over and covered her with a throw.

Stepping into the bathroom, Donnie made both the calls he'd been dreading—first Atlas—who answered on the first ring. Without waiting for Donnie to speak, Atlas launched into an update. It wasn't good news.

"Elana has a fever. It's bad, man. It's a fucking nuking day."

"An infection from the arm?"

"Yeah."

"Are you anywhere near Casablanca? Are you still traveling?" Donnie asked as he ran a hand over his neck.

"No, we've made it to El Borouj where I've had to stop to find a doc and a bed. I've used a good chunk of our money on paying for his services, and to shut him up. He's hooked up a line with antibiotics. We'll continue in the morning."

Atlas sounded concerned, more worried than Donnie had ever heard him. Updating his teammate on their diversion to Tinghir, Donnie discussed new exfil plans and their next check-in with each other. He prayed he'd made the right move by splitting up the group. If either of the soldiers failed, it could be their death sentence.

The call to Max had Donnie wincing. He was right in assuming that Max would be as livid as all hell. MIT2 were still stuck out in the field, on the Sudanese border and they were about to move in on a rebel extremist group who were radicalizing local school boys in the region. Max would reach out to their European counterparts—MIT4. They'd investigated mob links to extremist networks in the past and although this could be a stretch, MIT4 may have Intel on the *Crimson Quarter.* Any tie-ins could get the MIT taskforce investigating the Maltese angle. Donnie desperately needed back-up in the field, even from an intelligence-gathering perspective. Knowing his enemy was key to turning the tables. The hunter would eventually become the hunted.

Charlie woke from her nap to news of her ill friend. Donnie sat at the end of the bed as she hugged a pillow to her chest. She should never have let Elana go. Now she lay ill in a distant town, too far out of Charlie's reach. What if Charlie lost her? Elana had stood by Charlie through her roughest moments, and Charlie couldn't bear thinking of a world without her loyal friend. Then she'd be truly alone. All she had was her dad and Elana—and Jamie, but he didn't count. He was away most of the time and now he'd built a new life with Lizzy. Charlie sat up, trying to breathe. She coughed around her tightening chest as tears welled. Fisting the sheets, she tried not to think of a world without her friend.

"Easy, Sharls. I've got you."

Muscled arms wrapped around her as Donnie rocked her on the bed.

"Breathe slowly, in and out."

Panting, Charlie tried to slow her breathing. She clung to his shoulders as he whispered reassurances in her ear. Charlie had no idea how long they stayed there for, but when her hip began to ache, and her foot tingled with pins and needles, she let go and stretched out her leg.

"I've never experienced that before, was that an anxiety attack?"

"Probably—it's warranted. Do you want to eat something?"

She shook her head. "Too nauseous to eat. I want to rest—here—with you."

Looking up, she ran her gaze over his lips. Outlined perfectly by his goatee and stubbled beard, the top one bowed slightly, resting atop a full lower lip. Before she realized, Charlie cupped his jaw and traced his beard with her thumb. Then she slipped her hand behind his neck and pulled him in for a kiss.

With a growl, Donnie shifted over her and followed her down to the mattress. Charlie lost herself in his ravaging tongue and their instant hunger. He lowered himself until he fully covered her. His hard dick rested between her legs as he devoured her mouth, the warmth of his very male embrace had her sinking into the bed.

When his hand began to roam, she pushed it off her chest, down to the apex between her legs. He paused to stare down at her as she arched her hips and pressed his hand down.

"Touch me there, Donnie."

His intense stare never wavered, but he did as she asked. Cupping her over her jeans and rolling his palm once. The mere touch of his hand had her sighing in pleasure. Her trembling fingers reached between them as she unbuttoned and unzipped her jeans. He gave her room as he reclaimed her lips. Then in one swift move, he gripped her jeans and panties and peeled them off. She lay exposed as he stared down at her naked lower body.

The backs of his fingers stroked her inner thigh as he took her in.

"Open wider, Sharls," he said in a guttural growl.

She did as he asked. His hand slid up, but instead of touching her intimately as she expected, it traced over her hips, pushing up her vest to expose her pelvic bones.

"You feel like silk. So damn soft."

Kneeling on the floor, he gripped her hips and pulled her to the edge of the bed. Pushing her knees apart, he watched her again—his lips so close, that she could feel his hot breath against her folds. She waited for his touch, and when it didn't come, she shifted restlessly. He stilled her by gripping her hips and pushing them into the mattress.

That complete control had her throbbing for his touch. Her body flooded with desire as she watched his glittering eyes taking her in.

"Donnie." She moaned. "Please."

She expected a teasing touch, so when his mouth claimed her clit in a tongue swirling kiss, she jolted off the bed. In a full-on assault, he pushed a finger inside and stroked her inner walls. His finger stroked hard as his beard tickled the inside of her thighs. His lashing tongue made her moan as her body pulled tight— too many sensations bombarding her from all sides. He snarled into her heat, and the vibration almost had her sobbing. Another finger slipped in, and had her arching up.

With one hard lick and suck, her toes curled, and she exploded, thrusting into his hand. That was the quickest and most powerful orgasm of her life.

When she relaxed into the bed, he sat back—his fingers still buried.

His eyes burned as he looked at her. "I can feel you twitching and pulsing. I want to sink myself in that beautiful pussy."

He stood and used his immersed hand to push her back on the bed. Then he pulled out his fingers to unbutton his jeans. He dragged his shirt over his head, and Charlie took in his carved chest and stomach. The man had a serious workout routine. She wet her lips barely hearing his next words.

"Take your vest off. I want to see you naked."

When she didn't answer, he ran a hand beneath her shirt and tried to push it up.

"No. Don't." Her sudden shout had him pausing as she scooted back towards the headboard.

"Whoa. Easy. What just happened?"

"I can't do this. I can't do us. Whatever this is." She dragged the bed cover over her legs and pulled her knees to her chest.

Donnie stood frozen, and then cautiously sat on the end of the bed. "I've somehow walked into a minefield. Tell me what I did wrong."

"You did nothing wrong. You gave me a mind-screaming orgasm, but I can't do any more of this."

The stubborn man wouldn't let it go. She could see his mind working over the last few minutes, trying to find the cause for her distress.

"I'm tired, and I'm going to sleep. You can sit there all night if you want." She twisted away.

"Is this because of your fake boobs?"

"Excuse me?"

"I'm not an idiot. I can see you've had work done. I won't judge you."

Heat crawled up her neck. "You're judging me right now, just by saying that."

"I'm not—" He reached out.

"Women get breast augmentations for many reasons. Some to please a man. Some because a girl has such small breasts that she can barely fit in a training bra. Shopping for a bikini is a miserable experience, and maybe she wants to feel like a woman and not like a teenage boy."

He looked confused. "Is that why you—"

"Other women elect surgery because their breasts are so huge that it causes back issues and pain. Don't you dare judge—"

"Easy, Sharls. I'm sorry I brought it up. If it makes you happy, then that's all that matters."

"What do you know about what makes me happy?"

The poor man looked cornered and a little angry, but she couldn't tamp down the rage. Months, no years of frustration spilled out in front of the person who'd just loved on her; she craved a fight.

He spoke quietly, but all she heard was his annoyance thrumming beneath. "You're seeking happiness in all the wrong places. I know why you came on this trip—to feel excitement instead of pain. To have a fling with some European fuck-boy and run from your sheltered life. And—"

"You're a dick!" She kicked his thigh. "Sheltered life, my ass!"

As he stood, she dove into a tirade she'd been holding in for so long and said the words she'd never spoken to anyone. "You've made assumptions about me from the beginning. A wealthy farmer's daughter who's loud and what? Spoilt?"

"I didn't say that."

"Your eyes say it every time you look at me. My mama left when I was twelve. She wanted a life of fame. Not only did she

127

cheat on my dad, but she moved to Hollywood. My brother went with, and she tried to take me, but I refused to leave my heartbroken father."

"I'm sorry," Donnie said. "That's awful. I know what it's like to come from a broken home."

"Yeah, yeah. That's life, but my dad never hurt a fly. He is—was—a simple man who never got over his wife leaving him. For months he lay in bed, and I took over all the chores. I learned from trial and error—at twelve years old—how to run a sheep farm. I planted and grew vegetables. Planted that fruit orchard running below Jamie's property, and sold our wares at the market every summer to earn extra money. I thought life would be okay and that we'd be fine."

Something in her voice must've given her away and had Donnie sitting back down. "What happened?"

"I planned to attend veterinary school after I graduated, and I did. Except two weeks after my eighteenth birthday, I got sick."

◊ ◊ ◊

The way she'd said the words had the hairs on his neck standing to attention. She suddenly looked small and still in the bed. Johnny never mentioned her being ill. Donnie rubbed a hand over his mouth and asked the question. "Sick with what?"

"We were on health insurance, but it couldn't cover everything. Daddy wanted to put me on some fancy trial and at first, I refused."

"Sick with what, Sharls?" Donnie gritted his teeth.

"I think you know."

He shook his head as heat flooded his veins. "No. Don't say it."

"Stage Two. Invasive breast cancer." Trying to swallow,

Donnie stood. He clenched his fists as an onslaught of Sophie's last months almost brought him to his knees.

Charlie watched him with sad eyes. She knew of his wife's battle with breast cancer. And Charlie had gone through the same? His thoughts tumbled as he tried to catch his breath. Pacing, he ran his hands through his hair and paused to look out into the now darkened sky. Why hadn't Johnny mentioned it?

"Joh—James didn't say anything."

"Jamie doesn't know. I found out while he was on a deployment. He was in the regular military—like he said he was?"

"Special Forces. James was a Ranger."

"Well, he was gone a lot. And when he was in town, I knew if he found out he would've given up his career to take care of me. Dad and the farm hands told him that I was away at college."

"Where were you?"

"During the bad months? Lying on a mattress next to the toilet… when I wasn't passed out in bed."

"Jesus, Charlie!" Donnie swore.

"Yeah. It sucked, but you know what? I got through it. One double mastectomy, tons of chemo and a fancy drug trial later, and I came out the other side. I celebrated my twenty-first birthday with cake I could actually keep down. Weak and skinny and sad, but alive."

Leaning his hands against the window sill, Donnie asked, "Are you okay, now?"

"If you're asking if I'm cancer free? For the last six years, yes. I've never had time to celebrate. My father spent every last dime on saving my life. Four months after the doctors gave me the all clear, they diagnosed my father with heart failure. I've had to choose what was best for our family. I pulled out of veterinary school and studied to be a vet technician instead. Aside from my practical studies at a local shelter, I'd wake at three am every morning, study until five then start with my farm duties. At lunch, I'd squeeze in another hour of schooling, then work until dinner. Put dad to bed and study from nine until eleven."

She ran a hand over her neck and kneaded her fingers. The faraway expression meant she remembered her endless routines. Donnie ran his gaze over her chest, imagining the pain and all the surgeries. His eyes darted back to her face; she'd caught him looking.

"I considered reconstruction surgery from the start. I went with the staged approach where they insert a tissue expander under the chest muscle during the mastectomy. That preserves the shape of the breast and the skin. After all the treatments, we didn't have the money for it, but my father was determined. On my twenty-second birthday, he presented me with a gift. He'd submitted my name into a plastic surgery program that awarded five cancer survivors every year with reconstruction. I was selected. The program would cover the costs, and all I needed to do was show up. My father and Earl begged me for weeks, and I eventually gave in. I wanted to feel like a girl again. Breasts may be just mammary glands, but they're a big part of identifying as a female. Just like a man may feel attached to his penis—it defines his masculinity even though it shouldn't. And some survivors are okay with not having the surgery. I wasn't one of them."

"Was it a long process?"

"Not too bad as I'd already had expanders inserted. The recovery time wasn't that painful. I didn't opt for the nipple reconstruction; I went for a nipple tattoo instead."

"That's why you didn't want me touching your chest."

"Yes. You would've felt and known."

"Why keep it from me? Because of what happened to my wife?"

"That's part of the reason. That, and I didn't want you to see me as unattractive."

"Sharls. Are you kidding me?"

"You're freaked out. I can see by the crazy look in your eyes."

"I don't know if I can…"

"You don't have to explain. It's personal for you; I get it. It's personal for me too. I had a shitty decade, but I don't believe in waiting around for things to get better. I get better—and stronger and I'm in charge of my own path."

He didn't reply. Couldn't say anything. He stared at the wall as Charlie watched him.

"I met you a year after the final reconstruction surgery. At twenty-three years old, finally healed, I felt like a girl again. I'd emerged from a tunnel of horror, and when I heard about your wife… my heart broke for the both of you."

Three years ago. She'd worn her hair in a long bob-cut, and he'd noticed how the curls had traced her shoulder. At the time, her wide smile had ticked him off. He'd hated the farmgirl with the bright eyes and chipper attitude. God, and her only fault was that she'd been grateful to be alive. While his heart was being torn to shreds. His jaw ticked and Donnie turned his back.

"I'm going to shower again and get some sleep. What time are we leaving?" she asked.

He'd almost forgotten about their current situation; he couldn't think past the burn in his chest. "I'm not sure. Around five am. I'll be on the balcony if you need me."

Donnie welcomed the fresh air as he slid open the sliding door and took a seat. He flipped open his military grade laptop and checked his messages. New information leaked in, and he ran through the developing Intel. He paused to stare out over the wadi.

Every time he closed his eyes, he saw his beautiful Sophie wasting away from breast cancer. Flashes of her curled around the toilet, passing out on the living room floor, or too weak to stand or even climb out of the bath. Months of them fighting cancer together. Her devastating slide into a high care ward and her eventual death. Except now he saw Charlie in the same place. What if her cancer returned? Would he be able to live through it again? And why was he even considering that role in Charlie's life? They weren't even friends. Hardly even lovers. Sex would be a convenience in a foreign land. Except things had changed. She was his friend, more than a friend. He cared for her and every day he respected her a little more.

Her loud honesty grew on him. He liked knowing where he stood and he loved that she never played games. She'd been right in the truck; they shared similar traits. Aside from that, her kindness and loyalty were attractive qualities. He never tired of staring at her open face. That girl next door innocence combined with her full lips and the spattering of freckles across her nose was a dangerous combination. She was a tomahawk to his solar plexus, yet he couldn't resist standing up and walking back inside.

Golden light flooded the space from a corner lamp. Arabic music drifted in from a distance, and the cherry-like smell of sweet tobacco from a nearby hookah wafted on the air. Donnie crawled in the bed, and she stirred.

"Turn around and face me."

She did as he asked.

"Arms up."

"What are you doing, Donnie?"

"I want to see you. All of you."

"I don't know if I'm ready for that."

"You'll never be ready. Arms up."

She did as he asked, and he peeled off her dark vest. Then he straddled her, using his hips to fully twist her onto her back.

"Fuck," he breathed.

She tried to place her arms over her chest, but he secured them above her head with one hand.

The glowing light from the lamp lit the curve of her breast as Donnie ran a finger across it.

"You're beautiful. What is this?"

He glanced up long enough to see her swallow and then looked back down. Tribal flames snaked around and over her breasts. A bird emerging from a fire like a phoenix rising. Oranges, reds, and yellows danced together in intricate designs that took his breath away.

"I got the tattoo to cover my scars. I decided on a Firebird— from the legendary fairytales. It's a powerful source of light; even a feather can light up a whole room."

"It's you—you're the Firebird." The words slipped out before he could stop himself.

Her eyes widened, but she continued, "It makes me feel powerful after being weak for so long."

Stroking a hand over her breasts, he said, "This is a chest of a warrior, a beautiful woman who fought for her life."

Her eyes glistened at his words. "I'm far from done—in this life. I'll never stop fighting."

Donnie cupped her breasts reverently. The two perfect mounds felt soft in his hands. He stroked a thumb and she shivered.

"You can feel my hands?"

"Yes. Some spots are more alive than others. I never had radiation therapy—due to the drug trial they put me on—I've retained some of the nerves."

Donnie bent down and ran a tongue over the side of her right breast. "How about there?"

She nodded.

He moved to a new spot. "There?"

"Not so much."

He took his time exploring until he'd found every sensitive spot on her breasts. Then he cupped them again. "They're smooth; it feels weird without the nipple."

"I know. It took some getting used to on my end."

"You can go braless and not have to worry." He smiled.

"I do, often."

Heat flared, and he shifted on her hips.

She put a hand out on his leg. "You're hard—getting even harder—I can feel you through your jeans."

He didn't say anything, just continued stroking a beautiful breast. Charlie's hand moved to undo his button.

"Are you sure you want this?" Donnie asked.

She nodded and he rolled off to stand and pull off the sheet. She looked wanton in the soft light. The distant music rose, as Donnie pulled off his jeans and shirt. He walked over and slipped a condom from a side pocket of his backpack. Then he faced the bed, studying her as he rolled it on. Her fingers found her folds and he groaned, watching as she rubbed slow circles.

The time for games was over; he wanted inside. Pulling her hands away, he crawled up her body and positioned himself at her entrance. "I'm going to make this Firebird dance tonight," he said as he pushed in slowly.

"Donnie," she gasped as he fully impaled himself.

"How does it feel?"

"Amazing. Damn incredible. Now screw my brains out."

"Yes, ma'am." He pulled out and sank in. Leaning down to breathe in her scent, she bit his neck. Growling, he circled his hips, pulled out and ground back in.

"Holy smokes. Shit. That feels good."

"You like that?" He thumbed her as he repeated the action.

"Jesus. What are you doing to me?"

"Fucking you thoroughly, Miss Quinn." She moaned then sucked on his neck, and he buried his head in her wild hair, feeling himself coming apart. She consumed him and electrified him all at once. Thrusting in, he seated himself in deep. Then he pushed in, even more, their hips ground together. He pulled back and slammed back in, shoving as far as he could. He felt her clenching, and he stayed buried as he bit her earlobe. He repeated the action over and over. The music built along with their tempo. Charlie cried out, her nails clawed at his shoulders, and she tightened around him. He sank in and paused.

"Come for me, Sharls—while I'm balls deep, come around my cock." He slipped a hand between and stroked hard. Her hips jerked, she arched off the bed. Her spasms short-circuited his brain, and he moved, thrusting and pounding until he found his own blazing release.

Donnie turned them over, pulling her head to his chest. They were still joined, but he had no energy to move. He wanted to lie for a sacred moment with Charlie in his arms and forget the outside world. Forget about cancer and gun-wielding thugs and not being able to save her dead friend.

She nuzzled and kissed his chest as her hand played with the back of his neck. Who knew that Charlie Quinn was a snuggler?

He didn't complain. No-one had touched him in a very long time, and it felt damn good. His limbs turned to jelly as she danced her hand along his side and down his hip. Her hair tickled his nose; still, he didn't budge.

"Thank you for coming for me," she said softly.

He tightened his hold. "I'm glad I did."

"I'm grateful it was you."

He kissed her temple. "Let me get cleaned up and we'll talk."

Donnie disposed of the condom and wet a facecloth before wiping her and climbing back in. He rolled onto his back as she stroked a hand down his chest.

"I'm selling the farm."

"Johnny mentioned the possibility."

"I can pay off most of my debts. I discussed it with my dad before he died. He wants me to sell it to one of the established farmers in the area, not some fancy real estate developer."

"Good."

"I didn't pay for this holiday."

"Honey, it's none of my business."

"My father bought the tickets months ago and kept it a secret. Two days before he died, he told me to find joy and to explore with my friends. He knew I always wanted to go to Malta. I was fascinated with the Maltese Knights as a kid. And when it came to my dancing, he'd overheard me one day talking to my friends about learning more skills from the dancing group in Morocco. He always loved to watch me juggle fire."

"He loved you very much."

Wrapping an arm around his waist, Charlie resettled her head and stilled. He felt her relax and he ran through their exfil plan for the hundredth time. He'd protect her and make sure that she got back home to sell her farm. She deserved happiness in a life free from the burden of livestock and harsh winters plowing through debt. He'd gift her with security and safety—something he was trained in and could give her. After that, they'd go their separate ways. He wouldn't live through losing someone else to cancer. If Charlie relapsed... he couldn't think about it. It was best they parted before he did something stupid—like fall in love.

Donnie checked his watch; it was earlier than he thought. 2100 hours. He eased out from under her and got dressed. Next came a security check. He checked the street and perimeters outside their room before locking up. Then, he re-packed his equipment and cleaned his weapon. Unscrewing the suppressor he'd recently used at Ait Benhaddou, he checked for carbon residue. When he'd screwed the clean can back in place, he packed away his equipment. 2200 hours. Donnie couldn't settle, but needed to sleep. Placing his Glock on the bedside table, he climbed beneath the covers and pulled Charlie into his arms.

The ringing phone woke them. It took a second for Donnie to orient himself before deciding on answering the hotel line. He'd only slept for thirty minutes. He snatched up the receiver with a gruff hello.

"There are men—in my lobby—looking for your wife," Barb hissed. "And they have guns."

Chapter Eleven

Donnie swore and glanced Charlie's way. She picked up on his immediate tension, leaping out of bed to grab the shopping bag from earlier. Clothes spilled as she pulled out the jeans and ripped off the shopping tags before shimmying into them.

Barb continued, "I like your wife—if that is even who she is—the lumbering brute who just threatened to slice my throat? Not so much. Told them I've never seen her, but it's only a matter of time before someone recognizes her photo."

"Thanks for the heads up, and I'm sorry we got you involved. We're heading out now."

Charlie pulled a black fitted tee over her naked breasts, followed by a khaki button-up shirt and a satin looking olive green bomber jacket. Had she bought out the whole damn boutique? He didn't have time to admire her modern safari look. Instead, he turned to hang up.

"If you head up to my rooftop deck—on the south side—you could jump over to the next building and maybe then the next. Don't come down the stairs; there are at least eight of the bastards lurking around."

"Thanks, Barb. I appreciate it."

"No problem. Be careful, one is wearing a local police uniform."

Donnie hung up and shouldered his go-bag as Charlie pulled on new canvas sneakers. "The old shoes were giving me a blister," she replied when he shot her a frown.

"We can't leave them here. I want no trace of you left in this hotel."

She shoved her sling bag into a new girly looking backpack and slung it over her shoulders. Donnie glanced over the balcony, only seeing palm trees and thick growth near the water, on the back end of the Riad. "Let's not make it too obvious we were here." Donnie launched the sneakers into the night then stalked back and grabbed her hand. "Let's go. We're moving out."

Easing open the door, Donnie checked the passage. Shouting drifted up from below. They flattened against the wall and edged to the stairwell. With only a slight creak, the door opened, and he pulled Charlie up the stairs. Bypassing the second floor, they emerged onto an open terrace on the roof. A cold breeze blew through the tented space and clouds concealed the starlit sky. Tripping over a colorful rug, Charlie ran to catch up as Donnie looked for the best place to hop over to the adjacent building.

"Please tell me we're not jumping." She peeked over the side.

"More like leaping."

"Holy shit. I'm game, but if I twist an ankle, you're carrying my heavy ass."

Removing their packs, Donnie tossed them over the gap. A narrow lane ran between the two Riads, promising a three-story drop if one of them slipped.

Donnie turned to coach Charlie and stumbled back in surprise. She'd already backed up and now ran for the edge. His heart jackhammered as she flew through the air, landing on the other side in an awkward roll.

"That shit hurts," Charlie said, climbing to her feet and clutching her elbow. "Don't just stand there gaping—get your ass over here."

Grinning, Donnie jumped the gap, rolling to his feet in a graceful move.

"Well, look at you—an honest-to-God ballerina."

"Years of martial arts training." He grabbed their packs and looked for their next exit.

"You need to teach me some moves!"

"I already did. Head, elbows, knees and feet. Once we get back to Wyoming, I'll structure a decent training regimen for you." Throwing their bags for a second time, he grabbed her hand. "Ready to go again?"

"I guess this is what you mean by getting off the X." She stretched and clicked her back. "I'm going to be one swollen boo-boo."

"C'mon, Firebird. Jump the gap."

"Why don't you go first?"

"Because I'm watching your back. Go."

Grumbling, she positioned herself, ran and leaped. Charlie landed, rolling behind a potted plant. "Mother of God!" she moaned.

All he could see were her unmoving feet as she lay in a prone position.

"Sharls!"

She didn't move.

"Charlie!" Within seconds Donnie made the leap, running to her side. With a face scrunched in pain, Charlie curled in on herself. "Who leaves damn piping sticking up in the middle of a goddam roof." She kicked at a broken pipe extruding from the floor.

"Where are you hurt?"

"Screw you," she said through gritted teeth. "You made me jump and break my vagina!"

"Your what?"

"My effing vajajay! I rolled into that thing when I landed, and I got cooter punched!"

Donnie tried not to smile at her apparent agony. "Do you want me to shoot it for you? The pipe?"

"Can you? Just kill the asshole now… and don't make me laugh or I'll kick you in the balls and then we're even."

Hiding his smile, Donnie looked away. With a pained giggle, Charlie got to her knees. He helped her the rest of the way, trying to keep a straight face as she waddled the few steps to her bag. He dragged his attention away from his adorable partner and looked for the best exit. This was a private residence which conveniently had a ladder leading down to the alley. Waving her over, Donnie showed the way down.

"Thank God for the invention of ladders," Charlie whispered as she climbed down the rungs. Following, Donnie kept an eye on her progress, relaxing when her feet hit solid ground. His relief was short lived. She'd barely stepped aside when two men stepped around a corner, spotted Charlie and rushed her.

It took only a second for Donnie to analyze his targets. One had a knife. The other had nothing? From the way they moved he instantly knew that they weren't with the *Crimson Quarter*. The mercenaries were not well trained and not well armed, and they hadn't seen Donnie yet. He withdrew his tactical pen from a pocket.

The man with the knife reached Charlie first, swiping as she jumped back. When the thug stepped closer, Donnie let go of the ladder and let gravity do its work. Ignoring the impending pain, he focused on using his knees to strike the man's shoulders. Making contact, he drove the target straight down, riding the body to the ground. Donnie knew he'd severely injured the man's back, but he didn't pause. With a powerful punch, the tactical pen slammed into the asshole's temple, and he went limp.

Hearing Charlie shout, Donnie pushed to his feet, pausing as he took in the second assailant groaning on the pavement while clutching at his balls.

"Since I couldn't get even with that pipe, thought this bastard would be the next best thing. Don't grab a girl when she's hurting and mad." Charlie looked ready to land another kick.

The mercenary tried to roll to his feet, but Donnie gripped him in a headlock. "Did he lay a hand on you?"

"Didn't get the chance."

Kneeling and executing a chokehold on the carotid artery, Donnie waited the nine seconds it took for the target to pass out. Letting the body fall to the ground, he grabbed Charlie's hand then pulled them through a series of alleys and narrow roads.

"Did you kill him?" she asked as they ran.

He glanced her way, expecting to see disgust or fear. All he saw was a curious frown.

"No, he lost consciousness. He'll be fine. I'm trying not to leave a trail of dead bodies in our wake."

"And the other man?"

"He'll probably need to be hospitalized. I can't say if he'll survive, but he did try to gut you."

"I know." She squeezed his hand. "Thank you."

Slowing, Donnie glanced around a corner. "We're heading into that foliage, down by the creek. It's not much, but if we wind our way along, we can bypass the hostiles searching for us."

They kept to the shadows and moved towards the end of the alley. Five men slid out of the dark and blocked their way. When they turned to run, four more men trapped them from behind. Letting go of the small hand that clutched his was one of the hardest things he'd ever done, but Donnie needed both hands to fight. They'd have to kill him to get to Charlie. Donnie situated her behind him and pulled his Glock.

"Drop your weapons."

Four men had knives. One huge dick-weed had a bat but no gun, at least none that he could see. Again, they looked like untrained locals. He expected at least one Serbian mobster to join the gang, but still no sign.

"Take me. Leave him."

"Shut up, Sharls," he whispered. "Remember what I told you. Make the fuckers hurt and movement saves lives."

He'd shoot the knife-wielding bogies first; if they rushed him like he expected, he could still kill them without using bullets. As an edged weapons expert, the men didn't stand a chance against the Kali fighting system that focused on edged and impact weapons.

All nine charged and Donnie dropped three. Bullets struck the first two center mass, and the other hostile between the eyes. Moving quickly, he sidestepped the rush of bodies. Squeezing the trigger, he clipped another in the shoulder. The last knife fighter got too close. Donnie avoided the first jab, then chopped at the blade-wielding arm with the butt of his gun, breaking it at the elbow. Grabbing at that same arm, he twisted his assailant to the ground, snapping the bone all the way. A movement to his left indicated the target with the bat was swinging it at his head. Donnie ducked just as Charlie leaped on the huge guy's shoulder. Shit, he'd almost pulled the trigger. Since she was now in the fight, Donnie holstered his gun while kicking out at an attacker's knee, and slamming a palm upwards into the bastard's nose. A side blow to the temple had Donnie reeling. He staggered, trying to focus on the location of Charlie's battle cries. But they drifted farther away as he remained behind, fucking around in the alley. One wiry asshole left to deal with amongst the wounded and the dead.

Blood blurred Donnie's vision, and he swiped at his brow before slamming a hand into the enemy's skinny throat. The man fell, gasping and Donnie finished him off with a kick to the head.

Charlie. Donnie stumbled then ran towards the disappearing shadows. As he'd suspected, the behemoth with the bat had taken Charlie. Praying he'd get to her in time, Donnie pushed past concussive nausea, racing into the quiet city.

◊ ◊ ◊

The Goliath with the damn bat had her in a fireman's carry. Pounding against his muscled back did little good. The sour smell of his dirty shirt made her eyes water. She'd expected him to kill her, but instead, he ran with a destination in mind. Would he rape her first? Either way, she wasn't going down without causing bodily injury—starting with a human bite. Charlie sank her teeth into the back of his arm, biting down until she tasted blood. Howling, he threw her to the ground and raised the bat.

"Putain de chienne," he swore in what she assumed was French.

Remembering Donnie's advice, Charlie kicked out at the nearest shin. Twisting, she scrambled and ran towards the open field ahead. It was more like an abandoned lot between structures, and she had no idea which direction to take, but she threw herself towards the promise of freedom. It lasted all of ten seconds. His heavy weight slammed her to the ground. Her hands flew out from under her, grazing the dirt, and a knee screamed under impact. As he turned her over, Charlie coughed, tasting blood and dirt.

She tried to raise her head. He grabbed her hair and slammed it back down. Leaning close, he spat out angry words in languages she didn't understand and laid the bat across her throat.

"Let go of the bat and stand up." Donnie's timbered voice was like a morning hymn to her soul. He repeated the phrase in a couple of other languages while holding his gun to the man's head.

The giant's nostrils flared as he contemplated his next move. Finally, he stood. Donnie issued further instructions in a deadly manner. Charlie lay still and watched her partner with the suppressed weapon. The lot lay deserted. The drama played out in a vacant bubble, in a derelict space.

Goliath stepped back a few steps then lunged. Donnie pulled the trigger. The man's knee exploded. He collapsed, screaming in the dirt.

"Keep yelling, and I'll finish you off." Donnie's flat look silenced the man—almost—who whimpered as Donnie knelt over Charlie's prone form.

"How badly are you hurt?"

"I'm okay—nothing I won't be able to walk off. But I need water, quickly before I hurl."

"Your face is covered in blood." Donnie swung off his backpack, and reached into a side pocket.

"It's not all mine. I bit the asshole."

"Good girl." Unscrewing a bottle of water, Donnie's

glittering eyes ran over her as she rinsed out her mouth and splashed her face. Aside from a cut on his temple, Donnie looked unruffled, like he hadn't just taken on nine men.

"God. I can still taste his blood. I'm going to be sick."

"Not here," he said, glancing around. "We need to move."

"My backpack. It fell off somewhere back there."

"I know, I saw it."

Once he'd helped her up, she placed weight on her injured knee. Aside from a dull throb, it seemed okay.

Charlie limped but was mobile. Donnie looked ready to pick her up and carry her. Like hell, she'd had falls off stallions that were harder than this. She even insisted on carrying her pack once they'd retrieved it.

"I'm fine. Concentrate on getting us out of here."

With a brief nod, he morphed into "full-on operator" mode and cleared their path with clinical efficiency as Charlie concentrated on keeping up, and breathing through the shock. Via a new avenue, Donnie led them into the scrubby greenery near the creek. They picked their way through the brush, winding through palms and over rocky beds until he indicated that they change direction.

A tented campsite lay ahead, beneath a steep gorge. It looked like temporary lodgings for a tourist group who wanted an authentic Moroccan experience.

The quiet campground indicated that all were asleep. Still, Donnie waited and listened until he was satisfied with its conditions. Nudging Charlie, he pointed at the motorcycle parked on the periphery. Her eyes widened when she realized his intentions. He wanted the bike.

Back in Wyoming, Donnie always stopped in at the farm to visit Jamie when on a road trip with his biker friends. She'd seen him on a black Harley. Once he'd pulled in on a fancy superbike. Charlie didn't know much about the steel beasts. She'd been carted around once on her college boyfriend's Suzuki, but it hadn't lasted long. A couple of months. When she'd gotten sick, the dick conveniently disappeared along with his fancy new bike.

"Stay here," Donnie whispered before disappearing into the camp. What the hell was he doing? He moved so silently that she lost track of him immediately. Two minutes later Donnie returned with two helmets and a set of keys.

"How the hell—"

"I figured it was parked next to the owner's tent and their helmets sitting near the flap confirmed it. The guy's fanny pack sat just inside the tent. Easy pickings."

She'd almost forgotten what he did for a living. The man could probably pick locks, plant bugs and infiltrate most buildings. She was the sidekick to James freaking Bond.

Donnie placed the helmet over her thick hair, struggling to push it down as she groaned against the tight fit. Trying to clear the mashed-up strands from her eyes, Charlie ran alongside him to the bike. Instead of climbing on, he pushed it down the sandy path until they were a safe distance away. Then he swung a leg over, and she did the same, tucking herself to his back as the motorcycle purred to life. Soon the path became a smoother sand road, and then, as they sped towards the freeway, they eased onto a tarred surface. Charlie wanted to huff out a sigh of relief, but she knew they were far from safe. She also knew that driving the quiet freeway at midnight wasn't the best plan for staying under the radar.

As if sharing her concerns, Donnie pulled off at the first exit. A rough road that curved behind a hill and ended at a hiking trail. With her help, he pushed the bike down an embankment and covered it with palm fronds. Then they hiked a good fifteen minutes before Donnie spotted a sheltered area to make camp. He swept out the shallow cave with some fronds and Charlie gathered what little firewood she could find. Temperatures would drop, and they'd need the warmth. Thanks to the protected location in a small canyon, their fire would be safe from searching eyes.

Her knee burned with every step. That along with an adrenaline crash, had Charlie leaning against the rough wall as Donnie gathered more wood and started the fire.

Her feet and hands were numb from the cold, but she didn't care, she just wanted to sleep.

"Wake up. Don't close your eyes." Donnie—the annoying man—shook her hard.

"Leave me... me alone... tired."

"You're freezing and suffering from shock. Look at me."

"I'm too sob... sober for this sh... shit. Any beers stashed away?"

He wrapped her in something soft, then pulled her onto his lap. The warmth from the fire vaguely registered. Steel arms wrapped around her and she felt him at her back. Then Donnie rubbed her arms, unzipped his jacket and pulled her close.

"Sharls, don't fade out on me. It's cold, but we've got this."

The minutes ticked by and she began to thaw out. Her body trembled, and she knew it was more to do with her delayed reaction. They'd been attacked by multiple bad guys, many of which lay dead in the streets just miles away. They'd all been after her and Donnie was just an inconvenience that needed exterminating. God, he'd fought every one of them to keep her safe. Moving like a panther with sinewy grace in a choreographed death dance.

The last man—the titan—had scared her the most. He'd treated her like a lump of meat or like an inhuman speck he aimed to eliminate. She mattered. Her life meant something. If he'd succeeded, who would miss her? Elana and Jamie. Her foreman, Earl, and her staff would mourn her loss, but they'd move on. The only person who'd loved her to her core, who'd sacrificed everything for her was dead. Her father was gone.

Her brother and mother didn't feel the same. They'd left her and never looked back. Where would she go after this? She felt like an orphan in a cruel world and yet her life held new possibilities.

Charlie felt a soft kiss to her neck and her heart warmed. Right now, in this place, she wasn't alone. Donnie Wilson held her in his arms, and she felt safe. It felt right and familiar. Her shaking limbs calmed, and she looked down. Fingering the thin fabric draped over her, she asked, "What's this?"

"It's a microfiber towel. It's multifunctional, used for warmth, as a sling or an absorbent wrap. It packs up small, I can easily fit it in my go-bag."

"It is warm, thank you."

"I have a light sleeping bag which I'll pull out." He turned her in his arms and ran a hand over her forehead then down her cheek. "Where do you hurt?"

"I'm good."

"I have a medical kit. Let's take care of the cuts and scrapes to avoid future complications."

Without giving her time to agree, he pulled his bag closer and dug around.

"Do you have gum?" she asked.

"Erm. I might."

"I can still taste him." Charlie blinked back the tears.

"Shit, honey. Let me look. I have toothpaste and a toothbrush."

"Hell! I do too—from the hotel." Scooting over, she fished around in the front pocket and produced a travel kit. Donnie tossed her a water. "Go easy. I only have two bottles to last us."

After scrubbing her mouth twice over, Charlie rinsed then accepted the gum that Donnie offered. He cleaned up her scraped elbow and a torn shin. He then examined her swollen knee.

"How did it get injured? I need details." Firm fingers pressed around the kneecap.

"I landed on it when *The Rock* tackled me."

"I think it's more bruised than broken. Did it twist? Did you hear or feel anything snap?" Donnie rubbed a cooling gel around the joint.

"Thanks for that visual. Nope. I concur with your badass diagnosis; it's bruised."

"You must be feeling better if your smart mouth is kicking back into gear."

"Maybe my smart mouth needs attention." She grinned.

"Charlie," Donnie growled in warning as he threw her a granola bar before packing up the kit.

"If we're huddling for warmth, we might as well make it worthwhile…"

He didn't say anything, just pulled out a sleeping bag and continued packing away gear.

"That's the most organized backpack I've ever seen," Charlie said, tucking the protein bar away for later.

"I like order."

"Do you also iron your shoelaces?" She loved teasing that uptight side of him, always trying to loosen the carrot stuck up his disciplined ass.

"You're on a definite role." He smiled as he pulled out a second towel-blanket thing. "Now scoot into the bag and get comfortable."

Charlie did as he asked, then used her backpack as a cushion, and lay on her side as he covered her with both extra blankets. Donnie left the cave to do what she assumed was a security check.

Then he placed his gun nearby, climbed in the tight bag and spooned her. A hand cupped her jaw and twisted her head as he planted a blistering kiss on her surprised mouth. "Yum. Sweet spearmint heaven."

He dipped his head, deepening the kiss. Twisting, Charlie sat up, jarring her knee in the process.

Feeling the flinch, he pulled away. "You okay?"

"Knee," she huffed out.

"I think you've had enough for the night, lie down and ignore the anal jerk at your back."

She smiled as she settled, then tucked his arm to her chest. He dragged her hair up and out the way. "You're trying to suffocate me."

"I should be so lucky." Charlie loved their banter and found it settled her frayed nerves.

"Smartass." He gave her a squeeze.

"You were formidable out there. How old were you when you started learning those Chuck Norris Karate moves?"

"Chuck has nothing on me." She smiled at his small joke. "But seriously, I've never trained in Karate. I started Shaolin Kung Fu when I was five."

"Why so early?" she asked.

"As the smallest boy in the class, children pushed me around a lot. My mother would never tolerate kids who couldn't stand up for themselves. She enrolled both my brother and me in class."

"Why Kung Fu? Why not Karate like most kids?"

"My great-grandfather was Chinese—my mother's grandfather. He was a grandmaster in the Shaolin arts. The highest level you can get."

"You must be pretty high up?"

"I'm a master. I'm called a Sifu. Kung Fu was my starting base to many martial arts that I've studied, Krav Maga, Jujitsu, Muay Thai and Kali."

"Your mom must care for you."

"She does. My parents divorced for the same reasons as yours did. They were so different; my mother was also ambitious. She's now a fancy real estate guru. Unlike you, I wanted to go with her, to live that high life, but I stayed with my father instead. My parents are still good friends and my mother brings baked goodies over for my dad. My father has always needed us around."

"Why, is he ill?"

"Just eccentric. He's an inventor. Without my brother and I keeping him on track, he'd turn into a hoarder. He likes collecting knickknacks."

That would explain Donnie's drive for order and why he went for women like his mother. Ambitious, put together and graceful—the opposite of Charlie. She'd never met his mother, but Charlie would bet that she was an influence on how Donnie lived his life.

Changing the subject, Donnie tucked her hair behind her ear. "Back at the hotel, I was given more Intel. A Maltese family is involved with the Serbian attack. I suspect they're involved in organized crime."

"You mean like the mafia?"

"Exactly like that. We're narrowing down on the suspects,

and it's only a matter of time before we determine all the players."

Charlie only hoped the good guys caught the evil bastards before it was too late.

Chapter Twelve

They'd hardly slept. When a light storm rolled in, cool temperatures prevented them from finding comfort. Donnie's watch registered forty-two degrees in the early hours of the morning. They'd waited until an hour past first light, when there would be more traffic on the road. Now they made their way down the hillside in rain-dampened clothes. What Donnie thought was a hiking path the night before, turned out to be a herding path for local goat herders.

It took them a while to retrieve the bike. Their hands were numb, and exhaustion had them moving slower than he'd liked. They feasted on more granola bars before Charlie swung her leg over the seat. Her stiff movements spoke of all sorts of aches and pains from the night before. He doubted the three Advil he'd fed her would make much of a difference.

Despite the torturous night, she looked beautiful. Although he far preferred her natural red, the chocolate brown hair color made her eyes look larger and made him want to stroke her contrasting creamy skin. He'd stroked it last night. Well, more to keep her warm but nuzzling her soft neck had been heaven. And they'd talked—about everything. Donnie never pictured himself as a talker, but Charlie's relaxed manner had him revealing childhood adventures. Her husky laughs at him and his brother's antics had only encouraged him further.

Then she'd spoken about her father. How close they'd been and how he'd loved her. She was given her first horse when she was six—a pony called White Socks. He'd laughed when she told him how the small horse hated any show jumps and would turn and race the other way. That the pony bit most other animals and humans but adored Charlie. And how Charlie slept in the stables on warm summer nights. She'd fall asleep on the pony's back, and for a little girl, it felt like the safest place on earth. In the morning when she woke, her dad would be dozing in a lawn chair outside the stable doors. Always watching over his little girl.

That sweet story made Donnie's chest hurt. She'd equated losing her father to losing the only person to have ever cared for her. She must know that others cared—aside from her asshole sounding brother and mother. How had Donnie never seen her honest and open heart? Now it was hard not to notice. What started as an antagonistic affair had morphed into warm teasing and an alliance that felt more like an equal partnership. Donnie didn't like it. A potential future with the firebird would get him burnt. He couldn't afford to invest his heart in another human being. He'd done it once, and the resulting loss had brought him to his knees.

They'd have Morocco, and once he'd hunted down the threat to Charlie, they'd go their separate ways. It was the wisest option.

He climbed on the bike and checked the fuel. With under a quarter of a tank, they'd need to stop at the next gas station. Donnie hoped that the bike got them to Rabat. He drove them back onto the R703. Eighty-five kilometers until they reached the R317, then another ninety-five clicks until Khenifra. Six hours of travel lay ahead, and that was without complications. He'd need to check in—both with Max and with Atlas. Once they had better signal, the second new burner would be powered up.

◊ ◊ ◊

Two hours later.

"Pull over," Charlie shouted above the wind.

"What?" She heard the confusion in Donnie's voice as they rounded a bend through a quiet valley.

Considering they'd stopped only an hour ago to refuel, his query was warranted.

"Please, Donnie. I'm going to be sick."

He pulled onto a gravel shoulder. As soon as they'd stopped, Charlie ripped off the helmet and ran for the clump of bushes to the side. God, she hated that feeling of nausea, and wanting to barf her brains out. She felt a tiny bit better after hurling, but not by much...

"Sharls, how long have you felt ill?"

His concern had her swiping at a damp brow. "Since I woke. It's probably something I ate back at the hotel."

"That was over twenty hours ago. All you've had since are granola bars. Shit, I need to find you a solid meal."

"I can't think about food. Don't talk about it."

A hand stroked down her back as he passed her a bottle of apple juice—part of the meager provisions they'd picked up at the gas station. She twisted off the cap, and rinsed out her mouth before savoring the sweet refreshment. Trying not to waste any more time, she stood and walked back to the bike.

"Honey, you're so pale—you're almost blue."

Probably not far off the mark. Aside from feeling bilious, her body hadn't yet warmed up after their miserably cold night.

Although Donnie's bulk sheltered her somewhat on the bike, the biting wind still found its way to her numb extremities.

Ignoring his worry, Charlie lifted the helmet with shaking hands and he placed a hand on hers. How did he look that virile and unruffled? He seemed unaffected by the overcast day; even his hand felt warm.

"Stop. Just for a second and let me check you out."

"The longer we sit out here, the longer I'm exposing you to danger. I'm fine, Donnie. I want to get to safety and find a warm shower at the end of this road."

Her protest fell on deaf ears. Donnie ran a hand over her forehead. "You're freezing."

"Yip, I'm a block of damn ice."

He ripped off his jacket, revealing a white T-shirt.

"What are you doing?"

Donnie began stuffing her already layered arms into the sleeves.

"Stop. I'm wearing a winter jack—"

"Now you're wearing two."

"Are you crazy, you'll freeze!" Charlie said as he pulled up the zipper.

"Compared to temperatures I've worked in, in the past, this feels like Honolulu. It's sixty-three and warming up."

His military grade jacket warmed her limbs immediately, and they climbed back on the bike and headed onward. Despite his casual words about the weather, Charlie snuggled close and wrapped her arms around his muscled waist, trying to infuse warmth to his core. Although it was moving into winter, it should be warm, especially since they were still inland. They'd hit a week-long cold-spell.

As the day wore on, the temperatures heated, and they stopped at a small market. Shedding her layers, Charlie looked around. Nearing Khenifra, green hills and sedate valleys dominated the countryside. It looked like they were in Italy instead of North Africa.

Donnie stocked up on food. After buying oranges, they ate skewered chicken and corn as they sat behind a vendor's makeshift awning. The locals seemed friendly, and when a group of boys kicked a soccer ball their way, Charlie jumped up to punt it back. Donnie enjoyed watching her feint and pass the ball like a pro. Her knee still bothered her, but she worked around her limp. Charlie may be compact, but she had a powerful body. Years of dancing and physical activity had honed Charlie's muscles and meant she could easily star in the next Tomb Raider installment.

She seemed to have gotten over her bout of queasiness. Hating to leave but not wanting them to draw too much attention, Donnie signaled her over as he stood. She hugged the kids and slipped them a few dollars before he led them back to the bike. They'd parked down a sand road, under a wiry tree and away from prying eyes. The noise of the market faded as they rounded the last curve. Before they reached the bike, Donnie swung her around.

"What are you doing?"

"Taking a moment." He rubbed her cheek then planted a kiss next to her generous mouth. Before she could protest, he traced his lips over hers and pulled her hips to his.

"Can you feel how hard I am?"

She nodded.

"Once you're safe, the first bed we find is going to be our home for however long I'll need to explore every inch of you."

He pressed his lips to hers, caressing her mouth with deliberate strokes. God, she was like a drug, and he wanted to drag her to the grass and take her right there. Pulling away gave him pause. An odd look in her eyes had him frowning, but she looked away before he could decipher the cause. Grasping for equilibrium, he said, "I didn't know you played soccer."

She rubbed an eyebrow with her thumb. "As a kid, I played in school, but quit when my parents split."

"You're pretty good—for a girl."

He expected a snarky comeback to his silly jab, wanting to see her cheeks flush, as she rightfully kicked his ass with a verbal assault. But instead of rising to the bait, she stopped and turned. He almost plowed into her.

"We need to talk."

"I was just teasing—"

"Not about that." Sweeping her hair up, she clutched it in both hands and paced. She stopped beside the large tree to stare out over a field.

Donnie crossed his arms. "What's going on?"

"I haven't been entirely honest with you. I've been trying to find the right words. Something happened, when I was in Malta and I suspect…"

If she referred to Ruzar, he didn't want to know details of that relationship. He stiffened against an unwelcome and imminent confession.

Charlie turned, and all hell broke loose.

One second, she was about to make the biggest confession of her life, the next, a stranger stepped out from behind the tree and pulled her roughly against his broad frame. The primitive rage flashing in Donnie's eyes as he drew his weapon, didn't stop the man from holding a pistol to her head. A second mercenary walked up and pointed another gun her way.

"If you value her life, you'll drop your weapon." Another man said, stepping up from an adjacent trench.

Breath solidified in Charlie's chest. "Ruzar."

"Charlotte. Good to see you again. No sudden movements or my colleagues will be forced to hurt you. Tell your 'boyfriend' to drop the damn weapon."

Ruzar addressed Donnie. "I don't want to hurt her. If you give up your weapon, you'll both be safe. She has two pistols pointed at her head."

"Fuck you." Donnie's expression darkened as a chilled silence descended. The ferocity of his stance hinted at his bloodlust, and as if sensing imminent death, her captor drilled the muzzle of the gun into her temple.

Ruzar spoke again. "We're not here to kill her, I'm trying to help. The men that followed her aren't far off." Ruzar turned to her. "Firefly, tell him to stand down. I promise I won't hurt you."

"She's not a fucking fly!" Donnie said through gritted teeth.

"I'm not a Firefly or a Firebird. I'm just a girl who wants to live and I want to go home." Donnie swallowed as she made her plea. His hand shook slightly as nostrils flared.

"I'll get you there," Ruzar said. "I've come to warn you."

"Then why take her hostage?" Donnie asked.

"Because I don't know who you are, but I've seen what you can do. Those men in Tinghir didn't stand a chance and I value my life. Give up your weapon and allow my men to search you, and I'll release Charlotte back to your care."

Outgunned, Charlie saw the second that Donnie gave in. For the first time, he made eye contact and the agony in his gaze communicated a belief that he'd failed. He hadn't, because sacrificing his life wasn't acceptable. She knew Ruzar, or at least she thought she'd glimpsed a side of the real Ruzar, and it was now up to her to use that edge to keep them breathing.

Donnie threw his Glock on the ground and raised his hands. They directed him to throw his backpack down and move back from the guns and the bike. Now they were free to kill her. Panic welled, and her body quaked. Donnie's fear—stark and vivid—echoed her own.

Ruzar nodded, and the man released her. Charlie stood, knees wobbling like a newborn foal. She stepped toward Donnie. No-one stopped her, and she broke into a limping run, then stumbled into his arms. His crushing embrace made her gasp as she buried her face against his throat, feeling a pulse beating as erratically as hers. Donnie squeezed tighter before letting go and shoving her behind him. Her two assailants still pointed weapons their way.

Ruzar thrust his hands in his pockets. His gaze entirely focused on Charlie. Aside from the healing scar on his temple, he still looked as brawny as the first day she'd met him. He wore all black including the turtleneck sweater, overcoat, and black jeans. Except he now wore his long hair loose instead of pulled back in a low pony. That contributed to the dark and dangerous vibe he seemed to promote. The *Highlander* meets *Dracula*.

"Now that we're on even ground, let's talk."

Oh, she'd talk all right. "The last time I saw you, you were lying in a hospital bed in Malta and now you're hunting me?"

"Correct."

"Who are you?"

"I'm guessing he's part of the Maltese family trying to murder you," Donnie said as he clenched his fists.

"Correct again. Except I'm no longer supporting the contract. I pulled out of the family business."

"Contract?" Donnie asked at the same time as Charlie said, "Why?"

"Because of you." Ruzar checked his phone as he spoke.

"I'm guessing you set Charlie up." Donnie pulled her closer.

"I did, but I didn't expect to develop feelings for her. Before I could warn the women, my cousin and his moronic friend attacked us—well, her."

"You're telling me that you'd go against your family for a woman you hardly know?"

Ruzar shrugged. "We developed a connection. Where I come from—how my family raised me—my life is a deceitful game. Meeting Charlotte opened my eyes to a world outside of my dynasty. Look, we don't have much time. The *Crimson Quarter* are boxing you in and know where you are."

"How?" Charlie asked.

"Those were your men in Tinghir," Donnie said.

"Man. One man. Only one of the locals worked for me; my father hired the rest."

Charlie frowned. "Which one?"

"Let me guess, the Neanderthal who ran off with you and tried to strangle you with a bat," Donnie said in a dangerous tone.

"It wasn't my best move," Ruzar said. "I think I hired an imbecile. I asked him to extract you and bring you to the east side of Tinghir, where I could whisk you to safety."

"He tried to kill Charlie on the way. How did you know we were even there? How did your father's men find us?" Anger vibrated through the man sheltering her.

"I planted a tracking device in her cell phone and in one of her sneakers—the ones we found lying in the creek near your hotel. My father's men and his Serbian thugs have blocked off all routes between Tinghir and the coast. I took a chance that you'd head to Khenifra and I guessed right."

"What are you going to do with us?" Charlie asked quietly.

"Help you get to safety."

"Bullshit," Donnie said. "What's in it for you?"

Ruzar blinked then his shoulders hunched. "Redemption for my soul. I've done a lot of bad things—evil shit that I'll have to answer for one day."

His confession hadn't changed the tension rippling through Donnie's back. Charlie felt his muscles clench at Ruzar's next words.

"We have a minibus parked down the road. There are two groups of men closing in from either side of this location. If you stay here, you'll die. They'll shoot her on sight."

Donnie didn't reply, nor did he twitch.

"If I wanted Charlotte dead, we would've already executed her. Please—for her sake—come with us."

"And if we don't, you'll force us?" Donnie asked.

"No, I'll wish you luck on your journey and walk away. But I don't want Charlotte to die. We both care for her, let me help."

"It's not up to me." Donnie turned to Charlie. "You've known him longer than I have. He's a killer and the son of a powerful kingpin, what do you want to do?"

"If we go with him, swear that you'll never leave my side until we're safe."

"Never." He drew her to his chest. "They'll have to kill me to get to you."

"Nobody is dying. If what Ruzar says is true, we won't stand a chance against that many men. We need his help."

Gripping her arms, Donnie made a vow. "If he touches you, I'll rip out his throat."

She believed those words as she gazed into the face of the deadliest man in Morocco. Nodding, she grasped his hand and walked them over to Ruzar. "You have a deal. Now give Donnie back his guns and his pack. We have places to go and asses to kick."

"I'll pull the minibus around."

Chapter Thirteen

"Why such a big vehicle?" Donnie asked Ruzar.

"I'm delivering gifts to a friend."

Clambering into the black minibus with tinted windows went against every instinct that Donnie possessed. The men shuffled the couple past the middle seats, and Donnie restrained himself from raising his weapon and shooting a way back to open skies. Ruzar's men seemed relaxed and even joked amongst each other in Arabic. Bags of equipment lay across a few of the rows, along with a large cooler.

Donnie assessed the men. Judging from the way they moved and handled their weapons, they were average mercenaries. If they knew what he was capable of, they'd be pissing their pants. The man that had held a gun to Charlie's head stretched out his hand. "No hard feelings, mate? My name is Hakim, and this is Jamal." He pointed to his armed friend.

Turning in the aisle, Donnie grasped the offered hand and squeezed. When Hakim flinched, Donnie leaned in. "Fuck hard feelings, but if you ever wave a gun in her direction again, I'll crush your skull."

Releasing Hakim's limp grasp, Donnie guided Charlie into the back corner where he could shelter her if the shit hit the fan, or possibly kick out the back window. And it looked like that was a viable possibility as a second vehicle with two occupants rolled down the narrow path towards them. As the last to climb into the bus, Ruzar paused at the door then swore.

"Hide her behind the seats, quick."

Donnie pushed Charlie to the floor. As soon as the targets stepped out of the vehicle, he readied his Glock. Serbians. From the steel look in their callous faces, their economic movements, and their fancy hardware, there were no mistaking *Crimson Quarter* men. A thick beard covered the larger man's face, and a scar slashed at his eyebrow. He was the alpha of the duo. His pockmarked compatriot hung back—a skinnier soldier with buzzed cut hair and hollow eyes.

The next two minutes would demonstrate where Ruzar's loyalty lay. Donnie and Charlie may have walked into a trap or a shootout. Their steel cage provided zero protection against the AR-10 rifle held inside the open jacket by the lead target. Ruzar could serve Charlie up on a golden platter to the two mobsters standing behind him.

They greeted Ruzar in Serbian. Donnie didn't speak the language. He did speak Russian, but there were too many variances. Ruzar greeted them, then switched to Arabic.

The lead man followed suit. His mastery over the middle eastern language came as no surprise. He'd bet that the *Crimson Quarter* had business dealings with extremist friends. Over the last decade, thanks to the explosion of modern technology and the dark web, cross-pollination between global syndicates were now a standard practice. Extremists, poachers, mobsters all ran in the same circles. They shared a network of arms and drug dealers. It was the *You scratch my back and I'll scratch yours* mentality.

None of Ruzar's thugs knew who the American male at the back of the minibus was, or that Donnie spoke and understood Arabic. He did give Hakim and Jamal props for readying themselves and easing their weapons into positions. The Serbian spoke loud enough that eavesdropping now gave Donnie a tactical advantage. Ruzar looked relaxed, but appearances were deceiving. White knuckles clenching the bus door spoke of his underlying tension.

The bearded man stood near the front of the vehicle.

"Ruzar, aren't you supposed to be in Valletta? What are you doing here?"

"I thought I'd join the hunt."

"Does your father even know you're here?"

"I'm sure he does by now. I can't have others doing his dirty work. The bitch is my responsibility."

Donnie's pulse bounced erratically at Ruzar's words. He glanced down to check his weapon. Charlie looked up from the floor below. Fear glittered, and in that brief millisecond, Donnie wanted to sweep her away and teleport her to safety. Instead, Sharls cowered like a trapped rabbit as the fuckers outside the door debated her demise.

Donnie swallowed his rage and searched for an opening, a scenario where he extracted her from the impending violence.

The bearded dickhead now spoke. "Is she your responsibility because you fucked her brains out in Malta?"

Donnie's lips thinned. His grip on his gun felt like it would bend steel.

Ruzar shrugged. "Maybe. Perhaps I want to kill her for making me look like Frankenstein's monster." He pointed to the ugly scar.

"Let's hunt her together, we can take turns. I hear she has the

167

sweetest body. All ripe and firm. Once I've broken her, you can finish her off."

The words seared the corners of Donnie's control and murderous thoughts raced as he devised his next move. No matter what happened, that bearded asshole would die first.

"Vlado, I have my team. But I wish you luck in your search." Ruzar stepped through the door.

The target named Vlado called out, "I spoke with your mother this morning. She called to see if we've found the bitch yet. Your mother wants her dead after what she did to your cousin, and for almost killing you."

His words got to Ruzar. Donnie saw Ruzar's mask slip for the briefest of seconds. Nostrils flaring, he nodded and took a step away.

"You didn't find her at this market?" Vlado asked.

"It's a dead end. I've got to get going."

"Can I at least meet your team?"

Hakim stiffened, and Donnie shot him a warning look before pushing Charlie further into the corner and scooting his backpack in front as a shield.

Ruzar hesitated.

The skinny Serbian sidekick spoke up. "Maybe we can ride with you. That piece of shit rental car is giving us problems."

"I don't have room."

"Looks like there's plenty of room." Vlado pushed past Ruzar and stepped onto the minibus. Now Donnie was committed, and he worked over a tactical plan. Vlado's instincts must've kicked in as he half raised the AR-10 to a firing position while surveying the occupants. Vlado still hadn't spotted Charlie. Donnie registered movement outside the window but refused to take his eyes off Vlado's assault rifle. Hakim and Jamal introduced themselves. With a nod, Vlado stepped closer, now focused on the back-seat occupant. Donnie's pulse kicked as he shot Vlado a counterfeit smile. Then Donnie flexed to lift his pistol. Ruzar slid up behind the bearded target and raised a hunting knife. His muscled forearm wrapped around the Serbian's forehead.

Vlado's head jerked, and he fell face-first to the floor. Hakim darted forward and pulled the rifle from Vlado's nerveless grasp. Donnie took in the fatal injury, impressed and worried over the skill needed to sever a spinal cord in such a clean manner. To cut the cord, you'd have to know precisely where and what angle to insert the knife—cutting between the vertebrae and spongy discs to get to the cord. Ruzar accomplished this without breaking a sweat. He'd stabbed deeply into the back of Vlado's neck, angling the blade front and center before yanking back. The other skinnier target lay just outside the bus, with a gaping neck wound. Sightless eyes stared up at blue skies. Charlie whimpered, and Donnie drew her up to his chest.

Ruzar rolled Vlado over, not caring about the blood soaking his boot. "I'm not sure if you're still alive. You're unable to speak or move. All your body function has ceased to exist, and you'll die soon—in minutes. This is what happens when you threaten someone I care about. You'll never touch Charlotte Quinn, you dirty bastard. When I kill, I don't usually like a mess, but I think I'm developing a taste for it." Ruzar spat in the fallen man's face then cleaned his knife on Vlado's jacket before rising. "Let's get this party started. We've been here too long."

There were three alphas in the room. One lay dying or dead in a spreading pool of blood. One sat in the back contemplating the fact that he'd made the stupidest move by climbing into the minibus. And one was a raving fucking lunatic who could become Donnie's most lethal adversary. Charlotte Quinn was in Ruzar's crosshairs. What the crime boss wanted with her was anyone's guess and the only barrier standing in his way was Dave "Donnie" Wilson.

Donnie tucked Charlie in closer and rocked her while watching Ruzar Comino. The killer removed an elastic band from his pocket, tied back his hair and then climbed behind the wheel. With a three-point turn, he drove the large vehicle over the dead body lying in their path and headed back to the freeway.

Chapter Fourteen

"Where are you taking us?" Donnie asked.

"Fes," Ruzar yelled over the engine.

"We need to get to the embassy in Rabat."

"Yeah? The direct route is locked down. That's where they're expecting you to go. From Fes, we'll head to Rabat, but via train."

That wasn't a bad idea, except it added at least a couple more hours' worth of travel time. Plus, it meant that Donnie had zero control over contacts and equipment. That made his skin itch.

"Look, it's only three hours to Fes," Ruzar reasoned. "It's a big city, and I have a friend with secure accommodation. We'll stop for dinner, review our plans, and then decide on the best way forward. I think instead of pushing for the embassy you should head to Spain via boat. I have one available—a fancy yacht."

Charlie spoke up for the first time since the market. "Ruzar, this is happening too quickly. We need to talk. I don't know who you are, and this is all too confusing. Donnie and I need time to regroup."

"You'll get it. And you're right—we do need to talk. Firefly, you're safe. You need to trust me."

Gritting teeth against the affectionate nickname, Donnie folded his arms and stared out at the passing countryside. He'd have cell phone signal in Fes which meant he could use the burner phone to update his teammates on location and status. He needed every ounce of Intel he could get — both on Ruzar and on the men hunting them.

Donnie focused on that, instead of the possible history between Charlie and Ruzar. What had happened on Malta and what had she been about to confess before the ambush? Had she slept with Ruzar and if so, why did it feel like a betrayal?

It wasn't like she and Donnie were ever dating or had ever declared an interest in each other. Maybe Donnie should've reached out to Charlie in the States before she'd left for her trip. What did he think, that she wouldn't date? That she'd just put her life on hold for a grumpy operator that barely acknowledged her?

He'd known in the beginning that she'd liked him. Before he'd humiliated her at the Jackson Hole music festival gig, Charlie would blush and shoot him the sweetest smiles. Jesus, the timing had sucked. He hadn't been ready to date and hated the attraction he'd instantly felt for the red-haired vixen, and he'd shut her down so often that their friendship eventually turned bitter.

He guessed after the crappy eight years she'd had, that she'd just wanted a little fun, and Ruzar fit the bill. A holiday romance to sweep away the pain. But she'd been seduced by a wolf—a killer who marked her as prey.

Thinking about Ruzar's greasy hands touching her made Donnie's skin crawl. Although he could see the attraction, the dude looked like a male stripper. His long, thick hair added to the swagger and gave him an air of danger.

A small hand grasped his and Donnie looked over at Charlie's pale face. She'd dozed on the drive, all due to an adrenaline crash. According to the GPS on his watch, they were a few miles out of Fes. He'd kept her positioned in the corner. The smell from the deceased mercenary stunk up the vehicle, and Donnie tried to shelter her from the gory sight as best he could.

"You need to dispose of the body," Donnie said to Hakim.

"If we find a place."

"The smell is making her sick. If you don't, I will."

"Can we not talk of dead bodies? Please." Charlie rested her head back and took shallow breaths.

"Relax," Ruzar called. "We're almost at our destination."

Five minutes later they pulled up at a set of large gates. Two guards approached and Ruzar chatted with them. A call back to the main house, and they were through. Donnie didn't like the setup. They were prisoners more than guests, and claustrophobia set in as they drove around the cul-de-sac to the front of the sprawling home.

If he were in the jungles of Peru, this would look like a cartel leader's mansion. Whoever owned this estate had equally dubious connections. To his surprise, a middle-aged and elegant woman met them in the courtyard. She was a local and a wealthy one at that, flanked by two bodyguards and smelling like she'd broken into a French perfumery. Heavily jeweled hands patted coiffed hair, and her crocodile smile greeted Ruzar.

"My sweet boy." She swept into his outstretched arms, and he swung her around. She giggled like a small girl. Charlie stood awkwardly to the side. Donnie watched the display of affection with curiosity. The show got interesting when the woman pulled Ruzar's head down and planted a wet kiss on his lips.

"I've missed you, my Ruzzy. You've gotten bigger, those muscles have grown."

Ruzar's ears turned red as he introduced his Moroccan lady friend. "This is Amira. We've known each other for over ten years now."

"I was his first lover. I traveled to Malta for a vacation, and he was my towel boy."

Donnie felt his eyebrows rise. The woman was more than double Ruzar's age.

"I taught him how to treat a lady—how to touch her just right."

Charlie gaped, Ruzar's flush moved to his cheeks.

Had Ruzar used those techniques on Charlie? The thought made Donnie ill. Charlie's safety prevented him from going on a dick breaking rampage. The temptation was so strong that Donnie had to look away from the target—Ruzar's trouser shrouded package.

"Amira. You're embarrassing Charlotte." Ruzar rubbed his neck.

"Of course. Come here sweetheart, let me look at you."

Amira cupped Charlie's cheeks, and Charlie almost jerked away. A look from Donnie had her playing nice.

"Pretty and fresh-faced, I wish to be this young again. But you look tired."

"They've had a rough few days," Ruzar said before he turned to issue orders to his men. He swiveled back to Amira. "Along with your presents, we have an unwelcome gift in the vehicle. It's a few hours old."

Wrapping a hand around Donnie's forearm, Charlie scooted closer, obviously trying not to think of the rotting corpse in the minibus.

Amira glanced over at the body being dragged out of the vehicle then shrugged. "My men will take care of it. Come, I'll feed you and get you cleaned up."

She pulled Charlie to her side and walked ahead. Donnie followed and leaned into Ruzar. "What exactly does Amira do... for a living?"

"Arms dealer. Best reputation in Northern Africa."

"Does your father know about her?"

"Yes. But they haven't spoken in years. He's a dick and tried to fuck her over on their first deal, so she killed four of his men."

"And she knows you're his son?" Donnie asked.

"Sure does. Fucking me over the years is Amira's passive-aggressive way of getting even."

"You and Amira are still—"

"Yes. On occasion. She's a powerful ally. I keep her happy; she gives me what I want. Weapons, explosives, and men. Hakim and Jamal work for her."

"I want to know every detail about your elusive father." Donnie scanned his surroundings as they entered the mansion.

They walked into an airy foyer. Amira led them up a marble staircase and down a thickly carpeted passage. Donnie counted seven armed guards along the way and his gut clenched. They were deep in the lion's den and he prayed it wouldn't get them killed. He cataloged every exit, including windows, balconies, and doors.

Leading them into a bedroom with flourish, Amira turned to Charlie. "This is your room for the afternoon, stocked with amenities. Have a shower and relax." She smiled at Donnie. "Your room is down the passage."

"No, it isn't. I'm in this room—with Charlie."

Ignoring Ruzar's narrowed look, Donnie widened his stance. Tension coiled inside, begging one of them to challenge him.

"I think that's up to Charlotte," Ruzar said.

"I want him with me."

Ruzar clenched his teeth. "Fine, but your safety is now my responsibility. If the Serbian's attack, you're coming with me."

"Fuck that." Donnie got into Ruzar's face. "Let me make myself clear, anyone tries to separate her from me, and they'll end up very dead."

"Is that a threat?"

"The biggest fucking threat you'll ever receive."

"Do you know what I do for a living? I'm an assassin. Killing people is an art form. Don't fuck with me."

"I don't consider killing an art form. For me, it's an ingrained reflex. You want to test those reflexes?" Donnie pushed forward and Ruzar stepped back.

"Oh, for shit's sake," Charlie yelled. "Amira and I are choking on testosterone fumes. Head back to your respective corners and let's all get out of this alive."

Amira clapped her hands. "Ooh, I like this woman. She's got fire."

"When do we leave?" Donnie asked Ruzar.

"Two hours. I'm waiting on information. I've sent out scouts to check our routes."

"I don't like this," Donnie muttered, pinching the bridge of his nose.

"My men are reliable," Amira said. She seemed genuine but at that moment, all Donnie craved was a MIT2 teammate by his side. As soon as he had an opening, he was calling Max.

◊ ◊ ◊

They were alone. Donnie stood guard in the luxurious bedroom as Charlie freshened up. She sat in a daze on the toilet and stared at her backpack. Her clothes sat with her in the bathroom, but she dreaded pulling on her soiled jeans—covered in blood and dust. Donnie knocked on the door. "Can I enter? Amira brought fresh clothes. She says one of her daughters is about your size."

Charlie scurried to close her pack and drew in a deep breath. "Hell yeah, get your butt in here."

Slipping in, Donnie placed the clothes on the counter. He looked large and capable in the small bathroom, yet any minute, he could get injured or killed. Or she could be eliminated. The thought had her walking into his arms.

"Easy, honey, I'll get you all dirty again."

"I just need a hug." She held on and squeezed his muscled waist.

"Oh, baby."

Her towel slipped off between them, but she didn't care. Donnie lifted her like she was a rare and fragile being and placed her ass on the counter. Then he nudged open her legs and stepped between. The possessive move combined with his clothed cock rubbing up against her naked body had her groaning. But instead of taking her, instead of crushing his mouth to hers or reaching down between them, Donnie stepped back.

"I have to stay alert and keep you safe. You and I in this bathroom isn't a good idea."

"Then go."

He didn't leave. His hand ran along her hairline, then down her neck. He paused to rub a thumb over her tattooed breast before sliding between her legs. Charlie could barely breathe as his fingers explored.

"Does that feel good?"

"God. Yes. Donnie, first I need to tell you—"

"No talking. Open your legs. Wider."

She did as he asked, and he slid in a finger and rolled his thumb over her clit. Charlie arched, pushing against his hand.

"I could play like this for hours."

Her body shuddered as he worked his hand, rolling and pumping. His fingers pressed and pulled and her hips rocked as he increased the pressure.

"You're damn gorgeous—like a flame. My finger is burning up inside and the way your breasts move with that pretty bird. Shit."

His guttural words turned her on, and she felt herself clenching around him. Growling, he stepped back between her legs and unzipped his pants.

"Do you want this? Me inside you for the quickest fuck of your life?"

His words made her grin through her desire. "Quick and hard."

Within a second, he'd buried himself. He gripped her hips with both hands, positioning her on the edge, before shoving up and in, over and over. Charlie held onto anything that would secure her. A tap, a towel rail. But his control and strength were so exact as he angled her just right, that she need not have worried. He held her easily, his powerful thrusts had her need coiling and screaming within.

"Shit. Donnie. I need to come."

"Then touch yourself."

She did as he asked, and he looked down and watched her, green eyes glinting with desire. Watching him—watching her—was too much. She locked up in an upward thrust as her body exploded in blinding colors. She closed her eyes against her silent scream as he pounded his release.

Donnie pulled her off the counter and into his chest. His

heart raced in time with hers as they regained their breath.

She smiled. "Was that adrenaline sex?"

"What?"

"Adrenaline sex? You know—danger sex—like in the movies? Because if it was, then it's as good as they say it is."

"That was definitely adrenaline sex. It was amazing, and you're amazing."

She smiled at his compliment.

"But we didn't use a condom."

Charlie stiffened at his words.

"Sharls?" He drew back.

Shooting him a shaky smile, she said, "I can't get pregnant, and I'm clean. I was tested a few months ago and haven't been with anyone."

"You don't have to lie. I know what you were going to say. If you've been with Ruzar, it's none—"

She shoved at his hard chest. "I haven't. What the hell?"

"I didn't mean it that way—" He raised his hands.

"You mean the asshole way? And you know what, even if I had been with him, you never gave me the time of day. Not even after my father died."

"That's not fair. I had to attend a class in—"

"Yeah, whatever. A phone call would've been nice. 'I'm sorry about your dad. Can I do anything for you, Charlie?'" Tears burned.

"After what happened at Johnny's party in Wyoming, I didn't think you wanted to hear from me."

"You thought wrong. But that's always been our problem. We dance around each other like two inept morons."

"You're calling me a moron?"

"Yeah. A mean, angry moron. Don't laugh. It's not funny,

shithole." She punched him in the shoulder.

"Okay. I'm going to let you cool down in the bedroom. Take your clothes and here's the gun. Anyone enters and threatens you, aim and pull the trigger." Donnie checked the already locked bedroom door before walking back in the bathroom to take a shower.

He switched on the water, and instead of climbing in, he checked the bathroom for listening devices. Finding nothing, Donnie switched on the last burner phone and dialed a number. Max answered on the third ring.

"Hey, brother," Donnie said.

"Shit. I was about to send in the cavalry. Where the hell are you?"

"Fes. At a damn compound."

"You're supposed to be on US soil," Max said, referring to the embassy in Rabat.

"Yeah, things are a little bumpy. Have you heard from Atlas?"

"He'll meet you at the extraction point; he's providing backup. His package is safe and secure."

That meant that Elana had left Moroccan soil and Atlas had traveled to Rabat to meet up with Donnie. Donnie needed to contact him before they entered the city.

"Send him this number. Any more Intel?"

"Copy. The fours are already investigating. Luca Comino runs quite an empire."

Donnie wanted to tell Max that he was sharing the same space as Luca's son—Ruzar Comino—but couldn't risk it on an unsecured line. "I have to go."

"I'm worried," his team leader said.

"I'll clock in on time, this won't affect my job."

"You think that's my concern? I need you and Charlie to get

out of that death trap in one piece. I can't come for you."

Donnie heard the frustration in Max's voice. MIT2 were squatting deep in enemy territory on a mission, likely still in Sudan. The fact that Max answered his phone showed how worried he was.

"I can take care of myself. As soon as I get decent access to my equipment and good signal, I'm taking this Comino godfather bastard down."

After he hung up, Donnie washed off and slipped back into the bedroom.

Charlie sat on the edge of the bed. The Glock rested on her lap as she gazed at the door. At that moment, she looked vulnerable and tired. Her hair lay in a thick braid down her back. She wore a long-sleeved, white, button-up shirt and her still wet hair dripped a transparent trail to her ass. Her beige fitted pants looked comfortable. The Safari meets Sahara vibe suited her.

Bruised eyes looked his way. "Can we talk?" She bit her lip nervously.

Donnie walked over and took his gun. A knock on the door had Charlie jerking in surprise.

"Easy, I won't let anything happen to you. Who is it?" Donnie called.

"It's Ruzar. Dinner is ready."

"We'll be down shortly."

"Can I come in?"

Hell no.

"I need to know what happened in Malta, let him in," Charlie said.

Donnie unlocked and opened the door. Ruzar glanced at the weapon Donnie openly held.

"Are you going to shoot me—you don't trust us?" Ruzar asked.

"Maybe and nope. The only person I trust is sitting on the bed."

"What do you want?" Charlie's cautious tone reinforced Donnie's statement.

Ruzar stepped past Donnie, his focus on her. His hair, also wet from a shower, lay rakishly on his shoulders. "Can we talk in private?"

"That man—holding the gun—has saved my life numerous times. He's a friend from home. He didn't need to sweep in and protect me, but he did. He flew across the globe and tracked me down to a remote village. Then he fought like the damn devil to keep me safe. So, no—he stays."

"You seem like more than friends," Ruzar said, folding his arms.

"I don't know what we are," Charlie said, "but I trust him with my life."

Ruzar chuckled. "That's what I love about you—your open honesty." He sat next to her on the bed as Donnie leaned against the wall, monitoring Ruzar's hands. If the bastard got all touchy-feely, he'd break every one of those slick fingers.

"Well, spit it out," Charlie said impatiently.

"Fine. You killed my cousin. That's why my family is after you, but that's not the only reason."

Donnie's heart rate picked up.

"Wow, more than one reason? Lucky me."

"Let me guess, you're about to tell us why you seduced her." The Glock felt comfortable, but Donnie didn't need a bullet to kill a Comino. Bare hands would do just as nicely.

Ruzar grasped her hand and pulled it into his lap. "I'm a contracted killer, and you were my intended target."

Chapter Fifteen

Charlie tugged her hand from Ruzar and stumbled off the bed. Ruzar reached for her as Donnie stepped between.

"Not another move."

"Charlotte, I changed my mind the minute I got to know you."

"You're an assassin, and I'm your target. How do I know this isn't all a game, that you're not going to follow through?"

"Because if I did, you'd be dead already. I'm not a bumbling fool like Andrej."

"How many kills?" Donnie asked.

"Nine contracts. But I don't think I'm the only killer in the room. How did you take down all those men in Tinghir? Who are you?"

"Someone you don't want as an enemy. Why did you change your mind?" Donnie felt her hand at his waist, and every protective instinct surged. He stood between her and death.

"I don't believe in love at first sight. I don't believe in love—period. My family holds polite affection for me. I guess my mother loves me in her own way. She still cooks for me—fusses over both her kids. My father loves money and infamy. I grew up arrogantly thinking that if I tried hard enough to be a ruthless bastard, I could be like him. So, I used people to get what I wanted—including fucking pretty tourists along the way. Eye candy, you know?"

"What does this have to do with Charlie?"

"Everything. The minute I laid eyes on her, I knew Charlotte was different—so innocent. The people I have killed have never been innocent. Maybe some were, but she got to me and I cared. It was so damn quick. I wanted to hold her and—"

"Enough. Mention touching her again and I'll break you."

Ruzar smiled. "I think you would, and I think you know how I feel. She's easy to love."

Donnie wasn't ready to consider the L word. He cared for Charlie, more than anyone since Sophie. And the chemistry between him and Sharls scared him. He craved her like a drug and couldn't stop thinking about the Firebird, but that could just mean he felt infatuation.

Ruzar continued, "I realize that she doesn't feel the same for me. I don't exist for her when you're in the room. That's okay. Regardless, I cannot let my family destroy everything good in my world. I'm still young enough to leave them and to build a new life for myself."

"Would that life include more killing?" Charlie asked quietly.

"I don't want it to, but it's all I've known. Charlotte, I spoke the truth that day on the beach. I want peace. An ordinary job—perhaps building something instead of destroying others."

"Who hired you? Who sent the contract?" Donnie asked.

"Honestly, I don't know. It came through my father."

"Someone wants me dead." Charlie walked over to sit on the chair beside the window. "Who hates me enough to take out a contract on my life?" She folded her arms around her waist and rocked.

Donnie knelt beside her. "Sharls, I don't know, but I'll find the asshole."

"We both will." Ruzar stood and shoved hands in his pockets. "And that will be my last kill."

◊ ◊ ◊

Charlie picked at the Mediterranean cheese spread, barely tasting the food. Donnie looked as restless as she felt. They had to get to Rabat, but Ruzar and his men seemed to be in no rush. After ensuring that she ate something, Donnie turned to their host and her sidekicks. They'd gathered downstairs in the dining hall that led out to a sunny patio. Donnie warned her to stay away from the windows and doors. He'd decided, however, to join Ruzar's men; constantly checking the perimeter and their immediate surroundings.

Now he stood just inside the patio door. "As pleasant as this R&R visit has been, let's move."

With legs propped up, Ruzar lounged like a lion in the corner. "Patience, my American friend. We're here for a reason. I'm awaiting news on where my father's men are camped out. As soon as I have enough to go on, we'll move. It's only been two hours. Have a nice cold Pepsi and relax."

Rubbing his eyes, Donnie went back to pacing. The tension he emanated worked on her nerves. Charlie chose the comfortable-looking sofa in the corner to rest her head. The lack of sleep over the last few days took its toll, and within seconds, she'd fallen asleep. Her dreams were filled with foggy cliffs and dark alleys.

Firm hands shook her. "Sharls, it's time to go. Our bags are in the car." Donnie sat beside her and stared down with such warmth that she lost her breath.

She never got tired of staring at that strong face. The brooding energy combined with a warrior's intensity drew her in. Since she'd known him, sadness tinged the edges of that firm control. It egged her on, and she'd craved to hug the prickly stranger from day one. She'd discovered in Morocco that he gave good hugs, sheltered strength that gave her the courage to fight by his side.

Reaching up, she stroked a thumb over the two small frown lines between his brows. Donnie flinched then relaxed as she kept stroking. Men's voices drifted in from outside, and for a minute, she was alone with her serious sidekick. She had so much to say, but this wasn't the time.

"No matter what happens, I can never repay you for coming for me. Without you, I'd either be dead or lost out here alone."

Kryptonite fire leaped in those green depths. "You're not alone—never alone."

"I know. I think my father is my guardian angel. He left me, but I can still feel him watching over me."

"Oh, baby. That's not what I meant." He stroked a hand over a curl that sprang from her braid.

Charlie grasped his wrist. "If I survive this, my future is going to look very different. I want you to know that—"

"Are you ready?" Ruzar's gruff voice broke the moment, and Charlie swung herself up. She ignored Donnie's analytical gaze at the flush creeping over her cheeks. She stepped past to follow Ruzar to the new vehicle in the drive.

"We've swapped out transport."

Charlie felt relieved that she didn't have to climb back in the horror bus. Instead, she slipped in the back of a Land Rover and Donnie shifted up next to her.

"What's the plan?" she asked Donnie.

"The roads going into Rabat and Casablanca are being closely watched. But it looks like they don't know we're in Fes. We're taking the train from Fes to Rabat. Hakim will drive the route. If we have any issues at any of the train stations, we'll bail from the train and switch back to the Land Rover."

He didn't look happy with the arrangement and Charlie leaned in. "What's the problem with the plan?"

"It's not my plan, but based on Intel, we have little choice. If we do this on our own, we could get caught."

"Or killed," she added.

The four-wheel-drive vehicle rolled onto the road. All five occupants sat in silence, watching for tails or possible ambush vehicles. At the train station, they drove around a fountained circle and parked in the busy lot. The men watched for suspects from the vehicle as Hakim went in to book their seven pm tickets. He returned and gave the all clear.

Charlie knew that wouldn't appease Donnie. He didn't trust Ruzar and his minions, and his watchful eyes never rested. The group waited until the last minute before exiting the vehicle and rolling into the station. Donnie pulled her against him, tucking her face into his jacket and shielding it from cameras or prying eyes. They both wore their backpacks and Donnie rested his other hand on the Glock in his right pocket.

The short stroll up the palm-treed walkway and into the station felt like hours. They walked under an ornate cylindrical chandelier. If she were on vacation, she'd pause to admire the carved wooden ceiling and window frames. Huge arched doorways lit up the open space as Donnie maneuvered her expertly through the crowd. Ruzar walked ahead, and Jamal trailed behind. The station teemed with tourists and locals and suddenly, all Charlie craved was the silence of her farm.

"It's one of the older trains—I think it's a Grandes Lignes," Donnie muttered as they climbed on board.

"Is that a good thing?" Charlie asked.

He pointed to the door latches. "Easier to move around and exit if need be. Morocco is upgrading their trains and the tracks. High-speed rail lines will soon take over."

They navigated to a first-class compartment. Charlie made to sit, but Donnie stopped her. "Not yet. Stay near the door."

He scouted the other passengers as well as the boarding vicinity near the train and wasn't the only one on guard. Jamal looked nervous. The train began to move and still, Donnie didn't relax, instead he checked adjacent compartments. Eventually—tired of standing—Charlie sat tentatively on the edge of a seat. Ruzar had already stretched out next to the window. He yelled a few commands at Jamal in Arabic. When he'd scuttled off, Ruzar grinned her way and told her to relax.

Two Moroccan men pushed into their cubicle. Charlie froze as Ruzar stood. He spoke quietly, and both men backed up. Donnie walked up and shadowed them down the passage.

Ruzar sat back down. "Just men taking a chance to sit with a beautiful woman."

Not saying anything, Charlie stared across his stretched-out legs out the window. Her mind raced, and her chest felt tight. She wasn't built for subterfuge and constant danger—especially now. Charlie pulled at a button on her cuff.

"I'm sorry that they hurt you." Ruzar's dark brown eyes met hers.

"Bull, that was your original intention—my murder."

"I'm trying to make up for it."

"Why isn't your loyalty with your father?"

"Because he's a cruel man. He conditioned obedience into his rebellious kid and would beat me for hours. Then, he'd dunk me in a bath of icy water until I complied. As a child, I was a shell of a human being."

"That sounds barbaric."

Ruzar reached into his jacket pocket and played with something that looked round and smooth. "He raised soldiers—not sons."

"You have brothers?"

"One and he's the good child—the easygoing and complacent brother with all the business degrees. I was the foot soldier who deserved the weekly beatings. I didn't start out wanting to be a killer."

The killing bit was the part she couldn't wrap her head around. She found that she didn't have the same dilemma when it came to Donnie. Maybe because for Donnie, the killing was part of his job. He protected innocents against extremist terror and Donnie had a definite moral code in place. Ruzar lacked the same judgment. Still, she felt bad for the man. He'd been unlucky enough to be born into a family of organized crime. If he'd been born into an ordinary Maltese family, how would he have turned out?

Charlie placed a hand on Ruzar's shoulder. He hesitated then covered it with his.

"That's a hard life, I wish it had been different."

"Sorry to interrupt," Donnie said from the passage. He frowned as he sidled in and sat opposite Charlie. Donnie ignored her smile, instead glaring at Ruzar who raised a brow. Two fighting wolves in a space the size of a closet.

"Both of you, grow up. And shift your tree trunk legs, I need a little space." Charlie stretched her back. The next three hours would be as uncomfortable as all hell.

◊ ◊ ◊

As night fell, they stopped at Meknes, then at Sidi Kacem. Eventually, the train headed towards Kenitra. After that, they would enter Rabat and find a way to the embassy. Donnie stretched his neck and shoulders. The closer they got to Rabat, the louder the warnings—first whispering, then yelling in his head. Something felt wrong. It didn't help that they were jailed in on a set of tracks.

He didn't want to stray too far from Charlie but needed to check the other cars. He only half watched the now dark scenery flitting past. His instincts in the field had always saved his ass, and silent alarm bells screamed for him to snatch Charlie and disembark at their next stop. Then, he'd find a vehicle and drive them to safety. They'd need to be cautious nearer the embassy, but he'd infiltrated tougher roadblocks in the past. The train whistled as it slowed and entered the Kenitra station. As they waited, Donnie internally calculated a new route and possible diversions. He'd need to re-look at a map of the area. Minutes ticked.

"I need to use the bathroom." Ruzar shouldered down the passage to the small cubicle.

Jamal walked by and glanced at Ruzar. The look—so brief—that only a trained operator like Donnie would pick it up. Yeah. Time to go their separate ways. Jamal kept walking down the passage. When he was out of sight, Donnie pulled Charlie to her feet. "Bag. Now." He thrust her backpack into her arms. The train's air horn sounded, and he sped up, pulling them into the passage.

"Donnie, what are you doing?"

"We're leaving." He pulled her to a quieter cabin and opened the door. The train edged forward.

"It's moving!" she said.

"Barely, we need to jump." Donnie gripped her arm in one

hand and his pack in the other. "Quick, give me your bag." He'd toss their bags and then pull her out with him straight after.

Panic had her fighting his hold. "I can't."

"Yes, you can, I'll support you. Now, Charlie."

She dug in her heels and grabbed a side rail as he tugged her to his side. "I can't risk falling. I'm pregnant and it's yours. Don't hurt our baby!"

Her words had him letting go and stumbling back. He gaped at her teary face across the door. The train picked up speed.

"There you are." Ruzar's voice filtered through Donnie's shocked haze.

"Charlie…" Donnie gasped.

In ordinary circumstances, Donnie would've blocked Ruzar's powerful side kick to his ribs. But thanks to her revelation, he reacted a millisecond too late and found himself airborne. Time slowed. He registered Charlie's scream as the ground raced towards him. The train now moved a fraction too fast for a safe landing. The fall would hurt and might take him out of commission. Donnie tucked into a ball and tried to land on the center of his back. He allowed his body to roll from the forceful inertia. The impact drew air from his lungs. Donnie's head slammed into the concrete and a wrist twisted in the fall. Agony spiraled from his head and his side. He came to a stop facing the disappearing train. Charlie still hung out the door—trying to leap. If she jumped now, she'd die, and Donnie lay like a paralyzed fish watching his woman fight for her life.

His vision blurred but he could make out Ruzar's brawny arms snatching her back in. Her head slammed into the side of the train and then she was gone. He'd lost her—lost them. Black edges grayed Donnie's vision, and his last thoughts flitted back to the party, three months ago at Johnny's cabin in Wyoming.

Chapter Sixteen

Wyoming.
Three months ago.

Donnie reached down to switch on the radio as he drove the winding road to Johnny's cabin.

"I prefer it off." Margot continued swiping at her phone, never looking up.

Complying, he returned his hand to the steering wheel. The drive had been a quiet one, with hardly any traffic on the country roads. Ignoring the reticent energy that had remained throughout the four-hour trip from Salt Lake, Donnie tapped the steering wheel and glanced over to the woman beside him. Margot Barringer. Even her name sounded pretty.

Her legs were daintily crossed, and she sat with an elegant bearing that spoke of her part-time job as a ballet teacher. Her jet-black hair was styled in a sleek bob-cut with one side tucked behind a delicate ear.

They'd only been dating for four weeks, and she hadn't yet met his team. Hell, they hadn't even slept together. Easing into the dating game, he'd behaved like a gentleman, not sure if he was even ready for intimacy. Donnie hadn't been with anyone since Sophie. He'd introduced himself to Margot as "Donnie," even though he hadn't told her what he did for a living. As far as she knew, he was a sales consultant for an international military clothing company. That was the standard cover story.

MIT2 just returned home from deployment for training exercises, and as fate would have it, he'd met Margot.

She was precisely the type of woman he was attracted to—ambitious and focused—a hedge funds manager by day and a ballet instructor by night. She reminded him of Sophie—his deceased wife. Dipping his toes back in the dating pool felt daunting, and Margot was his first girlfriend since Sophie's passing over two and a half years before. Donnie smiled at the classy girl beside him. Dating wasn't that hard, he didn't know what the fuss was about.

Margot paused and lowered her phone. "Are you sure we have our own room? With a king or at least a queen-sized bed?"

"Uh. I'm sure James will put us up wherever he can fit us in, but he also has other guests. His girlfriend's parents are living there at the moment."

James "Johnny" Cane was the medic for MIT2. Growing up in Wyoming, the locals knew him as "James." In the field MIT2 referred to him as "Johnny" aka "Big John," because of his size. His land had an incredible view of the Grand Tetons, and although Johnny had also bought a home in Salt Lake City, the team regularly stayed over in Wyoming in the summer months.

As a "thank you" to the townsfolk in the area for helping him build an extension onto the cabin, Johnny decided to hold a party at the farm. It was a beautiful evening and Donnie looked forward to the festivities.

"Promise me that it's decent accommodation. I can't deal with creepy insects crawling about, or dirty linen."

If she only knew what conditions Donnie had slept in, in the past. Months curled up in a sleeping bag in deserts and savannah environments. Johnny's home was like a five-star palace.

"It's fine, Margot. He has a basic, but welcoming cabin. He's added a new wing with two extra guest bedrooms and a third bathroom."

She crossed her arms and stared out the window as he turned the last corner to the humble homestead. Rows of cars were parked up front, taking up much of the long drive and front lawn. It looked like many of the locals from town had come up for the evening barbecue.

As soon as they stepped out of the car, a gang of kids assailed them. Margot shrieked as the older kids ran past to retrieve a football, and Donnie recognized them as youngsters from a neighboring farm.

They slowly made their way down to the adults gathered around the cottonwood tree at the bottom of the backyard. Donnie estimated there were at least a hundred guests. He guided Margot to his team and introduced her. Johnny's girlfriend, Lizzy, ran up, slamming into Donnie's arms. He laughed. Although Lizzy lived with Johnny in Salt Lake City, she had an apartment in Kenya and spent months in Nairobi with the team. When MIT2 weren't in the field, they helped out at a Kenyan orphanage or lazed on one of her sofas. Lizette Steyn was now one of Donnie's dearest humans. Her endless optimism—despite what she'd lived through—and her easy smiles always brightened his days.

He turned as he released Lizzy, noting his date's sudden glare. He'd never thought Margot was the jealous type. Donnie quickly introduced Lizzy as the love of his friend's life.

Full of smiles, Lizzy led Margot to the rest of the women. Donnie ran to the kitchen to grab Margot a Perrier from the fridge. When he returned, she'd stepped away from the crowd, back to staring at her phone. Lizzy's service spaniel—Ray—trotted over. Her furious tail wagged as she greeted Margot. Without looking up, Margot nudged the dog away with her foot. Ray re-approached, tongue lolling, and Margot turned her back. Irritation rose as Donnie watched the scene unfold.

Perhaps she wasn't a dog person. He could accept that. Maybe cats were her thing. Except he loved the spaniel and planned on getting a dog one day. Tamping down his annoyance, Donnie handed her the glass. Taking a sip, she grimaced before placing it on the adjacent table.

"What's wrong with the water?" he asked.

"It's flavored—tastes like strawberries." She lifted her phone. "There's no damn signal here."

"There's Wi-Fi at the house. What's so important, that you can't put your phone away?"

"I'm closing a sale. This road trip may cost me a lucrative contract. If there's no phone service, I'll stay in Jackson."

Her statement had Donnie folding his arms. "You'll stay in Jackson... not we? Where do I factor into the equation?"

Her brows rose at his sharp tone. She opened her mouth to say something then reconsidered her words. "You're right. I'm sorry, I'm rude. I'll switch off my phone—at least for now."

"Thanks, babes. Tonight is important. I want you to get to know my friends."

Margot smiled and kissed him on the cheek. Taking her hand, Donnie led her back to his team. Max had arrived for the night without his family. Their newborn baby, Lucy, named after Abby's late grandmother, was still too small to bring on longer trips and his wife, Abby, stayed behind—along with Max's mother—to take care of the kids.

The afternoon light began to fade as they all chatted and ate smoked brisket and pulled pork from the smoker. A long table filled with an array of salads and jugs of lemonade occupied most of the shade of the cottonwood. Picnic tables and lawn chairs took up the rest.

Charlie's foreman, Earl, walked up. "I wanted to thank you for looking after Charlie a while back. I can't believe Billings laid his filthy hands on her."

"It was a lucky punch. I should've got there sooner."

Earl folded his thick arms and scanned the festivities. "See, that's the problem. All these new-age farmers and their spoilt kids are taking over our valley. I don't recognize half the folk at this shindig. A bunch of hippies thinking they know how to take care of this land, they're all in it for the money and the prestige. Billings' father has never farmed a day in his life. He's good at delegating. Don't you agree, James?"

Johnny nodded as Lizzy ran up, wrapping her tiny arms around Johnny's waist. The two of them were inseparable. Lizzy had even traveled with her dog, Ray, to Nairobi to her Kenyan apartment while the men were on deployment. Being in the same city as Johnny only strengthened their relationship. Johnny pulled her to his front and kissed the top of her head. His hand stroked her back as he closed his eyes and breathed in her scent. Watching that sweet moment brought a lump to Donnie's throat. He'd felt that way about Sophie. Their life together seemed so far removed from his current world. Too many lonely nights in country, on the back of his Harley or sitting in an empty apartment. Donnie missed having a partner—a woman who had his back.

There was no doubt that Lizzy had Johnny's back. She'd almost died protecting him and their friends from the Scythian a few months before. Her love for the big man echoed in that sacrificial act.

"Holy hot cannoli!" Lizzy pushed away and gaped at something behind Donnie. "Charlie Quinn! You go girl!"

Unable to resist, Donnie turned… and tried swallowing his tongue. Charlotte Quinn sauntered down to the gathering in the afternoon dusk. Her straightened flaming red hair fell in silky waves around her shoulders. Black leather tights encased shapely legs. She wore a matching leather half-top contraption that molded her perfectly shaped breasts. Donnie's gaze wandered down to defined abs. She had actual abs, and he couldn't look away. He knew she took dance lessons, but assumed it was line dancing or a country dancing gig. That sculpted body came from hours' worth of dance moves. That combined with physical work on the farm, and Charlie Quinn looked like a female superhero.

He'd never seen her dressed in anything other than dusty farm jeans and loose-fitting shirts—practical farm clothes. The few times he'd talked to her, they'd taken an instant dislike to each other. Her mouth was a weapon, and she knew how to rile him up with one look. Besides, her brash, rough around the edges attitude was the opposite to what he looked for in a woman.

The newly revealed Charlie distracted Donnie to such an extent that he barely registered the tall man loping alongside her or the stringed ball contraption she swung in lazy circles.

"Are you done staring?" Margot growled, and Donnie jerked his eyes away.

He acknowledged the physical attraction he felt for Charlie, fit and defined with a cute snub nose and full lips. But Donnie wasn't a fan of duplicity, no matter how unintentional. He suspected she'd had work done on her chest area and he secretly hated that she pretended to be an all-natural tomboy yet chose those cosmetic enhancements. It somehow didn't fit with who she was.

The fact that he judged her for that, also never sat well with him. Donnie believed that everyone had a right to choose what to do with their bodies. Cosmetic enhancements or surgeries were never issues for him before, so why now? He guessed it had something to do with his late wife, Sophie, and the way she'd passed. The breast cancer ripped her away from him. Sophie would've given anything for healthy breasts, for a healthy body. He'd have given anything to have her back. He loved her regardless of what she looked like and didn't bother over pretty breasts; he'd just wanted a healthy and happy wife. Cancer spread quickly, and the double mastectomy came too late. He hadn't cared that they'd taken that part of her. He just wanted her to live. God, he'd wished that so desperately.

"Are you all set up?" Johnny asked Charlie.

"Hell yeah. Just over the fence on that lower field."

Set up for what? Donnie scanned the unfamiliar bodies hovering around her. The dude next to her also wore black leather pants, with a black T-shirt. He stood way too close to the farm girl. A woman dressed in a similar fashion to Charlie chatted off to the side. The tall honeyed blonde placed a handheld camera on a chair. Donnie couldn't narrow in on her ancestry. Sultry eyes sized him up, as she rolled her heavy braid into a knot at the back of her head.

Donnie introduced Margot, and Charlie gave his girlfriend an awkward handshake.

Margot spoke up for the first time. "You're a dancer?"

Charlie eyed her, sizing her up. "Yup."

"What type?"

"For tonight's performance, a hybrid of belly dancing and modern dance."

Margot immediately lost interest and turned away. Donnie felt the snub and clenched his jaw. Unlike Margot, he was keen to watch the show they'd set up for the guests. From what he'd heard, Charlie had worked hard on her routines. He'd never seen her dance, but that dedication intrigued him. As a martial artist who spent hours perfecting his moves, he respected the hell out of that.

Charlie called her friends over. She introduced her male colleague as Zach. The statuesque blonde introduced herself as Elana Celik.

"Elana has not only taught us the belly dancing, but she's a fellow dancer and our videographer," Charlie said.

Elana's grip felt strong and capable. She looked like she'd walked off the runways of Milan. Her voice direct, she addressed Donnie. "So, you're the quiet nemesis."

"Elana—" Charlie raised a hand.

"It's all good." Donnie said, "I am, and Charlie is my loud nemesis."

"Screw off, statue boy." Charlie tried to elbow him, Donnie blocked the shot with his left hand. She stood way too close. Heat radiated off her body in the cooling breeze. A puff of a creamy rose scent teased his nostrils, and he inched away.

"Where are you from, Elana?" He couldn't pinpoint her slight accent.

"Jackson."

Donnie frowned.

"But I grew up in Turkey. My father is Turkish. My mother is from Wyoming." She glanced back to the lower fields. "Enough chitchat, we have fires to light."

Donnie frowned at her dismissal as she pulled Charlie away. Her standoffish vibes indicated she didn't like him much. He watched both women loping down the hill before ducking under a fence.

The crowd moved slowly down to the dance arena they'd set up—flattened soil spread out with four TIKI lights placed in a semi-circle. Margot grumbled beside him, first fussing about stepping in manure, then moaning about the occasional buzzing insect. He helped her maneuver best he could over the soft earth. She wore heeled sandals — not the most practical footwear for a farm. When they were situated, she turned to speak with Lizzy who immediately ran back to the house.

The dancers crowded around a far table; it was too dark for Donnie to see what they were doing. He waited patiently, chatting with friends in the crowd.

The male dancer moved up next to Charlie, tracing a hand along her back and Donnie looked away. Who she hooked up with was none of his concern. Lizzy slipped past Donnie with a glass of sparkling water for Margot. Instead of sending Donnie, or fetching the drink herself, Margot had asked Lizzy to run back to the house?

As Lizzy handed it over, Margot spotted Lizzy's still healing hand and flinched. Thankfully the slight blonde didn't notice, but Donnie took note. Lizzy still recovered from a brutal kidnapping in Africa. She'd barely survived the traumatic ordeal, earning nothing but awe and respect from his team, and they guarded Lizzy like she was their own. Folding his arms, Donnie turned away from his date, focusing attention on the imminent entertainment. He wanted to see Charlie dance, craved to know that side of her. He had a bad feeling that once the music began, he wouldn't be able to look away.

Margot tasted the drink that Lizzy had just brought down from the house. The fact that she'd asked Lizzy to replace the glass, still had Donnie's jaw clenching. The music began, building softly in the background.

"There's a lemon in this. It tastes like dishwater." Margot pulled a face.

He gritted his teeth. "Feel free to fetch another drink, you know where the house is."

Donnie wasn't ordinarily so rude, but he didn't like her as much as he did on the drive over. Aside from his physical attraction to Margot, how well did he know her? They'd had many conversations over the last month, but Donnie hadn't thought to delve beyond their mutual love of travel or her constant bragging about her prowess as a ballet instructor and her family's properties in California and Manhattan. Her narcissistic attitude was now getting on his last nerve.

"I'm your date. I thought you were a gentleman."

He took a bracing breath. "This is the second water you've refused to drink."

"The first one was flavored. All I need is plain sparkling water, and there's a lemon slice floating in this one. I'm not asking for the moon."

Lizzy and Johnny turned at Margot's raised voice, and Donnie shot them an apologetic look. "Stop being rude."

The music started up, and Zach positioned himself onstage.

"I'm rude?" she whispered. "You've ignored me all afternoon; now you're refusing to walk over and—"

"Jesus," he hissed. "I'll fetch your water. Calm down."

He turned to walk away, and she grabbed his hand. "I'm sorry Don-dons. Thank you for looking after me."

Not trusting a reply, he accepted her kiss to his cheek before walking back up the hill and taking a long swig of his beer. Maybe he was oversensitive. Donnie was tired. The last six months had been busy, and although he'd been back Stateside over the previous five weeks, he still worked nights on his laptop and after his next deployment to East Africa with MIT2, he was then scheduled to return to Fort Bragg to start training on the latest drone developments in the field. HQ would send a temporary replacement—another Intelligence Specialist—while he completed weeks of training at Fort Bragg. He hated being away from his team, always worried they'd need him in the field while he scratched his balls behind a desk back home.

Donnie shut off the frustration, cracked open another beer for himself, and loped back down the hill with a freshly filled glass of sparkling water for Margot. From the sounds of applause, the first act was complete, and he sped up to catch the second routine.

Charlie stood to the side of the makeshift stage. The TIKI lights and the last of the sun's setting rays provided a glowing backdrop to her beautiful profile. Her long lashes fluttered as she closed her eyes, readying herself for her routine. Her breasts rose and fell with each deep breath. Charlie stretched back her shoulders, raising her arms slowly in front of her. Donnie stood mesmerized by the mysterious picture she made.

Her fellow male dancer walked up, holding a flaming stick before touching it to her upturned palms. *What the living fuck?* Donnie rushed forward as flames leaped from her hands. The fire licking the air had Donnie's suddenly racing heart pausing in his chest. Charlie turned her head, smiled at him and curved her arms in a circle as she rotated her hips. Only then did he notice the handheld candles, strapped to her palms.

He slammed to a stop, a few feet away while swallowing relief.

Turning back to the makeshift stage, Charlie walked into the center of the crowd as the music rose in volume. A seductive song played, the words centering around "going up in flames." Her body undulated and twisted as she rotated the leaping candles in a synchronized act that kept him frozen on the periphery. She employed belly dancing techniques, along with traditional dance moves, melding the two together in a dance of heat and light. Occasionally, flames would almost lick up her arms or trace her cheeks, and his muscles would tense. He noted Zach standing on the periphery, with a precautionary fire cloth at the ready. Fire performances held great risk for the dancers; Donnie suspected that the danger element must be the allure.

He couldn't find a trace of the brash farm girl dancing in front of him. This woman was all sultry and sinewy sex. When she glanced his way with heat reflected in those warm eyes, she rolled her hips in a seductive circle, and his pants tightened.

Swallowing the hunger, Donnie drained half his beer, and turned away, walking up to Margot to hand her the cool drink.

"Like what you see?" she said nastily.

"Excuse me?"

"I saw you looking at her."

"Charlie's a friend. I've never seen her dance before, that's all."

"You don't look at me that way… when I dance."

"Of course, I do."

He regretted the words the minute they fell from his mouth. Her eyes lit with anger. "So, you find her what? Just as fuckable?"

And the evening had just gone from awkward to disastrous. The music faded out as Charlie leaned forward, swinging a leg back and arching into a final pose. Donnie ignored the dancers and concentrated on Margot.

"I'm sorry, honey, I didn't mean it that way. C'mon, let's go for a walk."

The crowd erupted with applause, and Donnie pulled Margot to the side.

Her face flushed. "Leave me alone. I'm going up to the house to make some business calls. Spend time with your precious friends."

The field fell quiet as Elana took up position on stage. She held a lit staff, slowly twirling it in circles.

Stepping away, Margot's shoe sunk into the earth and she toppled sideways. Donnie lunged to catch her, but Lizzy got there first, grabbing her arm for support.

"Don't touch me with that thing!"

Margot's shriek echoed through the silence as she wrenched her arm away from Lizzy's hand, tripping then rounding on the tiny woman. "I didn't ask for your help, did I? Did I ask you to touch me?"

Everyone stood frozen. Lizzy stumbled back, tucking her partly amputated finger to her chest in a protective gesture that broke Donnie's heart. He'd heard of people who had a fear of amputees—Apotemnophobia—but he'd never actually met one, nor could he ever make time for someone who found disabled veterans or friends detestable in any way.

Johnny growled and took a step. "What did you just say?" He pulled Lizzy behind him, protecting her from Margot's vile words.

"I'm sorry. I didn't mean it. I can't deal with…" Margot looked at Donnie for help.

"Deal with what?" Johnny asked, his voice a guttural growl.

Donnie knew that no matter how angry Johnny was, he would never physically threaten Margot. Still, Donnie placed a hand on her waist and turned to the giant warrior. "Take Lizzy inside. I'll be there shortly."

Johnny paused, reading Donnie's silent message before nodding.

Nudging Margot, Donnie said, "Let's go for that walk."

His team leader, Max, watched as they ducked under the fence, then walked towards the cobbled path that led around the front of the house. Folding her arms, Margot walked stiffly beside Donnie.

She turned to face him as they paused in the front yard.

"That was so wrong. I don't know what came over me."

Acknowledging her shame, Donnie looked down as he scuffed a boot in the dirt. "You're the first woman I've dated since my wife died." He ran a hand over his goatee, then stared up the drive. "I thought that you and I might've been good for each other. I was wrong."

"I'm only human. I made a mistake."

"That mistake hurt someone I care about."

"I can go to her and apologize." She shifted closer.

Flipping a stone with his foot, Donnie said, "I think it's best if you leave. I'll secure a hotel room in Jackson for you, and pay for an Uber to the airport and I'll get you a ticket. You'll be back home by tomorrow afternoon."

"Come with me." She leaned a hand on his chest.

He gave her a look that had her removing it.

"You have a great life, a busy one. You don't need me to complete it," Donnie said.

"You're wrong, I—"

Max stepped out the front door, keys in hand. "I'm heading into Jackson to pick up extra ice-cream for dessert. Need anything, brother?" Donnie knew that his team leader had purposely stepped in and he owed Max a five-course meal for treading on this landmine.

"Could you give Margot a lift into town? Give me five to retrieve her bags."

"Sure."

"Why can't you take me?" she asked.

"I need to speak with Lizzy."

"Fine. Whatever." Margot turned and stormed up the drive.

The next few minutes, loading her bags and getting her situated, felt awkward. Once they pulled way, Donnie sighed in relief before swearing soundly at the mess he'd caused. Trudging into the cabin, he cracked open another beer. He didn't usually drink this much, but Jesus, he needed liquid courage. Walking up the stairs took all of his willpower. Donnie followed the voices down the passage to the second bedroom on the left and stepped in. Lizzy hurriedly swiped at her eyes. *Fuck.*

She sat on the bed with Johnny. The spaniel lay with her head in Lizzy's lap. Johnny's jaw ticked as he held her right hand—the one with the amputation—in his.

"I brought her into your home, and I'm sorry."

Lizzy nodded. "I should've expected bias at some point. I didn't think it would be here or happen so soon."

"I broke it off with her."

"You didn't have to do that." Lizzy shot Donnie a watery smile.

"Hell, yes, I did." Donnie sat on the other side of her and pulled her in for a hug. "Did it bring back bad memories?"

She nodded.

"I'm goddamn sorry. What can I do?"

"Nothing… if you can give Charlie a hand. She needs to re-pack her equipment and clear the field—she's settling her dad in for the night."

"I can do that." Donnie would tightrope over the Grand Canyon if Lizzy asked. He'd spend the rest of his days making it up to her.

"Thanks, buddy," his teammate said.

Donnie nodded before stepping out the door. He paused to look back. Johnny buried his head in Lizzy's neck whispering sweet words as he stroked her hair. She cradled his cheek. The tender scene took Donnie unaware, and he closed the door, shutting out the memories of a love he'd once shared with a long dead wife.

Locating lodgings and making travel plans for Margot in Jackson took some time. Once he'd hung up, Donnie walked back outside. The place had emptied out. A few stragglers chatted by the fire pit. Ignoring them, he strode over to the adjoining gate and stepped onto Charlie's land. Donnie watched her disappear around the corner to the storage shed as he pulled on his beer. He felt the buzz from the alcohol and welcomed it. Could his night get any worse? He'd broken up with his girlfriend, damaged a friend in the process, and now he volunteered to help a woman who despised him on sight. Bracing himself for war, he slipped through the large shed's double doors. A couple of trucks were parked on the left side, shelving took up most of the back wall, and a large pile of wood was stacked neatly to the right. Music played softly from one of the trucks. A single light towards the back gave the shed an intimate feel. Donnie forced one foot in front of the other as he walked over to Charlie's kneeling form.

She sat on the floor with her head bowed, equipment spread in front of her. Fuel containers, the candle contraptions he'd seen her use, a whip-looking thing and various fuses.

"Charlie?"

She jumped at the sound of her name.

"For the love of God! Don't damn well sneak up on me." Her fingers wiped at her cheek and Donnie inwardly groaned. Now he was dealing with the third upset female for the night—this wasn't his forte. Finishing his bottle, he placed it on a shelf and walked over, stretching out a hand.

"Are you okay?"

"I'm fine. My daddy isn't."

"Sitting on a cold ass floor ain't gonna make anything better."

She ignored him. "Where's your girlfriend?"

"Margot and I broke up." He felt his face flush and shoved his hands into his jeans pockets. "She's staying in Jackson for the night."

"I heard about what she said to Lizzy. That's pretty fucked up. Can I punch her?"

"Easy, tiger. I'm thinking the whole town has heard by now." Donnie rocked back on his heels.

Charlie chuckled. "She'll be lucky to escape Jackson Hole in one piece. I'm sure there'll be a lynch mob gathered around her hotel by the morning."

Donnie didn't say anything.

"That's your type?" Bitterness polished over her words, and Donnie knew that she remembered his rejection, the year before at the music festival. That, combined with her father's illness, had her gazing up with such a bleak look, that Donnie's gut clenched.

"Get that raucous butt up."

He pulled her a little too hard, and she fell onto his chest. Bracing Charlie with his other hand, he felt her defined muscles pressed up against his. Her head came up just above his shoulder, which lined up his burgeoning erection against her pelvis.

Donnie's hand rested against the bare curve of her back and of its own volition, his thumb traced her spine. He needed to let go, and he did, but she held on.

"Charlie, what are you doing?" Donnie raised his hands.

"I need a hug. A long hug… from a friend."

He kept his hands up, trying not to gaze into those alluring eyes. "We're not friends."

"I know. Why not?" Her glazed look had everything to do with her dying father, and nothing to do with Donnie.

"You're just not my type, that's all."

"Your dick thinks you're my type." She reached down and stroked him through his jeans.

"Fuck. Stop. Shit. Charlie. You don't want to do this." They backed up against the cab of an old red truck as a new song played through its speakers. A slow belly dancing number. Charlie swayed against him, looking like cat woman. She still smelled like a rose garden, with the barest hint of fuel. He imagined his cock combusting with every stroke of her hands. She unzipped his fly, and still, he stood with his hands raised, afraid to touch.

"For one moment, let me forget about my shitty life, and you can forget that this is me."

"Sharls, don't—" His head swam.

She slipped his jeans over his hips. "I like it when you call me that. No-one ever needs to know about tonight, I want this and so do you."

He looked down, and his dick jumped in response. Her full lips sat an inch from his clothed cock. She leaned and kissed the tip through the fabric, and his knees almost buckled. He hadn't been with a woman in so damn long. A thumb ran up the underside and over his now damp tip. His hips thrust forward as his mind screamed for him to stop. He was drunk, but fuck, he'd never felt this good.

"Charlie—"

"Call me Sharls." She pulled his briefs down, over his thighs, and he felt the chilled metal of the truck against his bare ass. Her hot mouth closed over his cock and Donnie groaned. "Shit. Holy hell."

Cupping his balls, her tongue danced in delicious swirls. She circled his now fully erect cock with her hand and stroked him firmly before dipping her mouth down and up. The room seemed to explode as he bucked against the warm wet pleasure. Losing control, Donnie dragged her up and twisted her around. "You want this… Sharls? You want me to touch you."

Turning, she braced her arms against the bed of the truck. "Touch me. Stroke me. Feel me."

Donnie swore as he tore down her stretchy black leather pants from behind. He swept her hair aside, leaned over and sucked her neck. She shoved up against him, her firm ass cheeks clenching around his dick. A hand reached behind, and she positioned him at her entrance. Donnie welcomed the invitation, lifting one of her legs onto a tire and opening her up. The tip of his dick traced her folds. Throbbing music surrounded them, anchoring him in the moment, and with one long thrust, he drove inside. He took a moment to revel in their perfect fit. Her inner muscles clenched and they both groaned. Donnie began to move, then began to hammer into her, every thrust had her banging against the side of the truck. He slowed, pulling out then burying himself deep, grinding his pelvis against her firm ass.

"Shit. Donnie. Like that. Yes."

He reached around and stroked her clit. Slow strokes that matched his thrusts. First circling one way, then the other.

"Oh, crap!" She spasmed with such violence that he saw stars.

"Come for me, Sharls. While I'm buried deep." He rolled a thumb, and she cried out, pushing against him, begging for release. Swearing, he pounded her against metal with violent thrusts, and felt her come a second before savage pleasure exploded from the base of his cock. Biting her arched neck, he came down from the most violent high he'd ever experienced. He didn't want to pull out. He wanted to remain buried and take her over and over against the side of a farm truck, until they both couldn't stand. Her core still clenched and released around him as her chest heaved with exertion.

Then her breath hitched, and a sob escaped.

Donnie pulled out and stepped back. "I'm so sorry."

She shook her head, not looking his way. "It's not your fault. None of this is." She pulled her pants over her perfect ass, and he didn't know what to say.

"Thank you for giving me this small escape and forget this ever happened. Tonight was a mistake."

"I can never forget—"

"My father is dying and I'm damn scared. I have no-one." She folded her arms, curling inside herself, still not looking his way. "Please go."

"I can stay."

She shook her head.

"If you ever need to talk…"

"Charlie Quinn, remember? Annoying farm girl. You hate my guts."

Donnie clenched his fists. "I've never said that I—"

"You don't have to. Your eyes say it all."

For the first time in his life, he felt out of his depth. The unexpected connection with this woman, made him question everything he knew. Donnie didn't want to leave. He wanted to stay and to talk. He wanted to comfort her. He wanted something more.

"For fuck's sake, leave, Donnie! Leave!"

Against his better judgment, Donnie turned and walked out. It was easier this way. Charlotte Quinn had no place in his life. Only later, as Donnie lay in Johnny's guest bedroom, did he remember that they hadn't used protection. He'd speak to her about that in the morning. Except Donnie never did. Charlie's father died in her arms the next day, and MIT2 were called back into the field. Two months later, Donnie was back in country but only to begin the UAV course at Fort Bragg.

Chapter Seventeen

Ruzar's plans had just gone to hell. It all blew up when he went to the toilet. He'd used that as an excuse to escape from Charlotte and her lover boy. He couldn't bear seeing the way she looked at him, like the mysterious Yankee-shithead could slay her dragons.

What Ruzar wouldn't give for a woman to look at him that way—for his Firefly to gaze at him with such adoration. The kicker was that the American asshole barely noticed the love she had for him. The luckiest man on the planet whose head was stuck so far up his ass, that he didn't see the fiery beauty for what she was. Ruzar saw her, he saw all of her.

On the way to the lavatory, he'd changed his mind and turned to go back. He'd confess his love and tell her everything, about how he'd kill for her a thousand times over. When he got to their booth, it was empty. He saw Charlie and Donnie disappear up the aisle and he'd followed. A large man stepped in his way and as the train began to move, Ruzar's world stilled. Eddie Zarafa. How had he found them?

"You're letting her escape," Eddie said as he removed his

213

gloves. "Perhaps that was your intention. Is that why you're defying your father's orders?"

"No, sir. I was bringing her back to Papa."

"Now why would you do that? Smear Luca's front steps with murder. Retrieve the woman, and then we'll talk. You disappoint me."

Eddie's words ripped through Ruzar's chest like hot bullets. Swallowing defeat, he obeyed the order and walked down the passage to the couple about to jump ship. At that moment he stood torn—both the people he loved occupied the same space. He was about to sacrifice one to please the other. Ruzar committed to the cause and knew the only way he'd secure her was to kill the American fighter by her side. The guy was quick, and so Ruzar walked up, muttered something and kicked out. He used all his power to hit his target in the ribs. When the man fell from the train, Charlotte tried to leap out after him.

That sacrificial move annoyed Ruzar, and he saved her from a brutal fall by wrenching her back onto the train. Blocking out the sickening thud of her head hitting the frame of the door, he muffled her screams, and whispered in her ear, "If you fight me, you'll draw attention to us, and those men will kill you. They don't want the locals getting involved."

Three mercenaries stood beside Eddie, who waited until Ruzar led her back to the enclosed cubicle before they all took a seat. Jamal wandered up and lounged against the partition. He was the damn traitor.

Her cheek swelled, and Ruzar hated knowing he'd done that. He sat beside her and tried to shelter her. But he couldn't let on that he cared. She shook so badly that his leg vibrated. Charlotte flinched away—huddling against the window. Naturally, after tossing her boyfriend from the train, she'd placed Ruzar in the same category as his Serbian counterparts.

"What's your plan?" he asked Eddie in their language.

"The bigger question is what was your plan before we ran into each other?"

"I told you, I was bringing her to my father. I found her first. I wanted him to see that I'm a far better soldier than his stupidly trained men."

"I think you have feelings for the whore."

"She's a sweet piece of ass. I'm physically attracted to her," Ruzar said, forcing a smile.

"You want her before we end her, or have you had her already?"

Ruzar spoke through the rage. "Not yet."

Eddie ran an assessing gaze over Charlotte as she examined him like he was a rabid mongrel.

"My name is Eddie. If you try to fight us or escape, we'll take our time killing you."

To Charlotte's credit, she didn't blink or look away. Instead, she raised her chin in defiance.

Eddie smirked, switching back to Maltese. "If your father didn't want her dead, we could've sold her to the Russians. She'd fetch good money."

"So, you're planning to kill her?"

"Not here," Eddie said. "Too many witnesses. I hear you have a yacht docked offshore in Rabat?"

How had they found out about his boat? *Jamal.* Ruzar swore inwardly but knew that strangling Jamal or denying its existence would expose his allegiance to Charlotte.

"Yeah. I was planning to sail her over to Spain, then catch a private flight home."

"Let's make the trip together, except we'll drop her overboard on the way." Eddie adjusted his Rolex. "Use shark bait to bloody up the water. Then chop her up. That way, if chunks of her ever find their way to shore, there'll be nothing identifiable left." Eddie wasn't stupid and observed Ruzar for reaction.

Ruzar nodded. "Good plan. Let's get to the boat first without drawing attention."

Eddie stretched then pulled his phone. "I'll call Andrej's friends. They'll be glad we've found her. I'm sure they'll want to play with her first. They'll want revenge."

Clenching his hands to stop the tremble, Ruzar looked away. His eyes clashed with Charlotte's terror. She must've seen the horror reflected in his gaze because she paled before closing her eyes and praying.

◊ ◊ ◊

Charlie wasn't terribly religious, but she chanted the Lord's Prayer as the men spoke in their language. *Please let Donnie be okay.* She grasped for an escape plan that wouldn't endanger the tiny life growing inside her. After all the chemotherapy and treatments over the years, it was a miracle she'd fallen pregnant— an unplanned miracle. She'd felt so poorly. Although—after the cancer—she'd never had regular menstrual cycles. She'd bought a pregnancy kit while visiting Ruzar in the hospital, but kept it buried in her satchel. The doctors told her that the treatments for breast cancer would affect fertility and she'd believed them. But after the constant nausea refused to abate, and after three missed cycles, she'd finally used the pregnancy test in Amira's guest bathroom.

Donnie called her just minutes after she'd bought the test in Malta. She'd wanted to confess, but telling him over the phone from the other side of the planet felt wrong. *"I know it was just a one-night stand. Not even—more like a five-minute sesh—but I may be pregnant. No worries though, you stay there, and I'll see you when I see you."*

Then Donnie had come for her, and they'd formed a fragile connection. When she'd found out in Fes, she'd been terrified that her confession would push him away. He'd barely started dating, and the widowed man still had a long way to go. Panicked thoughts of Donnie leaving her all alone, stopped her from saying the words. The longer she kept the secret about the test lying amongst her things, the harder it was to tell him. And what would she have said if they'd had the luxury of time in Fes? *"Not only am I pregnant but I love you. You're the only man I've ever loved, and I can't imagine my life without you."* Yeah, that would go down well with the brawny commitment-phobe.

What if he'd died from the fall, or was severely injured? Charlie's confession on the train had thrown Donnie off balance. Had she killed him? She moaned against the mourning pain.

The only acceptable outcome was that he was alive and chasing them. She needed to do her part. For now, Ruzar's thugs outnumbered her, but the first opening she got, she'd fight for her baby and the man she loved. Head, feet, hands, knees, and elbows.

Chapter Eighteen

A rough hand grasped Donnie's shoulder and rolled him to his back. Chattering voices filtered through confusion. His head pounded and felt damp. Donnie shifted, and his ribs screamed. Something jabbed into his bruised back. He carefully slipped a hand behind him and touched the outline of the holstered gun.

Scuffling noises near his right side had Donnie opening his eyes. His go-bag lay a few feet away, and an abaya-cloaked lady bent to check it over.

"Mine," he said in a raspy voice, ignoring the gathering crowd. Rolling to his side and then his feet took way too much effort. The sprained wrist impeded his scramble to the backpack. Reality slammed in. Charlie. Morocco. The baby.

The woman raised her hands in compliance and tried to drag the heavy bag to his side.

"Merci," he muttered in thanks as a group of local men helped him to his feet.

Two well-meaning women patted his arm and gestured wildly at the now empty tracks. "Policier! Appeler une ambulance."

A "hell no" to police or anyone that would ask questions. Ignoring their shouts, he limped down the tracks, away from the crowd. One of the station workers called out to him. Donnie sped up and looked for an exit point on either side of the tracks. Spotting a low wall and ignoring his burning ribs, he jogged over and leaped. His wrist screamed in pain. He'd need to swap over to left-hand dominance. He could do that. Years of martial arts training honed his ambidextrous abilities. Not only could he fight with both extremities, but he'd trained himself to fire and use weapons using both left and right dominant hands.

Donnie moved through a rural neighborhood and located a reliable-looking vehicle. Hotwiring the sedan with his injured wrist took time, but soon he was on the road to Rabat. Donnie drove ten blocks then stopped in an empty lot to get his bearings. He'd allow a whole five minutes.

Clenching fists and sucking in shallow breaths, he tried to keep his shit together. For the first time since Sophie's passing, tears burned at the back of his eyelids. Sharls was pregnant, and they had her. They had his family which meant he'd go nuclear on the enemy.

He'd gone from being a lonely widow to being responsible for a tiny child and his sweet mother. His child. Oh, God. He was a father. If anything happened to them, he'd never recover. Thoughts of a second loss in his life—of one so great—had Donnie wrenching open the door and emptying the meager contents of his stomach.

How had he developed such strong feelings for Sharls in such a quick amount of time? Except it hadn't been fast. They'd built a prickly friendship over the years, as if she was readying herself to step into his life at precisely the right time.

Five years ago, Donnie envisioned his life turning out a different way. He'd been married to Sophie and imagined them growing old together. When he'd lost her, he saw a new future— as a military lifer—dedicated only to his brothers and sisters in the field. Now, a hope so bright lay ahead that it seared his soul.

What if it was some cruel joke from above? Would Sharls and their child be ripped away? Not on his watch. Donnie took a minute to ground himself and check injuries. His ribs didn't feel broken, just bruised. Same went for the wrist. He rinsed his mouth, then used the rest of the water to wash his face and arms. Blood and grit covered his body. Gravel embedded in grazed skin took time to rinse off. That flayed feeling—nerves on fire—only served to wake up the analyst in him.

He pulled on a fresh shirt and switched on his burner phone— a missed call from an unknown number. Atlas. He dialed the number back, and it went to a generic voicemail. The phone was either switched off or had lousy signal. Would Donnie risk asking Atlas to race to the Rabat station, could Atlas neutralize Ruzar and his men? Atlas was an excellent operator but if something went wrong, Charlie could get caught in the crossfire. Donnie dialed another number. Patrick "Rocky" Bauman, the team leader for MIT4, didn't pick up. Donnie hung up and dialed again. On the third try, a wary voice answered.

"Who is this?"

"Donnie."

"Holy shit, buddy. Are you still in Morocco?" Rocky asked.

"Yes."

"Right on. I'll call you back on a secure line."

Donnie picked up on the first ring. "I'm in trouble. Big trouble. Tell me you've spoken to Max and MIT assigned you to the Gozo case."

"I convinced the Colonel. The inquiry ties into a parallel investigation involving Jihadi counterparts. So yeah, I've spoken to Max and Atlas. We've exfiled Elana through Spain to Italy. We're on location."

That meant they were in Malta.

"Well, half their minions are running around the Moroccan countryside, and things are getting spicy." Donnie forced out the next words. "They have the asset."

"Damn. I spoke to Max. I believe she's a good friend?"

"She's more than that, and she's pregnant—they have my woman and baby."

"Um. Come again?"

"I think they're heading to a boat in Rabat, and I need help finding it. It's a yacht owned by a Ruzar Comino or Amira... I don't know her last name. She's a gun runner in Morocco. I have a tracker on the asset, but I'm not relying on that working."

"Copy that. Shit, I'm sorry man. Are you going to keep using this number?"

"I don't have time to change the burner out and don't give a fuck if the cell finds me before I find them—I welcome it."

"Buddy, don't do anything stupid. We're here for you—all the way to the end. Wait for us to come to you."

"It's too late for that. Check the location of the boat and send Atlas those coordinates. I'm also calling our embassy friend in Rabat. I need him to put me in touch with Moroccan Naval supplies and sea equipment. I'll need SCUBA gear, a dry bag for weapons, possibly an MK25 or Draeger rebreather."

"Not asking for a freaking miracle—you crazy MOFO."

"Your network is as extensive as mine. We both know Sam will do it. I'm calling him now, he owes me."

Rocky sighed. "Fine. You owe me dinner. Cupbop or Hawaiian teriyaki chicken, and I expect the works."

Rocky Bauman would come through for Donnie, MIT4 would access satellite and camera footage. They'd also dig into Ruzar Comino's records and history to find the name and description of the yacht. Hopefully, with a full arsenal of US military surveillance equipment at his back, Donnie could narrow in on Ruzar before the bastard left port. Rocky was a reliable friend and a kick-ass teammate. Although they didn't work on the same team, Donnie had trained with the MIT4 soldier in the past. The extrovert operator with the easy smile and fun personality was also a tough professional in the field and would have Donnie's back.

After hanging up, Donnie unpacked the Rabat map from his kit then accessed a number from his satellite phone. He pulled back on the road and called the one man in Morocco who could help him save Charlie. Samuel Batista worked at the US Embassy in Rabat as the SOFLE—the Special Operations Forces Liaison Element. He'd also served with Donnie as a Green Beret on an MLE team back in the day. They'd fought and bled together. Donnie didn't want to bring his old friend into the mangled hunt—thus risking Sam's career—but Donnie didn't have a choice.

When Sam answered, Donnie didn't waste time in outlining his predicament and requesting Sam's help. Sam didn't hesitate, listing how many times Donnie had saved his ass in the field. Thanks to Sam's close connections to the Royal Moroccan Navy, the equipment would be available.

Donnie then activated the tracker in Charlie's earring and called Atlas. If Atlas caught up to Ruzar, he could trail them to the yacht. Donnie hoped the targets weren't stupid enough to execute her on the train. If it were him, he'd wait until they were on the boat—away from prying eyes—and make it look like an accident. Ruzar wasn't a fool. The betraying bastard would want a clean kill. If Donnie was wrong, he'd already lost her.

Eddie—Mr. GI jerk—held Charlie close to his chest as they disembarked the train and made their way through the station. Two more men joined them. The mercenary team surrounded her, and the man-tools looked like they knew what they were doing. A sharp blade rested against her back, and Charlie took care not to stumble. Eddie held the knife with such ease that with one twist of his wrist, he'd slice through flesh and vital organs. The weapon resting against her waist was a Fixation Bowie Knife. Charlie had wanted to add one to her weapons collection for some time. Thanks to her current predicament, she'd changed her mind. Her fascination with knives didn't mean she'd ever used one. History was where her expertise lay. If she survived her Moroccan ordeal, she'd ask Donnie to teach her about knife defense.

At some point, Eddie would use the knife on her. She'd seen the promise in his eyes before he'd pulled her from the seat. Ruzar walked stiffly ahead. He hadn't looked in her direction since the train. She'd never hated before, but she hated Ruzar. He'd hurt and possibly killed Donnie. The thought of Donnie lying dead beside the tracks made her chest ache, and she wanted to bellow out the agony. If she got the chance, she'd rip out Ruzar's hair and claw out his eyes.

Her gaze darted around as they exited the Rabat Ville Terminal. The white building with arches and balconies led out onto a busy street. A cascading fountain blocked out the noise of a blaring horn. Families scurried by, and a couple of tourists argued with a taxi driver. A man stood just behind a column and Charlie almost tripped. He wore a baseball cap and glasses, but she couldn't mistake those broad shoulders or blond hair. Hands in his pockets as he chewed gum, Atlas watched them.

She wanted to break away and fight her way to his side. That move would alert the gang of armed thugs. Instead, she looked away and pretended not to notice—relief shot through her. If Atlas knew she was here, then he'd spoken to Donnie who was probably still on his way. Even if Donnie broke every speed limit, he wouldn't have reached her in time. He'd come, and Atlas would lead him to her, either through trailing them or through the tech-savvy earrings she still wore.

Eddie shoved her into the back of an SUV and his pumped-up brutes sandwiched her in from either side. Ruzar sat up front next to the driver, and stared out the window, not once looking her way. White architecture and modern buildings passed by in a haze. Instead of heading to a marina, they turned out of the city, traveling along a busy coastal road. Miles passed as they drove a straight line on a palm tree-lined highway through roundabouts and smaller suburbs, eventually turning down a roughly paved path that led to a rocky inlet.

It looked deserted, and although it wasn't the height of the tourist season, Charlie hoped for at least a few witnesses to her abduction. A man waited on the beach beside what looked to be a covered-up motorboat. They dragged her down to the water's edge. The rocky path had her falling to her knees. As Eddie pulled her up, Charlie ignored her torn up legs, instead focusing on the dark expanse of water that lay ahead. She didn't know how to swim. Thanks to living on a landlocked farm all her life, she'd never got the chance to learn.

Wetting her feet and wading in the sedate river at the bottom of her property didn't count. Now panic had her locking her knees and struggling against Eddie's brutal hold. Ruzar tried to calm her, and she twisted to fall at his feet. Looking up with tears in her eyes, she begged her traitorous friend.

"Please. I can't sw… swim, please don't do this. I can't swim."

He swallowed then grasped her arms and tried to pull her to her feet. "I know. Get up. You're causing a scene."

She didn't want to say anything, but it might be her only way to reach him. "I'm pregnant. Please don't let them kill my baby." Grasping his shirt, Charlie pulled his face to hers. "You need to save my baby."

Ruzar's eyes darkened and he squeezed her arms. "All this time, you've been pregnant with another man's child?"

"I found out in Fes... I had no idea."

"Is it his baby?"

"It's Donnie's. Yes."

Ruzar swore and let her go. She stumbled as he walked away. The men battled to start the motorboat. Three men argued as they worked on the engine and minutes ticked by. Every moment wasted was another win. She still breathed and that tiny life inside her still lived. Charlie covered her stomach and prayed that Donnie would get to her in time. Eddie shouted at his men and waved a gun around. When the engine purred to life, they all cheered and clapped each other on the back.

One of his soldiers dragged her towards the boat and handed her to Eddie and she kicked and screamed to no avail. Running his hands through his hair, Ruzar paced then joined them.

"Problem?" Eddie the toad asked.

"Aside from us killing the kid in her stomach?"

"You're not going soft on me, are you, Ruzar?"

"Tourists are pulling into the lot. I suggest we move," Ruzar muttered.

Eddie paid some of the mercenaries and dismissed them. Only two mercenaries remained with the motorboat.

A muscular arm shoved Charlie to the floor of the vessel. It smelled like rotten fish and her stomach rolled. They shifted into gear and roared into the surf. Every surge and fall slammed her into the side, and the sea spray and slapping waves soaked through her white blouse and pants. Protecting her stomach was the best she could do, and Charlie wrapped herself into a shivering ball. They must've passed the breakers because the boat eventually evened out. All that meant for her was that she moved closer to death. Charlie had no doubt that once she boarded the yacht, she'd cease to exist.

◊ ◊ ◊

After constant communications, Atlas followed the targets and Donnie stopped by an old dive shop to pick up gear from a Royal Moroccan SF "friend." They didn't want Moroccan forces involved, even though the Navy could easily pull up on Ruzar's yacht. Too many guns and risks involved. Sam could land in trouble for helping with an unauthorized mission in Moroccan waters, and Donnie owed him a huge favor.

The transmitter worked, and Donnie raced to meet Atlas at her pinging location. This would be a rushed op—too rushed for Donnie's liking—but they had no choice. Once Charlie boarded that yacht, they'd kill her.

And Donnie wasn't a damn frogman. Although MIT2 had some SCUBA and tactical water training, striking a target from the water wasn't their area of expertise—especially in the dark. But he'd make do. Donnie was a good swimmer and had used a rebreather many times before. The element of surprise was all he had.

The speedboat sat where the contact said it would be, and the keys sat in the ignition. They loaded up the gear, including a "borrowed" bolt-action M24 Sniper Weapon System with night vision optics.

Donnie eyed the rifle as they pushed into the surf. "You're not using that unless they're about to pull the trigger on Charlie. That sucker will bring way too much heat down on Sam and our Moroccan friends."

Atlas nodded. "I know. But just so that you know, the same goes for protecting your ass. If shit gets real, there'll be red mist on the water."

They swung into the boat and Donnie shouted over the surf.

"We need to stay invisible. If we are caught with that thing—"

Atlas grabbed Donnie's wrist. "Then I'll take the fall."

"No, I can't let—"

"Not only are we rescuing a pregnant American hostage, but I'm saving your woman, a woman who's now like family. I'll take the fall."

Donnie gripped the side of the boat as Atlas steered past a shallow reef. Ten minutes later, they spotted the white trawler yacht through their infrared binoculars. Atlas killed the engine as Donnie kitted up.

"Are you sure I can't join you?"

"You know the drill. We'll need a pickup, and you have an overwatch job to do from this end."

"Copy. I'll be watching through my scope. Good luck, man."

After slipping an additional knife in his wetsuit belt, Donnie stood. "If they've… if she doesn't make it…"

"This won't be a suicide mission. Dude, I can't let you do that."

"It's not up to you. If something happens to my little family, I won't stop until I've killed every one of the *Crimson* and Comino fuckers and I won't return to the MIT unit. If this goes to hell, you'll need to disappear."

Atlas squeezed his arm. "Drop your savage ass in the water.

I'm picking you and your girl up in thirty, and we will all exfil to safety."

Donnie adjusted his breathing apparatus and slipped into the dark water, grateful for the clear night and calm seas. He monitored the currents and kicked hard in an easy rhythm, ignoring his throbbing wrist and burning ribs. Every stroke and kick brought him nearer to his Sharls. The MIT master who specialized in death marked Ruzar Comino and his associates for extermination.

◊ ◊ ◊

Ruzar's mind swirled as they waited for the Serbians to arrive. Charlotte stood on the stern as Eddie yelled out orders. One of his goons held her in place and Ruzar watched from a few feet away. He didn't blink, and she met his flat stare communicating hate for the man who'd attacked Donnie and sacrificed her to his father's army.

He'd meant to rescue her from the violence. He should've saved her; instead he waited for the inevitable. They would hurt her before they killed her, and they'd make him participate. If that happened, he would never be clean. The longer he stood there doing nothing, the blacker his soul became. But this was Eddie, the man who'd raised him while his father jet-setted around the world. A surrogate uncle who sat down to Sunday luncheons and complimented Ruzar's mother's cooking. Ruzar's mama still cooked. That was the one task she still performed for her family. After the lengthy meals, the men would sit outside on the portico and Eddie would talk of his simpler childhood growing up in Mdina. They'd drink and play chess and talk of politics and of fucking women. Those days were over. Eddie had called the *Crimson Quarter*, now it was just a matter of time.

Ethical fading. That's what had happened to the Cominos. Years ago, they'd started out helping the Maltese people, through charities they'd erected. Then Papa had dipped a toe in the gambling pool. As his wealth grew, so did his unlawful prowess. He moved from illegal gambling to drug smuggling, then weapons. He justified the killings and greed by saying it was all to protect the family. Cominos came first. That was Eddie's favorite line.

Eddie pointed to a latch attached to the wooden deck and called over the other guard. Ruzar hadn't met either of the mercenaries before. "Open the lazarette and hide that AK47. If a patrol or a Navy boat sails abeam of us, I don't want them seeing those weapons."

The man bent over and opened the latched door to an empty storage locker built into the deck. He threw the rifle into the hole.

"Leave it open. Fetch the Berretta from the flybridge. Keep your pistol with you."

The soldier obeyed Eddie's command and ascended the ladder to the upper deck. Eddie whipped out an arm and pulled Charlotte to his side. She yelped then whimpered as he plastered her to his stomach. When she fought him and tried to kick him in the shin, he twisted her arm behind her back.

"Not long now, my cherry pie. The *Crimson Quarter* are on their way, and then the fun can begin."

Ruzar's pulse pounded, he'd never remembered Eddie being this cruel. But then again, this was personal. She'd unknowingly killed a family member and Eddie would make her pay.

"Your mother wants to see her die," Eddie said to Ruzar. "We'll record it on your phone."

Ruzar nodded, plastering a phony smile on his frozen face.

"You smell good. All woman and flowers." Eddie licked her neck. Ruzar snarled. "What are you doing?"

"Having fun while we wait, it's getting tedious. What do you say? My turn first? There's a bed in the cabin." Eddie shoved his tongue in her mouth. Charlotte struggled and tried to scream. When she kneed him in the thigh, he raised his head and backhanded her. The blow struck her already injured cheek and she fell to the deck.

Remaining still as she whimpered in pain took Herculean effort and Ruzar barely breathed through a sudden red haze.

Eddie knelt. "You will bend to my will. If you continue to fight, I'll slice that pretty belly open as I fuck you. Watching you bleed out, will bring me great joy." Eddie gripped her jaw and mashed his lips to hers. Then he grabbed her hair and pulled her roughly to her feet, before turning her towards the cabin.

Something snapped in Ruzar. He didn't care that this was a man he'd once loved. It was all wrong. Growing up—cruel as his family was—they'd always taught him to respect women. He never tolerated brutality when it came to the fairer sex. Women were beautiful and vulnerable. They were delicate flowers yet tenacious and tougher than most men.

How had his family veered away from those sacred values? His mama wanted to watch them torture an innocent woman? That wasn't the same mother who'd raised him. Greed and money had soiled her soul. Lately, all she cared about were fancy vacations and designer handbags. Wealth replaced humanity, and it saddened him. The Cominos were now a disgrace.

How could Ruzar help Charlotte before they brutalized her? Could he give her a quick death? He looked down at his weapon and knew what had to be done. He wouldn't let her suffer at the hands of monsters. Ruzar widened his stance, aimed and fired.

Chapter Nineteen

As Donnie neared the boat, he identified the vessel as a 35-foot trawler yacht. Swimming to the port side, he tossed a lightweight grappling hook over the rail.

He wore an immersible micro C4OPS comm system and clicked to let Atlas know his status. The sniper spoke immediately. "The asset is being sexually assaulted. Conditions aren't great, but if I have a green light, can I take the shot?"

Donnie's training flew out the window as his brain exploded. Would he come up on them raping her. The shattering thought had his control slipping as images of her assault ran through his brain. Taking a second to breathe, Donnie said, "Copy. If you have a clean shot, take it."

He pulled himself out of the water and silently swung over the rail. Readying the Valmet M76, Donnie prayed it would perform. It was an untraceable rifle supplied by their Moroccan Naval "friend." Donnie had the Glock on hand as a secondary weapon and aimed the assault weapon at the target on the flybridge. He pulled the trigger and the shot echoed through the night. The body fell. Simultaneously, another shot rang, and Donnie rushed to the aft cockpit on the yacht. That shot hadn't come from Atlas, it came from the boat. The sniper swore through the comms. "No clear shot."

Donnie rounded the corner and jumped down onto the stern. Ruzar stood, the M1911 Browning pistol pointed at the cabin doors.

"Don't shoot," Ruzar said. "Help me save her." The look on Ruzar's face gave him pause.

Donnie took in the blood-soaked deck and turned, heart pounding in a sick rhythm as he took in the scene. MIT training was on par with Delta Force's roster of repetitive training drills. Donnie was trained to eliminate targets quickly in hostage situations without injuring victims.

None of those scenarios prepared him for what he saw.

Heated adrenaline spiked through Ruzar. Charlotte's boyfriend leaped onto the deck and pointed a rifle his way. His eyes looked wild and Ruzar understood the rage. If Charlotte was pregnant with Ruzar's child, he'd tear Eddie apart with his bare hands.

"Don't shoot. Help me save her."

Donnie's gaze flicked to the dead mercenary lying behind Ruzar on the swimming platform. He then turned and took in the scene before swiveling his weapon in the same direction as Ruzar.

Ruzar released a breath before trying to calm his trembling hand holding his gun. He'd shot the guard first but hadn't expected Eddie to move so fast. Instead of confronting Ruzar, Eddie grabbed Charlotte's braid and jumped into the storage hole. She fell back. He rammed his pistol into the base of her skull and forced her to scramble into a kneeling position in front of the trapdoor.

She knelt—bent backward over the opening—with her head

facing up towards the sky and her arms stretched out for balance. He used her as a sacrificial umbrella to shelter his cowardly form while squatting in the deep space below. None of him showed in the tight space. They'd have to shoot through her to nail him.

Ruzar flicked a glance to his left, knowing Donnie ran through and dismissed all rescue attempts that involved blowing Eddie's head off. There were zero openings.

Ruzar spoke up as Donnie moved around the periphery, weapon focused on the action. "Eddie, you're outnumbered. Release her and let's talk."

"Fuck you—betrayer bastard. I should've known you'd turn against the family. What was your plan, to rescue this silly bitch? Now you can watch me blow her brains out."

"If you kill her, you'll die. Let her go and I promise to protect you."

"Your promises mean shit. The *Crimson Quarter* are on their way, and all I have to do is wait for them to board. Then, I'll watch them kill you both before I take her inside to play."

Ruzar stilled, but the quiet operator beside him never stopped moving, while looking for a gap. Eddie shifted for cover as he watched the deadly American moving to the right. A new plan formed. Ruzar's stomach revolted and he looked at Charlotte. Her eyes never left Donnie's face—hope mingled with the terror. When Donnie's eyes met hers for the briefest moment, she gazed at him with such love and sorrow that it broke Ruzar's heart. That's all he'd ever wanted. A woman to look at him that way. Someone who looked up to Ruzar and trusted him with everything they had.

That didn't happen in his universe. A devotion like that would never exist for a Comino. For a brief few days, he'd seen a flash of hope with a firefly, before his family ripped it away. The small part of Charlotte Quinn he'd fallen in love with was enough, and now it was time for atonement.

He studied the lines of her pretty face, absorbing every curve. The shape of her cheek and the trace of her brows. He wished he could see the fire of her hair beneath the brown, but it will glow again one day, taking on her inherent sparkle.

Ruzar smiled and shut down all emotion. One last kill. He took advantage of Donnie's pacing as a distraction and launched himself forward. Time slowed as he yelled Eddie's name. The sudden move resulted in Eddie's gun poking out and swinging his way. Eddie fired, and the bullet hit Ruzar in the shoulder. He staggered but then kept coming. Before Eddie could turn the pistol back on Charlotte, Ruzar dived onto the hole and mashed the man's gun hand against the wall and pointed his own Browning at Eddie. Ruzar squeezed the trigger, but nothing happened. He pulled again and still nothing. Swearing, Ruzar dropped the gun, reached back into his pocket and pulled out the mini grenade. He glanced back at the American. Donnie saw the explosive device and shouted, lunging to pull Charlotte clear.

"Take care of Charlotte!" Ruzar yelled. His body blocked any kill shot from Donnie, but he didn't care. It would end now. "Take her and jump!"

With Eddie's gun hand still trapped, Charlotte elbowed him in the nose. Eddie let go of her hair just as Donnie wrenched her across the deck. Eddie wrestled his hand free, but before he could shoot, Ruzar dropped on top of him and pulled the pin.

Find happiness, my firefly.

Ruzar closed his eyes and the world exploded.

◊ ◊ ◊

Donnie launched them into the water. The concussive blast from the grenade slammed into the couple as they hit the surface.

Charlie's hand slipped from Donnie's hold as they sank. Kicking hard, he searched for her outline in the murky depths. Seeing nothing, he surged to the surface and pulled in a long breath before diving again. He needed to drag her away from the boat. If the fuel caught alight, the whole thing would blow.

A white smudge to his left had him cutting through the water. He grabbed the back of Charlie's shirt and pulled her to the surface.

She choked and struggled as he held her to his chest and stroked backward.

"Calm down, honey. Concentrate on breathing."

"I… can't swim. I can't."

"Well, I can, and we need to swim away from the boat. Just relax your body. I won't let anything happen."

She shuddered and coughed as he cleared some distance. A motorboat zeroed in on them.

Donnie slipped his earbud back in position, reached down and activated his comm unit. "Tell me that's you, brother, bearing down on our asses."

"In the flesh. But those *Crimson* turd-biscuits are heading this way."

"Well then, hurry your ass up."

"Ruzar sacrificed himself for me." A sob wracked Charlie's shaking body.

"I know, Sharls." Donnie had to get her warm. Even though the water temperature sat at sixty-eight Fahrenheit, she was both in shock and pregnant.

"Why. Why would he… b… blow…himself up?"

"Because he felt like he didn't have a choice and with you in the mix, I didn't have a clear shot." Donnie tucked her closer.

"I thought he was a bad guy… he pretended?"

235

"They would've killed him if they knew he was protecting you."

"But why?" Charlie asked.

"Because he loved you."

"Could… could he still be alive?"

"No chance, honey."

"I didn't tell him…thank you…or that I cared," she said on a sob.

"I think he knew." Donnie pulled wet strands of hair off her face and kissed her ear. "I'm sorry, baby." He kissed her again. "Are you hurt anywhere else besides your sore cheek?"

She shook her head. "What about you… after… your fall?"

"Just bruised. Nothing ibuprofen won't cure."

Atlas slowed and pulled alongside. With Donnie's help, Atlas pulled Charlie into the boat. Donnie rolled in after, and immediately got to work on drying her off.

Atlas handed over a second towel. "I'm sorry, dude. I couldn't pull the trigger. That asshole grabbed Charlie and disappeared before I could take a shot."

"He jumped into a damn lazarette—he hid in the hull of the boat."

"What happened, did you set that explosion?" Atlas asked.

"No. Ruzar did. He had a fragmentation grenade in his pocket. Ruzar saved Charlie."

"That's some gnarly shit. Where are we heading, Spain or the embassy?"

"We're meeting Sam. I don't feel like being hunted on the water by our *Crimson* buddies. We'll head to the nearest marina—one closest to the embassy. Do you have a spare t-shirt?"

Atlas nodded and pointed to his pack. Donnie unpacked a navy shirt and unbuttoned Charlie's blouse. She didn't say anything—didn't protest—just sat limply, allowing him to pull her arms into the dry clothing. The blue tinge to her lips worried him, and he wanted a doctor to check her out. He scanned the scrapes and bruises on her arms and frowned at the blood on her pants. He wrapped her in his Arcteryx jacket and slipped a hoodie over her head that he'd found in Atlas's go-bag.

Donnie hoped she hadn't sucked water into her lungs, a secondary drowning was a valid concern. Donnie also wanted an ultrasound to check on the baby. He rubbed a towel over her damp legs. She had to wear the wet trousers; they had nothing else. The mercenaries must've dumped her backpack along the way, or it still sat on the burning trawler.

"How's Elana?" she asked through chattering lips.

"She's safe in a clinic—in Italy—and doing well. Friends of ours have men watching over her. She has two bodyguards." Atlas referred to friends of MIT4.

When Donnie had done all he could, he tore off the wetsuit and changed back into his clothes. Then he pulled Charlie into his lap for the rest of the journey to shore.

"Do you have any pains or cramps?"

She shook her head.

"Are you sure you're not injured?" he asked again.

"No, and I'm alive, you're okay, and the baby is hopefully fine. That's all that counts."

She sounded calm, and he knew it was shock. Donnie checked her pulse then pulled her to his chest.

The moment felt surreal. Donnie held the mother of his child in his arms. After Sophie's passing, he'd retreated emotionally from the world. He'd lost his wife to death, and he'd lost himself to life. He'd worked hard at his job, but outside of that, Donnie had been an empty shell.

Suddenly his life was way too full. A week ago, he'd been in control of his sedate personal life, and now he felt like a spinning top. Too many sensations assaulted him, yet he was terrified they would spin away into the dark. That if he let go for just a second, Charlie and their child would slip from his grasp. He squeezed tighter and prayed he could hunt down the individual who sought her death before it was too late.

Souissi area, Rabat.

An hour later, they pulled up to the Wifaq Tennis Club's empty lot—four blocks from the embassy—and waited in the car. At one in the morning, silence from the deserted roads settled into the small space.

Charlie sat curled in Donnie's arms in the backseat. She felt good snuggled against his side. Her reassuring warmth had him stroking her arm. "Why can't we just go to the embassy?" she asked.

"This is a high-profile investigation that will bring a behemoth bureaucratic machine down on our heads. We're talking the CIA, the State Department, and Washington DC bigwigs. We've all killed in country. Not only would we be tied up for months, but I won't be allowed to return to work. More importantly, I won't be able to use MIT resources to shut down the Cominos and find who took out the contract on your life."

"I've got you into deep trouble."

"I've been in tighter spots before. Relax, I have friends watching our backs."

"She needs to be checked out," Atlas said from the front. Donnie wanted that badly. If hostiles weren't hunting them, he'd carry her through the nearest hospital doors himself.

"I've recovered. I'm fine."

"Those men roughed you up, and your chest sounds wheezy. You'll need a general check-up at a clinic."

"Donnie, I said I'm fine."

"You're covered in bruises."

"So are you, you stubborn man."

"I'm not the one who's pregnant." He frowned.

"But you're the one who has the most to lose."

In a flash, Donnie grabbed her shoulders and pulled her to him. "I don't give a fuck about my job. If you think I'd not take care of you so that I can save my ass from an investigation, then you don't know me at all."

"Okay. I trust you and Atlas to protect me; I don't want to take unnecessary risks."

"Incoming," Atlas said as a black SUV pulled in beside them.

Donnie drew his weapon then relaxed as Sam Batista eased out of the driver's seat.

Atlas unlocked the doors and Sam slipped in the back, beside the couple. Donnie leaned over Charlie to give him a pat on the back.

"Hey, bro," Sam said. "What the hell is going on, and why are you bringing carnage into my city?"

"It's your city now? You've been here all of six months?"

"Hey, it beats Islamabad. That assignment was a long two years."

Donnie introduced his calm friend to Charlie; then they got to the meat and bones of the debacle.

"She took in water during the rescue, and those assholes roughed her up. We need a safe clinic for a general once over and an ultrasound."

"Aside from the equipment I've arranged, I've called in a favor with the Moroccan Naval unit. You'll need to tell them that you're an active duty officer and that you can offer them future tactical training via MIT. For valuable field training, they'll provide a protection unit to accompany us to the clinic, and eventually the airport. In the meantime, I'll arrange a temporary passport for Charlotte. You can stay on my rental property. I have two spare rooms and I'm hardly ever there. I stay over most nights at the embassy."

"Will your wife mind?" Donnie remembered the philosophy professor that Sam had married a couple of years ago.

"Ex-wife. Nope, she moved out two months ago."

"Shit, I'm sorry, man."

"I'm not. She was sleeping with some hippy that runs a cafe in town. That's the price you pay for a seventy-hour work week."

Sam turned to Charlie. "When you're settled at my place, we're having a debriefing. I need to know everything from the time you booked your tickets to Malta until the moment I slid into this vehicle."

"What exactly do you do for the embassy?" She looked suspicious, and Donnie couldn't blame her.

"I train up local Special Forces units in host nations—making them self-sustainable. In some countries, I have a team, other times like in Rabat, I work alone."

Donnie squeezed her hand. "Sam and I go way back. We served in the same unit for many years. I trust him, Sharls."

"Then it's time to shut down the shadowy shit show. Point the way, boys."

Chapter Twenty

Her mind drifted as she listened to the nurse bustling around. The door shut, silence fell as she waited for the doctor. They'd been here for the past two hours, and Charlie wanted to sleep for days. It probably had something to do with the lack of sleep and her adrenaline crash. They were safe, at least for the moment. Three armed men stood outside her door along with Atlas. They'd concealed their weapons, and all wore civilian clothing. They had the same watchful look as Donnie. She opened her eyes, and the room swayed, and she closed them again.

Fingers stroked the back of her hand and she jumped.

"You're sneaking up on me again."

"Sharls, you're too pale."

"No shit, Sherlock. I need a bed and food—lots of food. Oh, and clean clothes. Clothes that come with tags, not borrowed clothes. I'm thinking sweats. Super comfortable and soft sweats—with fluffy socks."

Donnie kissed her cheek, and she felt him grin. "I'll send Atlas on a shopping run."

His hand wrapped around hers as he pulled up a chair. Charlie shifted impatiently, looking down at the gown. "Is this necessary?"

"The ultrasound?"

"All of it. I feel fine, except I really need to pee—the nurse made me drink so much water." She opened her eyes and glanced around the examination room—just the two of them. Donnie occupied so much space next to her, contrasting with the room's soft tones. His sinewy muscle, battered face and fierce energy dominated the sterile room. And the way he looked at her, drilling her to the bed with such earnest ferocity. She knew it was because of the baby.

"You jumped from buildings, thugs threw you to the ground numerous times, you almost drowned and were held hostage by men intent on killing you. You're getting checked out."

His other hand slid over to hover above her stomach. Donnie hesitated and almost drew back.

"You can touch it—me—the baby."

His hand descended reverently on her still flat stomach. A bump had begun to emerge. Only she was aware of the slight sloping and the softening around her hips.

"Can you feel him or her?" he asked as he stroked.

"Not yet. Apparently, it feels like little butterfly wings at first. It's too soon, though, maybe in a month. I have no clue what to expect."

His stroking fingers felt warm and comforting against her still chilled skin and Charlie covered his hand with hers.

"When did you find out?" He didn't look at her as he asked the question, but she sensed the tension behind the words.

"In Fes... At Amira's mansion. I bought a pregnancy test at the pharmacy in Malta when I visited Ruzar, but I kept it in my bag. I guess I was in denial. I convinced myself that I wasn't pregnant, but the nausea wouldn't go away. I realized I'd missed my period three times. The first and even second time wasn't a big deal. Since my cancer, I haven't had regular cycles."

"You didn't know about the baby before the trip?"

"No, I swear. I would've told you right away."

"Yet you didn't say anything once you'd taken the test?"

"I couldn't find the right time. Then we…"

"Had sex in the bathroom—straight after you found out?"

"Um. Yeah."

"Nice, Sharls. Real smooth."

She threaded her fingers with his. "I didn't want to ruin things. We made a connection and—"

"So, you elected not to speak about our even bigger connection?"

"I'm sorry," Charlie said. He still didn't make eye contact.

"And it's because of that night after the party… the barbeque?"

"If you're asking if I'm sure it's yours. Yes, Donnie, the baby is yours and was conceived in my shed. Unless I'm having a four-year gestation period."

"Don't act all prickly. It's been four years for you?"

"Are you wanting to start a fight? Why are you angry? I'm sorry I didn't tell you straight away, I should have." She shifted and her bladder screamed for release.

"If I'd known, maybe I could have protected you better. You should've taken the test when you first bought it."

"How would it have changed things and how would you have protected me better? Beam me up on a spaceship? You were thrown off a train while trying to watch over me."

He swallowed and looked down at their clasped hands. A clock ticked in the corner as Charlie tapped her foot and watched the door.

She forced out the words. "This is a lot for you to take in. I understand if you're confused and once this is over, I won't be mad if you decide to—"

"You aren't about to say what I think you're gonna say."

"I'm strong enough to raise this baby on my own."

"Shit, Charlie. What kind of man do you think I am?"

"The kind who might not be ready for this mess—after what he's lived through—but will be a good father, regardless."

"Regardless of what?" Donnie asked.

"Of what happens between you and me."

The door opened, and a female doctor walked in. "I'm Dr. Hanin. I'll be examining you today. I'm schooled in obstetrical ultrasound, but I suggest that once you're home, you'll need to book an appointment with your ob-gyn for a full work-up."

She shook both their hands and sat down behind a computer screen. "I'm sorry about your ordeal. How are you feeling?"

They'd told the hospital that they were mugged at the port.

"Considering the circumstances, I'm feeling all right," Charlie said.

Donnie leaned in and tugged Charlie's hand. "Are you okay with me staying?"

"Do you want to stay?" Charlie referred to the ultrasound, but somehow the question felt bigger than that. She held her breath as she looked into his black-lashed eyes. Looking past his concern and searching for something… something more?

"If you promise to be nice to me." He smiled.

"Just because you're the baby daddy, doesn't mean you acquire new privileges."

He chuckled at her joke and kissed the back of her hand. The moment felt perfect. Too perfect for the likes of her. Maybe they could pretend that they were a couple, expecting a child together. Like they'd dated and taken their time falling in love. A man who wanted to be by her side and who had said yes to dancing with her under the stars, who saw her as a best friend and not a bickering enemy—although they hadn't argued all that much over the last week. Aside from the danger, she'd enjoyed his company and felt too reliant on the quiet warrior.

But for a moment she would pretend that people hadn't died or that she hadn't killed two men. Or that there wasn't a contract out on her life. That farm debt didn't rest on her shoulders along with the welfare of all her staff, or that cancer might return one day to finish her. For now, she was another expectant mother waiting to hear her baby's heartbeat for the first time, and that felt like the best feeling in the world.

The doctor asked Charlie a barrage of questions, then checked her over physically.

When it was time for the ultrasound, Charlie situated the gown above her stomach and waited.

The doctor paused before slathering gel. "I'll be listening for a heartbeat. I'll estimate age by measuring the length of the fetus. I also want to rule out an ectopic pregnancy and will check if you're pregnant with multiples. I can't do a nuchal translucency test here, but you're due for that ultrasound. That evaluates the risk of Down Syndrome or chromosomal abnormalities. It will also rule out heart defects."

Donnie swore softly. "How soon will she need that done?"

"Are you the father?"

"Yes, ma'am. I didn't realize there was so much that could go wrong."

"Small risks in the bigger scheme, but I'd schedule that test within the next two weeks. Let's begin the ultrasound."

The moment she placed the wand on Charlie's stomach, Charlie's eyes filled. Donnie's grip tightened on hers. They heard the heartbeat. Then with the doctor's directions, they saw the baby's outline on the screen.

The doctor chatted as she clicked and measured. "Your baby is as big as a plum. 2.2 inches and I'm thinking 50 ounces. All the organs are developing nicely. You'll start to feel movement in the next couple of weeks, and your stomach will begin to grow considerably. The good news is that you should be moving past the morning sickness."

"I've had some nausea."

Charlie looked over at Donnie who seemed to be taking internal notes while cutting off circulation to her fingers. His bottom lip twitched, and she wanted to kiss the concern off that pouty mouth.

"And watch for dizzy spells."

"There've been a couple," Charlie said.

"What?" Donnie growled the word.

"It's normal," the doctor said quickly. "And they'll pass. Drink plenty of water and eat smaller meals."

Donnie reached for the water bottle on the side table and Charlie grabbed his wrist. "No. Stop. I've just drunk a borehole's worth."

Chuckling, the doctor promised to print out the images she'd captured and then cleaned Charlie up. When they were alone, Charlie swung her legs off the bed and stood. Donnie wrapped an arm around her waist and tried to carry her to her shoes.

"Oh, for the love of God and country. Back up. I'm pregnant, not paralyzed." She shoved with all her strength, but he barely moved.

Hovering, he asked, "What do you need?"

"To use the bathroom and pee out the Niagara Falls. I'll meet you out front."

Were bathroom breaks the only escape from the man? Charlie had acquired a human-sized leech, and that made her uncomfortable. His concern was for the baby and not for the female incubator that carried his offspring. Charlie was back where she'd started. Invisible as an attractive woman to her quiet crush that always stood in the shadows.

◊ ◊ ◊

She slept in the opposite room at Sam's place. Two soldiers watched from their vehicle below. By nine in the morning, they'd been processed, checked out physically and had time to rest. After a shower, Donnie stared at her door from the hard sofa in the corner. He'd just wrapped up the second call to Max. For now, they'd keep Donnie and Atlas's involvement out of the case.

Charlie's attack in Gozo would remain classified and work its way into the now official MIT4 investigation.

Atlas threw his jacket on the bed along with a couple of shopping bags. "Dude, you need to blink. I'm starting to think one of the extras from *The Walking Dead* has taken up residence in my room."

Donnie didn't move, just kept gazing at the door across the way.

"Earth to Donnie…"

"Vaccinations," Donnie said.

"Vacci-what? When last did you sleep?"

"I can't remember. She's had her vaccinations for the trip. Oh shit. Do you think that could affect the baby?"

Atlas leaned against the bed and folded his arms. "Not sure… but why are we suddenly talking about vaccinations?"

"It means she could come to Kenya. Lizzy's there, and we'll

247

all be in Nairobi for at least a few weeks, especially once MIT2 returns from the mission."

"Okay, you've lost me, why would she not just go home?" Atlas said, scratching his neck.

"Whoever put out that contract on her is from Wyoming. Until we determine who's behind Charlie's assassination attempt, she won't be safe. This way, she'll be closer to me while I investigate."

"Buddy, this sounds complicated."

"Charlie has two killers after her. The person who paid the Cominos and Luca Comino himself. By the time we're due to re-join the team, I want Luca Comino neutralized." Donnie's wrist still ached and he flexed his fingers.

"MIT4 is handling the Comino investigation. You can't become any more involved," Atlas said.

"This is my child's life on the line, and Sharls…"

"I know. That's what worries me. You're in a weird headspace. You've spent all of four days with her. And I know you had a one-night stand but—"

"Don't. I've known Sharls longer than that. I met her over three years ago."

"While losing your wife, and you're only just ready to start dating again. How do you think that's going to work out for Charlie?"

Donnie launched to his feet. "Don't fucking talk about my late wife, or who I'm currently seeing. You and I have been on one deployment together. And as the new guy, my private life is none of your concern."

"Yeah? Well, I just risked my ass to save you and your friends." Atlas didn't back down, instead stepping forward.

"Do you want a medal?"

"Fuck you. I would've done it a hundred times over. But only for those two kick-ass chicks. I'm not sure about your bad-tempered ass. You and I both eliminated targets on an unauthorized mission to protect them—not even an actual mission, on a damn vacation."

"Again. Do you want a medal?"

Atlas picked up Donnie's pack and the shopping bags and tossed them towards the door. "Hey, dickhead, get a few hours' sleep. Oh, and get the hell out of my room."

Chapter Twenty-One

The matching sofa in Charlie's room looked just as uninviting as the one in Atlas's room. His mind spun as he ran over the last chaotic few days. Donnie needed time alone to think, but when he glanced over at the bed and saw Charlie sit up, he only wanted to pull her close.

"Why are you still awake? You look like crap." She held the sheet to her neck.

She always made him chuckle. "I'm making a nest on the couch."

"What the hell is wrong with you? Climb under the covers, now."

He couldn't make himself move. "We should talk."

"Probably. We have a lot of shit to shovel, but we aren't doing that today. I need you to hold me in those sexy arms. I keep hearing the explosion and feeling myself sinking into that cold sea. I see the bullets slamming into Zach and—"

"Enough. I'm here." He slipped off his jeans, slid between the sheets and pulled her to his chest.

"You're wearing too many clothes," she said.

"Sharls."

"Not because I want to jump your tired bones. I like the feel of your bare chest. Your skin on mine."

"I like that too. Fine." Donnie pulled his shirt off and re-settled. He froze when he felt Charlie's breasts mash against his side.

"Please stroke my back. Yeah, just like that." She snuggled in and rested her head on his chest.

"You're gonna be the death of me. How am I gonna sleep with your naked tits in my face." Donnie brushed his hand up and down her spine and heard her sigh.

"After today, we should abstain from cuddling and sex."

Had he heard her correctly? "Excuse me?"

Her finger stroked over his nipple. "If we decide to make a go of it—for the baby—then I'd like us to date like a normal couple and take our time getting to know each other. If you don't want that, then we need to decide on how we'll raise this baby as separate entities. Either way, we both need time to think without adrenaline clouding our decisions."

"What if I already know what I want?" Donnie said.

"You don't."

"You know me that well, wench?"

"I think I do." Her hand slid lower and slipped into his boxers. "And I think someone's happy to cuddle." Circling him, her thumb slid up and traced his tip. Donnie no longer felt tired.

"We can't. The baby?" He stiffened as she worked his shaft.

"Is fine, this won't harm the kid and look at the bright side, at least you can't knock me up." Her head brushed against his hips as she slid down his body and Donnie jerked. He felt her hair sliding across his stomach; then her tongue traced his inner thigh. With every touch, she lit him up. He was addicted to her scent, to the way she moved and how she tasted. Warm lips closed around him, and Donnie groaned out his pleasure. She took her time, taking him in with such care. When she pulled her hair to the side and looked up at him with chocolate brown warmth, Donnie snapped. He pulled her up and rolled them over.

One hand pulled down her panties and the other spread her legs. He bent down and licked her hard—once then twice. Then he positioned himself and eased in. Wrapping herself around him, Charlie pulled him down for a kiss. He began to move. She stilled him with her legs and leaned back to look into his eyes.

She spoke so softly that he strained to hear. "Whatever happens, you tracked me down and saved me. I never knew what it was like to be sheltered by such strength until you, and I want to fight by your side. I have to give our jellybean inside me a better life. You make me believe that everything will be all right, that I have a future with this angel in my stomach."

The trust in her eyes undid him. A cloud of hair nestled around her strong face, and Donnie traced the bruise on her cheek, then the pretty bow of her top lip. How had he not seen how perfect she was? If the nipper growing inside her turned out to be a little girl, would she have her mommy's lovely lips? Or her open countenance? Her cute nose? Her beautiful hair? He hoped so.

Donnie traced the healing scar on her neck, bent to kiss the bruise, then traced his lips over her eyelashes and the tip of her nose. He began rocking his hips but took his time exploring every curve of her face. Burying his nose in the crook of her neck, Donnie pulled out and thrust in with long strokes. She kept pace, and when he bit her neck, he felt her explode around him. Donnie stilled and then buried himself as far as he could. Everything inside him clenched then blew like a grenade. Immediately, he pulled her to him, wanting to feel every inch of her skin against him.

The intensity of their joining scared him. The connection he'd felt, was like nothing he'd known before. And that felt like a betrayal. Sophie. He'd already found and lost the love of his life, so what the hell had just happened with Charlotte Quinn?

Five hours later, Sam sat down with them. Charlie ignored her silent ally in the corner and tried not to think about the few hours they'd spent in each other's arms.

Sam's watchful eyes were set in a harsh face. She liked him—a no-bull-shitter like herself. She relaxed in the chair opposite and waited for the interrogation to commence. He'd already spoken with Donnie and Atlas. Now it was her turn.

"Do you need anything before we begin? Aside from the water."

"I'm all good."

He'd re-assessed her from head to toe when he'd entered the room, and those deadly eyes continued with their visual examination.

"I'm sorry you were hurt," Sam said.

That was something she didn't expect to hear.

"I wasn't hurt, aside from the stitches in my arm." Charlie waved about the injury. "Daily chores on the farm cause more bruises than this, especially when I take a rare tumble from a horse."

"You're not riding while you're pregnant," Donnie said.

"Technically, I already did—in Malta."

His frown deepened. Sam ignored the glowering man beside him and leaned forward.

"Donnie and I combed through the last few days and chatted about the players involved. You're not in a good place. Someone close to you who knew you'd be visiting Malta, planned ahead and contacted the Comino family to eliminate you. Ruzar was the assassin on that assignment but developed feelings for you. We're not sure why his Serbian cousin—Andrej Borjan—was brought in."

Charlie broke in. "Ruzar mentioned his cousin to me once, saying that his father didn't respect him enough and was forcing them to work together. I assumed it was a business deal. I think that Ruzar wanted to break away from the business. Perhaps his father sensed his son's rebellion against the family. I believe that he changed his mind about killing me. At least initially."

"I concur," Donnie said as he paced the living room. "And I think he felt that way, until the end. He wanted to protect her."

Sam drew her gaze. "Then you killed Comino family, or family by marriage. Ruzar's mother is originally Serbian— Milena Borjan—before she married Luca Comino. Her family runs the *Crimson Quarter*. You have some big guns after you."

"Do I change my name? Fake my death? Go into hiding?"

Donnie placed a hand on her shoulder. "Not necessarily. It seems as if the attempt on your life has uncovered a nest of criminal syndicates. The MIT4 team has made good progress. They've already linked the Cominos and the *Crimson Quarter* to a jihadist foundation in Palermo. With their extremist links, we'll take them down quickly."

Sam smiled then grew serious. "My question for you is, why would somebody from your hometown want you dead?"

Her heart pounded, and Charlie clutched the edge of her chair. "I've been thinking about that, and I have no idea. I think I'm pretty likable and I haven't pissed anyone off recently."

"What about Peter Billings?" Donnie volunteered, and Charlie considered the possibility.

"He has the means. I know he's inherited a fair amount of money, even though he's a delinquent."

"We'll start a list of suspects. Anyone else stand out?"

"There was this guy that I dated—about eight months ago—that wouldn't take no for an answer."

"What!" Donnie erupted and swung around.

"Relax, Chuck Norris; I took care of him."

"What happened?" Sam asked, ignoring the fuming soldier.

"I went on a blind date and met him at a coffee shop in town. He seemed nice and even walked me to the car. Then when I said no to a goodbye kiss, he persisted. I slapped him, then he grabbed me around the neck—"

"What the living hell?"

She'd never seen Donnie flush that red before. The muscles in his neck pulled taut as he placed his fists on the side of the sofa. She imagined steam pouring from his ears.

Charlie continued, "I grabbed his nipple through his shirt and twisted. Then I finger punched him in the eye. I finished him off with my trusty bottle of mace."

"Who is the fucker?"

"Did you report it to the police?"

She ignored Donnie's question and answered Sam's. "Drove straight over and filed a report. He was arrested and ended up getting six months' probation."

"You didn't think to tell anyone, like James?" Donnie said as he swung back into pacing.

"I was swamped with my dad and the farm."

Sam placed a paper and pen in front of her, and she began scribbling down an extensive list of family, friends, and acquaintances. Aside from the two morons she'd had a run in with, the rest were well-meaning and kind members of her circle.

Donnie added Elana to the list which almost earned him a punch to the face.

"Sam, can I call my brother and Elana? I'm sure my family has heard about Zach, and they must be worried."

"Possibly, but you can't tell them where you are until we clear up this mess. Once we have a lead, we'll see about getting you back home or at least over to Kenya. Donnie says you'll stay with a friend in Nairobi."

Charlie choked on a sip of water. "That's news to me. Seriously, Donnie?"

Sam gestured for Donnie to sit back down before he could answer. "You can hash out accommodation logistics once this interview is complete. Charlotte, I want every detail from when you boarded the plane to Malta. I need airlines, times, dates and who you spoke to."

Charlie settled in and began talking.

Chapter Twenty-Two

Nairobi, Kenya.
Two days later.

Before they'd even parked the rental car, Lizzy came rushing down the steps, tripping in her haste. Charlie laughed at her energetic friend and welcomed the enthusiastic embrace. Blonde curls impeded Charlie's vision as Lizzy chattered away. "I can't believe you're freaking here. In bloody Kenya!"

"Careful, Lizzy," Donnie said. "You look like you're wrestling Sharls to the damn ground. She's still tender in places."

Charlie rolled her eyes. "Lizzy's the size of a flea. I'm fine."

Lizzy grabbed Donnie's sleeve as he shouldered the two packs. "Wait. Did you call her Sharls?"

He grunted as he ran up the stairs.

Big blue eyes widened. "What have you two been doing?"

"Getting knocked up." Charlie grinned at Lizzy's shocked expression. "Come, I'll tell you everything."

"Lizzy, don't you dare take Charlie to the orphanage if there are sick kids around with contagious superbugs," Donnie called from the top of the stairs.

"You're not the boss of me," Charlie called back.

"What have you done to Mr. Cool, Calm and Collected?" Lizzy asked Charlie in a whisper.

"I removed the stick from his ass."

Laughing, they made their way to Lizzy's front door. Ray sat at the entrance, her tail working overtime as she greeted the new house guests.

"Is there a shopping mall nearby?" Charlie asked as she bent to greet Ray. "I have two pairs of sweats to my name."

"You betcha. But your looming bodyguard will insist on tagging along."

"Damn straight," Donnie said before sinking onto the couch.

"How long are you here for?" Lizzy asked.

"Until we can pinpoint who's trying to kill me. Donnie wants me close to his shadowy alpha-male unit." Charlie nuzzled Ray's neck and received a wet lick as a reward.

"You mean MIT2." Lizzy laughed. "Hopefully, John should soon be returning to Nairobi."

"You mean Jamie. It feels weird to think of him as John."

"I'm running back out tonight—to Malta," Donnie said. "Atlas will swing by and stay with Charlie while I'm gone."

"How long will you be gone for?" Lizzy asked.

"I want to leave and return before MIT2 arrives back at base. MIT4 has gathered enough Intel to move in on the Cominos. I'll help to take Luca Comino down. I can add my analyst skills to the mix."

"You're not allowed to kill any more boogeymen," Charlie commanded as she sunk onto Lizzy's furry beanbag. "You're in enough trouble already."

"Yes, snarky pants."

Charlie smiled at the exhausted warrior spread across the couch. They'd kept to their word and hadn't performed any "jiggery-pokery" since the first night at Sam's place. She missed knocking boots with her stern champion, but he needed time, and she needed time. She loved him. The realization battered her cautious heart, and she had to look away. He could break that same heart badly. She'd always loved him. Ached for him from the first day she'd seen him, and Morocco had set that silly crush in stone.

Later that night, Charlie waited in the guest room for Donnie to step out of the shower. He paused when he spotted her on the bed. She admired his well-muscled body with a towel wrapped around his athletic waist. He looked like airbrushed perfection.

"Looking for a free strip show, Miss Quinn?"

"I won't say no."

He quirked his lips as he pulled a pair of socks from his bag. "Sharls, what's bothering you?"

"Am I that transparent?"

"I'm guessing you're worried that I won't return from Malta with my ass intact."

"If you get hurt because of me…"

He sat beside her. "None of this is on you. It's on the asshole dickhead who wants to harm you. You're not responsible for Zach or Ruzar or for the choices that I'll make in the coming days. Besides, I train for this shit—it's what I do."

"If you don't come back, I'm going postal on their mafia asses."

"Copy that." He leaned and kissed her jaw, then her mouth. "Is kissing off the table?"

His magical mouth nibbled her lip as she whispered, "Goodbye kisses don't count."

"I'll be back in a few days. Catch up on sleep and don't let Lizzy drag you around the city." Donnie grabbed her face in both hands and ravished her with his mouth. He took his time, and when he pulled away, he placed a kiss to her brow.

"Don't go out unless Atlas is with you. He also has work to do at our base a few miles away. You should be safe here and I'll keep in contact."

Two hours later, after he'd left, she sat with Lizzy on the balcony. The city lights twinkled in the distance as Lizzy uncapped a beer and Charlie sipped on a lemonade.

"I can't believe you're pregnant. How are you feeling?"

"Good. Like myself, aside from some slight queasiness."

"So, Donnie, huh?"

"Yeah. It's complicated. He's not ready for an instant family. I'm waiting for the impending freak-out."

Lizzy picked up Ray and snuggled the pup on her lap. "Now that you know what the guys do, I can tell you how I lost my finger and how John saved me."

"You told me you caught your hand in a fence."

"Nope. Also, I shouldn't be saying anything yet, but we're adopting."

"Uh. Adopting…"

"A little boy from *Teens and Tots*— the children's home that I work at."

"No shitting way."

Lizzy's eyes sparkled with tears. "Yes, ways. John and I can't leave him here. We love him so much."

"A little boy, huh?" Charlie asked.

"Yes. His name is Valentino, and we've just filed the paperwork."

"Oh, honey."

"And John's going to kill me for saying this." Lizzy ran inside. A short while later she emerged waving her hand in the air. "We're married."

Charlie stared, tongue-tied.

"We got married on the shores of Lake Victoria, just over a month ago. It was just the two of us. We haven't told anyone outside of his team—we wanted to tell our family and friends all at once."

"Jamie got married without me there?" Charlie said in a choked voice. He was like her big brother, and she'd always imagined seeing him walk down the aisle. The exclusion hurt. Her life had changed so much over the past year and her farm family had disappeared.

Lizzy must've seen her distress, and pulled Charlie in for a hug. "Sweetie, we're planning another ceremony back in the States—a big affair with my parents and all our friends. John wants you there. He says you'll be like his best man—best girl. We want the full shebang but with Valentino by our side. I promise, we haven't forgotten about the people that mean the most to us."

Charlie couldn't stop a sob from escaping. She hadn't truly let go since her dad's passing—all the stress from the past month culminating into hiccupping wails which morphed into giggles. Lizzy leaned back, took one look at Charlie and joined in. Ray's puzzled expression from the corner had them laughing even louder.

When they'd wiped their tears, the girls settled back and chatted into the early hours of the morning.

Qormi, Malta.
Fifteen hours later.

The warehouse was a basic structure that easily held the nine men and their equipment. Along with MIT4 and Donnie, were two members of the Italian Special Intervention group—the Special Forces unit of the Italian Carabinieri. Two Maltese lieutenants had just joined the black ops mission. One led a Maltese Rapid Deployment Team in the Maritime Squadron, and the other ran a C Company's VPD team.

Instead of attacking the Cominos' gambling syndicates or drug trafficking, MIT4 focused on their arms trafficking operation. More specifically, they zeroed in on one shipment that had occurred earlier in the week with the Palermo extremist group, using a local mosque as a front. The Italian Carabinieri had already run a four-month surveillance operation on the jihadist mercenaries and tracked a weapons shipment via a fishing vessel from Malta.

Fake certificates and forgeries were beginning to surface. The Cominos had a reach that extended all the way up into the chambers of government. Thanks to wiretaps set up by the Italians and MIT4, Luca Comino would take the fall. They not only had his voice on the recordings, but they had surveillance photographs of him and his wife with the smuggling vessel at the harbor.

Now, as the sun sat low in the sky, they were planning the takedown of his empire. The Maltese military wanted to run with the mission. MIT4 and the Italian SF team would provide back-up. There would be four assault teams in place.

Donnie held raw emotions in check. Luca Comino could not escape. If he and his wife disappeared, Charlie would always be in danger. Donnie wanted to be the point man on the mission—the first in the door. The pulsing knot in his stomach demanded vengeance. He wanted Comino blood spilled for attacking Charlie and their child.

Donnie studied the area via satellite as they planned the

assault on Luca Comino's large villa, located beside his vineyards in Mgarr—a small rural town in the northern region of Malta.

When they'd wrapped up and began readying MIT4 weaponry and equipment, Rocky walked over to help Donnie prep the comms.

"I can't have you going demonic on Comino ass on this mission. If you tag along, you have to play nice."

"Bro, as long as you do your job and neutralize this asshole, I'll behave. But if I confront his evil ass, I'm pulling the trigger."

"Don't give the targets or their dirty friends a reason to wriggle away. This is my mission, and it will run like clockwork. Stand back or stand the fuck down," Rocky said, his good-natured countenance nowhere to be found.

"Copy that, sir. I'll be a choir boy."

Donnie ignored the primitive bloodlust pounding through his veins and concentrated on the task before him.

◊ ◊ ◊

Mgarr, Malta.

Donnie eased around the sprawling pool that looked out over the valley. The limestone home lay before him. A double story structure with white shutters, terraced gardens, and palms leading up the walkway. Luca had quite the army. Mostly Serbian guards, who put up a good fight but were no match for four strike-units that broke silently through the barrier of averagely trained mercenaries.

Donnie counted ten dead tangos, and still, the teams hadn't fired a shot. He'd hung back as commanded, and along with a small contingent of the Italians, he checked the side buildings.

Gunfire erupted from the main house. Ignoring the sounds

of battle, Donnie moved in on the tidy-looking shed next to the garage. It sat dark and off to the side, yet a small glow flickered from beneath the door. A heat signature registered. When the men were in position, Donnie breached the already unlocked door.

Ignoring his surprise, Donnie zeroed in on the target slumped on the stool. Unshaven with a bottle of whiskey in one hand and a gun resting on his lap, Luca Comino looked up with bleary eyes.

"You've found my workshop."

A vintage Maserati A6 sat behind him with its hood propped open. Tools lay scattered at Luca's feet.

"Ruzar and I would work for hours on cars in this shed. He liked Fiats. I like Maserati. It was how we connected. Then, I got busy and life got in the way."

Luca sniffed and rubbed his nose with the back of his hand, the bottle still clutched loosely. Donnie never took his eyes off the gun hand. They could easily eliminate him, but the Maltese authorities wanted Luca Comino to stand trial. So, Donnie waited to see what the kingpin would do.

"I destroyed my family. My son… my son is dead. I should've taken more care—watching over him. He should never have left the hospital in Gozo…"

Donnie recognized grief. He'd lived through it. Luca's sorrow surprised Donnie. He wondered what Ruzar would think. The young man had craved his father's attention, and now he had it.

"Did my wife put up a fight? Milena is a viper. She's the strong one. She'll go out fighting, killing, and maiming."

Five weapons pointed at Luca Comino. He carried on talking like he was chatting to old friends.

"I'm guessing I can't pay you off. I bet you're a bunch of

noble assholes." Luca shrugged. "Do you know how my son died? Who killed him?"

The devil in Donnie spoke up. "He killed himself and used a fragmentation grenade."

"You're a fucking liar. My son would never kill himself. He's no coward." Bloodshot eyes shone with rage.

"I saw it with my own eyes, and he did it to save others."

"You're... you were with the tourist bitch?" Luca laughed. "How is she still alive? I hear she's pregnant. Eddie told my wife just before he died. Maybe I'll send a *Crimson* man to cut that baby out of her. You think I can't do that from prison, arrange her death?"

Donnie turned to stone, then felt his blood scald as rage soared. "Who paid for her murder, who arranged the contract?"

"Interesting reaction. Are you the father? I'll never tell, and I'll have fun sending exterminators to her door."

"You won't get the chance," Donnie growled, stepping closer. "Your woman is dead, and I'm her executioner."

Chapter Twenty-Three

A deadly silence fell as Donnie's craving for vengeance took over. Luca's gun hand twitched. That's all it took. His head evaporated in a red cloud. Donnie turned to the Italian soldiers at his back.

"Who pulled the trigger?"

"Fanculo," the team leader swore then shrugged. "The bastard threatened your family. He cannot live. Now, you go home with clean hands and keep your lady safe."

Donnie chuckled. "I owe you, buddy."

"I come to your country, and you buy me—how you say—a corn dog? Then we see an American football game?"

"You got it. Name the time and day, and I'll make a plan."

The men laughed and exited the structure. Rocky walked down the path to meet Donnie. "Comms tell me that Luca Comino is dead. Tell me you didn't shoot the dickhead."

"Nope. It was close, but I obeyed the order."

"Thank God. You're already buried up to your eyeballs in bodies, which stays between us."

"What about the wife?" Donnie asked.

"Milena Comino sleeps with a gun under her pillow. Before she could aim, we took her out."

◊ ◊ ◊

Nairobi, Kenya.
Two days later.

Charlie stood in front of the full-length mirror, tracing the lantern sleeve, deep emerald chiffon blouse she wore. Blue jeans and nude sandals finished the look. Lizzy had shown Charlie how to emphasize her eyes with dark green shadows and Charlie wore a plum lipstick that felt luxurious on her lips.

"See, the shopping trip this morning was worth it." Lizzy draped a dangly necklace to Charlie's front, then moved to the back to fasten it. "Donnie is going to flip his lid when he sees you. Fiddlesticks, this damn clasp."

"This feels weird," Charlie said, before biting her lip.

"Relax, he's the one that called and asked you on the date. Atlas says Donnie is stopping by their base to shower, then he's heading this way."

Charlie admired her wavy hair. "The poor man probably hasn't slept. He's only just landed."

"I know. And now Donnie wants to take you on a date. It's darn romantic."

It was sweet. Charlie smiled as Lizzy added the last finishing touches to the outfit. She'd enjoyed the previous few days with her friend. Lizzy had taken Charlie to the children's home where she worked. Seeing all those orphaned children had broken Charlie's heart. A lady called Esther ran *Teens and Tots* and the kids seemed happy. Well, as comfortable as they could be, growing up without parents or a home of their own.

Valentino was constantly by Lizzy's side. He looked up at her with the biggest brown eyes. His adoration had brought a lump to Charlie's throat. When Lizzy held him, he would play with her hair and rest his head in the crook of her neck. They sang softly together as Lizzy went about her day.

He didn't know about the adoption. They'd elected not to say anything in case something went wrong, but it was clear that Lizzy adored the little tyke.

Charlie loved her stay in Nairobi so far. It was a bustling city, surrounded by African savannah. She wanted to explore the area, even though she had no idea how long she'd be staying. She also needed to contact her friends and family from back home, check on the farm and reassure her family that she was all right. Atlas told her that Elana had flown to Turkey to stay with family. Knowing her friend was safe, helped her to relax.

Except now Charlie wasn't relaxed. Nerves had her stomach fluttering. Even though she'd spent a solid week with Donnie, this felt different. They were going on an actual date. Charlie couldn't remember the last time she'd dated a man aside from a brief relationship with an idiot boyfriend in college, and an even briefer fling with a stuffy banker from town. Fighting cancer, then running the farm and caring for her ailing father had canceled out any girly plans with the opposite sex.

The knock at the door had her sucking in deep breaths. Lizzy grinned. "The look on your face is priceless."

"Screw off. Answer the door and let me pull my shit together."

Giggling, Lizzy disappeared down the passage. Charlie traced a hand over her stomach. "Are you ready, jellybean? It's time to hang out with your daddy."

Charlie walked to the living room. Coming around the corner, she paused. Donnie wore dark blue jeans with a black button-up shirt. Standing in the small hallway, he looked so virile and dependable that she wanted to launch herself into his arms. Restraining herself, she walked towards him.

Donnie pulled a bunch of orange roses out from behind his back. "You look pretty... damn amazing. And your hair?"

"Lizzy mixed Vitamin C powder with shampoo. It removes semi-permanent hair dye without damaging your hair." Charlie took the flowers with trembling fingers.

"I've missed this incredible red." Donnie traced his finger through her hair.

"It's almost back to my natural color."

He continued playing with a strand and Charlie floundered under the intensity of his gaze. Goosebumps broke as the back of his knuckle brushed against her neck.

"Jeez, will you both evacuate the premises already. With all that staring, I feel like I'm in a Twilight movie." Lizzy took the flowers from Charlie and nudged them to the door. Donnie placed his hand at Charlie's waist as he led her down the stairs.

"How are you feeling, any cramps or spotting?"

"Wow. You know how to charm your date."

"I worried while I was gone that—"

Charlie stopped and turned. "We're not talking about the baby or men chasing us this evening. I might ask what happened on your Maltese trip, but then we drop it. I want to feel like a girl on a first date, and we should be exploring our connection."

"You got it."

"Where are we going?"

"Now that's a surprise."

They drove for over thirty minutes. Donnie filled her in on the mission. Although she hated that Ruzar's parents had died, she knew it was for the best. From the sounds of things, the Cominos destroyed so many lives and were behind numerous assassination attempts throughout Europe.

"We've cut off the head of the Comino cobra. The body will die. The *Crimson Quarter* will continue with their syndicate, but without the Cominos' support and funding, I doubt they will continue to chase you. We'll keep an eye out, just in case."

Charlie settled back in her seat. She'd enjoy the evening knowing that there was just one killer left on their radar. She knew Donnie wouldn't give up until he'd tracked the bastard down.

Donnie steered them up a winding sand road to a wooden cabin and it looked inviting. It was still light out as they walked into the foyer and waited to be seated. As they followed the server, he led them out a back door along a sandy trail. Donnie threaded his fingers with Charlie's and smiled.

"What?"

"Look to the left," he said.

She did, and her eyes widened. "What is this?"

There were luxury wooden treehouses built on stilts and set amongst the trees. They winded up a path to a distant treehouse and Charlie stumbled as she looked around. Donnie pulled her to his side.

"There are a few treehouse chalets or hotels scattered around Africa, but this is different. It's a stilted restaurant. You dine in a private treehouse where you sit in the treetops, under the stars." Donnie pointed to the structure up ahead. "That's ours for the night. It's built around a Marula Tree."

Lanterns hung from the branches and white curtains framed wide wooden windows. A ramp led up the two stories to the treehouse.

"Oh, my hell. This is... you've blown my mind. Donnie, you're a romantic."

His face flushed and he stumbled. "I'm not... I... It's a quiet place to talk."

They walked up and ducked through the doorway. Charlie felt like she was in a Tarzan movie—if Jane was used to five-star luxury. A table sat out on a wide deck that looked out over distant mountains and the savannah. Suspended in the corner were two hammocks and a set of folded blankets. A watering hole lay below, and warthogs and an antelope stood near the water's edge.

Donnie pulled out her seat and Charlie sat while taking in her surroundings. A waiter immediately introduced himself and presented her with an array of drinks. She chose an apple juice as Donnie settled opposite.

"We should have a perfect view of the sunset. They have a set menu, I've checked—everything listed is safe for the baby."

They watched the sun dip as they chatted. Charlie asked Donnie about his brother and she, in turn, spoke about her adventures on the farm. They discovered that they both shared a passion for old artifacts and weaponry and had even visited the same museums near Wyoming.

As the stars came out and the waiter placed the dessert before them, the conversation turned to Charlie's travels.

"Why Malta?" Donnie asked. "Not many Americans choose Malta as their first travel destination. You could've chosen Italy, France, or Spain?"

She played with her water glass as she spoke. "Dad loved to read. He loved history, and mostly collected books on the wild west—the history of the cowboy. But he also had books on the World Wars. He subscribed to the National Geographic magazine. My brother—Nate—and I poured over those books for hours. There was this one set which we loved. It was a history of the Knights of the Order of St. John."

Leaning back, Donnie took a sip of water as he listened. His foot rubbed along Charlie's calf, doing naughty things to her nether regions.

Continuing with her story took concentration. "We would make Daddy read the Maltese Knight adventures to us before bed every night. Nate was much older, and I always begged him to play swords with me. I even carved the Maltese Cross into a piece of wood and hung it around my neck on a dirty string."

Donnie smiled. "Did he play with you?"

She hid the hurt. "Nate said he was too busy for a little brat." She stared into the night. "I'm glad he's helping me on the farm. It was good to see him again. He's done well for himself. I'm hoping we can re-establish a connection. I always got along with him, even though Daddy disowned him."

"Why would Jack do that?"

"Nate was a difficult teenager. He drove home drunk one night and had a car accident."

"Was he injured, was anyone else hurt?"

"He hit a tree and broke his arm. Unfortunately, I was in the car with him."

Donnie grasped her hand. "How bad?"

"It happened a long time ago, on the way back from a dressage competition. Daddy always kept the photo from that day on his nightstand. The last photograph we took as a family. My mom and dad took the horse trailer home, and I rode with Nate. He'd been drinking behind the stadiums that day. We didn't know. I don't remember what happened. Apparently, he rounded a corner too fast. I wasn't wearing a seatbelt and hit my head on the windshield. I was in a coma for a week."

"Sharls, that's crazy."

"Yeah, well, I recovered. My family didn't. My mother fell apart and confessed to having an affair and Nate moved away to culinary school. My father never forgave him."

"It's truly been just you and your dad."

"And Jamie… Johnny… whatever you're now calling him." She breathed in the fresh air and looked up. "Look at those stars. Aren't they incredible?"

"I love that you do that." Donnie stroked her arm.

"Do what?"

"Find the beauty in every moment."

"I survived cancer. It was like the universe gave me a blank sheet of paper. We only have a certain amount of breaths left on this incredible planet. How can I not see the beauty?"

Donnie blinked then looked down at their clasped hands.

"I'm sorry. I shouldn't have mentioned cancer. Your wife…"

"I don't want to talk about that or Sophie."

"You miss her."

"Sharls."

"Do you ever feel sad that I survived, and she didn't?"

"Why would you say something like that?" Anger flashed.

"I don't know—survivor's guilt. She had everything, including your love. She should've lived."

Raw hurt glittered beneath the sheen in his eyes. His bottom lip twitched, and he let go of her hand to lean back. Footsteps indicated the waiter approaching with the check. Donnie pulled out his card and signed, as Charlie concealed her inner turmoil. They walked down the ramp in silence. When they got to the car, Charlie paused. "We're stepping into a minefield, and I can't risk a broken heart. Love is a choice that you're not ready to make."

"I need time to get used to the idea of us, and of having a

child with you. All I need is a moment. Sharls, my head is spinning."

"I'll give you that, but we're not forcing this relationship. It doesn't have to be a package deal. You'll always be a father to this jellybean regardless of whether I'm in your life or not."

After a silent ride, Donnie pulled into a parking space and switched off the engine.

"Thank you for dinner under the stars. It was special," she said.

Donnie stared ahead. His grip tightened on the wheel. "The feelings I have for you—"

His phone rang, and he swore. "Give me a second. Rocky, what's up?"

Charlie fiddled with her necklace as she waited.

"When?... Are you sure?... Send me the details.... I'll tell her. Yes, her family is worried."

Donnie hung up and looked at Charlie. "Rocky—the MIT4 team—traced a money transfer from an offshore account to the Cominos."

"Okay. I'm guessing this relates to me?"

"Peter Billings opened the account last month. He transferred over fifty thousand dollars."

"Only fifty? That's all I'm worth? Relax, I'm joking."

Donnie shook his head and smiled. "Rocky is red flagging him with a local FBI office. They'll issue a warrant and have him arrested within the week."

"Holy shit. So, it's over? I'm safe."

"Not until he's behind bars. I'll reach out to some law enforcement buddies back home to keep an eye on him. You're not going anywhere until he's been sentenced."

Charlie planted a kiss on Donnie's cheek. "Thank you. Crap.

I need to make a bunch of calls, and check on the farm and call my family. Lists—I need to make checklists."

She was already out the door and stalking across the lot. Locking the truck, Donnie walked up beside her. Later that night, she lay in bed and wondered what Donnie wanted to say to her in the car before his phone rang.

Chapter Twenty-Four

Donnie laughed while watching the giraffe tongue playing with Charlie's hair. They stood on the feeding platform at *The Giraffe Centre*, a sanctuary located twenty clicks out of Nairobi.

MIT2 had returned to their base. The men were due to begin work later that day. As Lizzy worked at the orphanage, she was allowed to take Valentino out for the morning and had chosen a trip out to *The Giraffe Centre*. Johnny looked relieved to be back with his wife and with Valentino.

Charlie had fed the Rothschild's giraffes a literal bucket load of pellets. Now she'd run out of food, but two giraffes wouldn't leave her alone and ignored the other visitor's outstretched hands filled with pellets. Their long tongues played along her cheek and neck. Charlie's deep laugh had Donnie grinning in response. He snapped more photographs then stood back to enjoy the show.

Charlie was like damn Snow White. Animals followed her wherever she went. It was the oddest thing. When they'd visited an elephant sanctuary the day before—*The David Sheldrick Wildlife Trust*—a baby Ellie had veered away from his keeper to follow her around. Wild squirrels ran up to her on the walk around *The Giraffe Centre*, and the warthogs trotted behind her on the way up to the platform.

This was technically their third date over the last three days. Hanging with Charlie was fun. She never stopped smiling, and her innate curiosity with her surroundings fascinated Donnie.

One of the *Centre's* educators walked up to stand next to him. "Your woman has a way with the animals."

"I noticed." Donnie chuckled. "She's worked with animals all her life, plus she went to veterinary school, it's part of who she is."

The guide pointed at one of the taller giraffes. "That giraffe—allowing your girl to stroke her neck—is called Kelly. She doesn't come to visitors unless they have food, yet she's enjoying the attention. And the one giving her sloppy kisses is Salma. She's a love hog."

Donnie smiled. "The sanctuary looks well run. I believe the Rothschild's giraffe is endangered."

"It is. We've raised the numbers from 130 to 300 giraffe in various Kenyan parks."

On the other side of the deck, Valentino squealed in Johnny's arms and wriggled to climb down. "You dwopped it. It's gone. Get more. Get it."

Johnny laughed and grabbed another handful of pellets to feed to a huge male giraffe.

"Don't dwop them dis time. Feed him nicely." Valentino shook a finger in Johnny's face.

Donnie called to his teammate. "Yo, Johnny. I think the kid's gonna be as bossy as Charlie. You're whipped, man."

Johnny slipped him the middle finger, and Charlie stuck out her tongue.

At least Donnie received a response from Johnny, the giant. His friend had given him the cold shoulder since returning from the field. Donnie guessed it had something to do with the fact

277

that he'd knocked up Charlie—a woman who was like a sister to the big man.

They'd have a sit down at some point if Johnny didn't try to beat the shit out of Donnie first.

Despite the brotherly tension, Donnie enjoyed the day. He couldn't remember when he'd last had this much fun. After Sophie, happy moments hurt the most—the guilt of experiencing an inkling of joy after your beloved wife had suffered and passed away. So, Donnie had deprived himself of happiness. It served as a punishment of sorts. But as he stood there watching Charlie glow in the morning sun, laughing with Lizzy and tracing her stomach with a sure hand, he realized the guilt was no longer present.

"Valentino needs his lunch," Lizzy said as she walked to the stairs. "Let's head home. Plus, you guys will need to check in with Max."

Reluctantly Donnie filed in behind the petite blonde. Then he reached back and grasped Charlie's hand.

"My hand is covered in giraffe goo, are you sure you want to hold it that tightly?"

"That's what makes it all the more special."

Charlie smiled at his words. Johnny grunted from behind. You couldn't please everyone.

Lizzy's apartment.
Later that day.

Leaning over the balcony railing, Donnie watched the women playing soccer with Valentino in the dusty field below, admiring Charlie's sinewy lines. Donnie scanned the adjacent parking lot, not expecting any trouble but still searching.

"Sit your shifty butt down. We need to talk."

Johnny was ready to rip his ass in two. Donnie took his time settling in on the balcony chair opposite Johnny, and the stare off began.

"When did you decide to sleep with her and not use protection?"

"The night of the barbeque bash."

"You mean the night you brought your other girlfriend to my home?"

"When you say it like that…"

"Can I be honest?" Johnny asked.

"I thought that's what we were doing?"

"You're a standup guy, you're solid, and I trust you with my life. You also don't sleep around, and you're an honest and loyal individual."

"But?" Donnie asked, trying not to shift on the chair.

"Your head is fucked up, which means you're going to destroy Charlie."

"How can you say that?"

"Because I know you. You're barely standing after what happened with Sophie. It's taken you this long to start dating again."

"You only see what I choose to show you, and you don't know what Charlie means to me." Donnie rubbed a knuckle with his thumb.

"Then tell me."

Donnie kept quiet. His jaw ticked as he glared at the potted plant in the corner.

"She's having your baby. Are you ready for marriage? Another marriage to someone other than Sophie?"

"Screw off. What do you want? Would you prefer that I walk

away? Charlie needs me—"

"Bullshit." Anger smoldered in Johnny's golden eyes. "She's strong enough to raise this kid on her own. I'm guessing she'd rather do that, then marry a guy who doesn't love her as much as she loves him. And shit, dude, she straight up loves you."

"You don't know that. What do you know about her? You were away for the last decade of her life. She's had to carry everything on her own." Donnie saw surprise registering in Johnny's eyes, but he couldn't think past the rage. "Where were you when the farm nearly went under, or when Jack got sick, when a first date assaulted her."

"What?"

"Or when she got canc… never mind."

"Got what?"

"Nothing."

Johnny stood, his lips thinning. "No. Tell me. Tell me before I pound you into the floor. Got the what? Were you about to say cancer? Fucking cancer?"

"She didn't want you to worry." Donnie stood and ran a hand over his mouth.

"Charlie had cancer? The hell she did. You're a damn liar." Fury yielded to shock and Johnny grabbed the railing as he staggered back.

"I wish it were a lie. I want her to be my wife. Both she and the baby need to be on my health insurance. If her cancer returns…"

"You told him?" Charlie stood in the passage, and Donnie's heart stuttered at the look on her face.

"Sharls. What are you doing here?"

"I came to change my shoes. You told Jamie about my cancer. How could you? I told you that in confidence." Her eyes darkened with pain.

"Sharls, I didn't mean to."

"Charlie, how could you not tell me. When was this?" Johnny's broad chest heaved like he'd run a marathon.

Donnie didn't like her sudden gray pallor. "Honey, sit down. Let me grab you something to drink."

"I don't want anything from you—not water or an apple juice or a damn marriage. I don't need your hefty insurance. You can stick it up your bum along with that snotty carrot."

"I know you're mad—"

"I'll marry you… when you tattoo my name on your stupid ass. Until then, you and that sneaky mouth can leap off the balcony." She turned and stalked out the front door.

Johnny grabbed Donnie's arm as he pushed past. He looked as shell-shocked as Charlie. "What kind of cancer? Is she still sick?"

"No. She's been in remission for the past six years. She had breast cancer, that's why she had a reconstruction."

"I had no idea. I thought she'd had implants, but I wasn't sure and I didn't want to ask. She never seemed sick."

"She hid it well. Listen, this is a conversation you'll need to have with her. I need to make things right." Pulling his arm away, Donnie exited the apartment and ran down the stairs.

How had he let the cancer thing slip? Donnie guarded everything that came out of his mouth. He'd gotten defensive and let emotion take over, and now he'd hurt her. His betrayal stung, and he'd do anything to make it right.

He caught a glimpse of her scarlet hair in the parking lot, and then saw the tall blond man holding her by the arm and shuffling her towards a Toyota. Donnie took off, drawing his handgun. He stumbled over the pavement in his haste to catch up. Her captor turned her around, and Donnie caught a glimpse of her face just as Donnie raised his weapon.

She was smiling. Then the target pulled her in for a hug. Re-holstering his Glock, Donnie walked up to the embracing couple.

"Everything all right, Sharls?" Fingertips still tingled from adrenaline.

Pulling away, she turned to introduce her companion. "This is my brother, Nate, and my mother, Darla."

An elegant blonde woman slid out of the car and stood. She wore a tailored navy dress. Aside from the mouth and nose, she looked nothing like Charlie. Her collarbone stood out along with emaciated cheekbones. The woman had obviously starved herself, and Donnie wondered if it had to do with her Hollywood lifestyle.

Darla swung a strappy Gucci-looking bag over her shoulder and gave him the once over, pausing at his crotch area before focusing back on Charlie. Why did Donnie suddenly feel defiled? He ignored the urge to cover his family bits.

Nate sidled near. His hair, a white blond. His complexion seemed pallid next to Charlie who had a natural tan to her skin whereas her brother looked practically anemic. "Ignore her," Nate said. "Mother likes young meat. She's a predator and always looking for her next meal." Brown eyes twinkled, and those reminded him of Charlie. The combination of pale hair and brown eyes was a rare trait. Charlie's mother shared the same mix.

"Nate, don't be cruel." Darla glared his way "You only have one mother."

"Yes, and I'm stuck with her for life."

Charlie looked down, hiding the hurt. Donnie had a feeling that Nate purposely placed the jab.

"How did you know that Charlie was here?" Donnie asked.

Charlie folded her arms. "I called them and explained what happened. They've arrested Billings, and I needed to speak to my family. I also called Elana to see how she's doing. Atlas gave me her number."

Darla wrung bejeweled hands together. "We were all worried. Nate says all your farm hands and the whole town were in a tizzy when the Moroccan authorities contacted Zach's mother. I feel bad for that family. When you disappeared, we were beside ourselves. I went straight back to the farm—to Nate. When Charlotte called, we came running."

That seemed odd. They'd never bothered with her in the past, and now they scurried to her side?

"Where are you staying?" Charlie asked. "And for how long?"

"At the Hilton, and for as long as you need us."

"Mummy," Nate said. "that's not true. You need to fly back for that shareholder's meeting on Friday."

Darla nodded. "We'll be staying for two days."

Nate looked at Donnie. "Now, who are you and what do you want with my sister?"

The second grilling of the day, except this time Donnie had little respect for his interrogator. But before he could strike, Charlie dropped the baby bomb.

"He's the father to your niece... or nephew. We haven't found out the sex yet." She smiled at the angular woman beside her. "Congratulations, Darla. You're going to be a grandmother."

What Donnie wouldn't have given to snap a picture of the horrified look on Darla's face at that exact moment.

◊ ◊ ◊

Donnie left with Johnny for the afternoon. He was back in work mode, and Charlie doubted that she would see much of him before she left for the States. Lizzy mentioned that they might go back to Sudan later in the week. It was better that way. Charlie needed to focus on her next steps and not on the handsome brute. The future of her little jellybean depended on the goals she'd now set.

She'd never used her vet technician degree, and although she wanted to work with animals, she wasn't sure about being a technician. If she could sell the farm for a reasonable price, then perhaps she might consider going back to college to study veterinary science. Opening a practice one day seemed appealing. It would be a long road, but it was a dream she'd had all her life.

Perhaps she could open an online antique weapon store on the side. That would be fun. She'd built a small collection and had vendors she could contact. And where would she live? She'd always wanted to experience city life, but nothing too overwhelming. Maybe Denver or Salt Lake City?

Charlie couldn't sit down with her thoughts until her family went on their merry—more like miserable—way.

They'd insisted on accompanying Lizzy and Charlie to the orphanage to drop Valentino off, but the pair hovered near the car the entire time.

Now the four of them sat down to dinner at some fancy restaurant that Nate had read about online. Charlie had to admit that the food was good, but she preferred a burger at Lizzy's friend's place downtown. Nate worked through a seafood platter, and the fishy aroma made Charlie want to dry heave, the smell reminding her of the floor of the motorboat in Morocco. She ignored the memories flashing through her mind.

The awkward evening dragged on. Darla spoke about her

latest facelift, and Nate bragged about how well his restaurants were doing. Then they moaned about the facilities in their hotel. Not once did they ask Lizzy about her life or make any effort to catch up with Charlie, or ask about her pregnancy. How was she even related to these shallow pricks?

They meant well. She'd visited them in California a couple of times but could only take them in small increments. She should never have told Nate where she was staying. Trying to clear her mind of toxic thoughts, Charlie re-focused on their conversation. They loved her in their way, and she felt guilty for judging them.

"Did you speak to Charlotte about your proposal?" Darla asked Nate.

"What proposal?" Charlie sat up, taking shallow breaths. Nate's half empty plate sat under her nose. She glanced around for a waiter to remove the dinner course. Her jellybean reacted to the smell of lobster and Charlie needed air.

"Not yet, Mother." Nate fingered the rim of his wine glass and turned to Charlie. "I'm thinking of opening a restaurant in Jackson Hole."

"Good for you. It will do well over the tourist season." Charlie smiled as she stretched her back.

"What kind of restaurant?" Lizzy—who'd been unusually quiet—asked.

Nate barely glanced her way. "French."

"Like those fancy Parisian places that offer a mouthful of pate on a leaf of lettuce? Or the more rustic restaurants that serve larger organic dishes like from the South of France? You know— roasts… stews… cheeses… vegetable soups."

If looks could shred, Lizzy would be dead. Charlie smothered a giggle then answered her friend's question. "The former. My brother excels in sprigs and leaves and fancy contemporary concoctions."

"Charlie, just because you don't like the food… I'm a Michelin Chef. I've served the president." His face turned ruddy.

"I'm sorry. I'm just teasing."

"I'm trying to make a point—if I'm going to be staying in Jackson, why not the farm?"

"Um. Okay."

"We're thinking of pulling down the old farmhouse and building something better," Darla said, folding the napkin in her lap.

Charlie couldn't think of anything better than the humble and warm home where she'd grown up. Bile rose as she thought of her father's house being torn down. Yes, she wanted to sell, but it would be to a local farmer like her father — someone who'd farmed the land for generations and would continue the legacy. Her current staff members could retain their jobs, and the land would be preserved.

Nate took a sip of his wine. "We could sell the sheep and most of the land. There are plenty of developers looking at that prime location."

"That's my land. Daddy left it to me. Can someone remove these plates?" Charlie pushed Nate's plate towards the center of the table.

Her mother leaned and grasped Charlie's hand. "I know, sweetie, but our priority is your child. Let us help you to provide for the rascal. We could be a family again, just like before."

Charlie stared at the bony hand clutching hers. She'd wanted that for so many years—a mother by her side. Darla left without a backward glance when Charlie was twelve. She'd never bothered to visit, not even when Charlie was sick. As a teenager,

Charlie would watch the commercials where mothers and daughters baked together. There were kisses and laughs and hugs.

As Charlie stared at the manicured fingers stroking hers, she realized she would never have that. Darla wasn't capable of that kind of love. She wanted the farm because of her greed, not because she wanted to help Charlie in any way.

"I had a family. He died. Daddy was my mother and father and best friend, and I won't sell out his soul so that you can make a quick buck."

Darla withdrew her hand.

"Charlie, are you okay?" Lizzy asked. "You look pale."

"You're being unreasonable," Nate said to Charlie. "Grow up and accept our help."

"She doesn't have to accept anything," Lizzy said, standing. "And she's been through a lot over this past week. It's time for us to go. I'll call you both a taxi."

Nate's round face twisted in anger. "Who do you think you are, sweetheart? Don't stick your nose into family business."

Charlie stood, and her knees felt weak. She swiped at her damp forehead. Did they not run air conditioning in the place?

"She is family," Charlie said. "She's Jamie's wife."

"I don't need a stranger telling me what to do, and who the hell is Jamie?"

"The man who's more of a brother than you'll ever be." Charlie grasped the table.

"Charlotte!" Darla threw down her napkin. Her mother's antics had little effect as the room spun. Charlie felt herself slide sideways. Lizzy yelped. Plates and glassware crashed, and the world went dark.

Chapter Twenty-Five

Donnie rushed from the elevator and zeroed in on Lizzy. "Where is she?"

"Relax, she just fainted. She fell pretty hard, so they're checking her out."

He barged past as Johnny came up from behind. The couple then joined him at the nurse's station.

"Charlotte Quinn. I'm her fiancé."

Donnie ignored the tension rolling off his teammate. "Fiancé huh?" Johnny muttered then said to the nurse, "I'm her brother, and this is my wife."

The nurse directed them to a curtained area, and Donnie rushed down the passage.

"Fudgebuckets," he heard Lizzy mutter from behind. "This isn't going to go well."

Donnie pushed the curtain aside and visually ran over the woman in the bed. He couldn't see any apparent injuries, but her eyes filled when she saw him. Charlie never cried. Ignoring etiquette, he shoved her brother aside and grasped her hand. Darla stood at the head of the bed like a matriarch.

"What the hell? Did you push me out of the way?" Nate said as he shifted around the cot.

"Are you okay? Where do you hurt?" Donnie asked as he stroked her cheek.

"I'm fine, I passed out. It was stupid. I've already had the ultrasound. Jellybean is perfect. I couldn't get air, and the fishy smells made me ill. Fainting can happen in a pregnancy."

"Aside from the fight with your family," Donnie said.

Charlie winced. "Lizzy told you? I feel bad that you left work to come here."

Johnny stepped in. "Hey, bruiser, how do you feel?"

"Jamie. I feel fine, ready to break out of this joint."

"This is Jamie," Nate said with a sneer.

"You've met him before, plonker. At least a couple of times." Charlie glared, and the heart rate monitor sped up.

"Okay. We're done for the evening." Donnie faced Nate. "You're upsetting Charlie; it's time for you to leave. If you want to see her in the morning—before your flight—then your attitude needs to change."

"You're issuing orders? This is our fault?"

Donnie stepped up in her brother's face. "Charlie may have fainted from the pregnancy, but you did nothing to help. That's my child that you're putting at risk. If you flew over to Nairobi to offer her support, then offer support. Otherwise go home."

Nate responded to the alpha vibes pouring off Donnie and stepped back. "Charlie, we'll swing by in the morning to say goodbye. Get some rest." Darla pecked Charlie on the cheek.

Donnie didn't relax until the duo were gone.

"Wow," Charlie said. "You faced down the Piranhas. Impressive."

"I don't like speaking to your family that way, but your health comes first."

"Sorry that I blabbed, and told the guys," Lizzy said from the corner. "I didn't like the way they treated you at dinner."

"Or you," Charlie said as she raised herself to a sitting position. "That's what made me angry. You didn't deserve that. I guess a general apology is in order. I have a messed-up family. I'm sorry, peeps."

"Phewy. You're calling me messed-up?" Johnny grinned, and Charlie smiled back.

Later that night, Donnie led Charlie to the bed in Lizzy's spare room.

"I don't need a shadow. I'm fine. Just tired. And I'm sorry for dragging you away from your secret spy work."

"It's all good. We were just prepping equipment."

She settled under the covers, and Donnie sat beside her, noticing the dark shadows beneath her eyes and the sad droop to her shoulders.

"They hurt you."

"I always dream of a life where they care. I realized tonight that it's a foolish fantasy. I'll never understand them, and they'll never love me."

Donnie's chest tightened. At that moment—as she looked down and her lashes traced her cheeks, and as a small frown creased her pretty forehead—he knew he loved her. Standing, he turned to the wall and placed his hands on his hips. How could that be? He wasn't supposed to fall in love. Never again. When Lizzy had called Johnny to say that Charlie had collapsed at a restaurant, Donnie experienced a helpless terror that he hadn't known since Sophie's death.

He shouldn't be here. Loving Charlie wasn't meant to be.

"Donnie, are you okay?"

"Fine… I'm good." He could barely utter the words. "I need to go… I have work stuff to do."

"It's midnight."

"Yeah. Uh… well, Max asked me to come in and finish some paperwork."

"Okay."

He couldn't look her way. If he did, he'd never leave, and they needed distance, he needed space.

"You take care. I'll check in tomorrow." He waved a hand in her vague direction and almost ran from the room.

You take care?

Charlie frowned over Donnie's words for the hundredth time.

You take care.

Who said that? Ninety-year-olds about to hang up the phone? Long-distance pen pals who skype once a month? An insurance broker talking to his customers? Donnie Wilson—of all people—told her to take care? Charlie mulled over the words as she climbed out of the shower and got dressed in sweats. Pulling her hair into a messy bun, she stared out the window and marveled at the bright clouds drifting across the morning sky.

You take care.

Oh, she'd take care all right. She'd take care of herself and the little tyke sprouting body parts within her. They'd be just fine. She was never good at man-game-speak. Hot and cold bullshit wasn't her thing. He should take care. If he pissed her off enough, he'd get a knee to his nuts. Shaking off her frustration, Charlie walked to the kitchen to cook up some breakfast. Jamie leaned against the counter, smiling and drinking a coffee.

"You look pleased about something."

"I just love my wife." Jamie smiled.

"I don't want to hear about your bedroom gymnastics. I'm queasy enough as it is."

Jamie shrugged. "How do you feel?"

"Better after a good night's sleep, and I'm tired of hearing that question." She placed a pan on the stove and turned to stare at him. "So, do I call you Jamie or Johnny?"

"Whatever you want. James is my name. Johnny is my call sign."

"Lizzy calls you John."

"She does. It's the name I used when we first met."

Charlie listened as she slid butter into the pan.

"Why didn't you tell me about the cancer?"

"Jamie, why didn't you tell me you were married?"

"I'm serious. You could've died."

Charlie paused. "What would you have done? You would have quit the military to take care of me and I would've destroyed your dreams."

"Probably. It doesn't make this any easier. I failed you. I've failed the only family I've ever had—aside from Lizzy."

"You didn't know."

"That one time I saw you—just after your twenty-first birthday—you'd cut your hair in a pixie cut, and I asked if you were on a diet. You were skinny. I should've known you weren't yourself. Were you still in treatments?"

"No. That was six months after my last chemo session. It all happened forever ago."

"I was gone a long time, and I neglected the farm and my family." Swallowing, he placed down his coffee.

Charlie walked over and slipped a hand around his waist. "You're the best brother in the world. Even if we're not blood relatives, you'll always have my back, and I'll have yours."

Jamie wrapped her up in a bear hug, and Charlie squeezed him as hard as she could.

"You're the only woman that's allowed to hug my beast of a husband," Lizzy said as she walked into the kitchen with mussed hair, old leggings, and a Nirvana shirt. "And don't stop. I want in on the action."

She wrapped tiny arms around them both, then began to tickle.

"Shit." Jamie jumped away.

"He's ticklish," Lizzy said grinning before he swept her up and swung her over broad shoulders.

"I'll give you ticklish." Jamie chuckled.

Charlie avoided the wrestling match and got back to cracking eggs when the phone on the wall rang.

Jamie answered, comfortably holding a giggling Lizzy in one arm.

He swore and gently placed his wife back down. "It's Nate and Darla. Do you want to speak to them?"

"Damn. Let them up." Charlie took the eggs off the stove.

Two minutes later, the duo stepped into the passage.

Her mother gave Charlie's sweats a disapproving look. "Have you just risen?"

"Nope. Had a shower and I'm relaxing for the day."

"Aside from teaching me how to belly dance," Lizzy called from the kitchen.

"We came to apologize," Nate said, scratching an ear. "We don't want to leave on bad terms. And you're always welcome to come and visit us in Cali—bring the kid."

Charlie nodded politely. "Do you want some breakfast?"

"We'd better go, don't want to miss the flight." Darla reached out and then pulled back.

"Oh, for God sakes, Mom." Charlie pulled her in for a quick hug.

With uncomfortable goodbyes all around, her family walked to the car. Charlie watched them drive off. Back to limbo, except she needed to move on with life. Her father was gone, and she had new responsibilities. Peter Billings sat in jail. The only reason that Charlie hung around Nairobi was to be close to Donnie. She'd never chased a man—her desperate craving for his love needed to stop. She couldn't compete with his past and never wanted to.

Charlie needed a distraction. Staring at the walls wouldn't do, and Lizzy had bought a light-dancing poi kit online. Instead of juggling fire, she'd juggle psychedelic lights on a staff attachment. Eager to learn Charlie's trade, Lizzy had bounced up and down with the Amazon delivery.

Charlie could use the kit and an additional plain staff to practice her dance moves. She wouldn't overdo it, and she wouldn't juggle fire while pregnant. Fuel vapors and risks of getting singed weren't worth risking the baby. If Charlie received a bad burn, she couldn't get it treated properly until after the birth. Not that she'd received any injuries in the past, only a mild first-degree charring once when she'd first started using real fire. For the next six months—or longer—psychedelic light dancing would have to do.

After breakfast, Charlie grabbed the box of equipment and chose the soccer field as their practice area. Lizzy was a natural and a bit of a clown. Charlie laughed at her friend's antics and finally relaxed under the shade of a Jacaranda Tree.

Two days later.

He missed the hell out of her. How had they grown so close? Donnie went back to gathering Intel on a new terrorist cell in Ethiopia. He still sat in the briefing room. MIT2 had just finished with a rundown of the prep they'd need to do before leaving their forward operating base, and heading to Jimma in three days. Donnie couldn't focus on anything else but the scarlet-haired woman on the other side of town. It had been another long day and Johnny was tired of relaying constant updates to Donnie on what Charlie was doing.

They stayed in the same city, yet he avoided Charlie like she was a Medusa. Donnie tapped his finger on his keypad and stared down the long, empty conference table. He allowed his mind to drift over the last two weeks—from the moment he'd seen her lying on the dusty ground in Ait Benhaddou to their mad rush to the embassy. He thought about her bright smile and vanquishing attitude, how she'd kept up through alleys and markets and down river creeks.

His mind turned to Peter Billings. According to Wyoming authorities, Peter Billings still denied taking out the contract. Donnie had run a background check on Billings, but something didn't feel right. From their brief encounter, Donnie profiled the man as being a hands-on bully who would do his own dirty work. He came from a wealthy family in Jackson and did have the financial means to take out a hit. Deciding to dig deeper, Donnie sifted through files. With military grade access and his hacking prowess, Donnie finally paused on what he needed. He leaned back and swore. Johnny and Max walked in at that exact moment.

"Hey, analyst asshole, you look beat," Johnny said to Donnie.

"Are you getting any sleep?"

"Donnie, what's up." Max was already sitting beside him. Reading body language and emotion was Max's specialty, and he focused in on Donnie's concern. Donnie returned Max's pale regard and said, "I've fucked up."

Chapter Twenty-Six

Donnie needed to be logical. He swallowed down the panic and rubbed a hand over his face.

"How?" Max asked.

"We've got the wrong man."

"I gather we're talking about Charlie's case."

Donnie nodded as Johnny took the other seat. "Let us help, man. What do you have?"

"Peter Billings has never traveled out of the Midwest. He doesn't even have a passport. His parents have their travel documents but not him. They interviewed a friend of Billings this morning, and the guy says that Peter is deathly afraid of flying. Two months ago, he'd even refused to fly to Vegas for a boy's weekend."

"And that means?" Max asked.

"If he didn't open the Swiss bank account, then who did?"

"Do you think his father is working with him?"

Johnny interrupted. "I know his father well. He's a standup guy. He doesn't want anything to do with the kid."

"How did the money appear in an account in Peter Billings' name?" Max asked.

Donnie slammed a fist on the table. "Billings was set up to take the fall."

Max rubbed a brow. "Okay, so the question is, by whom? Who has the most to gain by Charlie's death?"

"Her mother or her brother?" Donnie said immediately.

"The farm was left entirely to Charlie?" Max asked.

"Yes," Johnny replied. "Her father disowned the rest of her family. I don't know of any extended family."

Max rubbed his chin. "And if she dies? Where does the land go?"

"I don't know, but we'll uncover the truth." Donnie picked up the phone and dialed her new burner phone's number. "No answer."

"I'll call Lizzy," Johnny said. "She's heading to the orphanage this evening, but I might be able to catch her."

They waited in rigid silence. Johnny hung up. "No luck. Are we taking a drive into town?"

Donnie was already standing and addressed Max. "Sir?"

"Move your asses. I'll handle the meeting with the Colonel."

They'd scheduled an online briefing with their MIT boss. All Donnie could focus on was Charlie's safety, but he paused and turned to Johnny. "Do you know who the executor is handling Jack's estate?"

"I think it's Sutherland Estates. Charlie mentioned their name once."

"Leave it up to me," Max said. "I'll learn who the second beneficiary is on his will. I'll contact the firm then I'll call you."

Donnie knew that Max wouldn't fail. He'd use any means possible to find that name; threats be damned. The two men took a minute to grab some gear—rifles, handguns, and knives. Johnny climbed in the passenger seat as Donnie started the truck. "The girls are probably practicing their dance moves. Lizzy's decided she likes the belly dancing. I don't have the heart to tell her that she looks like a teeny fairy—shaking her hips—and trying to sprout wings. Dude, it's fucking cute."

Donnie tried to smile, but the lead ball in the pit of his stomach made him want to hurl. "Try her again. I'll call Charlie."

Both phones went unanswered, and Donnie tried not to lose his shit. The big warrior beside him shifted restlessly. "Speed up."

"I have," Donnie said as he negotiated the dark streets.

Johnny tried Lizzy again, and this time she answered. The call filtered through the speakers.

"Where are you, Lizbug?"

"I'm heading back home to the apartment. I've just left Valentino. I know you've told me not to travel at night, but I ran late and—"

"Is Charlie at home?"

"Yeah. I left her snoozing on the couch."

"Sweetie, I don't want you going home. We're checking on her; she may be in trouble. Can you head to the base? I'll meet you there later."

Lizzie had visited the forward operating base a couple of times. Johnny liked her knowing where it was in case of emergencies. Due to extremist threats, Nairobi wasn't always the safest city. After she'd agreed and they'd hung up, Johnny relaxed slightly. He still looked like Donnie felt and instinct screamed for Donnie to get to Charlie.

Five minutes out, and his phone buzzed. *Max.*

"Talk to me."

"You ain't gonna believe who's second in line for that damn farm, and I checked flight records. The fucker has been in Nairobi for the past two days."

Max said the name and Donnie's muscles locked. "Buckle up," he said to Johnny as he pushed his foot down on the accelerator.

◊ ◊ ◊

After Lizzy left in the late afternoon, Charlie decided on a quick nap in front of the television, only waking when it was dark outside. Thanks to the pregnancy, all Charlie wanted to do was sleep. She stood from the sofa, looked down and grinned. Lizzy must be rubbing off on her. Charlie wore mismatched fluffy socks, pink sweatpants, and a purple tank top. At least she still wore a bra.

A glass of orange juice quenched her thirst. Charlie grabbed a handful of grapes from the fridge and decided to head to the balcony. Sitting down, Charlie acknowledged the fact that Donnie had entered the freak-out phase of the relationship with the mother of his child. He was officially ghosting her. She knew it would happen, but it still hurt. She also knew that he needed time. He'd come around—at least as a father. He'd never neglect his kid, Donnie wasn't built that way. Their child would have a loving father, but it would've been nice if he felt the same way about Charlie.

She was over waiting and crushing on a man that kept her at arm's length. You couldn't make someone love you, and Charlie was done trying. It was time for her to leave and face all her responsibilities back home.

The doorbell rang, and Charlie stretched before walking to the door. It was strange that the guard hadn't rung up from the front gate, but maybe it was a neighbor. She looked through the peephole and growled before throwing open the door.

"Holy crap. What the hell are you doing here?"

"I came to see how you're doing."

Charlie gaped at the man in the doorway. "Earl, who the hell is taking care of my farm?"

He stepped in for a hug, pulling her against his broad chest. "God, it's good to see you, I was so worried." The smell of pine and soap wrapped her up in the comforts of home and Charlie squeezed back. Not only was Earl her foreman, but he was a good friend who'd worked tirelessly to help with the farm. He had an old school work ethic which she appreciated. His loyalty over the years earned him a place as her father's sidekick, and that made her frown. Why would he abandon the farm he so clearly loved, to climb on a plane and fly halfway around the planet. As far as she knew, the furthest he'd ever traveled was to his vacation cabin in Colorado.

Earl let go and slipped past into the passage. "I'm darn thirsty. Tell me you have beer."

"You're not getting anything until you tell me why you're in Kenya and not looking after my livestock in Wyoming."

"Relax, I've left Butch in charge," Earl said, and he scratched an unshaven cheek.

"Butch is a lazy nincompoop."

"He's learning. Besides, it's only for a few days. I'm heading back tomorrow." Earl prowled the living room then wandered down the passage to the bedrooms. His large stature consumed too much space in Lizzy's tiny apartment.

"What are you doing?"

"Checking out your digs. Are you alone?"

"Um, yeah. Why?"

"No reason. We need to connect." He opened up the fridge and took out a beer. "You want one?"

"No. I'm pregnant."

Earl froze, then slowly closed the fridge. "You're shitting me."

Something about him seemed different, and Charlie had the urge to pick up the nearby broom and chase him out the door. That sudden swaggering arrogance seemed out of character to the man she'd worked alongside for many years. Earl wandered into the living room and chose a sofa. "Sit, Charlie. We need to talk."

He was now issuing orders? Holding onto her temper, Charlie chose a seat opposite and leaned her elbows on her knees. "I'm not sure what's going on, I trusted you with my staff and livestock. I'll need to book the soonest flight out to sort out your mess."

He didn't say anything, just raised a brow.

"I pay you handsomely. I'm not unreasonable. Earl, why are you here?"

He placed the beer bottle carefully on the table before leaning back. "Do you know how your father found me? Why he hired me all those years ago?"

"He never told me. I'm assuming that you answered an ad in the local paper?"

"Your land was once mine."

Charlie couldn't suppress a snort. "That was old Tom's land. His family farmed it for generations."

"Most of your acreage is Tom's, but a small portion belonged to my father. Originally to my grandfather. I grew up in beautiful country and had a tough but happy childhood, until our herd of sheep fell prey to Thin Ewe Syndrome. Disease wiped them out and left us with nothing."

"I had no idea. I'm sorry."

"I'd just graduated college. Jack swept in like a superhero and offered to buy the land. My foolish father said yes and gave away our Teton legacy to buy that fancy cabin in Colorado. Jack offered me a job, and I turned it down. I told him I wanted to travel throughout the Western states."

Charlie didn't know what to say. His underlying bitterness seemed apparent. Feeling cornered, she scanned the room for her phone. She wanted to call Donnie and remembered leaving the device on the bed in the spare room. Continuing his story, Earl watched her intently.

"I have an aunt that lives in Tuscany. We rarely saw her, but she invited me over to Italy when she'd heard about the land sale. She runs a stud farm, and I spent two years learning how to breed and raise horses. I also visited nearby countries and made many friends. My favorite spot is Malta—beautiful—don't you think? Only a stone's throw from Italy."

Swallowing past a suddenly dry mouth, Charlie tried to stand.

"Don't twitch. Sit back down."

The large revolver suddenly pointing her way had Charlie complying.

"I lived a good life in a pretty villa. I drank wine, studied poetry, ate cheese and pasta. But I couldn't let it go—the land that was rightfully mine was gone."

"It was a fair sale."

"Except no-one consulted me." Earl stood and towered above her. "That's the place where I was born, and I fucking tried to buy it back. When my daddy died from a heart attack and I returned to the States for the funeral, figured I'd become your father's best friend and work by his side. After you came along, I made him an offer on a thousand acres, but he whined about building a home for you and your spoilt brother. So, I waited and got rid of your brother when the time was right. Hoped I'd killed him in the accident."

"What are you talking about?" Charlie said in a choked voice.

"The night of your car accident. Nate wasn't drunk. He'd had two beers. I spiked one of them."

"You were responsible for the crash? You shitting asshole," Charlie said in a clipped voice.

"You both survived, but at least your daddy dearest disowned Nate. I felt bad about almost killing you. You were a sweet kid and you made me care. Nate was a dick from day one, but 'Charlotte Quinn' was the apple of Jack's eye, and I couldn't get rid of you in the same way. I hated that I prayed you'd die when you got sick. I thought about poisoning you, except your father never left your side. I never could quite build up the courage to kill you myself. There are so many accidents that can happen on a farm. You made me damn care, Charlie—up until the day your father told me that you would sell the farm after his death."

His confession made her ill and Charlie gripped the sofa, trying not to panic.

"Before that, I thought maybe we could get together. We'd marry and I'd have my land back and a hardworking wife by my side. We could have a family of our own. The land would keep the Taylor name, and everybody would win."

Was he crazy? He was old enough to be her uncle—he'd been like an uncle. She'd never sent any romantic vibes his way. Not even remotely shown an interest in the older overseer. How had she worked alongside such a delusional monster, and never seen the madness lurking beneath?

"And Jack was all good with you selling his pride and joy. He didn't care if you sold my land. It was all about your fucking happiness."

"If you'd come to me and explained your situation, I

would've given back your land," Charlie said.

"Bull crap. You want to sell."

Charlie spoke carefully. "I do want to sell, but you were like family. I'm not as stubborn as my father, and if I'd known your history, I would've gladly helped."

Earl frowned and shook his head as if clearing a mental fog.

"How do you know the Cominos?" she asked.

"Luca was a friend of my aunt's. When you thought I was on my annual vacation in Colorado, I traveled to Europe a month before your trip. Setting up Peter Billings was pretty easy. Luca helped. I planted the seed in your dying daddy's head—wouldn't a ticket to Malta be nice for poor hardworking Charlie? If you died overseas, the authorities wouldn't trace your accidental death back to the farm. And how do you think your father came by those old books on Maltese Knights? I brought them from Italy with me when you were just a babe. Your father assumed that they came from my father's cabin in Colorado. Like Jack, I love collecting history books. I gave them away when I ran out of space."

Charlie's phone rang in the bedroom. The fear for her child and Earl's warning glance held her immobile.

"If you die, I'll inherit the estate—all of it. Now stand up." He wrenched her around the coffee table, his fingers marking her arm with an iron grip.

"Where are you taking me?"

"We're going for a walk. The field below is nice and quiet."

"You're going to shoot me on the soccer field?"

"I'm not going to shoot you, honey. You decided to practice your fire dancing all by yourself. I'm going to light you on fire and watch you burn."

Chapter Twenty-Seven

Johnny slipped in the key and slowly turned the lock. Pushing the door open, Donnie took point and eased up the passage. Only the hum of the fridge broke the silence. An open Windhoek beer sat on the coffee table, and the balcony sliding door stood open. Moving quickly and both carrying M4s, the men cleared the apartment. Nothing.

"Buddy, calm down," Johnny said, trailing behind Donnie as he stalked to the living room. Donnie ran a hand down the side of the bottle, and his fingers came away wet.

"Obviously, that's not Charlie's. Earl was here, and we've just missed them."

Barely pausing, Donnie exited the home and raced down the stairs. He ran through the parking lot towards the guard's room at the boom gate and check-in point. Like in many African cities, with apartment blocks and Western housing, security checkpoints protected the residents. High walls, barbed wire and alarm systems surrounded the apartment complex. The only way that Earl could leave was through the front gates.

Wrenching the door open, Donnie pulled the guard from the hut.

"Jesus!" Johnny said as Donnie held the struggling guard by

his collar, while fishing in his own pocket for his phone.

Donnie addressed the struggling man. "Don't move. I'm asking questions. There's been a break-in while you've been sitting on your ass. You know this woman?" He shoved his phone in the guard's face.

"Yes…y… yes. She's Miss Lizzy and Mr. Johnny's friend… like you are."

"Did you see her leave tonight?"

"No. Mr. Johnny, help."

"Hold him," Donnie said to Johnny. When the big warrior took over and spoke quietly to the guard, Donnie searched through social media sites until he found what he needed.

"This man? The one with the cowboy hat? Have you seen him? Look properly."

"Um. Maybe. Earlier. He drove in behind a delivery truck. I think. He had a mustache."

"When?" Donnie asked.

"Around lunch."

"Did you see him leave? What car was he driving?"

"He hasn't left. A black Honda Odyssey. Only the old lady from 307 and Miss Lizzy left so far this evening."

"Find it—in the lot—now."

Hurrying the guard along, they searched the rows. He pointed at the vehicle parked in a dark corner. Johnny thanked the guard and slipped him a generous wad of cash. They circled the locked vehicle. Donnie pulled out his knife and used the back end of the weapon to shatter the passenger window and search the car. What he saw on the floor of the back seat had terror slamming through his chest.

An open fuel container, wicks and fire dancing paraphernalia littered the vehicle.

Donnie scanned the area. "If they haven't left the compound, Earl has her nearby."

"Another apartment?"

Donnie shook his head. "He's setting up an accidental death. They'll be in an open area, a place where Charlie would normally practice."

Both men paused, then ran for the field below.

Movement on the opposite end caught Donnie's attention. A shape shifted under a far tree. Nodding to Johnny, they readied their weapons and split. Crossing the stretch of open ground would draw attention, and the target might panic. Donnie worked the shadows on the periphery, frustrated with the delay. Rushing in like a raging lunatic would get Charlie killed.

Earl Taylor had shitty situational awareness, his entire focus was on Charlie. Donnie's heart thumped painfully as he took in her predicament. Earl had taped her arms in front of her with duct tape. Her feet were also bound together. She sat on the fuel-soaked ground. The noxious liquid dripped from her drenched hair as her captor hovered like a rabid predator. Earl held a lit wick on a dancing staff, and a large gas container lay on its side nearby. He still stood too close; the fumes could catch the flame at any moment.

Earl twirled the wooden pole standing beyond the circle of fuel, as he spoke. "Do you think I want your money? You want to sell my rights. It's my fucking property, and you have no right. That land is more valuable than all of us combined. It will live on for decades, millenniums to come, worth way more than your dirty family."

The guy was insane, and that made Donnie's job more difficult. Earl wouldn't back down which left Donnie in a dangerous corner.

"I just care about my baby," Charlie begged the crazy cowboy, her voice croaking through the fumes. "Please, I'll give you whatever you want. Don't hurt my angel. Please, Earl."

"It's too late. I'm sorry it must be such a painful death. This way, no-one will ever know."

"I will." Donnie stepped into the moonlight. "And so will James. He's standing somewhere to your left."

"I'll burn her. One more step and I'm lighting this bonfire."

"Do it, and you die." If Donnie fired his rifle, the bullet wouldn't ignite the fuel, but a spark from the discharge might. The chances were low, but Donnie wouldn't risk Charlie's life on guesswork. And if he shot the target and the burning staff fell to the ground, it could be just as catastrophic. Any fuel splatter on the ground could trigger a fire ball.

For a second, Donnie took his eyes off the flaming stick and looked at the woman he loved. Time slowed as he absorbed every feature. She panted through parted lips while squinting through bloodshot eyes. The fucker had thoroughly soaked her in gasoline. Even if they exfiled her safely, the exposure could still harm her and the baby.

"I love you," she mouthed.

Fear blew his heart apart, and control shattered.

"Sharls. Get off the X," Donnie ordered, then moved quicker than he ever had in his life. He used his legs to launch forward, and rushed the target, plowing his shoulder into Earl's stomach while grabbing the wooden rod with his other hand. Both men flew back—away from the circle. Earl stumbled. In a fluid motion, Donnie twisted the bastard's arm, wrenching the staff away and tossed it with all his might. It landed thirty feet away from the fuel.

In Donnie's peripheral vision, he saw Johnny charging

towards Charlie who hopped then rolled away from the combustible ground. Johnny hoisted her up and kept running. Donnie rounded back on Earl who scrambled back and produced a gun from a belly holster. He tried to aim for Donnie but never got the chance. In one smooth move, knowing that Charlie was now safely away from the fumes, Donnie raised his weapon and blew a neat hole through Earl's forehead. The world didn't explode. Still, Donnie chose to step back—way back—before edging around to extinguish the burning staff.

◊ ◊ ◊

Jamie didn't pause, not even to look back when a shot was fired.

"Donnie," Charlie managed to whisper.

"He's fine. He can take care of himself." Jamie kept running. "We need to get you clean. Now Charlie."

She'd sat way too long after the fuel soaking, while Earl raged and ranted. Her skin felt like it was on fire and it hurt to breathe. Charlie took shallow breaths as her head bounced on Jamie's shoulder.

"Sharls!" Donnie called from somewhere behind them. "Sharls!"

Jamie ran up the steps and paused to kick in his door. Charlie vaguely wondered why he didn't use keys, but she guessed it was down to the urgency of the situation. He sat her on the toilet, pulled out a knife and sliced off the duct tape. Jamie then began ripping off her socks. "Get your clothes off, now." He coughed, she knew it was from the vapors.

Her head felt muggy and her lungs burned. Another set of hands grabbed at her shirt. "Johnny, call an ambulance. And get garbage bags for her clothes—and ours too. Call Max. We have that tango to deal with."

Jamie stepped outside as Donnie turned on taps and ripped Charlie's clothes off then lay her in the bath.

"Towels, face cloths." He called to Jamie, "Where's a fucking facecloth?"

Battling to draw in breath, Charlie gasped and coughed.

Jamie stepped in and pulled a bathroom cabinet open. Donnie grabbed a handful, then shoved one under the running water. He squeezed it out with shaking hands and gently wiped her face.

"Did you get fuel in your eyes?"

Charlie tried to talk but wheezed instead. She shook her head then attempted to speak again as he climbed, fully clothed into the tub. Donnie scrubbed her down with soapy water.

"Can't breathe."

"I know, shallow breaths." He poured a wad of shampoo in her hair. "You've breathed that toxic shit in. We'll get you to a hospital."

Charlie concentrated on pulling in air. Donnie held her to him and rinsed her off with the sprayer. Charlie closed her eyes against the spinning room. Her world tilted as her chest tightened.

"Sharls. Stay with me. Open those pretty eyes. Sharls."

His voice faded—splashes and shouts drifting away, as Charlie huffed out one small breath.

Chapter Twenty-Eight

Donnie stared at the numerous monitors. He didn't want to think about the past twelve hours. First the race to the private hospital, then she'd been torn away as they rushed her to a room. Next came the questioning. He'd been forced to leave and meet Max at a local police station. The big brass from Fort Bragg stepped in to defend their million-dollar soldier. Hours of questioning had Donnie almost howling to get back to the ward. Thankfully, they'd trained nearly every officer in the police station and MIT2 had built a personal relationship with the men. They'd let him return to Charlie.

After the Pulmonary Aspiration she'd experienced, Charlie was diagnosed with mild chemical pneumonitis from exposure to the fumes. They'd hooked her up to oxygen therapy and IV fluids. Thankfully she'd improved enough that the prognosis was good. They'd also checked the baby, which seemed in excellent health.

Donnie studied the sleeping patient and knew it was over. Charlotte Quinn had won. She had him firmly by the balls and Donnie couldn't imagine a world without his Firebird. Everything that came before Sharls seemed dull in comparison. She kept him on his toes, ready to spar and he loved every minute.

Donnie swept hair off her cheek and winced. Red patches marred her skin, places where the fuel had burnt and made its mark. Coughing through the mask, Charlie jerked awake and mumbled something. A struggle ensued where she tried to raise the mask and Donnie wrestled to keep it in place.

"Stop, you're such an annoying man."

"Keep the oxygen on."

"Bleh. I can't sleep with this shit on my face." Her voice sounded raspy, and her breathing—way too choppy.

"You slept just fine. A whole two hours that time."

"Are you sitting there watching me sleep—like a creepster-stalker?" she asked.

"I have nowhere else to be. Now put it back on."

"You're deploying to shadowy lands in a couple of days and—"

Donnie shoved the mask down.

"Yod nedgthral. I'm grong to beat yur ash."

Donnie chuckled. "Stop talking. I can't understand you."

She raised her hand and he lunged to place it back down. "Tell you what, you lie there like a good girl, and I might nibble your ear—like this."

He kissed her neck then worked his way up her jaw. She smelled like fresh shampoo and warm spice.

Relaxing back in the bed, Charlie allowed him to play with his lips and tongue. Occasionally she'd mumble inarticulate words when he found a sensitive spot. Her cute verbiage encouraged him to continue his trailblazing on her other side. He worked down her arm, avoiding the red and burnt areas and nipped the skin on her wrist. That earned another murmur. With a quick movement, he captured both her wrists in a firm hand and leaned over her masked face.

"Now that I have your full attention, I want you to know how much I love you."

Charlie gasped then choked into the mask.

"I know, it came as a surprise to me too. I don't know how I've lived this long without you." Donnie stroked her brow. "I already adore that kid growing inside, but nothing is more important to me than my Firebird. I experience life in an entirely new way with you, and I'm an idiot for not seeing your blazing beauty from the first moment. And... now that I've said my soppy shit, I'll need to check in with Max."

He planted a kiss to her forehead and stood. "I'll stop by later. Johnny—James is grabbing a coffee and then he'll be back by your side."

Charlie sputtered. As soon as Donnie let go of her hands, she yanked off the mask. He was halfway out the door.

"Did you just spring the L-word on me?"

"Yes, ma'am. I love the shit out of you. Now get some rest."

"Donnie!"

He ignored her shout and headed for the elevator. No longer trapped in the past, Donnie stared at a future so bright that it made his grinning face hurt with the widest of smiles.

Epilogue

Wyoming.
Three months later.

Donnie followed Johnny's truck into the drive and parked his SUV alongside, carefully avoiding the snowbank. Slater walked around the side of the cabin and thumped both operators on the back.

"Good to see you, brothers."

"No sling. Way to go, Slate." Johnny stepped back to study their former teammate.

Donnie liked what he saw. The arm looked functional, and Slater didn't look as pale. He'd also filled back out with muscle, but there was still a pinched look around his eyes.

"Bro, thanks for letting me crash at your cabin. I'll be heading back to Salt Lake tomorrow."

"Anytime," Johnny said. "When do you start the fancy new FBI job?"

"Next week. It's more a training gig. Thought I'd do a little hiking and snowshoeing before the big day."

Donnie looked in the direction of Charlie's farm, restless to find her. She'd sold the farm a month ago to a local farming friend, but still ran it until the day the new owner stepped in. Donnie would help her with the clean-up, chores and the transfer of ownership, but he first needed to get through something important.

"Does Lizzy know I'm here?" Johnny asked Slater. The guys wanted it to be a surprise.

"She has no clue. She's in your room getting ready for the *Jackson Hole Winter Fest*. We're planning on heading that way."

Lizzy had flown back to Wyoming—along with Charlie—in November to spend Christmas with her parents at the farm, while the men hunkered down in Ethiopia. And Johnny had good news for her; they'd been given the green light on the adoption papers and they'd fly back together to fetch Valentino in two weeks. They'd need to wait for his travel papers and passport.

Johnny turned to walk in with Slater, and Donnie caught his arm. "Can we talk, big man?"

Slater blew into his gloves. "It's fucking freezing out here, dude."

Donnie maintained eye contact with Johnny. "It's important."

"Give us a minute," Johnny said.

Slater ran up the porch and slipped inside. Donnie felt his lip twitch and sucked in a bracing breath. He willed his usually steady hands to stop shaking. The last three months—sleeping in tents and living on MRE's—were the longest of his life. Not being able to check in with Charlie had driven him insane. He'd spoken to her four times in twelve weeks. The last being when he'd landed back in Nairobi. The constant worry over the health of both her and the baby had drained him of all energy.

"You're a best friend and a brother. I'd kill for you and die for you."

"I know that, buddy. I'd do the same." Johnny patted him on the back.

Donnie sucked in a breath. "And I feel that way about Sharls. I can't imagine life without her, I love her so much. I'm asking for your blessing in marrying your sister."

Johnny stepped back, and opened his mouth to say something. He swallowed and ran hands through his hair. "Shit, man." He turned and walked in a circle.

Donnie swallowed past the lump in his throat. "Since she doesn't have her dad—and the other dickwads don't count—you'll be giving her away."

"Bro, I'd be honored to have you as my brother-in-law." Johnny pulled Donnie in for a firm hug. "And hell yeah, I'm walking Charlie down that aisle. She is my little sister in every way that counts."

"I fucking love you, man." Donnie squeezed his friend hard.

When they'd both gathered their composure, they headed indoors. Halfway down the stairs, Lizzy saw Johnny and ran squealing into his arms. Johnny kissed her hard on the mouth, then cupped her face and traced her cheeks. He kissed her again before pulling back. "He's ours."

"Uh, what?"

"Val is ours. We have our little Valentino."

Lizzy cupped her mouth as tears rolled down her cheeks. Johnny picked her up and swung her around. "We have our little man. God, I've missed you."

Donnie left them to hug it out and walked over to the kitchen. Slater ate a sandwich and threw back a glass of milk.

"Have you seen Charlie?"

"Sure, man," Slater said between bites. "She's in town already—warming up for her dance routine—that's where we were heading."

"Her what?"

"That fancy fire dancing shit."

"Wait, she's six months pregnant, and she's fire dancing?"

"I guess. The Winter Fest committee asked her to perform. It's in honor of her friend that passed away. She's due on stage in an hour."

"Oh, hell no." Donnie headed out the door to his SUV.

"You need me to ride shotgun?" Slater grinned as he carried his glass of milk and half-eaten sandwich to the car.

"Don't mess up my car with that shit. Milk and upholstery don't do well together."

"Copy. Hey, I know where she's setting up, I drove her equipment over earlier."

"Get in and keep that glass upright."

Donnie pulled onto the road as Slater barely kept the milk from spilling onto his lap. "Jesus, don't land us in a ditch."

Donnie ignored Slater as he negotiated the slippery roads. Slater downed the rest of the milk.

"So, Salt Lake, huh? Are you planning on seeing Kat?" Donnie asked.

"You had to say her name. Screw you."

"She was the best thing that ever happened to you."

Slater placed the now empty glass between his legs. "And I fucked it up. And then Kat had her revenge by giving me the giant finger from across the Atlantic—as I lay dying in Germany."

"Dying? That's a little dramatic."

"Yeah? Have you had your entire arm smashed to smithereens?"

"I'm sorry, man, I'm a dick. Listen. Reach out to her and take her for coffee. You never know. Look at Charlie and me. Four months ago, we wanted to scratch each other's eyes out."

"It's different." Slater stared out the window. Donnie wished he could take his friend's pain away. The PTSD and the heartache. But it was out of his hands, the only thing that mattered was getting his own girl and making her his wife.

Oranges and yellows swirled around her as Charlie flipped the staff. Due to the now substantial belly bump, she had to adjust her dance routine. She'd chosen a simple black outfit—flared tights, and a long-sleeved fitted shirt. Her hair pulled into a high bun gave her a ballerina vibe—aside from the watermelon silhouette extending from her abdomen.

Charlie loved this part of the routine. The swinging lights mesmerized the audience and put her in a similar trance. So what if she performed in a beer tent. With one last flourish, her routine ended. *That was for you, Zach.* It was the routine he'd created and performing it in his hometown felt right. The audience erupted.

His mother had elected not to come tonight, and Charlie didn't blame her. It was too painful. Perhaps in time, she'd sit down with his family and tell them what an incredible and brave friend he was.

Strong male arms reached up to help her off the stage, and Charlie rolled her eyes. They'd scheduled in this earlier performance that coincided with a group of male gymnasts that next took the stage. Charlie allowed the gymnasts to lift her down and they took a minute to compliment her performance.

One of the performers refused to let go of her hand. "You're incredibly talented. Maybe we can perform together sometime?"

"I already have a dance group." She tried to pull her hand from his monkey grip.

"But fire combined with gymnastics… I can teach you some moves," he said.

"I'll teach you some moves." Donnie slid between them. "Let go of her arm."

Charlie's heart turned over as she ran a hand down Donnie's spine. He was there, in the flesh. She barely noticed his silly testosterone posturing as she wrapped her free arm around his chest and stepped into his back. Donnie smelled male, all amber and wood.

The gymnast released her hand and stumbled over his apology. When he'd left, Donnie grasped her hand and brought it to his lips, then he turned and faced her. His eyes clung to hers. Powerful arms pulled her in, and his demanding mouth captured her lips. She tasted a desperation that mirrored her own.

Donnie pulled away. "God, I've missed you."

"I've missed you too."

His eyes flashed. "And you're juggling fire?"

"Did you not see my performance? Not even close. It's a psychedelic light staff."

"Thank God. I only just walked in." He placed his forehead on hers. Fingers cupped her neck, and Charlie frowned at the trembling vibrations.

"Are you okay?"

"You told me once that the only time you'd marry me was if I tattooed your name across my ass," Donnie said.

"I vaguely remember that."

"I took you at your word." Donnie unbuttoned the button on his jeans and turned to show her the top side of a butt cheek. The letters "arls" peeked out. Donnie ignored the wolf whistles from the nearby crowd.

"It says Sharls. We stopped in at Fort Bragg and I found this excellent tattoo artist."

"Are you freaking crazy?"

"I am, and I got this." He pulled up his shirt and lifted an arm. A tattoo of a Firebird snaked around his side and over his chest. Now there were more whistles of the female variety.

"Not only have you marked my body, but also my heart." Donnie knelt, and Charlie covered her mouth with her hand. He pulled a box from his pocket and presented her with a diamond and orange stoned ring.

"The stone is called Orange Citrine. It sparkles with fire— just like you." His bottom lip twitched, making her smile. "Marry me, Sharls."

Charlie said the first thing that came to mind. "Are you going to give me a hard time? Boss me around like you do now?"

"You bet."

"And will I still have to deal with that carrot stuck up your ass?"

Donnie grinned. "It's lodged in there like a giant orange weed."

"That sounds like a fair deal, for as long as you love me and put up with my rowdy ass. Just so you know, I love the hell out of you, Donnie Wilson."

The crowd cheered. Slater slapped Donnie on the back as he stood.

"Come here, Firebird." Donnie pulled her to his chest and began to sway.

"Are you dancing?" Charlie whispered against his shoulder.

"Dancing with my woman. Something I should've done a long time ago." Donnie buried his nose in her neck, mumbling, "Mandarin, roses, hope, and light."

Charlie smiled at new beginnings. With Donnie by her side, they'd set fire to the damn sky.

The End.

Watch out for "Jade in the Snow." This is Slater and Kat's story, packed with action and the biggest climax of the series!

Jade in the Snow (MIT Book #4)

Prologue

Salt Lake City, Utah.
The day they met.

Derek should've come earlier. He swore as he shifted through the mass of runners. Most operators hated crowds, and Derek Banez was no exception. The bodies crowding around registration tables made his skin itch, and he kept reaching for an imaginary holstered weapon. When he saw a flash of neon pink hair in the crowd, Derek zeroed in like a missile.

"Casey," he called.

His cousin didn't hear him. Derek yelled her name again as he dodged an elderly lady stretching in line. Casey turned and squealed. He hadn't intended on participating in the 5K race, but as he planned to stay with his cousin for a week, and since it was for a good cause—a charity called sweat4schoolsupplies—here he was. Sponsoring school backpacks for underprivileged kids in the area was a no-brainer, so he'd run his tired ass down to the local park. He'd just returned from deployment, the last one serving as a Green Beret. Now, Derek was about to join a newly formed covert Taskforce—Mobile Intelligence Team—as their Protection Specialist and Sniper on Team Two. MIT2. Even the name sounded bad-ass, and he'd just met the first members of his team. His team leader—Erik Andersen—seemed solid, and a little anal. James Cane was the team medic, a huge beast of a man.

They were still selecting a fourth team member. At least Derek had some time off, and he supposed he'd need to up his already strenuous fitness game. A leisurely Saturday morning jog wouldn't hurt, especially at such a pretty location. Early June saw blue skies, green fields and avenues of leafed trees.

Casey jumped into his arms, and Derek staggered under her enthusiasm. As kids, they'd always been inseparable. She wasn't just his first cousin, she was one of his closest friends, and he hadn't seen her in over two years.

Derek stood back to assess his short and curvy sidekick. Her blonde hair was now cotton candy pink. A colorful tattoo wrapped over her right shoulder, and yet another piercing decorated her left ear. She grinned up at him. He forgot how darn cute she was.

"You're back from crusading through mysterious lands." Her eyes sparkled.

"Aye, Aye, milady, and I bring gifts. They're in my car."

"Two years, that had better be a big-shitting gift."

Derek laughed. "Damn, I missed your clever ass. Now where do I sign up for this gig?"

"Relax, we've got you covered. Here's your race number."

"We? Hell no, I'm donating to those kids."

"There's a separate donation table towards the back of the pavilion." Casey pointed to a teeming table. "And there's one at the finish line. And 'we' as in Kate's cute derriere and my reluctant one. Kate is my best friend in Utah, you haven't met her yet—she's walking up behind you."

Derek turned, and for the first time in his life, words eluded him. Derek wasn't a recluse. When he wasn't deployed, he dipped his toe rather generously in the dating pool. He enjoyed women and prided himself on never getting too involved. Some might call him a commitment-phobe, but Derek's first priority was his career. He was one ambitious son of a bitch. Criminal Justice classes on the side, and Counter Terrorism studies kept him busy. He didn't have time for relationships.

The goddess stretching her shoulder spoke. She had a slight Irish lilt, so subtle, it was barely noticeable.

"Case, don't try and pee. That bathroom is a disaster zone. Find a bush, it might be more sanitary. And I'm not using a porta-loo, not after the last time."

Her skin glowed, it literally glowed like an angel—a stark contrast to her blue-black hair. Derek studied her ultramarine eyes framed by dark lashes and brows. A stubborn-looking chin jutted out slightly, matching a gaze so direct that it took his breath away. His eyes ran over her hourglass shape. She looked like a 1940's pin-up girl.

Casey giggled. "That was different. It was a rock concert." She turned to Derek. "While Kate used a porta-potty at a Twin Peaks gig, a bunch of drunk dicks decided to brawl and fell into the potty, almost toppling it over."

"Thanks for the reminder." Kate shuddered. "And you're spilling my secrets to a random jogging dude? I know he's a hotty, but seriously?"

Derek felt himself blush—that was a first.

"My mute sidekick is actually my cousin—Derek." Casey nudged him. "Say something so she knows you're real. Not just a six-foot cardboard cutout for a Calvin Klein commercial. He talks, I promise."

"Six-two, and are you girls done with making me feel like a piece of meat?" He elbowed Casey back and put some power behind the move.

"Ouch. Stop, you big lug."

Kate didn't say anything, just studied him. A couple more of Casey's friends joined the group.

"Kate, don't wait for me. I'm walking the 5K." Casey grimaced. "And I'm taking my time."

The announcer came over the system and told everyone to shuffle to the starting line. Kate turned and walked ahead. Derek's eyes drifted to her shapely ass molded by athletic leggings. She had an ephemeral quality, yet she was curved in all the right places. He lengthened his stride to catch up. A beefy-looking man pushed past her, and Derek glared his way. The eager beaver barely noticed. With long strides, Derek caught up to the raven-haired beauty and watched her six. The crowds lined up as Derek stepped up behind her. A river ran along their right side. The route would follow the water all the way into the city.

"Do you jog on a regular basis?"

She looked back and raised her brows, pausing before answering. "Often enough to complete a 5K. Try to keep up."

"Ouch. Why do you run?" Derek jogged on the spot and shook out his arms.

Kate sighed. "Because I love chocolate milkshakes and beer."

"My kind of girl."

"I doubt that. I think a Victoria Secret model is your kind of girl," she said, stretching her thigh.

"You think I'm a player." Derek grinned.

"I think you're dangerous."

"You don't like danger? I can be a meek little lamb. Or a puppy? A Golden with a waggy tail."

She tried to hide a smile. "Oh, you're something else—I'm more of a cat person."

"Liar. I bet you love all furry beasts."

She shook her head and let her smile show. "Are you calling yourself a beast?"

"You said it, baby. I'm the beast to your beauty."

"I think it's the other way around. That girl over there—just walked into a tree while gaping at your pretty ass. No thanks, I like my men a little rougher around the edges."

Leaning down, Derek whispered in her ear. "I can be as rough as you want me to be."

He was close enough to see goosebumps break out on her arm. Her chest rose, but she kept her eyes trained ahead.

The gun went off and they shuffled forward. As Kate broke into a run, the overexcited dick-bag from earlier cut past, shoving a child aside, then ploughing past Kate. She stumbled, and Derek saw red. Surging ahead, he smoothly tripped the bastard, and the guy rolled into a ditch. "Oops," Derek muttered as he kept running.

"I saw that," Kate said from behind. "I also saw the dirtball push that kid."

"Don't know what you're talking about. Poor guy tripped over his own feet." Derek dropped back beside her. She set a comfortable pace, and they ran in silence. It felt right, a symbiosis that needed no words. He kept looking her way, her breaths came out in quick rasps, and her nostrils flared slightly with each breath. For Derek, a 5K run was the warm-up to an additional two-hour training session.

"Kat, are you okay? Do you want to slow?"

She glared at the nickname. "You're seriously trying to have a conversation while jogging, and you're not even out of breath. Are you secretly Superman?"

He grinned. "C'mon, don't let me jog alone. My poor heart won't take it."

"I need to babysit a big, brawny man's heart?"

"Maybe. It doesn't like to eat alone either. In fact, it's craving a juicy burger—with fries."

She snorted and rolled her eyes. "You've got some plums on you."

He grinned at the Irish saying but still persisted. "What do you say? After the run, we grab lunch, with a double chocolate milkshake on the side?"

"Oh, you're dangerous all right."

"Is that a yes, Kat?" Derek jogged backwards and clamped a hand on his chest. "Be still, my brawny heart. You're smiling. That's a fucking yes!" She couldn't stop a giggle, and Derek whooped, running silly circles around his gorgeous jogging partner.

**

Three and a half years later, December.
Denver, Colorado.

Kat stood in the rain. Warm tears leaked from her eyes, as drizzle cooled her cheeks. It was dark out, too dark for the team to see her hovering on the sidewalk as they sat in the warm booth of the restaurant. Agony ripped through Kat's chest as a hard knot balled in her stomach. It was meant to be a surprise. She'd canceled the last day of her workshop seminar to be with him—Derek *Slater* Banez—on his birthday. The love of her life. The man she'd shared a bed with for the past three and a half years. The asshole who now swayed in his seat while a brunette colleague pawed at his chest. Kat recognized the woman, some work friend from Fort Bragg. Derek and Kat had run into her once at a dinner.

Another minute ticked by, and Kat couldn't tear her gaze away. The rest of the team seemed pissed, and Max and his new fiancée, Abby, stood. Abby glared at the woman as she gathered her coat. The bitch didn't seem to notice. She whispered something in Derek's ear. Clearly drunk, he leaned back and laughed, and the sound felt like knives to Kat's heart. Johnny and Donnie exchanged words, then also stood. Johnny grasped Derek's arm and Derek jerked it away.

The team took offense on Kat's behalf. She knew they felt protective towards her. They'd all been that way since the Black Friday bombing. Thanks to that tragic day, Derek's PTSD slowly expanded until it had taken over their relationship, and now it ran the show, destroying their love connection months ago. Although they still lived together, Derek avoided Kat whenever possible. When he was Stateside, he made excuses about catching up with the boys, while she sat at home. Always hoping he'd come around and let her into his damaged heart. She should've fought harder. Kat kept hoping that things would get better, that Derek just needed time to heal and he'd come around.

Except they'd drifted farther apart, and her training schedule didn't help. Kat was a corporate trainer who helped entrepreneurs grow their business. Derek's covert team had just held a training exercise in Colorado near Derek and Kat's hometown of Denver. When they'd finished up a week earlier than planned, he'd called Kat and asked her to meet up with him and the team—to celebrate his birthday. She'd felt overjoyed that Derek had reached out, but was already setting up workshop trainings in California. After months of avoidance, he'd contacted her again—earlier in the day—and told her where they'd be in case she changed her mind. Kat's workshop was too important to cancel. Still, she'd regretted her answer almost immediately after hanging up with Derek, so she'd re-scheduled her workshop and caught the first flight back home. With Derek's last deployment, and her tight schedule, the last time they'd seen each other was three months ago.

Kat looked down at her red heels. One of the birthday presents she'd bought earlier in the week for Derek. He loved her in heels—wearing nothing else. They'd always had an explosive sex life, even through the rough patches. That was their safe place, fucking each other's brains out without saying a word.

"Fuck him." Kat turned away from the skinny woman sliding closer to her soon to be ex-boyfriend. Forcing one foot in front of the other, Kat walked to her car. She didn't want his friends seeing her this way, broken and standing on the street like a pathetic stalker.

Climbing in her Mercedes took effort. Kat eyed her luggage in the back seat. That would stay. Kat swiped at her wet cheeks and headed home. No. Derek's home, not her home. Not anymore.

***

The car sat in the shadows but offered an excellent view of the apartment steps. Picking at a scab on his finger, the man watched the drama unfold. His heart rate sped up as the woman emerged with a second load of bags, slipping on the sleet-covered steps. Her lover tried to help, and she shrugged him off. He could see the allure, a dark angel with plum red lips and flashing eyes. He hadn't meant to eavesdrop, but he'd swung past to see a friend. Now, he picked up his digital camera, and slid down his window to catch the couple's angry words only a few yards away.

"How did you even know I was there?" she said through tears.

"Donnie saw you as he walked out the restaurant. I'm so sorry. It's not what it looks like. When she tried to grope me, I—"

"Derry, how could you let it get that far?" She tossed a pillow into the front seat. White snowflakes clung to her damp hair. Zooming in, the man snapped a photo of her flushed cheek, watching how the wet flakes melted on her skin. He then zoomed in on the shape of her full breasts, peeking from her jacket. They heaved with each breath. So damn pretty.

"I arrived early and sat at the bar. It was a coincidence that she was there. We both drank too much. She invited herself to the dinner. It's not a big deal, she knows the team."

"That's our problem, you drink too much. You're angry all the time. You barely look at me anymore, and I feel like a naïve fool."

"Kat, please—"

"You need help. I'm not enough, and I never was. I want you to find peace..."

"Don't, baby. I love you. Please don't leave me—"

"Derek, you're breaking me. I cry all the time and I worry that you'll hurt yourself every time you drink too much or sink into that depression. We're both sad and I need to smile again. You need to get help—professional help. I love... love you so much." She swiped at her eyes. "I need you to be safe. Derry, promise me that you won't do anything stupid."

He pulled her into a hug, muttering unintelligible words. She drew back and placed a hand on his chest. "I have to go. Keep that brawny heart safe."

"You're my angel, please don't leave me." The tall man rubbed a hand over his eyes. "Baby, stay. I'll try harder and I'll get help."

Ignoring his pleas, the girl got in the car. With one last look she pulled away. The man swayed then collapsed on the steps, swearing then howling. Finally, he rested his head on his hands, rocking as the snow began to fall.

Heartless bitch. The scab came away and the man sucked at the welling blood. He reached over and checked the photos he'd captured. A good angle, she was a pretty one. Six girls in six months. Each kill was a cleansing. His next target was a man in Texas, the first male kill. Then, he'd write this snow-covered darling into the schedule. She needed to be taught a lesson in respect. He wasn't sure when he'd purge the black-haired beauty, but he had a feeling that the feisty girl would sanitize his soul.

Jade in the Snow.
Book Four.
The Mobile Intelligence Team Series.

Check out the rest of the MOBILE INTELLIGENCE SERIES series!
Heart pounding romantic suspense. Highly trained covert SF soldiers who will fight to the death for the ones they love.

SIREN IN THE WIND ($0.99) - Book One
An MIT Team leader on the hunt tracks down a woman, hiding from dangerous enemies.

.

STAIN ON THE EARTH - Book Two
A Special Forces Medic watches over a flight attendant exploring dangerous territory.

.

FIRE IN THE KNIGHT - Book Three
She's getting lost in Morocco, and he's finding her.

.

JADE IN THE SNOW - Book Four
A sniper trying to forget will fight for a woman in the crosshairs of a determined killer.

KITE ON THE ROCKS - Book Five
Friends to lovers face dangerous foes on a collision course with fate.

Also, check out the STRIKE ZONE SERIES!
The Strike Zone Series follows a group of Diplomatic Security Agents and the women in their lives. Romantic suspense with a political thriller edge.

STRIKETHROUGH (3.99) - Book One
A Special Agent and his team protect the US Ambassador's daughter.

ACKNOWLEDGMENTS

Writing *Fire in the Knight* was a bumpy journey. Starting this novel took patience through heavy research and plenty of hair pulling. But after finishing my first draft, I knew that I'd written a gem. I aimed for a brutal yet fun ride. It doesn't carry the darkness of *Siren*, but *Fire in the Knight* covers some serious themes. My loyal friends and beta readers—Joyce, Summer, Jolene, Tracy, and Colleen—you're on this journey with me. Derek from Cali, again, thanks for your help. To my family—mom, dad, and Colleen—I can't do this without you. Tammy—I love you sis. Mamello, I miss you so damn much. Lastly, to my editor, Joan Turner at JRT Editing. Thanks for your incredible work. My cover artist—Syd Gill—rocked this cover. Onward and upward!

Louise Dawn writes heart pounding romantic suspense. She's also a corporate trainer in Utah. Louise loves travelling and has lived in many countries before choosing the States as her home. Her passion is reading and writing fast paced stories simmering in romance. If you enjoyed this book, consider leaving a review. It's appreciated by authors both new and established.

Chat with her on Facebook @
https://www.facebook.com/authorlouisedawn
Follow her on Twitter @ https://twitter.com/louisedawnwrite
Or check out her character's developments on Pinterest @
https://www.pinterest.com/louisedawnwrite/boards/

www.ingramcontent.com/pod-product-compliance
Lightning Source LLC
Chambersburg PA
CBHW020245200626
46816CB00001BA/134